MW01133985

Kipjo K. Ewers

Copyright © 2013 by Kipjo K. Ewers

THIS IS AN EVO UNIVERSE BOOK

PUBLISHED BY EVO UNIVERSE, L.L.C.

All rights reserved under International and Pan-American Copyright Conventions. Published in the United States by EVO Universe, L.L.C., New Jersey, and distributed by EVO Universe, L.L.C., New Jersey.

www.evouniverse.com

The First

ASIN: 0615836690

Printed in the U.S.A. by EVO Universe
Email: info@evouniverse.com

On-Line Chat: go to our website, **www.evouniverse.com.**

For Sophia...

OTHER WORKS

EVO UPRISING: (THE FIRST SERIES BOOK 2)

GENESIS: (THE FIRST SERIES BOOK 3)

EYE OF RA

FRED & MARY

"HELP! I'M A SUPERHERO!": BOOK ONE

THE ELF AND THE LARP: BOOK ONE

WAR OF MORTAL GODS: BOOK ONE

ACKNOWLEDGMENTS

I would like to thank God Himself for giving me the gift of words and blessing me with the breath of life and longevity to make sure it did not go to waste.

I would like to acknowledge the two women who inspired this book.

First, my mom, Kimba Ewers, held down a house of four men and gave a kid like me everything he could ever want; I can say I was born to the greatest mom ever. Thank you for loving me.

Last but not least is my wife, Jacquelin Franklin-Ewers. You are the epitome of "Beside every good man is a great woman." Thank you for giving me the privilege of sharing my life with you.

Finally, I'd like to acknowledge all mothers, daughters, sisters, nieces, aunts, grandmothers, and women of the world. God may have made Eve from Adam's ribs, but women have proven they are also the backbone of the family and us men. Thank you for holding us down.

CHAPTER 1

Monday 11:30 P.M., Mountain View Unit in Gatesville, Texas:

Prisoner 28301:014 stared at her prison door as if she were watching a movie. She barely touched her meal of medium-rare steak, mashed potatoes with chives, and macaroni on the side. She mostly ate her dessert, a double chocolate banana fudge sundae with sprinkles on top. Quietly, she sat holding a thick leather Bible in her tiny hands. As she waited, the sound of heavy boots and chains grew closer. She stirred not an inch through the clicking and clanging of the cell door opening as a shadow cast over her.

"Dennison, it's time," a rough voice announced.

Her arms, waist, and legs were in restraints in less than two minutes. After confirming her shackles' security, the group's female correctional officer handed her back her Bible. She pulled several envelopes from it, giving them to the female C.O.

"Could you please make sure these get mailed? They have stamps and addresses on them."

The female correctional officer took them with a silent nod.

Dennison took one final deep breath as she gazed out into the hallway of the prison.

"Okay, I'm ready."

Monday 11:35 P.M.

Dennison walked the halls of Cellblock D, clutching the black leather Bible tightly as if to crush it while flanked by two large male correctional officers from behind and the female correctional officer in front. The sound of her chains rattling like Marley's ghost, along with the heavy boots and gear of the officers, was the loudest thing on the block that night. As she walked, she could feel the eyes on her. She could hear the sniffles and the whispers; she started to count her steps in her mind. The procession stopped at thirty paces as she reached her first destination.

The correctional officer to her left turned to her.

"Five minutes," he sternly reminded her.

"Thank you." She gratefully nodded.

Quickly, Dennison shuffled over to the bars of cell 28.

A young woman barely in her twenties with raven-colored hair in cornrows trembled, her head bent as she gripped the bars sobbing. Resting the Bible between the bars, Dennison placed her hands on top of the young woman's hands as best she could despite the hindrance by the bars and her restraints.

She leaned in close, kissing her on the top

of her head, causing the young woman to whimper.

"No more tears now," Dennison whispered to her. "Two more weeks, and you can see your babies, and God help you if you ever come back here... because I'll be watching. Car boosting days are over... you hear me?"

Her words only made the young woman cry more as she fought to hold Dennison's hands through the bars. As Dennison tried her best to comfort and silence her tears, the young woman's cellmate, a woman two shades darker than Dennison with longer dreads than hers, walked up to the bars and stood next to the young woman. She stood a thick, yet fit, four inches over Dennison. The prisoner had a chiseled face and demeanor, but it could not take away the motherly eyes she looked at both of them with.

She playfully nudged the young woman in mourning from behind.

"Come now; soldier up," the older woman softly ordered. "Our girl's going home; she got too much on her mind than to deal with your tired ass and the waterworks."

She placed a gentle hand on the sobbing young woman's back, then put her other hand on top of Dennison's hand.

"I shall miss our talks with one another," the older woman uttered in her best Tom Cruise impersonation.

It was enough to make Dennison burst into laughter and respond in her best Ken Watanabe voice.

"I shall too, they were just... perfect..."

The two women laughed over the young woman's whimpering sobs.

The older woman finally choked up. She quickly swatted away her tears so they would not flow.

"I'm sorry," her voice cracked, "I know you don't need this shit now."

"It's okay, happy tears," Dennison said with a trembling smile, fighting back her tears. "Remember, I'm going home..."

"Yeah, you are," her elder tried to match her sad smile, "you're going home…"

"I'm going home," Dennison said again, attempting to use a more convincing voice.

It did not work as her body violently began to tremble, which made the older woman hold her hand tighter.

"Dennison, two minutes."

Dennison turned to nod to the correctional officer, reminding her that her timed request was almost up. She quickly took the Bible, handing it to the older woman.

"This belonged to my mother. She's not going to need it back. She's got like a ton of them. Something to remember me by…I left you both a little goodbye note on the inside; please read it."

"Dennison…"

The second warning came from the female correctional officer.

Dennison nodded a second time and

attempted to leave, pulling her hand away, but the younger woman, still clutching her left hand, refused to let go.

Her elder stepped in to pry her off of Dennison before the guards did.

"Come on, Bishop," she gently coaxed, "you got to let her go. You got to let her go, honey."

"No! No! It's not right!" Bishop hollered, holding on for dear life, "No! No! No!"

With bitter reluctance, the young woman, forced by her older inmate, broke her grip. Collapsing to her knees, she curled herself into a ball and emitted a gut-wrenching howl as if she were dying. Dennison gave a final wave as she shuffled off, falling back into line and led off by the guards.

The silver-haired woman quivered as she finally allowed her tears to fall. She gripped the bars, screaming.

"An innocent woman right there! God help you all! God help you all!"

11:50 P.M.

Dennison walked through the door, held open for her by one of the officers. As her eyes winced while adjusting to the medical lights' harshness above, she finally saw the table.

"Oh, dear God…"

Dennison whimpered as her legs went out from underneath her.

As she was told by many, almost everyone went down after seeing the table; it was the final gut check, etching the cold, hard realization that what was happening was real. On instinct, the male officers caught her as she went down; it was the only time they showed compassion as they allowed her to compose herself before helping her back up to her feet.

As they led her to the table, she started to chant her mantra.

"I'm going home… I'm going home… I'm going home…"

Dennison kept repeating the exact words to herself as they removed her shackles for the last time. They allowed her to remove her shoes and socks before positioning her on the table and strapping her down. She liked being barefoot and wanted to be so one final time; stretching her toes and the chant helped keep her from breaking into tears, but it could not stop the uncontrollable shivering her body was going through. Finally, the lab technician walked over with the needle. She closed her eyes as he found her vein and stuck it in her arm; she barely felt it going in as he checked it before taping it down to her arm. Silent tears poured from her eyes, blurring her vision as she shook her head. But this was not a bad dream. She was not going to wake up.

With the final checks made, the warden stepped in to begin the proceedings.

"The time is now 11:55 P.M. as we prepare to proceed with the execution of Prisoner 28301:014, Sophia Dennison, by the state of Texas, by lethal injection for the crime of capital murder. The condemned will be allowed to say a few words at this time."

Sophia drew a quivering breath as she

looked at the double mirror hiding from her the witnesses sitting on the other side, listening to her final words and who would watch her draw her last breath.

"I… stand here before you… declaring my innocence," Sophia began to find her words, "As I did four years ago… I now go to my Maker in peace… knowing despite all my other sins… which I have owned, the one sin that I am truly clean of is the one I am condemned to die here… for… tonight…"

Her body shook violently while her tears rolled heavily as she fought to get out her final words.

"I… did not… murder my husband, and I forgive you all… for what you're about to do… to me…"

Timidly, she nodded, cueing the lab technician to flick the switch, lowering the table to a horizontal position; her vision became blurrier as her tears flowed like a waterfall. Despite being nearly blind, she could make out the three clear canisters lined one after another… all she focused on… was the one that would put her to sleep.

"I'm going home… I'm going home," Sophia softly sang, "I'm going home… I'm going home…"

Midnight:

The warden nodded; as the executioner pushed the button pumping the sedative within the first cylinder into the tube heading for her arm, a final soft smile appeared on her face as her eyes began to flutter. She continued to sing to the end.

"I'm going home, I'm going… home… I'm going…"

The machine then pumped the fluid from the second cylinder.

It was now Tuesday 12:01 P.M…

CHAPTER 2

Tuesday 6:30 A.M., Mountain View Unit, Gatesville, Texas:

S.A.C. (Special Agent in Charge) Mark Armitage had seen it all.

His ten years in the army and his almost fifteen-year career in the F.B.I. had exposed him to terrorist cells that threaten national security, drug cartels, missing and exploited children, things that would leave lesser people with eternal nightmares.

Nothing surprised him these days, especially when he came home to an empty house and divorce papers on the bed his wife and he used to share. Neither did the 2:30 A.M. call from his executive assistant director to get on the first plane from Washington to Gatesville ASAP.

He should have his job by right, but Armitage chose to remain a field agent. He knew a desk job would see him one night with his service weapon in his mouth, blowing his brains out the back of his skull. In the field, he was in the shit, which meant his mind was preoccupied with other things besides ending his existence.

He slowly drove his rental car up to the Mountain View Unit's metal door entrance, the Gatesville women's prison section created solely for prisoners on death row. The usual media whores were out in full force, taking pictures and video footage and waving their microphones while screaming questions, expecting answers they had no business getting. This was usually a familiar scene for him, except for the National Guard, keeping the inquisitive media and residents at bay instead of the local police or state troopers.

A Private First Class in full gear holding his M16A2 walked up to the window of his rental car, cueing Mark to flash his badge and credentials.

The Private nodded and radioed to open the doors blocking the outside world to the prison, letting him in; then, Armitage realized the need for the extra firepower.

Inside the Mountain View Unit was a war zone. There was a huge gaping hole in the main building's side and a massive hole in the side of the forty-foot wall that enclosed the facility. A large personnel vehicle blocked the cavity, keeping residents and nosey reporters from getting in. There was also an obliterated watchtower and two destroyed cars, one smoking and one still on fire, covered in debris from the tower partially brought down. The local fire department continued to put the hose to it to kill the flames from one of their trucks. The compound included local police, state troopers, special agents, correctional officers, and the National Guard. Paramedics were also on-site attending to the wounded, comprising correctional officers and local police.

Mark had to admit rioting was a common thing that could break out in regular prisons, both male and female, but this was a battlefield, something he had never seen in his career.

As he parked and stepped out of his rental, looking around, a familiar face amidst the chaos fueled his sentiment with a look as he walked up to him.

"Ain't never seen no shit like this in my life, Mark," Dustin greeted his partner.

Mark looked around at the damage for a second time before asking his oldest friend the question on his mind.

"What the hell happened here?"

"Prison Break, one dead C.O., several guards, and police badly injured."

Mark scanned the yard again, surprised that the damage around him only caused one fatality.

"Only one dead?"

"Yeah, what's left of the poor bastard on

22

top of the smashed squad car over there."

Dustin pointed to the caved-in Impala with the Gatesville police colors smoking and covered with debris from the massive hole made in the building's front from the eighth floor.

The only thing of the dead seen from Armitage and Mercer's distant view was a leg as forensics took pictures of the scene before the paramedics removed the body. Mark asked as he walked with Dustin to the prison.

"How many broke out?"

"One," Dustin dryly answered.

"Just one," Mark asked, stunned, "so what are we looking at, an organized gang or a terrorist cell?"

"No one broke in to break her out," Dustin nervously returned. "She broke out all by herself."

Armitage gave Mercer a look that it was too early in the morning for jokes; Dustin returned the gaze, meaning that he was not yanking his chain this time.

"Dustin, you're telling me one inmate did all this damage?"

"Just walk with me." Dustin motioned.

Mark followed him into the facility, where they went through security and saw some of the injured who were brought down from the eighth floor; some were talking to field agents and accounting their version of what they'd seen, while others just sat there with blank expressions on their face unable to speak much less comprehend what they saw.

Armitage continued to follow Mercer as they took the elevator heading for the video surveillance room on the second floor. Dustin began to run down the events of six-and-a-half hours ago.

"At 12 A.M., now escape convict Sophia Dennison was scheduled for execution by lethal injection."

"What was she in for?" Mark asked.

"Four years ago, she murdered her husband, Lieutenant Robert Matheson, a former decorated Iraq War Marine Vet in cold blood, stabbed the poor bastard like forty-one times in their bed. Bitch was found two states away in an airport hotel in Oklahoma with a one-way flight to Brazil."

"Why'd she do it?"

The motive did not mean anything to him. Mark wanted info to understand the mental state of the fugitive he would be hunting.

"Two- point-five-million dollar trust fund," Dustin responded.

"Say what?" Mark furrowed his eyebrows. "You mean insurance…"

"No, trust fund," Dustin clarified. "Kid got it when he completed boot camp. Father is a well-known four-star general who comes from old money, and I mean money after the Civil War. He's also got a lot of connections in both the military and private sectors. Did very well for himself in both; the poor kid was so trusting he dumped all the money into their joint savings and checking accounts. Red flags went up when it was all transferred into her personal account within the same bank that she got a month prior. She transferred the money the same night she killed him. They had footage of her withdrawing cash from an A.T.M., driving through a toll heading to Oklahoma, and checking into a hotel near the airport."

Mark and Dustin got off on the second floor of the building, walking to the surveillance room.

"Was he crippled or something?" Mark asked.

"Took shrapnel to the chest from an I.E.D., badly burned left arm, and lost sight in his right eye... other than that pretty healthy," Dustin responded.

"So how did she overpower a Marine? She kills him in his sleep?"

"Worse," Dustin answered with a face of disgust, "she injected him with a serious paralyzing neurotoxin. Numbs everything except for nervous system... poor bastard felt everything… and get this… she did it after she banged him."

"How did she get a hold of…?"

"She's a licensed neurosurgeon, graduated with a full scholarship to Texas Southwestern," Dustin answered Mark's unfinished question while rushing to get to the surveillance room. "She did her residency at Memorial Hermann till graduation and got a position there. Records show she lifted it from their research facility."

Mark nodded before throwing out the driving question.

"Okay, so how did she escape before her execution?"

Dustin uneasily hesitated again before he answered.

"She didn't escape," he fumbled with his words, "she was executed."

His answer stopped Mark dead in his tracks. He held his hands up in frustration.

"Wait! What? What the hell do you mean

she was executed? Then what the f…"

Dustin grabbed his arm, ushering him to keep moving.

"Just walk with me, man," he growled.

"Dustin, so help me if you don't start making some damn sense."

Were Mark's thoughts as he snatched his arm away and continued to follow him into the security observation room. One of the correctional officers in the room tensely monitored the series of screens as they walked in.

"At twelve midnight, Sophia Dennison was executed," Dustin finally began explaining, "she was pronounced officially dead by the local county coroner at 12:05 P.M… then this happened…"

Armitage watched the video feed at 12:07 P.M.; one of the room officers walked over to remove the thick leather restraints from a now-deceased Sophia Dennison. Out of nowhere, the pronounced dead arched her back, gasping for air, almost scaring the life out of the six-foot-two-inch correctional officer, who reeled back in fright. As the pastor fainted, everyone else in the room and on the other side of the observation window began freaking out at the terrifyingly miraculous resurrection.

Mark watched in disbelief as the five-foot-six, one hundred-ten-pound woman in a hyper-hysterical state fought to sit up, ripping her six-inch thick arm restraints from the same table while screaming three words in a rant.

"Get me out! Get me out! Get me out! Get me out! Get me out!"

Armitage would have thought it a fluke, a rush of adrenaline, if his still 20/20 vision did not show the same woman snapping the restraints from her chest and waist right from the table itself, sending pieces of metal flying. As she sat up, a correctional officer, overcoming his shock and fear, rushed over to restrain her. With a swipe of her arm, she swatted a man who had at least one hundred fifty pounds on her clear across the room, slamming him violently into the wall behind him. He dropped face-first onto the ground like a slab of beef.

After effortlessly popping the last two restraints from her legs, Sophia rolled off the table, dropping to her knees.

"I remember! I remember! I remember! I remember!" Sophia snivelingly repeated. "I remember! I remember! I remember! I remember!"

"Dennison! St... stay down!"

The order came from a frightened second male Correctional Officer.

Sophia ignored his order as she fought to her feet, stumbling and falling against the glass partition that separated her from the audience who had watched her execution on the other side.

"I remember! I remember!" she continued to babble. "I remember! I remember! I remember!"

The witnesses scattered in terror and disbelief as a second officer lunged to tackle her to the floor. Much to his own shock and dismay,

Sophia's apparent adrenaline rush allowed her to stop him in his tracks; in the struggle, she managed to grab him by the front of his shirt, lifting him off his feet.

"No!" Sophia screamed.

Sophia threw him backward as if tossing a stuffed teddy bear. His near bone-crushing blow against the wall behind him was anything but that of a stuffed bear launched. He, too, dropped face-first, hitting the concrete floor with a sickening thud while pieces of the wall crumbled from the impact.

Sophia stood there, clutching her skull; she appeared in excruciating pain, shaking like a leaf. In frustration, she shrieked, pounding on the reinforced observation glass and cracking it.

"I… got… I got… to get… out."

She hit the glass again with a more massive shot, giving it a large shatter pattern. It looked like an aluminum bat hit it; one more shot would send shards raining everywhere. On the other side of the glass, people screamed, backing up, terrified at what they witnessed. As a disoriented Sophia looked to deliver another blow, four guards swarmed on her for a dog pile attempt… it went horribly wrong.

Armitage, beside himself, now witnessed one woman tossing around highly trained correctional officers like rag dolls. There was no finesse to what she was doing, making it evident that she was not a trained combatant, but her strength was beyond what the four guards could handle combined.

With one swipe of her hand, she accidentally backhanded a male guard into a tailspin; to break free, she threw an elbow into another guard's chest.

The shot lifted him off his feet and folded him in half as he hit the floor back first; he rolled to his side, gasping for air as if she broke his sternum; reports would later show that she shattered it. The female guard in the mix hung desperately onto one of her legs in a failed attempt to bring her down. Dennison's movements thrashed her around like an ankle-biter holding onto a mop. Having enough, the last standing male guard grabbed his baton and let loose a skull-crushing shot to her skull. It staggered her and drew blood, but she remained standing as he stood, taken aback that his metal baton was now bent in half.

"What the f-?" said the stunned male officer.

Before he could finish his sentence, a bloodied Sophia with a possibly fractured skull and a severe concussion swung for the hills, hitting him dead in the chest. The force of her punch sent him flying through the shattered glass into the observation room, hitting a couple of witnesses and knocking them down like dominos.

She was in a daze as she wiped the blood off her face while superfluous yelling and screaming now filled the lethal injection room; realizing the window was broken, she advanced to freedom but felt a weight on her right leg. It was the female officer still holding onto her.

"Let... me go... please... let me go..." a disoriented Sophia pleaded.

"I can't do that, Sophia..." a terrified

female correctional officer bound by duty returned.

Sophia grabbed the guard by the front of her shirt, lifting her into the air with one arm.

The officer screamed and held onto Sophia's arm for dear life.

"Please, Sophia," she pleaded, "you know I got kids… please…"

"I… I'm not…" Sophia tried to reassure her.

Before calming down the officer and explaining that she only wanted her to let her go, a voice called out, "Dennison!"

BLAM! rang out as she staggered back, releasing the officer who scurried away for cover. She looked down to see the front of her green prison scrubs become red. As she tried to advance, gunfire erupted into the lethal injection room. Armitage watched in disgust as the young woman's body was torn apart via panic fire. It took twenty shots to bring her down to her knees and five more to drop her, one hitting her skull, which snapped her neck back as she crashed onto the now bloody floor, lifeless once again.

It should have been over, but Armitage remembered what Mercer said. Dustin watched the godfather to his children turn to him with a visage he had never seen on him before, one of fear.

"You said... she escaped," Mark uttered with unsettling nervousness.

Dustin turned again to the correctional officer.

"Fast forward the tape."

The officer, sweating bullets, turned the dial, making the video fast forward in dual-time mode. The guards who did the shooting came in to check if she was dead for a second time while securing the room. Additional guards now came in along with the Warden himself. The witnesses on the other side tried to move closer to look, but the officers moved them back and then ushered them out of the room altogether to safety. County and state police now appeared along with local detectives. The on-site forensics doctor walked in to inspect and pronounce her dead for the second time. Additional forensics now came into view, taking pictures. Armitage's eyes widened as the fast-forward feed revealed something happening underneath everyone's noses within the room.

Armitage shuddered as he tried to believe what he was seeing.

"Is... is she growing?" he stammered.

"Now I know I'm not still drunk," Dustin said, reaffirming his suspicion.

The two agents and the C.O. watched in disbelief as the "corpse" in the room went through a severe growth spurt; the video feed showed that about two hours and fifteen minutes had passed.

"Stop right there... move in... now play it," Dustin commanded the officer. "Mark, tell me what do you see."

Armitage realized what his friend wanted

him to see as the footage began to play with a closer shot at Dennison's lifeless face. Through the thick, partially dried blood on her forehead, the bullet wound that pierced her skull was no longer there. Five more minutes had passed as a hand reached over to close her eyelids in preparation for placing her in a body bag. A scene out of a horror movie ensued as the dead came back to life again, emitting an inhuman blood-curdling scream that took ten years off Armitage's life just standing there.

"Jesus…" Mark yelled while jumping backward.

He was visibly shaken, as if he had seen a demon.

"You wish," Dustin responded, shaken despite this being the second time he had seen the footage.

Armitage watched as the dead rose back to her feet for the second time. Screaming once again filled the room, mostly from grown men. Those armed did not ask questions as they drew on her, ordering her to get down and surrender. The prison scrub pants she wore looked like knee-high shorts, confirming that she definitely went through a growth spurt while "dead." Her first barefooted step sounded like a diesel hammer smashing into the concrete floor. Someone freaked out in the herd of officers and opened fire without order, causing panic fire to erupt within the room again, hitting her from all directions. Sophia instinctively covered up as gunfire smoke filled the room.

The shooting was more vicious than before, but something was evidently wrong. Ricocheting bullets hit two officers, one in the arm and the other in the leg. Someone screamed an order through all of the mayhem.

"Cease fire! Cease fucking fire!"

The majority of the gunfire ended because of empty ammo.

The surveillance room was filled with the audio sound of cursing and the relock and loading of weapons.

Time felt as if it stood still; Mark leaned in, attempting to see through all the smoke and chaos. At that moment, a black and green blur came from the smoke, emitting the same high-pitched inhuman scream.

The sound of seasoned guards and officers screaming and the sound of soft bodies hitting something hard rang from the speakers. It was as if an F-1 tank was rolling through the halls. The gunfire erupted again but grew less and less as the echoing of destruction increased from what the audio picked up.

A shaken Mark bore witness on the other screen as something swift and powerful smashed through concrete walls, tearing open steel doors on its way to freedom.

Mark gave a wave to shut it off as additional gunfire, and yelling came into play; he now got the picture of what went down. He leaned up against the console of the observation room, rubbing his jaw, trying to process what he had just seen.

Finally, after taking it all in, Mark looked up at Dustin.

"This can't be happening... right?"

"Look at this poor bastard, Mark."

Dustin gestured to the equally unnerved correctional officer running the surveillance system.

"He was here when it was happening, and he's seen the footage… how many times have you seen it?"

"Four… four times," the correctional officer answered while holding up four shaking fingers.

"Four times," Dustin threw up his own four fingers. "I'd be the first guy to call bullshit on this, but as you can see, he and several other people who were in the middle of it upstairs just saw super-bitch bust out of prison!"

Mark lowered his head and dug deep to find his buried nerve. He asked a question, switching the topic for a minute.

"Who was the C.O. she killed?"

"Dennis Buck Wilford," Dustin rattled off. "Sixteen-year career, ten between here and the

Gatesville Women's Prison, father of two…
husband; you don't want to see that footage…
shit was brutal. Bitch singled him out and put
him through three concrete walls, including the
one she smashed through to break out. He lost
one of his arms during the second impact and is
now a puddle of goo on top of the obliterated cop
car you saw outside."

Mark rubbed his chin one more time. He
got up, left the room to clear his head, and
returned to the game as his partner followed.

"I want to know who she is," Mark
ordered. "Every detail… most importantly, any
medical records… if you can find out when she
got her first period, I want that too."

He snapped his fingers, thinking, going
down the standard list of protocol and field
training gained over the years.

"I want to know who came in to see her
during her time here, conjugal visits if she had
any, and anything in her prison cell is ours. I
want to interview anyone she spoke to and made
friends with here. Call brass and put her on the
terrorist watch list underneath Bin Laden… with

a precaution not to engage. We need to know who or what the hell we're dealing with first. Family and friends, where is she originally from?"

Dustin recited the information on his notepad that he pulled from his jacket.

"Mount Vernon, New York... a small town outside the Bronx... Parents are still alive; father is from Belize, the mother is from Jamaica... she's a first-generation U.S. citizen of three children, eldest to a brother and a younger sister."

He had the skill of gathering vital Intel at the drop of a dime.

"So, she met her husband here in Texas?" Mark rattled off another question.

"Correct, the late husband is from Houston; they went to the same college; they got married and resided there," Dustin confirmed.

Mark did not need Google or an F.B.I. database with the big man at his side.

Mark then began to set up his ability to strategize, ignoring that he was dealing with an individual who could be on a superhuman level.

"So she's either heading back to Houston or New York. Either way, find out where else she traveled to… vacation… business… whatever. Did anyone see her bust through that wall last night from the outside?"

"You mean like the NCADP?" Dustin scoffed. "Bro, this is a red state. A local news team was in the front doing a story about her execution. No one saw anything, nor did they get any footage. We checked."

Mark nodded, continuing his course of action.

"Then we need to keep this inside here," he commanded. "Speak to the Warden and the Chief of Police, tell them to convey to their people that no one is to talk to anyone about what happened here; failure to comply means being charged with obstructing a federal investigation. The last thing we need is mass hysteria in the streets. What are the chemicals they used to administer the execution again?"

43

Dustin quickly searched his mini notepad, running through the notes he had taken earlier. He squinted to read his own writing.

"Usual stuff, sodium thiopental used to induce unconsciousness, pancuronium bromide for paralysis and respiratory arrest, and potassium chloride to stop the heart."

"Chemical residue to the lab," Mark ordered. "I want to confirm if that's what they really are, on top of what she ate for her last meal."

"You might want to speak to this guy over here," Dustin said while motioning to another agent.

The Agent brought forth one of the watchtower guards stationed earlier that morning.

"This is Sergeant Michael Wexler," Dustin introduced, "a guard and tower watchman #2 of the four towers, also a former Army Ranger and Sniper."

"Army… infantry," Mark addressed a

fellow military man. "What can you tell me that I don't already know?"

Sergeant Wexler responded as a man still military forged despite not wearing the colors.

"After the escaped inmate exited the building from the eighth floor of the facility, destroying the squad car she crashed onto on the way down with Office Wilford killing him," he began his rundown. "She hit the quad running. I tracked and hit the target with an Armor-Piercing M2 round to the back of her skull."

"What are you doing with that type of round in this facility?" an inquisitive Mark asked.

"Being prepared for anything, sir," Sergeant Wexler calmly responded.

"Continue," Mark nodded.

Sergeant Wexler went on with his assessment.

"She went down hard but was up again in less than a minute. I believe the round barely pierced her skull. I then fired a total of eight rounds after that, hitting the target in different parts of her head, neck, and chest, and that was in addition to the other rounds fired from the other three-tower guards. Each round after the first initial one was ineffective until she threw a patrol car at me, and I had to bail from my nest."

Mark held his hand up, stopping him while attempting to wrap his brain around what the sergeant just said.

"She threw... a car... at you?"

"Yes, sir," Sergeant Wexler responded without hesitation. "The smashed-up Charger outside buried by part of the tower. I believe it was on instinct since it was the closest thing to her at the time. The shot also appeared to be lucky; she seemed disoriented all the way till she smashed through the courtyard wall."

Mark began to wonder if Sergeant Wexler was superhuman.

"You don't seem the least bit shaken," he raised an eyebrow.

"During my tours, I've seen a lot of things, sir," Sergeant Wexler smirked, "nothing much shakes me."

Mark gave a slight smirk himself, nodding again out of respect.

"Stick around," he instructed Wexler. "May have some more questions for you... is that a helicopter, I hear?"

Armitage looked at Mercer, who shrugged his shoulders. They walked to one of the windows to see a jet-black twin-engine Sikorsky private helicopter descend into the battle-ridden Mountain View Unit courtyard.

"Who the hell?" Mark asked with an irritated, twisted look on his face.

He was not ready for any more surprises.

Dustin wore a matching visage of irritation.

"Damn if I know..." he shrugged.

The helicopter landed, sending dust and fresh smoke from an ousted fire everywhere.

After winding down, the door opened, and the automatic steps folded down. A tall, well-built man in a black, crisp, tailored suit sporting horn-rim glasses and a buzz cut stepped out first.

He waited as a medium-built, clean-shaven man with a two hundred dollar haircut and a ten thousand dollar light gray suit stepped out, looking around at the mayhem as officers, soldiers, and agents looked back at him in bewilderment.

Additional suits, all in black, stepped out and stood behind him. The last to exit the helicopter was a near dwarf-like elderly man with a Santa Claus disposition sporting a clear bald head, long white beard, and bifocals. His suit looked cheaper than Armitage's and reminiscent of the 1950s. Following him were three people in lab coats carrying silver cases.

"Who is that?" Dustin sneered like a wolf defending his territory from an invading pack.

"Don't know," Mark replied while grinding his teeth, "but I smell asshole…"

Armitage watched as the mystery man

looked up in his direction, brandishing what appeared to be an obnoxious smile. He proceeded to walk with his team, following into the prison.

Not liking the look he gave him, Mark motioned to his partner.

"Five bucks says where he's headed."

"Lethal injection room," Dustin answered.

"Let's get up there and greet our mystery guest…" Mark gestured to Dustin, "Make sure he doesn't piss all over our crime scene."

"This'll be fun," Dustin snorted.

They left the second floor, taking the elevator to the eighth, which housed the lethal injection room. Once both men stepped onto the floor, Mark could see the damage worse than he saw on video footage.

He looked around to see walls obliterated and steel doors ripped from their hinges; his feet kicked around shell casings, which littered the floor from shotguns, semi-automatics, and handguns, and used tear gas and smoke grenades. The lingering smell of the gas made his eyes water a bit as he looked around in disbelief. Having seen enough, he and Dustin marched to the lethal injection room to see their own team, initially working the room, now standing outside. The new mystery team was now inside, taking pictures and samples. Mr. Mystery stood in the middle of the room with his back turned and arms folded, taking it all in.

The scene pissed Mark off to no end.

"What the hell is going on?" he barked.

"Uh… the gentleman there identified himself as a Director," answered a nervous F.B.I. forensics agent, "and told us our services were no longer needed. He instructed us to pack up and leave."

Mark looked like he wanted to tear the Agent's head off with his bare hands.

"Director of what?!" he scowled.

Armitage palmed the Agent out of the way, not giving him a chance to answer. Mark walked, wearing blinders, toward the man in the room.

The six-foot-five-frame bruiser first exited the helicopter with a clean look down to his crew cut, and the MIBensemble stepped in Mark's way.

"F.B.I.," an unimpressed Mark identified himself, "which means get the "Fuck" out my way... before I "beat" you within an "inch" of your life."

"I know who you are, Special Agent Armitage," returned the man in black, unintimidated by Mark's threat. "You and your team's services are no longer needed here."

"And who the hell are you?" Dustin chimed in.

The man in black pulled out his credentials, identifying himself.

"Special Agent Stanley Slater."

Mercer eyed along with Armitage the shiny chrome black and silver badge with

Slater's I.D. identifying him as a Special Agent of the United States Government. It, however, did not specify his division or branch.

"Never heard of you, Special Agent Slater," Mark replied with narrowed eyes.

"And you never will," Slater coldly responded, "all you need to know is my division and credentials trump yours as far as this case is concerned. Now I will repeat it again: you and your team are officially relieved of duty."

Mark sarcastically scratched his chin as he gestured to Dustin, who looked ready to pounce on Agent Slater. Mark wagged a finger at his friend.

"What was that cool line from that crazy robot movie we watched at your house with your kids before the boxing match on cable last month?"

"You mean the one where the robots change into stuff," Dustin returned, building on Mark's skit. "While hanging out with the little half-Jewish kid?"

"Yeah," Mark snapped his fingers, "when the soldier put his gun in the face of the doofus with the Superman-looking shirt, and the Aloha draws. I think he said, 'We don't take orders from people that don't exist.'"

"Yeah, that's right," Dustin smiled before turning to Agent Slater with a sarcastic grin. "We don't take orders from assholes that don't exist."

"Is there a problem, Agent Slater?" a calm, elevated voice rang out.

The question came from the man in the gray suit standing in the middle of the lethal injection room, stopping the ensuing brawl about to take place between Armitage, Mercer, and his muscle in black.

Armitage pushed past Slater to confront his apparent boss while Agent Slater continued to have a staredown match with Mercer, who was only an inch shorter than he was and ready to go.

"Yeah, you can say there's a problem," Mark fired at the man in gray. "This is an official F.B.I. investigation, not M.I.B., so what the hell are you doing at my crime scene?"

"Director Arthur Rosen," he finally introduced himself, "I am here running my own investigation with my team."

"Who is your "team?" What department do you come from?" Mark demanded to know.

"Unfortunately, I cannot divulge that to you, Agent Armitage," Director Rosen answered with a half-apologetic tone. "What I can tell you is that my department is better equipped to handle this situation than you are. So I am asking you to please stand down and allow us to work."

"What situation may that be?" Mark asked, pretending to be ignorant of what was going on.

"No need for cynicism, Agent Armitage," Director Rosen smirked, "you know very well what the situation is."

Mark moved closer to the Director, giving him his trademark 'fear of God' look.

"This is what I do know," he sneered,

"you fly in here on your fancy helicopter outside, with your 'team' and Jason Bourne reject over there impeding in a Federal Bureau investigation and contaminating my crime scene. You flash a badge I've never seen before and a suspect title, and you refuse to tell me what department or organization within our United States Government you claim you hail from so I can check your so-called credentials. That gives me probable cause to arrest you and your whole party and throw you into a deep dark cell until you decide to tell me or until I can verify if you're bullshitting me."

Director Rosen openly laughed at Armitage's attempt to intimidate him.

"I can assure you that won't happen," he smiled.

"You think not?" Mark snarled while advancing forward again.

He intended to yoke the good Director up in his high-priced suit and slap some cuffs on him to prove who was in charge.

His ear caught the sound of a firearm

pulled from a leather holster. Part of him thought he would see something shiny and high-tech like in the movies. Instead, Agent Slater, who had drawn on him, held a standard-issued Glock 23 sidearm with a laser sighting pointed at the side of his head.

A livid Dustin stunned that Agent Slater had the gall to attempt such a thing, pulled out his sidearm four seconds later, pointing it at the Agent's head. Agent Slater does not flinch from the apparent threat to his life.

"Drop it, asshole! Drop it now!" Dustin roared.

It was a chain reaction as fellow F.B.I. agents, the Director's agents, and local authorities in the vicinity went for their service weapons.

Armitage had been in some messed up situations, but this was apparent insanity on top of insanity. Any second, he thought he would wake up from a horrible dream, except he kept catching a whiff of the Director's early morning coffee breath.

"That also is not going to happen, Agent Mercer," Director Rosen responded. "Instead, what's going to happen is Agent Slater will shoot and kill your partner and friend of twenty-four years while you, who hasn't fired your service firearm in ten, watch. He will then probably kill you despite your current "advantage" over him and anyone else who draws on him until finally, I give the order for him to stop."

"We will most likely be arrested by whoever is still alive on your team or the local authority present. We'll probably spend no more than three hours in a holding cell before being released with no charges while you and your partner share toe tags in the county morgue. Your family, friends, and associates will mourn and bury you; nothing further will come from this incident. Or Agent Slater kills your partner, you kill him, arrest me, I still spend three hours in a cell, and you get to watch me released with no charges brought against me while your partner here lies in a morgue with a toe tag."

"The other alternative is you lower your weapon. We take what we came for, leave, and in a couple of hours, you will receive a phone call from your Executive Assistant Director Douglas Edward King, who will tell you he just received a call from his boss, telling him he received a call from higher authorities within our government ordering you to neither engage nor interfere with us ever again. I will be proven correct in either scenario I just presented; you decide which one plays out."

"How about the scenario where I blow your goddamn head off after killing this son of a bitch?" Dustin bit back.

"Interesting scenario," confirmed the Director, "but your partner is still dead in that one. Oh, and I forgot, a gun is also pointed at your head."

Mercer was reminded by the clicking sound of a Sig Sauer P226's hammer cocked back by a female agent on Director Rosen's team. She held it steadily and trained at his head from behind. Two more of the Director's agents covered her in a standoff with two of Armitage and Mercer's agents, along with a couple of Gatesville's finest in the hallway. Checkmate all around in the Director's favor.

In the middle of the commotion, the short Santa-looking man in a white forensics lab coat and his three-person team huddled together with nervous looks in the middle of a stalemate. He swallowed hard as he announced with his thick German accent.

"We have acquired the samples…"

"Thank you, Doctor," Director Rosen acknowledged.

He gave Armitage a "your move" look.

Mark locked eyes with Dustin, communicating that even though they were the designated law and order in the vicinity, it was best to fight another day. Armitage did not fear a gun pointed at him, but Dustin had a family. Although Dustin did not care about getting into a fight, testing the alleged Director's prophesies was not worth the Agent's blood, especially his friend's. It also did not help that he knew so much about them, which unnerved Mark.

Dustin motioned to the other agents under him.

"Stand down, everyone... stand down."

Everyone slowly lowered their weapons except for Agent Slater and his agents, whose guns remained raised; Mercer kept his finger on the trigger, ready to go, despite the gun pointed at the back of his head.

"Please know, Special Agent, it was not my intention to undermine your investigation," Director Rosen gave a somewhat sincere apology, "but due to this being an extremely time-sensitive matter, you left me with very little choice."

"Who the hell are you?" Mark pressed, demanding to know.

"I'm just like you, Special Agent, the good guy," Director Rosen smiled. "You must have seen the footage already... look around you. This woman is extremely dangerous, and you are not equipped to deal with her. I am. She's my problem now. I advise you to finish your investigation here, file your report, and walk away from this case for your own sake."

Not waiting for Mark to tell him to screw

himself, the Director walked away, followed by the doctor and his technicians. Agent Slater waited for the Director to leave the vicinity before him. The agents under his command moved in unison, creating a protective perimeter around the Director and everyone with them, heading to the elevator. Armitage and Mercer forgot they had guns pointed at them and walked out to the hallway with their agents to watch them depart.

"Gentlemen."

These were Agent Slater's last words before lowering his gun with the rest of his agents, bidding farewell as the elevator door shut.

Mark and Dustin raced to the nearest window to see the Director and his party heading to the helicopter they had traveled in.

Dustin turned to Mark and asked the obvious question.

"What the fuck just happened?!"

"We just got punked," Mark muttered.

"Did we just let them walk out of here?" a dumbfounded Dustin inquired.

"This place has seen enough mayhem. Something in my gut is also telling me as much as that piece of shit down there is a grade "A" asshole... he's no bullshit artist. The doctor said they got the samples they needed."

Mark walked away from the window, executing some quick contemplation, with Dustin following him.

"Get the team back in there now, scour this place from top to bottom... blood, skin, hair samples if you can find it, I want it... all of it. Call the Houston office; we're setting up camp and grab all the footage. We're also starting interviews ASAP. I also want to know who Director Rosen and Agent Slater are by the time I walk out of here. No one points a gun in my face and gets away with it."

CHAPTER 3

She appeared to be running until the breath ran out of her, except she was not getting winded. Her bare footsteps sounded like a wild stallion charging across the open plain. Part of her screamed to stop realizing how fast she was actually moving, that what she was doing, what she had been doing, was inhuman and unnatural.

By right, medically speaking, her heart should have popped several hundred miles ago, and her leg muscles should have torn off her bones. The opposite happened as she clocked speeds of almost seventy, possibly eighty, miles an hour with a heartbeat as if she was taking a leisurely walk while her muscles did not cramp.

Fear was the rider that kept her moving; images of what happened at Mountain View flashed before her eyes, forcing her to move faster and faster. She had to get as far as her legs could carry her so that she could sort out what was happening. She did not realize that she had gone exceptionally far at her current speed. Her tattered, bloodied, bullet-riddled clothes felt like they would be torn from her body. It was then that things also got blurry. Superhuman speed did not translate to superhuman eyesight, which would have allowed her to see and maneuver at such breakneck speeds as she charged into a wooden area.

Logic would dictate stopping at this point, but Sophia, trying her best to maneuver around the trees, was not even sure she knew how to stop, not that she really needed to, as she clipped and smashed through any and everything getting in her path.

"Oh, Shit!" she yelled.

The mammoth oak tree had probably a century on it within those woods; its trunk was clearly six times the width of Sophia's body. Age gave it the strength and density close to steel, making it strong enough to stop anything made of fiberglass and even some things made of metal. Sophia barreling through obliterated an enormous portion of the trunk on impact, sending chunks and splinters flying everywhere. She would have been fine if she had not tripped over what was left of the tree trunk, sending her into an awkward roll, tumbling down an embankment, and destroying all in her path, whether it be wood or stone. What was left of the tree could no longer support its weight, as it burst in half and fell to Earth with a ground-shaking thud.

Sophia screamed and cursed as she tumbled down the steep embankment, falling in ways that should have snapped her neck or split her skull. She shrieked again as the deadly roll flung her off a cliff at the bottom of the embankment, falling a good fifty feet, hitting the river down below hard like a two-ton Mack truck.

Minutes went by as she finally got her baring underwater and battled against the currents to come up. Her new powerful lungs kept her from drowning as she emerged. Her gag reflexes made her throw up half of the river she took while going under. As she finally made her way to the shoreline, she continued to puke up what was left of the water in her lungs. She was still human, she thought to herself, and the fact that her heart was still beating in her chest meant she was not the walking dead. Sophia instinctively checked herself to ensure she did not break a bone, only to find there was not a scratch on her despite her life-ending tumble.

She looked around in wonderment as the morning sun shined down on her. The realization of what happened several hours ago caused her to emit a nervous laugh mixed with sobbing tears as she clutched her chest.

Several hours ago, the state of Texas had executed her. A couple of hours ago, she was brought down by a hail of bullets; after each death, she was resurrected stronger than the last time, giving her the ability to physically break out of prison, fighting through a brigade of heavily armed and highly trained correctional officers, police, and, from what she could tell, a SWAT team. Four years ago, she was sure she would never see outside those walls alive, and there she stood on a riverbank free underneath God's blue sky.

Painfully, Sophia remembered why she was there—distorted images—memories she had no knowledge of flashed before her eyes. Pieces of an apparent puzzle hidden from her for years, Sophia grabbed her skull, trying to sort through the visions. It was then she realized that around her wrists were the restraints from the lethal injection table.

Sophia went to unbuckle the wrist restraint on her right wrist when she was hit with the vision of being on the lethal injection table, going to sleep, feeling herself suffocating and dying despite the assumption that lethal injection was the most "humane" and "peaceful" way to be executed before everything went dark. She could feel her lungs filling with air again, more distorted memories flooding her mind, the skull cracking strike of the baton, bullets ripping into her body, and choking on her own blood before the piercing pain of a bullet penetrating her cranium, destroying her brain sending her into the black for a second time. She did not know how long she was in the black until air violently rushed into her lungs again. Sophia's heart pounded as if it would explode from her chest while all her veins were on fire. The last pain she felt before escaping Mountain View would be what felt like another bullet striking the back of her skull.

Sophia quickly ripped both restraints from her wrists like paper, throwing them as far away as possible. She crouched down in the freezing cold water of the river, trying to get it together. It was terrifying; she felt everything again, except she was not dying.

Sophia gripped a nearby stone about four times her size, not realizing her hands were imprinted into the wet rock. She began to count backward to herself from twenty, taking a deep breath while focusing on the stone; slowly, the visions disappeared, and she could see straight again.

"It's not real... it's not real... you're alive... you are alive," Sophia reaffirmed to herself.

She submerged herself in the river to shock her system with the ice-cold water.

Although it was not the teeth-chattering hypothermia cold felt after dunked into a surging river, she could still feel cold and wetness. It meant her nerves were still intact. Not that it mattered since the heat from the Texas sun would dry her off once she started moving again.

Sophia rose to a standing position with her senses clearer and more focused. Slowly, she looked around in bewilderment, pondering the one question in her mind since stopping at the riverbank.

"Where the hell am I?" she asked aloud.

CHAPTER 4

Gatesville Women's Unit of the prison was designated for regular prisoners and lifers instead of Mountain View, strictly for death row inmates. Agents Armitage and Mercer sat in the interrogation room, reviewing the files and pictures they had of Sophia, attempting to piece things together when the door opened. The silver dreadlock-haired woman Sophia had said her final goodbyes to walk through in shackles flanked by two correctional officers. She had a slight permanent limp on her right leg due to a prison altercation some years ago. Armitage looked up while Mercer continued to go through the files.

"Shackles aren't necessary, boys; you can take them off," Mark requested.

She stood taller and more distinguished as they removed the restraints from her wrists, ankles, and waist. Armitage motioned for her to sit, which she did as the correctional officers took their leave waiting outside.

Mark picked up her file, quickly scanned it, and began to read it out loud.

"Agnes Shareef Wilcox, also known as "Sister Shareef, head of the Sisters of Islam, convicted of murder and sentenced to forty years to life in prison with eligibility for parole after twenty. My name is Special Agent Mark Armitage, and this is my partner, Special Agent Dustin Mercer."

"How can I help you, Special Agent?" Sister Shareef asked, getting down to the point.

Mark took a photo of Sophia, sliding it in front of her.

"Do you know this woman?" Mark asked, pointing.

Sister Shareef glanced at the picture.

"Her name is Sophia Dennison. She was murdered a couple of hours ago."

Dustin snorted in disgust.

Sister Shareef narrowed her eyes at Mercer, who shot her back a dirty look.

Mark spun around the laptop on the table to face her. He fumbled a bit to bring up the video function.

"We'd like you to watch something," Mark requested. "The footage you're about to see is a bit disturbing, but we ask that you please watch."

As the video played, Sister Shareef's chiseled expression quickly softened at the footage of her friend lying lifeless on the execution table. As she swatted away the tears, twenty years was scared out of her witnessing the supposed dead corpse of her friend rising back to life, gasping for air.

"Jesus…" a shaken Sister Shareef uttered.

Dustin gave her a sarcastic, perplexed look.

"Thought you prayed to Muhammad?"

Sister Shareef ignored Mercer's snide remark as she watched her friend rip through her restraints and overpower five correctional officers, punching one through two inches of solid glass. She then cringed, letting out a yelp as she watched her friend savagely gunned down on the screen.

"Sophie…"

Sister Shareef whimpered, witnessing Sophia's bloodied and bullet-riddled body as she lay dead for a second time.

A stone-faced Armitage with full knowledge of the end story walked up and fast-forwarded the video.

"Keep watching… please."

Sister Shareef gave him a quick look of disgust until she glanced at the speeding footage, seeing what they saw a couple of hours ago.

Mark stopped the video just before the second resurrection. It removed another twenty years from her.

Sister Shareef watched in horror as what used to be her friend rose once more, now impervious to gunfire, and proceeded to tear through a hallway stuffed with correctional officers, local police, and SWAT.

Mark allowed her to listen to the screams and yells and the background sounds of smashed concrete and bending steel before shutting the video off. Sister Shareef lowered her head, attempting not to appear shaken after absorbing everything she had seen.

"If you're expecting that doofy looking white kid from "That Seventies Show" to come running out and tell you you've just been punked… he's not," Dustin said, coming out of leftfield with a zinger.

Sister Shareef tried to compose herself as she raised her head, looking Mark in the eyes.

"What do you want from me?"

Mark started his interview.

"Aside from her attorney, during the almost four years Ms. Dennison has been here, she has not had contact with family or friends in any shape or form. No phone calls, personal visits, or emails; she refused all mail sent to her. The only people she's had contact with during that time are the people in this prison, and I have it on good knowledge that you and she became bosom buddies during that whole time."

Shareef shrugged.

"And? Yes… we were friends… good friends… sisters, but if you want to know if I knew she was stronger than a friggin' locomotive, leaping tall buildings in a single bound, no, I did not know that, nor did she display that ability in the four years she was here. I don't know what that is… but that is not the Sophia I knew."

"We're wasting our frickin' time," Dustin muttered, burying his head in his tree-trunk arms.

Mark moved closer to Sister Shareef, sitting on the table's edge, looking down at her.

"Ms. Shareef, let's put aside the unexplainable insanity that has happened in the last couple of hours. The reality is that your friend seriously injured several people in her escape, men and women with families. She even murdered one."

He hoped his song and dance would get her to open up and give him a shred of clue or idea about what happened in Mountain View.

"Who did she kill?" Sister Shareef jeered.

She leaned back in her seat, folding her arms with the knowledge that the Sophia she knew would never hurt a tick, much less another human being.

Mark began with his violin speech.

"Officer Dennis Wilford… husband… father of…"

With widened eyes, Sister Shareef shot up in her seat, holding a hand up, halting him before he could finish his tune.

"She killed Big Buck?"

Before Mark could answer her, Sister Shareef hunched over, cackling. It grew louder as she stomped her feet with apparent joy.

Her full-blown hysterical laughter royally pissed off Dustin. He sprung to his feet, violently slamming his fist on the table.

"You think this shit is funny, convict?! How about I..."

"What exactly do you think you can do to me, F.B.I. man?" Sister Shareef snapped back at Mercer, looking dead at him.

Mark stood up, holding a hand to Dustin, telling him to settle down.

"If Sophia killed Buck," Sister Shareef bit back, "**trust me**... he deserved it and then some... and as far as whatever plans she might have had, she didn't mention any on the count that she was supposed to be **dead.** But good luck when you find her because judging from what I just saw..., you're gonna need it. Now,... unless you have any more '**questions**' for me, may I go now?"

Armitage, seeing that the interview was officially going nowhere, got up and knocked on the steel door for the guards to come in and escort Sister Shareef away.

As they came in, placing her back into shackles and proceeding to lead her away, Mark stopped her for one final question.

"What do you mean, Officer Wilford, got what he deserved and then some?"

"I find it very ill to speak of the deceased," Sister Shareef returned sarcastically, "but if you did some "real" F.B.I. work, you'd find out that the dearly departed Wilford wasn't only a husband and a father."

As the guards escorted Sister Shareef back to her cell, Mark sat back on the table, feeling a migraine setting in due to the interviews' apparent pointlessness; he massaged the bridge of his nose.

"Guess she told you," Dustin muttered while doodling in his notepad.

Mark turned to look at him as if he wanted

to pull out his service piece and shoot him.

Dustin raised his head in bewilderment, feeling the negative vibe his partner was emitting toward him.

"What?"

"Get off your ass and get me Officer Wilford's file of his entire career," Mark barked, "and not just the bells and whistles."

The door opened before Mercer could get up as a blonde-haired, green-eyed female agent in her mid-twenties popped her head in.

"Um... sir," she sighed, "we have a new problem."

"What is it?" Mark dryly asked, not in the mood for more problems.

"The Warden just informed me Ms. Dennison's parents just called. They're here in Gatesville, asking when they can take possession of her body."

Mark grabbed his skull as if to crush it in his own hand.

Dustin let out a sarcastic chuckle.

"Just keeps on getting from bad to worse."

CHAPTER 5

September 3, 2008, 0200 A.M. in the
morning, Cypress, Texas, twenty-seven minutes
away from Houston and three hours and five
minutes away from Gatesville driving, Sophia
actually made it in less than an hour-and-a-half
despite crashing and burning in Birch Creek
State Park at a steady pace of an estimated
seventy miles an hour taking the woods and back
roads to stay ahead and under the radar of, local
law enforcement on the hunt for her.

Sophia remained in the woods on the
outskirts of town until nightfall, moving
whenever she felt a patrol was coming her way.
With her newfound speed, covering a lot of

ground was simple. It was all too clear that the word was out that she had escaped, but the patrol was light, probably believing there was no way she could have made it from Gatesville to Cypress on foot, covering that amount of distance without getting caught.

Sophia quickly learned to use lighter steps while moving, although she made a few necks snap and dogs bark. Eventually, if she kept this up, someone would catch her, and for now, she wanted to avoid getting into any form of confrontation until she figured out what was happening to her. First, she needed to get out of her tattered, blood-soaked, river-drenched prison gear and locate some warm, inconspicuous clothes. After another ten minutes of ducking in and out of alleyways, Sophia came upon the only Goodwill store in town.

"Well… there's no one more in need of goodwill than me…" she whispered with a shrug.

As Sophia made her way to the back alley of the building, her first thought was to rip the door off the entrance until she saw the sign warning of a security alarm. She considered going to the roof when she noticed the large Goodwill drop box at the side of the building.

"Jackpot," Sophia murmured as she cautiously trotted over to it.

Sophia gave a quick look around, stooped down a bit, and proceeded to try to slide her hand between the gap of the locked door; the fit was tight until she gave it a bit more force and realized that the metal was actually bending like clay underneath her hand. She took a deep breath, bracing her other hand against the box and slowly pulled. The thick steel locking mechanism creaked and groaned as Sophia stretched it.

Sophia could have easily ripped it off with a yank but feared the popping sound would attract attention. Besides, she was fascinated at how she felt no pain from the harsh metal against her fingers and how the metal literally bent akin to laffy taffy to her strength. Questions about her strength level flooded her mind as the lock finally gave in, snapping in two. She exhaled with a half-nervous laugh, which she halted by covering her mouth, remembering where she was. Aside from a small bag of paisley slippers, the box was empty; she muttered a curse, realizing she had no choice but to break into the store.

Noticing the fire escape ladder at the side of the building, she began to form a plan. Looking around to ensure no one was coming by, she quickly gripped the colossal and awkward dropbox.

Sophia took a deep breath, remembering what her father told her.

"Lift with your knees."

As she raised her feet, the steel box that had to weigh at least fifteen hundred pounds went up quickly. Sophia trembled with a flood of emotions. Her mind was not playing tricks on her, nor was this some freaky unexplained adrenaline rush; what would have taken a forklift to pick up, she held in her hands like a paperweight.

"Focus, girl... focus," she told herself.

Now was not the time to be amazed; she

did not know when a patrol would come her way. She carried the dropbox to the fire ladder as quietly as possible, placing it underneath it. She then hopped up on top of the box with relative ease.

She breathed, rubbed her hands together, and leaped from the box to the ladder.

The push-off left a big dent in the box.

Sophia's new predicament was the ladder bent in half after catching the rung.

"Aw shit!" she whispered.

Praying for it not to snap under her weight, Sophia quickly scampered up the ladder in a panic for the platform section, which violently shook and felt like it would rip off the concrete wall itself.

Pulling herself up, she finally made it to the platform. She thought she was safe until she heard the snap of steel. Sophia dove, catching what was left of the ladder before it hit the drop-box below, echoing her position to everyone in the town. However, the force with which she hit the platform pulled the steel bolts that held the ladder against the wall halfway out, bringing the structure closer to the Earth.

Sweat added to the blood and river water that soaked her tattered clothes. She was tired of taking deep breaths as she pulled the piece of the broken ladder up, catty cornering it through the box entrance of the platform before laying it down. Sophia whispered every prayer her mother taught as she moved up the rest of the ladder.

As Sophia trotted up the rungs, her movement violently shook the fire escape. With each step, she felt it would tear off the wall and come crashing down with her.

Thankfully, she made it to the roof of the building with no further incident. Now, she had to move extra fast; the mess she left at the side of the building would surely draw attention to her.

Sophia first examined the emergency roof door and skylight window with warning signs of a security alarm waiting to go off if tampered with. No, go there. She stomped with frustration, unknowingly creating a footprint in the dry concrete of the roof. Realizing what she'd just done, she smiled, getting low again to remain undetected as she came up with another idea. Sophia thought there was no way the charity Goodwill would rig the entire roof. She stomped down with her heel, making a sizable hole that only a jackhammer could rival. She repeatedly stomped, making the hole bigger and bigger.

A few more stomps, and she would break through, creating an entrance big enough for her to climb down into the store.

"Oooooooooooooh shiiiiiiiiiit!"

Her perfect plan had a snag; on the fifth stomp, a portion of the roof underneath her gave way. She came through the ceiling, falling a good twenty feet, smashing through some racks full of clothes at the bottom.

It sounded like the Dropbox outside was tossed off the roof. Sophia lay there for a minute due to wounded pride, not pain or injury, which she no longer felt or sustained. She waited to see police lights shining through the windows and Cypress's finest breaking down the doors, drawn to the commotion she made.

Two minutes had passed; she apparently was in the clear. Slowly, Sophia rolled to her feet, looking around to find no security guard or a night watchman. She spied a few security cameras, but she was doubtful they patched into the nearby police station, seeing how they would have been there already. She remembered from movies that if she found the tapes and destroyed them, they would not have any footage of her to go on while she would be long gone.

The first thing was to clean up. It took Sophia a while, but she found an old rag and towel set. She went to the bathroom, peeled off her butchered prison garb, and used the sink to wipe off the remnants of blood and funk on her.

As Sophia went through the cleaning task, she also took the time to examine her body. Except for her original scars and birthmarks, there was no bullet wound or scratch on her body. Sophia then ran her hand across her now washboard stomach, where once was a little pouch. Her eyes watered, and emotions washed over her; she was alive and breathing when she should be dead. Sophia quickly dismissed it, enthralled with how solid and muscular her body was now. She shuddered when she finally realized that she went from being five-foot-six to a near six-footer.

"I'm Sasquatch…" Sophia said to her reflection.

Feeling clean for the first time in almost twenty-four hours, she timidly stepped back into the store wearing nothing but a bath towel, keeping it low again, searching for new clothes. This proved difficult because she had to work in the dark, and everything about her was larger. Underwear proved a problem, especially for the up-top; in the end, she had to settle for a sports bra and thong bottom. The store filled with profanity as she destroyed two pairs of jeans in her original size. Luckily for her, a couple of light blue jean leggings were in an XL size. She was officially in the red when it came to shoes, as she no longer wore a size six.

"Aw, hell no!"

Sophia growled in disgust as her feet ripped through a pair of white Reeboks sneakers in her original size.

Realizing she was wasting too much time, she sneered and reluctantly hunted for a bigger size, coming across a pair of black and white Converse size nine, which fit perfectly. After going through several colorful shirts, she settled on a simple white tank top and a weird black Goth-style hooded jacket that caught her eye. It was more like an oversized hood with just sleeves and a midriff top with a small zipper that fastened over her chest. The rings and studs on the arms gave it a unique look.

It was not practical, but Sophia liked it, and she figured if she appeared to stand out, it would actually make her appear incognito. Her last accessory was a small black shoulder book bag she would use to carry her bloody prison gear, which she placed in a plastic bag. She knew that if she was going to find out what exactly happened to her, Sophia would find it within the blood once she got it tested.

With new clothes checked, she went about looking for money; the registers were open and empty, so she made her way to the main office in the back of the store.

On the way there, Sophia stopped in the small break room, looking for something to eat. Surprisingly, she was not famished after going almost an entire day without anything, but she felt a little hunger setting in. Inside, Sophia copped a can of Sprite, some French fries, half of a chicken sandwich, and one-half of a peanut butter and jam sandwich. She started with the P&J, throwing the rest in the microwave while sucking on the Sprite. She munched on the grease-saturated meal while heading to the office in the back of the store. The locked door meant nothing to someone of her ability as she used a little force to push the door open, breaking the lock and cylinder while cracking the door frame. Once inside, she put the food down to case the office.

Luckily, the office had a window, so she searched around via moonlight; Sophia was careful to ensure she did not move anything out of place. She first found the video recorder linked to the surveillance cameras outside. Sophia pulled out the tapes and thought about destroying them but remembered seeing enough cop shows to know they would find a way to view the footage regardless. She stuffed them into her bag, taking them with her. The next thing she had to find was money.

Sure enough, like all small towns, there was still some trust. There was a safe underneath the manager's desk. Like the Dropbox, but with more confidence, she quickly ripped the door off. She pulled out the cash box and opened it as if it had never been locked. It was packed, probably all of the cash from last week and yesterday. As she pulled out the twenties, tens, and fives to count them, her eyes glanced at the picture of the manager on the table.

He was a stocky, cheerful, elderly man, probably in his early sixties, with white-silver hair and some silver horn-rimmed spectacles. There were pictures of him with his wife, children, grandchildren, and employees. In every picture, she could feel the happiness pouring out, the sense of family, even from the people who worked for him.

Sophia sadly sat down in his chair, riddled with guilt. Aside from the paddling she got from her mother for attempting to lift a stick of bubble gum from the local convenience store when she was six, she had never stolen anything. She was accused and punished for many things that she was innocent of; she was guilty of this crime.

~ ~

Her mind began to wander back to almost four-and-a-half years ago. The grueling trial and the looks of disgust and hatred she had to endure, the district attorney wove a story to the court of how she was an evil, conniving woman who grew tired of taking care of her badly injured, mentally traumatized veteran husband who served honorably for his country.

She acquired a personal checking account a month before in the same bank as her husband and kept their joint accounts, which she had no knowledge of. Evidence, namely video footage, showed otherwise. There was also evidence of the neurotoxin she smuggled from the hospital's experimental facility where she worked. She used the drug on her husband after making love to him. As he lay both powerless and defenseless in their bed, she savagely murdered him.

The district attorney then accused her of transferring all the money from her and her late husband's joint accounts to her personal bank account and purchasing a one-way flight to Brazil that night while he lay dead in bed. The IP address from her laptop was the additional damning evidence.

The next day, she withdrew two thousand dollars in cash from an ATM and then drove to Oklahoma, checking into the Four Pointed Hotel near the Will Rogers World Airport using her credit card; tollbooth cameras also caught her and her Nissan Maxima during the drive there.

Aside from the DNA from the murder weapon, their wedding cake knife, she had to sit there and watch damning video footage of herself doing these things. Things she had utterly no knowledge of doing.

It was like watching another person who looked exactly like her wearing her exact clothes and jewelry down to her wedding ring. She almost came to believe she had gone crazy because, in her own mind, the events she watched were a complete utter blank.

The medical examiner's testimony was additional compounding evidence of how the forty-one stab wounds on her husband's body were slow, deliberate, and precise, hitting vital veins and organs so that he bled out slowly. He linked her skill and knowledge as a neurosurgeon, making her capable of doing it. It was a slam dunk for the prosecuting district attorney.

Despite the mountainous evidence against her admitting to the only thing, she feverishly denied everything. She did make love to Robert the night he was murdered.

She could still remember the cries and wails of her family, especially her mother when the lead juror read the guilty verdict on all charges; a week later, she heard the chilling words during her sentencing.

"Has the jury reached a verdict?" the judge asked.

"Yes, your honor," the lead juror announced.

The judge motioned for the bailiff to take the paper from the lead juror so that he could read their judgment against Sophia. Time literally stood still for her at that moment. After reading, he looked at the jury again, then turned to a trembling Sophia waiting for sentencing.

"Usually, I would disregard what is on this paper and hand down a life sentence with no promise of parole," the judge began. "Being that this is your first brush with the law, Mrs. Matheson."

"But the evidence of your crimes is so… disgusting… so heinous… I have no choice but to make an exception here today."

He shook his head as he continued.

"You not only planned out the murder of your husband, but you butchered him while he laid very much coherent and defenseless… as a former Marine … I find this the most dishonorable and cowardly way to be murdered.

And so I have no choice but to go with the jury's decision and levy the ultimate punishment on you. Sophia Matheson, you will be remanded to the Mountain View Unit for Women in Gatesville, where you will be sentenced to death by lethal injection. May God have mercy on your soul. Remand Mrs. Matheson into custody. This court is adjourned."

Sophia had collapsed at the word "death" as the wails grew louder in the courtroom; her mother was rushed to the hospital for a mild heart attack. After three months of prison time, she had cut off all contact with her family and friends so they could not see the state she was in. She changed her name back to Dennison, and after her first and only appeal that took an agonizing three-and-a-half years, she gave in and waited to die.

~ ~

She did not know if it was one of her abilities, but her mind was like a DVD operating in 4D mode. It was playing back events in her mind in precise detail where it felt like she could smell, hear, and touch things as long as she focused on that time. Sophia tested it by concentrating on the night in the hotel. She remembered waking up groggy with a massive taste of cottonmouth. She did not understand how she went from being naked in her bed, wrapped up in Robert's embrace, to one of her business suits as she tried to sit up.

Looking around the room, she only recognized her laptop on the desk and her luggage. Who packed her bags, and why was it there? Why was she there, for that matter?

Sophia stumbled to the bathroom to run her face with ice-cold water in hopes it would wake her up and shake the fogginess so she could figure out what was truly going on. Halfway there, her soul leaped out of her body, startled by the door to the room slammed open. Men flooded in, screaming at her. As her focus cleared, she saw they were police officers with their guns pointed at her.

"What… what's happening…" Sophia managed to get out amid the chaos.

The officers ignored Sophia as they barked orders at her.

"Police! On the ground! Get on the ground now!"

She raised her hands in the air, terrified.

"I don't understand what's happening? What's happening?"

Realizing she was not armed, two officers rushed her, throwing her violently to the room's carpet floor. It felt like they were attempting to snap her arms in half like twigs. She sobbed and wailed uncontrollably. Why was she in that room? How did she get into that room? Why were they hurting her, and why was no one answering her? Most importantly, where was Robert? She tried to search her memory, but everything between the night she slept in his arms and when she woke up in that room was completely blank.

As she felt the cold steel of one of the officer's handcuffs clamp down hard on her wrists, the officer with the words "Detective" written across his bulletproof vest finally gave her an answer.

"Sophia Matheson… you are under arrest for the murder of your husband Robert Matheson… you have the right to remain silent…"

She did not hear him reading her the rest

of the Miranda rights.

"What? Robert is dead? No! No! No! Tell me what happen?!" she screamed incoherently. "Tell me what happened?! Please! Please!"

She went on like that as they pulled her to her feet and dragged her out of the hotel.

Bringing her back to Houston through a horde of reporters asking questions she could not answer.

She did not bother reliving the hours and hours of brutal and relentless grilling from a chain of detectives and the sleepless nights of bitter crying in a cell.

~ ~
~

Sophia focused on what happened after that night in the hotel, but it was all blank again. The length of the blankness told her she was probably out for a day or two. She focused harder to get to that night; on the verge of giving up out of frustration, an image appeared in her head.

It was blurry and dark, but an image was still coming through. Sophia could see the moonlight coming through the windows of their room. The cottonmouth had returned just like in the hotel, but she was home in her bedroom this time.

Sophia was not lying next to Robert in their bed. She was propped up against a wall, covered in her bedsheets, sitting on the cold cherry oak floor they redid together. She looked around, wondering how she got there when she heard the voices. Three distorted and one muffled, she looked up to see Robert lying on the bed looking straight at her.

His eyes were full of tears; it looked like he was fighting to move but could not. Why could he not move? Why could he not even speak, for that matter?

His mouth looked like it had a case of lockjaw. Sophia then realized she could not move either; she did not feel paralyzed, but her body felt like a ton of bricks. Her voice was gone as well, filling her with fear. It felt like she was in the middle of a nightmare and could not wake up. She tried to calm herself and focus on what the voices were saying.

"Of all the things," said a first distorted voice, which sounded like a man, "…a fucking wedding cake knife…"

"What?! It's symbolic!" returned an entirely different, distorted male voice.

"Whatever… let's get this over with," the first man said.

Their voices sounded Vader-like without the heavy breathing.

"Playtime, big boy…" came a third distorted voice that sounded like a woman.

Sophia concentrated on the female voice; she could make out a slender dark figure straddling her husband on their bed. She could not see her head because she could barely raise her neck up, but she could see what appeared to be a patch on her shoulder. It was dark and embossed, but the moonlight revealed to her what seemed to be the Grim Reaper sitting on a colossal skull, holding a scythe in one hand while holding a skull in its other hand. Sophia's eyes traveled lower to see her running something silver and pointy across her husband's stomach. It appeared to be the cake-cutting knife from their wedding.

Her eyes returned to Robert, who remained fixed on her, while he mouthed, "I'm sorry... I am so sorry..."

Still unable to find her voice, she groaned, catching everyone's attention.

"Holy shit... she's awake," Man #2 announced.

"Impossible," Man #1, the group leader, said. "She should be out for at least thirty-six hours."

"Just cut her fucking head off," hissed the woman of the group.

Sophia struggled to lift her head to see who the bitch was, only to see that she was wearing some high-tech-looking helmet that covered her entire head attached to an equally tech-like suit.

"No, you idiot, we need her alive for this to work," the leader reminded the woman. "Just hit her with another dosage and some of the pink stuff; that'll make sure she won't remember any of this."

She struggled to move and tried to make her voice louder so someone could hear her, but it was useless. The next thing she felt was a leather hand grabbing her arm and a sharp prick. She groaned again as things began to get foggy; her little consciousness was focused on the female figure.

Sophia felt her looking at her before everything went black, and she was sure she heard her say, "Get ready for your life to change."

~ ~

Sophia woke from her trance with a gasp, and her eyes were blinded with tears. She scrambled to her feet in confusion, crashing into the nearest wall, effortlessly caving it in. She steadied herself, forced herself to breathe normally, and to stop the damn shaking. As crazy as it was, it was now clear what had happened on

104

that night all those years ago.

Rage now stoked her heart; somehow, someway, she had to find out about that morbid patch, and then she would find them. First, she grabbed the cash from the box, counted it, took half, and put the rest back. She then tore a piece of paper from a tablet, grabbed a pen, and wrote.

"I'm so sorry for taking your money and the damage. I promise I will pay you back and fix everything. You have my word."

As she finished her letter of apology, an earth-shaking crashing sound of metal-on-metal from outside made her leap out of her skin.

"Jesus!" she screamed.

She quickly stuffed the money into the bag and zoomed out of the office through the store. She broke through the emergency exit door without thinking of the alarm. Not that it mattered; she could hear sirens getting closer.

Sophia cupped the top of her head, gritting her teeth. The fire escape ladder finally ripped from its fixings and crashed into the alleyway atop the dropbox.

"Not… good," she said before turning on her heels.

With her newfound ability for speed, she jetted out of town before anyone could see her. Her destination was the only place she knew she could find her needed answers. Back home.

CHAPTER 6

September 2, 2008, 11:56 AM, several hours before Sophia visited Cypress, the jet-black twin-engine Sikorsky private helicopter from the incident in Mountain View Unit soared over the gigantic trees of Upper Klamath Lake in Oregon.

It no longer made the loud whirling sound that came with its entrance at the prison. It appeared to be in stealth mode as the blades continued to spin without emitting any noise, while reflective panels at the bottom made it a ghost to virtually anyone looking up.

Its destination was the top of Mount McLoughlin. Carved right into the mountain, a sixty-foot security wall masked the only entranceway for transporting equipment to enter or exit when needed.

On top of the wall, holographic projectors and reflective panels provided camouflage against unsuspecting hikers or campers looking outside as it hid the security detail in high-tech armor, gear, and weapons never seen before in modern warfare.

Not that they really had to worry; three hundred meters ahead of the wall were patrols on off-road highly advanced ATVs minus the loud, obnoxious sounds they usually emit, wearing similar armor to the ones on the wall, but with camo color that allowed them to blend in perfectly with their environment.

They, along with the network of hidden cameras, mini-bird-like drones, and motion sensors, ensured that no one either unintentionally or deliberately got within the eyesight of the facility.

Finally, two hundred meters ahead, a security detail of phony park rangers intercepted hikers and mountain climbers, feeding them false information or redirecting them to the other side of the mountain not located near the facility. The aircraft made its final descent at the top of the snowcap of the once volcanic mountain; the very top, though covered in snow, was also a massive platform helipad, which the copter smoothly landed on despite the wind conditions.

Upon confirming a secure and safe landing, the platform lowered the helicopter into the mountain. A massive lid door on hydraulics ascended as it descended, closing the mountain base entrance while new snow spewed out through vents to cover the entry.

In her late twenties, a woman stood waiting near the helipad's main entrance, clutching a computer tablet and dressed in a jet-black, slightly form-fitting business suit. She wore her silky brunette hair in a bun as she adjusted the black and silver high-priced name-brand glasses on her face, which amplified her bright green eyes.

Her demeanor commanded professional respect despite wearing colorful pink flip-flops, revealing her rose-colored toenails. Briskly, she walked to the Sikorsky as the platform finally reached its resting spot. The lights turned red to green, confirming the platform was locked and secured.

She stepped onto the platform, now waiting at the vehicle entrance, quickly scratching the back of her left leg with her right big toe. As the doors opened and the steps flipped down again, the Director stepped out, followed by Agent Slater, the Santa-looking man with the German accent, along with his staff and the agents under the Director.

"Welcome back, Director," greeted the young woman.

"Status, Ms. Barrett," Director Rosen commanded, getting down to business.

Ms. Barrett fell in line with Agent Slater as they followed the Director, making a beeline into the facility.

"A couple of hikers came close to the perimeter; our "park rangers" met them and sent them to the "safe side" of the mountain," she began her report. They were informed they were too close to black bear territory and a family of bears, and then Mr. Dunbar showed up again."

Director Rosen drew a sigh.

"Did the men stomp him out as ordered?" he calmly asked.

"Yes, sir," she confirmed. "Before the usual "tranq and wipe" followed by dumping him on his lawn for an umpteenth staged drunken stupor."

Director Rosen smiled.

"We have it recorded?"

"Yes, sir," Ms. Barrett nodded.

"Good, I'll watch it later," he said as he continued to his destination within the facility.

"I still don't understand why we continue doing this instead of eliminating him altogether," Ms. Barrett said. "He just won't stop."

"I keep telling you, Ms. Barrett," Director Rosen lectured, "one local drunken conspiracy theorist nut keeps the regulars skeptical and

away and reduces an unnecessary body count…
not to mention I just love messing with him.
Remember, we're in the business of killing the
enemies of our country."

"Not our citizens… except when
necessary," Ms. Barrett recited.

"Correctamundo, now are they here?"

"Yes, sir, they arrived an hour ago.
They're in debriefing room one with the updated
files."

"Thank you, Ms. Barrett."

Director Rosen motioned to the others
following.

"Mr. Slater, go grab breakfast, Dr.
Zimmerman; I believe we have no further need
of each other till later."

"Of course…" Dr. Zimmerman nodded as
he broke off with his staff, following him to run
further tests on the samples in their possession.

Agent Slater and his team briefly followed
Dr. Zimmerman and his team before making

their way to the mess hall. Ms. Barrett followed the Director, striding with him to debriefing room one. The sterile white walls, ceiling, floor, and dull chrome silver finish on the doors they passed made their outfits pop out against the stark background.

The only other color in the hallway was the surging blue motion sensor strip on each side of the walls and the textbook-large black global surveillance cameras stationed in the ceiling down the end of each hallway.

The Director and Ms. Barrett did not break stride as they neared the debriefing room doors, which parted open perfectly, allowing them to walk vigorously through. Waiting for them in the front of the college campus classroom set up with the big theater-style video screen sat four individuals, three men and one woman.

The midnight black military fatigues they wore could not be associated with any of the five US branches or any military force on the planet. No nametags, call signs, or badges of rank. The only symbol they sported were black embossed patches on the sleeves of their fatigue jackets; the emblem was of a Grim Reaper sitting on a skull, holding a scythe in his right hand and a small skull in his left hand.

From right to left, a man in his mid-thirties was sporting a sharp blond crew cut attached to a well-groomed blond beard with piercing blue eyes lazily flipping through the computer tablet before him reading the data. Next to him sat a younger man in his late twenties with brown hair cut low into a Caesar style, clean-shaven with a nasty disposition, sporting shades in the darkened room. He was not a bit interested in the data on his tablet.

Next to him sat a young woman in her mid-twenties with dirty blonde hair sitting Indian style with her tablet on her lap, more interested in balancing her jet-black stiletto boot knife on the back of her hand. Finally, next to her was a man in his early thirties with fiery red hair and a matching long beard playing Angry Birds on his tablet.

Everyone came to some attention as the Director took the podium. He pulled out his reading glasses from his jacket and put them on.

He began the debriefing.

"The files you have in front of you will outline the details of the target; in this debriefing, we will focus on the essentials."

The theater-sized screen behind the Director came to life, showing Sophia's prison profile and her picture.

"Subject's name is Sophia Dennison, the married name was Matheson," Director Rosen explained. "At age thirty-four, she was convicted of the capital murder of her husband and sentenced to death by lethal injection. The State of Texas executed her almost twelve hours ago. Seven minutes after she was pronounced dead, the subject resurrected, breaking through her bonds and taking out five correctional officers before being gunned down."

Rosen stopped to adjust his reading glasses before continuing.

"After being pronounced officially dead for a second time, the subject resurrected two hours and fifteen minutes after her second death impervious to gunfire taking out between fifty to sixty armed correctional officers, local police, and SWAT, destroying a majority of the eighth floor of the prison before smashing through the wall dropping several stories into a parked squad car. She killed a correctional officer in the process of doing that.

As she proceeded to run the yard, a high-caliber bullet from the watchtower guard brought her down to one knee. She returned to her feet less than a minute after the initial hit. The same guard fired several of the same rounds at her. They were ineffective. She picked up and launched a police car with relative ease, taking out the watchtower. She then ran the yard's length, almost half the length of a football field, in less than ten seconds before smashing through a concrete and stone security wall where she is now on the run. It is believed that the subject has been infected by the EVO Virus."

"How do you know it was the virus?" the first man known as #1 asked.

"Because we were able to test the sample of blood we acquired after she was "shot to death" inside of the prison," Director Rosen returned with stone-cold irritation. "Please do not interrupt me again unless it's with an intelligent question.

Now, as you can see based on the footage, the subject displays the following superhuman abilities… strength allowing her to lift possibly several tons, smash through solid concrete, and rip through pure steel with considerable ease and durability; she's impervious to armor-piercing rounds, all forms of blunt force injuries and falls that may prove fatal. Superhuman speed… top speed, however, is unknown to us.

She also possesses regenerative healing, which we believe heals her from wounds and gives her new abilities to not be injured the same way again. This ability seems to vary in recovery time, depending on the injury. Prison records reveal before her "execution" her original height of five-foot-six inches, weighing in at one hundred and twenty-five pounds; however, the footage we have acquired suggests an alteration to her current physiology.

We estimate her to be almost six feet tall with a weight of several hundred pounds."

The theater screen broke into smaller screens, showing footage of Sophia either smashing through brick walls or ripping off steel doors. At the same time, correctional officers and SWAT fired round after round at her from various firearms, proving ineffective in bringing her down. The outside courtyard's footage showed the side of the eighth floor exploding as Sophia, holding a correctional officer with a missing arm, fell crashing into a squad car, almost creating a crater.

She crawled out of the wreckage only to go down to one knee from what appeared to be a high-caliber bullet. She raised again as similar rounds fired at her bounced off her now impenetrable skin. She then grabbed a sheriff's Dodge Charger squad car, lifting it clumsily from the back end, and launched it like a shot-put, taking out the watchtower as the security guard jumped to safety to avoid the hit. The four individuals looked at each other, visibly concerned about how to deal with such an individual.

"One more thing… almost four and a half years ago," Director Rosen remembered, "you all murdered her husband and framed her for it."

Usually, information like that would not bother a couple of highly trained killers if their targets were regular.

"Well… that's good to know," the red-haired man, #4, said sarcastically.

"So now that you've dropped the mother of nukes on us," #1 asked, "how do you expect us to kill her?"

"I don't expect you to kill her," Director Rosen answered. "I expect you to bring her in."

It was as if someone sucked the wind out of the room; #3 let out a nervous laugh as she played with her long hair while picking at her boot with her knife.

#4 lowered his head down, stroking his fire-red beard, while #2 stared at the Director through his dark shades.

#1 does not even look at the Director as he flipped through Sophia's profile on his tablet.

#4 finally decided to raise his hand,

flailing it around like in elementary school.

Director Rosen finally recognized him.

"What is it?"

"Just curious, sir," #4 innocently asked, "us and what friggin' army is supposed to bring in the bitch of steel carrying the mother of all grudges against us?"

Director Rosen removed his glasses and exited his podium to stand before #4. He looked down at him as if he were an ant he was about to step on.

"My apologies," he said with a stern, sarcastic tone, "I've seemed to have given off the impression that you all had either an opinion or choice. Do you need re-education?"

#4 looked at Ms. Barrett and the tablet in her hand as she raised an eyebrow.

He swallowed hard.

"No, sir," he shook his head.

The Director turned his back to #4,

returning to his podium as the other teammates gave him a dirty look for agitating the man.

#4 returned the look in kind.

"What? Fuck y'all lookin' at?"

"If we are done playing games, let us make one thing clear," the Director sternly delivered home to the team of four. "Sophia Dennison is more valuable than all of you and everyone else who has come before you... and just like you, she is my property that I want back... like yesterday."

"But not to worry," Director Rosen said, giving them a fatherly smile of reassurance, "as usual, Daddy has some toys that will put you on equal footing with her so that you can carry out your mission."

The screen went black and then came on again with an expansive view revealing four gigantic metallic monstrosities in separate clear glass cylinders of some mysterious solution with various wires attached.

#4 was the first to echo the team's

sentiment. "What the...?"

"Biological Assault Mechs," Director Rosen answered, "BAMs" for short, the perfect mixture of cybernetics and living tissue."

"Cyborgs?" the silent man known as #2 asked.

"Mechs," Director Rosen reiterated, "Instead of hydraulics and servos, these machines move via genetically altered muscle, sinew, and a nervous system that is part organic and part cybernetic integrated with a virtually indestructible metallic bone structure, giving them not only exceptional superhuman strength and speed but superior agility and reflexes for their size.

An operator via controls and a neural uplink commands them from within. You each will be fitted for an uplink and calibrated to each machine within the next eight hours; you will then have the next forty-eight hours to master each of your units before engaging the subject."

#4 held his hand while asking his question, not waiting for the Director to call him.

"So, when are these coming to a store near you for Christmas?"

"If you're asking if these will be standard issue for the military, they won't... our government can't afford these. Not to mention the "ethical" retaliation we'd get if the public knew what it took to create such a machine."

"I don't follow," a curious #1 asked.

"For the operator and machine to calibrate perfectly, the organic material has to be first taken from the operator for altering and cloning," Director Rosen explained.

The woman, known as #3, narrowed her eyes as she thought she had figured out what the Director was saying.

"You mean..."

He answered, not waiting for her to wrap her brain around it.

"The DNA used to grow the organic materials for each of these machines was taken from each of you."

Dead silence filled the room for a second time; it was hard to tell whether each member had a look of violation or fascination.

Either way, the look on the Director's face showed he did not care.

"Now, if there are no further questions… prepare to be prepped for surgery in the next six hours."

CHAPTER 7

September 3, 2008, 0830 AM, Armitage
stood in the alleyway near the Goodwill. It was
the first sighting of Dennison since she broke out
of prison. In the alley, he looked at the dropbox
that required a forklift to move, buried under a
couple thousand pounds of steel from the
emergency escape ladder that collapsed on it. It
had been almost a day and a few hours since the
manhunt started. Here, in front of him, was
another sign that the madness was far from
ending. He left his agents and the local forensics
team to take pictures and collect evidence
outside while he went in to see the full extent of
the damage inside the building.

Mark stood next to Dustin, looking up at God's blue sky through the hole in the ceiling next to a small crater and a couple of destroyed clothing racks.

"Self-explanatory, isn't it?" Mark asked with a sigh.

"Yep," Dustin reconfirmed. "Made her way to the roof with that unstable setup outside, punched a hole through so as not to trip any alarms, got cleaned up, picked out some clothes, got something to eat, and broke into the manager's office. She took the videotapes for the surveillance cameras, then broke into the safe, taking some of the money."

Mark furrowed his brow.

"Some?"

"There's still cash in the box," Dustin sneered in disbelief. "It looked like she counted it and took half; she left a note to the manager apologizing for the damage, taking the money, and said she'd pay him back."

Mercer pulled out the letter in a sealed

evidence Ziploc bag, which Armitage took, giving a quick read. He came up, giving his partner a look of total confusion.

"She kills a C.O. in prison," Mark ran down, "breaks into here, and yet leaves half the money and an apology note for the damage she's done."

"There's no end to the weirdness, man," Dustin said while shaking his head, "I figured she booked out of here when the ladder outside fell; that's what prompted the locals to show up."

"Considering the ground she covered so far," Mark estimated, "she could be halfway to Houston by now."

"She could also head to Mexico," Dustin added.

"Good point," Mark agreed, "we'll need to set up a grid from here to there, get some agents down there with the border patrol to try and keep her from going over."

Dustin furrowed his brows at the "Keep her from going over part" of Mark's sentence.

"You did see that she lifted that dropbox outside by herself, right?"

"I'm trying to handle one problem at a time, Dustin," a frustrated Mark returned. "We need to find her. We can figure out how to deal with the superhuman factor after that."

Armitage spied a stocky older man with white-silver hair and some silver horn-rimmed spectacles in a light fall jacket with a checkered shirt underneath and khaki tan pants held up by a belt and suspender combination. He calmly walked around, inspecting the damage.

Mark pointed.

"Who's that?"

The man with the answer looked over to where Mark was pointing.

"Manager of this store... Thomas Ward," Dustin confirmed.

Out of nowhere, Mercer's phone rang; he looked at it and sent it to voicemail.

"Is that Bethany?" Mark asked pryingly.

"Yeah, I'll call her later," he grumbled.

"What'd I tell you about that shit?" Mark came out of nowhere, lecturing him. "Answer your phone, man."

"She's just calling to bitch about my cholesterol and the kids!" Dustin yelled. "I'll call her later!"

"Call her now, dammit!" Mark ordered him, "I'm going to talk to the owner; handle your business!"

"Alright, "ma"! Alright!" Dustin yelled, flaring his arms.

Mark waited until Dustin picked up his phone and called his wife back.

"Bethany? Yeah… what's up?"

Dustin rolled his eyes as she answered.

"I had egg whites and orange juice today; you want me to bring home a stool sample? Well, that's what you get for dick-riding my ass! What?! Well, call the plumber and tell him the toilet can't take him to China!"

Dustin mouthed the words to Mark, "I fucking told you!" as he continued to bicker with his wife.

Mark walked over to Thomas Ward for the formal Federal Bureau assurance that they were on the job with the promise of apprehending the fugitive eventually, etc.

"Mr. Ward," he introduced himself, "Special Agent in Charge Mark Armitage."

Mr. Ward extended his hand for a shake.

"Nice to meet you, Special Agent."

Mark gave a textbook apology for situations like this.

"Sorry about the damage to your store. And everything else."

Mr. Ward shrugged with a smile.

"Well, you didn't do this, and that's what insurance is for."

"Still, we're pursuing the fugitive and should have her in due time," Mark reassured.

"May I ask if all of the cameras in this store work?"

"As I told one of your agents," Mr. Ward confirmed, "two are dummies... two are working... we don't get a lot of thievery in these parts. You're welcome to the tapes, but I heard the young lady took them."

Mark nodded with appreciation.

"Thank you. Um... here's my card; please call if you can think of anything or need anything."

"Thank you, Special Agent. Oh, and if you do happen to catch the young lady who did all this, tell her I forgive her... and I am praying for her."

Thomas Ward gave Mark a smile and a nod as he walked away, leaving him bewildered and unable to process what he had just heard.

"Okay... the whole world has officially gone mad," he muttered, shaking his head.

CHAPTER 8

11:45 PM, Sophia stood in the backyard of her and Robert's home. After four years, she thought someone would have made it the family home she always wanted it to be. She thought she would see bikes, a swing set, and maybe a puppy. Instead, it sat there as dark and empty as a tomb almost four years later, and it was still on the market. Considering what had happened there, she understood why it was so hard to sell. The place where she dreamed about having a family was now a real estate agent's virtual nightmare. An image flooded her mind as she neared the stone fire pit, one of the key selling points for them wanting the house. It was of her and Robert curled up in a blanket on one of the patio chairs. They looked at the stars while the warm fire blazed in the lit pit. She could hear the fire crackling, feel the heat from it, and Robert's warm embrace. She could taste his lips as they kissed and hear his heartbeat as she nuzzled against his chest.

Sophia shook herself, regaining her senses as tears once again filled her eyes, a painful reminder that she had to get control of her new ability. All she had to do was think of a memory long enough, which activated in 4D, making her feel like she was there. So much so it left her in trances if Sophia was not careful. She destroyed a couple of trees and a concrete wall on the way before she figured out how to get somewhat of a handle on it. One of the memories that caused the wall fiasco was a sexual nature with Robert in a movie theater.

As Sophia neared the patio, she grabbed a stone from the waist-high wall entrance that surrounded it. Sure enough, no one found the fake stone with the spare key. She placed the false back where it originally rested and tiptoed to the back patio doors. She prayed that whoever was selling the house was too cheap to continue to pay for the alarm system while it was on the market. Jackpot again as the door opened, minus the one-minute warning beep to enter the disarming passcode into the keypad. She entered slowly, closing the door behind her. With her eyes closed, she reminded herself to stay focused; a treasure trove of memories was in that house.

Birthdays, football games, a couple of firsts, arguments, and every good and bad memory came simultaneously, and she had to shove them all back. Apparently, if she was not near something familiar, she could pull a memory by choosing and viewing it. However, the memories spilled like an over-packed closet when she came across or touched something familiar. The original plan was to stay the night in their old home. Clearly, that was no longer possible; she would go insane by dawn. She was there because she wanted to know if her memories gave her the same clear-cut image when Sophia selected them or if it was more intense in her former home; she was looking for clues.

Sophia trotted upstairs, where she was barraged with more memories ranging from moving in new furniture, the water fights in the hallway, the time they could not wait to get to their bedroom to have each other, and arguments with slamming doors. She weathered through them, trying to get to the master bedroom. She forced herself to stop at one particular bedroom beside the master.

~ ~

They did not change the paint; they probably wanted it to be the selling point for a house fit for a new family. Sophia could smell the sea-green paint as she applied it to the wall on her side; on the other side, Robert put on the yellow.

"So, if it's a girl?" she asked.

"Rebecca, Sarah, Mary..."

"Anything other than Biblical names?" Sophia sneered.

He thought about it and rattled off some more.

"Erica... Stephanie... Alize... Porsha."

"Alright! Alright!" Sophia stopped him. "What if it's a boy?"

He contemplated with a smile.

"Well, I was thinking about Rob Junior..."

"No... oh no, just because it's coming out of me doesn't mean you get a mini-me!"

"Oh... oh... real nice, you just came up with that on the spot?" Robert asked sarcastically.

"I can't help that you're kind of slow in the wit department..." Sophia returned with an underlined, yet blatant, diss.

"I'm slow now?" Robert asked, slowly turning around. "You calling me slow? Do you want to see how slow I am? You think this is slow?"

She did not have time to react as he walked over and picked her up, whisking her around.

136

Sophia burst out with a shocking scream of laughter.

"What are you doing? What are you doing? Put me down. You're going to make me drop the paint!"

"Am I still slow? Am I still slow?" Robert asked, playfully demanding her to recant her comment.

"There are pineapple shrimp, lemon shrimp, coconut shrimp, pepper shrimp, shrimp soup, shrimp stew, shrimp salad, shrimp, and potatoes," she answered with her best Bubba voice in a playful taunt.

"You doing Bubba again?" Robert said. "You doing Bubba?"

He grabbed Sophia, throwing her over his shoulder, grabbed her legs, and began to paint her feet with the paintbrush tickling her.

"No! No!" Sophia laughed. "You know that makes me pee! No! No!"

~ ~

Sophia painfully recoiled from the memory, a happy memory with a heartbreaking reminder that only paint filled the room. She pulled herself away, finally making it to the master bedroom.

She braced herself, psyching up before she walked through the doors.

"One memory… focus on that one memory… focus on that night…"

~ ~

As Sophia touched the double doors to the main bedroom, her memory transported her to that night, hours before her world changed. She was going to leave him that night; almost six months after he returned home injured from Iraq, they had been arguing nonstop, and when they were not fighting, they were barely talking to one another.

Sophia's psychology background made her understand Post Traumatic Stress Disorder, especially with soldiers injured in combat; however, it was a completely different story, being the wife of a soldier suffering from it.

138

Money was never the issue. They had more than enough, especially with his trust fund, military pay, and her work; she also could live through the night terrors.

She could not live through the nights of silence, being in the same house with the person she was in love with, and feeling so lonely; there were no talks of children or starting his custom auto restoration business. Instead, there were late nights alone at home or him stumbling in drunk after a night with his friends.

Then there were the days when he was just angry and would snap at her, especially about stupid things. She asked him to go to counseling, and he flat-out refused. She started taking extra shifts at the hospital so she did not have to come home and deal with him.

Sophia couldn't live like this; she needed time to think, so she decided to take a couple of weeks off work and stay with her parents in New York to determine if this life was worth continuing. She did not expect him to be home; she thought it would be a long night of waiting before she could confront him. The master bedroom doors were rarely shut. Sophia listened at the door briefly in case someone was there with him. It sounded like it was just him. With a deep breath, she opened the doors to every wife of a veteran worst nightmare.

Robert sat on the bed hunched over, sobbing uncontrollably, holding his Beretta M9 locked and apparently loaded... a horrible combination.

Sophia thought it was best to postpone telling him she was leaving him as she slowly entered the room with her heart in her throat and fresh sweat soaking her doctor scrubs. It was like walking into a field of landmines as she neared her husband.

"Robert... honey... what are you doing?" Sophia asked with a calm innocence.

He sobbed harder as she edged closer to him, unsure whether or not she should call the police.

She breathed and decided to see if she could defuse the situation.

"Robert... baby... give me the gun," she gently asked.

He blubbered with his chin buried in his chest.

"I'm gonna burn, I'm gonna burn... for what I've done... oh God, forgive me, I'm gonna burn..."

His finger was not on the trigger, but the safety was off, and Robert was a quick shot.

"Robert, give me the gun," she gingerly asked again, standing before him, "give me the gun, baby..."

At that point, Robert went into a near-hysterical state, flailing his arms around with the gun, forcing her to back up a bit.

"All that blood! All those people!" He howled. "I'm gonna burn! I'm gonna burn..."

Sophia decided best to take a more direct approach, not going for the gun as she knelt before him.

She cupped his face, looking him dead in

141

the eyes.

"You're not going to burn, you hear me… you're not gonna burn…"

"Sophia… you don't know," Robert sobbed, dropping his shoulders, "you don't know… what I've done… you have no idea what I've done."

Sophia shook his face, fighting to get his full attention.

"You served your country, you gave them everything… but you're mine again… you hear me?"

Tears now poured as she lost control of her own emotions.

"You are mine again," she cried, "and they are not taking you away from me… Do you hear me? They're not taking you away from me…"

As Sophia kissed him, he pulled away. She kissed him repeatedly and ripped the front of his shirt open, kissing his shrapnel-scarred chest.

"Sophia… stop… stop… please stop,"

Robert growled.

Refusing to be rejected, Sophia jumped up, straddling him, holding on by his ripped shirt, sparking his now hair-trigger rage.

"I said, stop!!" Robert screamed at her.

"I'm not stopping!" she shouted back. "You are mine! You hear me… you are mine… so hit me… throw me off… shoot me… do what you have to do, but I am not stopping till you put down that goddamn gun… and touch me! Please! Just touch me."

Sophia continued to kiss and nibble his torso and neck, holding onto his ripped shirt for dear life. She reached his lips as he weakly attempted to fight her off. Robert laid down the gun, lifting Sophia into the air, unable to fight anymore.

Sophia wrapped her legs around his waist, letting him take her as willingly as she came to him. He quickly ripped the front of her medical blouse as she did his shirt. A night of trembling passion from bodies that had not touched in so long; they slept that final night entangled in one another.

~ ~

Sophia pulled out of the memory, knowing
what would happen next. She clutched her chest,
trembling and weeping; it was a thousand times
more intense being there and reliving it. She
should not have returned, but she had to discover
why Robert was so distraught. What was he
going to burn for? The answers to her questions
were not there. As she opened the doors to an
empty bedroom, the entire room was bare; their
furniture and belongings were gone, God knows
where. This was no longer her home, and she had
to leave it again for good this time.

Sophia snuck out of her home with a
clearer vision of a gritty memory but no clues.
As she locked the door for a final time, she took
the key as a keepsake, the only thing she had of
her old life. She prepared to retake flight to
figure out her next move until another familiar
sound pierced her ears like nails on a chalkboard,
planting her in her tracks. A screaming woman
and glass breaking; the Martins were at it again.

Craig Martin was a senior executive for a

major insurance company in Houston; she remembered him as an abusive prick who liked letting his hand fly, especially against his wife, Tammy. Tammy was a stay-at-home wife and mother, by Craig's choice. Sophia rarely saw Tammy because of her sometimes long work hours as a surgeon, but she remembered the shy smile that went with the light blue eyes when she saw her.

She remembered how that smile would disappear when Craig pulled up, and the first time, her scream woke both her and Robert out of their sleep.

They either went there or called the police to deal with the situation. Sometimes, the officers walked away, just giving him a warning; they walked him out in cuffs a couple of times.

Tammy, however, would go and bail him out an hour later. He would stop for a couple of weeks until Tammy supposedly did something to set him off again.

The redundancy made the neighbors decide not to get involved anymore; Tammy became the neighborhood's joke and gossip, while Craig became the person to avoid altogether.

It did not stop until Robert finally had enough and decided to take matters into his own hands, having a little "man-to-punk" chat with Mr. Martin.

He gave Craig a warning that made him stop cold turkey. He did not detail what he said, but the gist was that Robert refused to live in a neighborhood with a wife-beater living next door to him, and since he was not moving, Craig had three options.

Option one was for Craig to move. Option two was to stop hitting his wife. If he refused the first two, alternative three was vague, but the gist of it was Robert was a Marine with Marine friends, Special Forces friends, and Black Ops friends.

He knew where Craig worked and could easily track his routine, whether going to the strip club or hotel to meet whatever whore he was screwing behind his wife's back and something about never finding the body. He also hinted that his father was a highly decorated four-star general, so there was no way he would do any jail time, much less see the inside of a prison.

Craig, needing to be as close to work as possible, decided to take option #2. Apparently, it lasted until Robert's death.

Sophia narrowed her eyes and hissed her teeth in disgust.

"Dumb bitch…" she muttered.

In her head, Sophia thought that her now-dead husband was the reason Tammy's psycho for a husband ceased and desisted, pounding her face into Play-Doh. Four years later, she was still too stupid and weak after his death to leave his friggin' ass. It was unfair, and Sophia had her problems, which were mountainous to another late-night ass-kicking session at the Martins' house. She went to slink away in the dark, never to return, when a squeal once again stopped her from taking another step.

"Daddy! Please stop!" A crying child wailed. "Daddy! Please!"

"Shut the hell up and go back to your room!" Craig Martin barked back. "Come here bitch!"

Little Ethan was one year old before she was locked up; she remembered him being delivered at her hospital. Tammy was by herself. Craig did not show up until the afternoon the next day.

Sophia looked up into the dark, starry sky, cursing the heavens. This had to be a cosmic joke. God was up there, pissing Himself with laughter, spraying all over her. As the second cry was louder, radiating down her spine, Sophia marched through their yard, heading for the back door. As she neared the door, Sophia hesitated; doing this would alert everyone to her whereabouts, making it extremely difficult to do what she came to do. She still had time to walk away until she heard a fist pounding flesh like a hamburger, followed by a pleading yelp, followed by another fist and another.

She growled as she stabbed the custom cherry-wood door through with a knife hand before gripping it and ripping it out with part of the frame. She tossed it into the yard, where it tore chunks into the freshly cut lawn while breaking into pieces as she entered the house.

They forgot to arm their system, probably due to the hell going on, which meant she had time to get out of dodge when she was finished. She was surprised no one heard her rip the door off as she rushed to the living room area only to find no one there. Her ears popped up to the near-hoarse cries of little Ethan over the commotion going on upstairs.

Sophia darted up the stairs; each step she took caved in whatever wood step she hit, sending splinters flying. She turned left, running down the hallway toward the noise from the master bedroom. Stopping, she saw something no decent human should ever see.

An animal standing over a woman barely half his size with a now unrecognizable bloody and beaten face as a little boy bawled uncontrollably in the corner of the bedroom. She found it ironic to be sentenced to death for a murder she did not commit when she wanted to commit murder at that moment.

Huffing and puffing, Martin looked up from his dirty work to see a lioness standing at the door of his bedroom.

"Who the fuck are you?" he asked. "What the hell are you doing in my house?"

He did not recognize her because of the oversized hood covering the upper half of her face. Not to mention, Sophia was initially much shorter, with long, curly black hair instead of dreadlocks before going to prison. She did not answer him as she broke into a stride, intending to break his neck.

"Crazy bitch!" he yelled.

Craig proved an equal opportunity woman beater as he hauled off and slugged Sophia, not expecting to hit skin denser than steel.

He hollered, coiling away as he broke at least three knuckles on his right hand. Sophia stood there stunned with disbelief, not that she felt a thing but that he hit her. Aside from Mountain View, which was sheer chaos, she had never been in a fight in her life, not even as a child. Except for a couple of paddling from either her mother or father when she was naughty, no one had outright hit her before. Superhuman or not, it was still startling.

"Wha... what the hell are you?" Craig groaned, clutching his hand.

The startling was fleeting as Sophia turned to beat Craig into pink sticky stuff when he grabbed his wife's vanity chair, damaged hand and all, and delivered a cliché chair shot to her skull.

Obviously, it smashed to pieces on impact, but the sheer gall that he up and hit her again made Sophia lose it.

In the middle of it all, Sophia did not notice a badly beaten Tammy crawling out of the way of the new commotion in their bedroom.

With her one good right eye and whatever senses were not knocked out of her, Tammy witnessed a woman three inches shorter than her husband grab him by the front of his shirt and charge, shoving him back first into one of the walls of their bedroom putting half of his body through it. She then pulled him out of the hole she made with his body, hoisted him effortlessly into the air, and, with a swing, hurled him back-first through the door and part of the main bathroom wall.

Part of his shirt was torn during the throw, which she still had in her right hand; she gave it a quick look before letting it fall on the hardwood floor.

"Oh… oh god… my back," he gasped in excruciating pain. "I think you broke my back…"

Sophia went in after Craig stalking him; her Hippocratic Oath was officially tossed out the window as she cared not for how much agonizing pain he was in, the same way he did not think about when pounding his helpless wife like a heavy bag.

"Come here, you filthy son of a bitch," she seethed, "you like beating on women?! Get your ass up!"

She ripped him off the floor with one arm, ignoring his cries, dragging him effortlessly by his torn shirt out of the bathroom back into the bedroom. Tammy huddled into a corner, watching her haul what was left of her husband to their balcony. Sophia booted the doors open, snapping the lock that held them together.

The force of the kick shattered the glass doors while ripping them partially from the hinges they were on, waking part of the neighborhood. She then dragged him over to the front of the balcony. Sophia grabbed the guardrail with her left hand, ripping it out of the patio's cemented concrete.

She then chucked it down, making sure it smashed out the windshield of his Mercedes-Benz below. Sophia really did not have to do it; it was extra, but Sophia wanted to put the fear of God in him, not to mention Sophia knew how much he coveted his car. She then pulled him up, facing her, grabbed him by his throat with her right hand, and proceeded to suspend the broken and beaten man, ready to drop him two floors to his death.

Craig weakly grabbed her forearm, holding on while begging for his life.

"Please... please... don't... please..." he

groaned.

"You will leave... tonight... never to come back," she ordered. "You will give your wife a divorce... you will leave her the house... her car... you'll pay her for the pain and suffering every year she had to put up with your miserable ass, along with alimony and child support. You will do everything I told you to do because if you do not... I will hunt you down and find you underneath whatever rock you crawl under. I will rip each of your limbs off by the joint one by one... nice... and slow... and with your last dying breath, you will watch as I beat you to death... with a limb of my choosing... do you understand?"

Craig Martin whimpered and sobbed, nodding his head with tears and snot pouring down his face, which only enraged Sophia further.

Sophia wanted to hurl him to death and watch his skull crack open like an egg on the concrete below, but witnesses were already peeping out their windows. Some stuck their necks out of their doors, and she could hear police sirens getting closer and closer.

"Do... you... hear... me?!" Sophia screamed, hoping to blow out his eardrums.

"Yes... yes... oh god... yes," Craig Martin acknowledged with a saliva-spitting whimper.

She pulled him back in, dropping him onto the balcony deck, where he curled up into a ball, trembling as he sobbed and cried; it only made her want to kill him. However, she had no time; she had to leave before Houston's finest swarmed the place. She went to go back out the way she came when her ears heard the most unbelievable thing.

"What have you done?" a badly beaten and barely coherent Tammy uttered.

A borderline postal Sophia, who did not want to get involved in the first place, slowly turned to her.

"Say what?"

"What have you done?" Tammy Martin

babbled, "You ruined my marriage… because of you … my marriage is over…"

Sophia's lips quivered; she no longer cared about the sirens getting closer. She lunged for Tammy, ripping her off the floor. She screamed as Sophia dragged her in front of a full-length mirror, forcing her to look at herself.

"Look at your face!" Sophia screamed at her. "Look at it! Look what he did to you in front of your son!"

Sheepishly, Tammy looked at her face, literally destroyed on the left side. She broke into bitter tears.

She wrapped her arms around herself, trying to stop the violent shaking as embarrassment and shame washed over her. She wanted to die right there on the spot. A part of her wished that Craig had killed her. She came from a typical happy family one could have; her father never raised a hand to her mother, much less an unkind word, and they both loved her very much.

She was the girl who came from a

Midwest lower-income home with laughter and love. She moved to the closest big city to further her education and fell for a charming prince story that was a life of upper-class misery, humiliation, and sorrow.

Her father had warned Craig that the next time he put his hand on her, it would be the first and last time Craig would see him with his shotgun. The fear of not wanting to see her father possibly go to prison stopped her from going home.

She never finished her nursing degree because Craig demanded that she stay home, and he paid for and dealt with everything. The common rational sense was to leave him, but she did not know how to survive without him.

"Look at me," Sophia said softer, realizing she had enough of being yelled at. "Tammy... look at me."

Tammy turned to look at the woman before her; it did not click that she called her by her first name. She was everything she was not a billion times over, intimidating, tall, and powerful. The hood covering the upper part of her face made her look like something straight out of a comic book, but there was something eerily familiar about her.

Sophia motioned to little Ethan, standing in the corner, crying and shaking.

"If you love your son, you don't want him to see you looking like this ever again. You also don't want him to grow up to be like that," Sophia said while pointing to Craig, still sniveling on the floor outside. "It's time to draw a damn line in the sand and fight for him if not for yourself."

She probably had less than a minute before the vehicles pulled up, but she could not leave just yet as she walked over to little Ethan. She knelt down to his height as he stood in the corner, sniffling while tears continued to pour from his eyes.

She gently rubbed his little bicep to give him comfort.

"I promise you," Sophia reassured him, "Daddy won't hurt Mommy anymore... okay?"

Ethan nodded, wiping his eyes. Sophia whispered to him to go to his mother. He timorously obeyed, walking over to her, no doubt fearful of the state of her face.

It only broke her heart more as Tammy embraced her son tightly.

"I'm sorry… I'm so sorry…"

Ethan hugged her back, which made her cry harder; Sophia realized she was out of time and headed to the smashed-up balcony for an exit.

"Wait," Tammy mustered enough strength to answer a question. "Who are you?"

"It doesn't matter," Sophia said, not looking at her. "You'll never see me again."

She continued to head for the balcony but stopped for one more second to deliver a message to a still-cowering Craig Martin.

"But you'll see me "real" soon if you don't do what you're told," she scowled.

Craig curled deeper into his human ball,

thinking she would put a boot on him. Instead, Sophia ran quickly and leaped off the balcony; she imagined all the action movies she had seen where the hero or heroine jumped from dangerous heights, making a break for it, and landed safely on the ground.

She stuck the landing, much to her surprise, only causing slight damage to the concrete on impact; she figured she would crash and burn, sprawling out in the middle of her former street, which would have been downright embarrassing.

Sophia made a break for it just as the patrol cars turned the corner. She ran darting through the Morrison's yard across the street.

As Sophia neared Anderson's eight-foot gate, she envisioned she had to clear it like Lolo Jones.

To her shock and surprise, her body instantly kicked into overdrive, speeding toward it. With a leap, she cleared the gate, mirroring the form of the famed track star. Sticking the landing again, Sophia stopped briefly, marveling at the feat.

"Whoa," Sophia uttered.

The sound of the sirens broke Sophia out of her euphoric moment and got her running again. She would be long gone before the officers stepped out of their cars, but they would now know she was in Houston, meaning she had to act fast on whatever she planned.

CHAPTER 9

AT 1:05 A.M., Charles Hampton yawned as he entered his building, checked his mailbox, and proceeded to take the elevator to his studio apartment. He did not look like it, but the word doctor followed his name. Although Charles was one of the leading doctors in Stem Cell Research and biophysics, Hampton had a face that belonged in a boy band with his five-o'clock shadow and long, slick, jet-black hair. He was fumbling with his blackberry as he searched for his keys to enter his apartment. It had been a long day for him, especially with the FBI walking into his facility asking him a million and one questions he had no answers to. In particular, one question was the whereabouts of his good friend-now-escaped-convict, Sophia Dennison, who apparently broke out of prison before her execution. Obviously, the FBI did not tell him the whole story.

Even though he would never give her up, he did not know her whereabouts. She cut off all contact with him three months after her sentence to Mountain View, right up until then after locking his door, flipping on the lights, and turning to see a tall, dark figure with a hood standing almost nose to nose with him.

"Sweet baby Jesus!" he screamed, falling back against the door.

Sophia calmly approached him, cupping his mouth and removing her hood from her head.

"Ssh…"

Charles calmed himself as she removed her hand from his mouth; he winced his eyes to ensure they were not deceiving him.

"Sophia?"

"Hi, Charlie." She smiled.

"How… how… did you get in here?" Charles began to babble. "Do you know everyone is looking for you?! How the hell did you escape from?!"

She calmly shut his mouth again.

"I climbed up here… sorry about the window… yes, I know they're looking for me… I was executed… I came back to life… twice… I broke my way out… no, I am not a zombie… nor am I crazy… and right now… I need your help."

As she removed her hand from his lips again, he slowly looked her up and down, realizing the severe changes in his former friend.

"You're a lot… taller than I remembered…"

Sophia breathed, finally in front of a true friend again.

"You don't know the half…"

About an hour-and-a-half later of explanation and showing him that she was not jerking his leg by crushing two of his sharpest cutlery knives with her bare hand without drawing any blood, Hampton sat in his chair across from her, sitting on the arm of his sofa with a blank dumbfounded expression on his face unable to understand or comprehend what he just heard and witnessed.

He began summarizing her entire ordeal.

"So you were executed, and then you came back to life… then you got shot… several times… and then you came back to life again… and then you broke out of prison… and now you have super strength, and you're bulletproof…"

"And I can run… really… really fast," she added.

"How fast?" Charles inquisitively asked.

"I ran from Gatesville to Cypress in under an hour and a half… barefoot… to Houston, I think only took forty-five minutes," Sophia estimated.

Charles sat there with a blank, stunned look on his face.

"Okay," he swallowed, "add superhuman speed… Can you see through walls? Heat vision? Freeze things with your breath?"

"No, you jackass." Sophia rolled her eyes. "And I can't fly either… I also don't get tired."

"You don't get tired?"

"I've been up for over twenty-four hours, including the Guinness Book Human Land Speed Marathon I just ran," Sophia estimated again. "I didn't get winded after the run, and I haven't hit the fatigue wall yet. In fact, I feel the opposite… like I can go and keep going."

"Could be your body no longer produces fatigue toxins," Charles guessed. "Do you eat?"

"Like a horse."

"Do you feel weakened if you don't eat?"

Sophia shrugged.

"No, just hungry."

"Anything else?"

166

Sophia leaned forward with a stone-cold look on her face.

"My memory... I remember... everything."

"About the night?" Charles nervously asked.

"Not just the night. My entire life until now... I remember being in my mother's womb and being born."

Charles leaned back in disbelief, even though she had shown him the impossible already.

"That's... not... possible," he stuttered.

"Dude... I had a four-inch growth spurt," she said with a bit of frustration, "and I can javelin a cop car, so don't tell me about "not possible" anymore."

Sophia fought to find the words to explain.

"I can't explain it, the first time I woke up, it was like my brain got rebooted, and memories of things I'd forgotten or shouldn't even remember just flooded my skull all at once all the way up until now. All I have to do is think of something, and the memory pops up in detail. And I mean, I can see, hear, even remember the scent, touch, or taste of anything with a memory."

She paused to give Charles a demonstration.

"From birth, I can literally see inside my mother's womb... feel the contractions pushing me out. I could feel my lungs' scorching after breathing air for the first time and the cold air within the room. I saw my mother drenched in sweat and crying as she looked at me while Dr. Roper, with his huge bi-focal glasses, cut my umbilical cord.

The nurse with this big Afro wrapped me in a green hospital blanket and handed me to my mother. My dad came into the room crying, fell on his ass, and crawled over to the bed. My mom laughed like crazy as she held me, then he kissed my mom and took me in his arms. He kept kissing me on my nose until I fell asleep, and it smelled like he was drinking a lot of coffee.

I can break down in detail what the room looked like and what everyone was wearing. The memories are also more intense if I'm near something familiar. Sometimes, if I'm not careful, more than one memory will come out at once. Sometimes if it's too intense, it can leave me in a trance that I have to forcefully pull myself out of."

Hampton leaped out of his seat.

"Okay… there's a way to test that."

He walked over to his library, pulling out a massive medical book with tabs sticking out. As he opened it, it appeared seriously marked up due to various study sessions.

"Remember this monster?"

Charles smiled, flipping through it to find a page.

"Read me chapter… 27."

Sophia glanced at the book's name, shrugged her shoulders, and turned her back to him. She began her recital.

"Chapter 27, page 246 on DNA…
Deoxyribonucleic acid (DNA) is a molecule
encoding the genetic instructions used in the
development and functioning of all known
living organisms and many viruses. Along
with RNA and proteins, DNA is one of the three
major macromolecules essential for all known
forms of life. Genetic information is encoded as
a sequence of nucleotides
(guanine, adenine, thymine, and cytosine)
recorded using the letters G, A, T, and C. Most
DNA molecules are double-stranded helices,
consisting of two long polymers of simple units
called nucleotides, molecules
with backbones made of
alternating sugars (deoxyribose)
and phosphate groups (related to phosphoric
acid), with the nucleobases (G, A, T, C) attached
to the sugars. DNA is well-suited for biological
information storage since the DNA backbone is
resistant to cleavage and the double-stranded
structure provides the molecule with a built-in
duplicate of the encoded information."

Hampton's face had unnerved written on
it.

She paused, sure that he got the idea now, but to make sure, she asked.

"Shall I keep going? I can say it in Spanish… also remember all the words from what my grandma taught me, on top of high school and college classes were I got a C. Capítulo veintisiete, página doscientos veinticuatro sobre ADN… El ácido desoxirribonucleico (ADN) es una molécula que codifica las instrucciones genéticas utilizadas en el desarrollo y funcionamiento de todos los organismos vivos conocidos y de muchos virus. Junto con el ARN y las proteínas, el ADN es una de las tres macromoléculas principales esenciales para todas las formas de vida conocidas."

"Um… no… no need to…"

A wide-eyed Hampton slowly closed the book he knew his friend had not seen or read in over eighteen years.

"By the way," Sophia added, smiling, "we read that chapter on October 16, 1990, at 7:30 P.M. during a study session with you, me, Chris Parker, and Denise Oswald. We had Chinese Kung-Pow chicken, General Taos, and beef with broccoli with chicken lo Mein and garlic dumplings. You were going through your Public Enemy phase, rocking the cap, hoodie, and black military pants with black Gore-Tex boots, and Denise Oswald, who had a crush on you, was wearing that tight..."

"Okay! Okay!" he cut her off. "I remember! No need to rehash."

He sat on the arm of the sofa this time and got serious again.

"So... what do you remember?"

"I saw who murdered Rob," Sophia said, still visibly unsettled. "I can clearly see them as if they were right in front of me."

She paused, taking a deep breath before continuing.

"I woke up unable to speak or move, but I saw the three of them... in black... two men... one woman. The woman was sitting on top of Rob in our bed, holding our wedding cake knife in her hand. They wore weird black rubber suits and helmets... nothing I ever saw before... as if it came out of a sci-fi movie… they had distorted voices… but I could make out their gender. They were shocked that I woke up… like I wasn't supposed to… one of the men came over and shot me in the arm…it felt like a high-powered syringe, and then everything went blurry… the last thing I heard was the woman say."

Sophia's face went blank, almost mechanical. As she spoke, her voice sounded distorted and identical to the woman's voice in her memory.

"Get ready for your life to change."

Dead silence covered the room as Charles almost fell off the arm of the sofa. Sophia covered her mouth as her eyes widened.

"Oh… my god," she stammered under her hand-covered mouth.

Swimming in a vat of shock, fascination, and fear, Charles just uttered one word.

"Wow."

Sophia shot out of her seat. Hysterically

pacing back and forth.

"Oh god... oh god... oh...god!"

Charles sprang to his feet to put her at ease.

"Calm down! Calm down! Makes sense... super memory equals vocal mimicry. No different from African Grey Parrots, so... what else do you remember?"

Fear made her hesitant to continue; vengeance made her dive back in.

"An embossed symbol on the woman's left shoulder," she said slowly. "Saw it through whatever moonlight was in the room... it was a Grim Reaper sitting on a large skull while holding a scythe in one hand and a smaller skull in its other hand... I think they're either military or mercenary."

"So... what do you need from me?" he asked. "I'm a doctor... like you, you know I don't have any military ties."

Sophia retook her seat, leaning forward.

"I need to know what's happening to me. On a physical and what is clearly a cellular level."

"How am I supposed to do that when the needle will either bend or break off your skin?"

"Hello, you forgot to be a doctor?" Sophia asked with joking disbelief. "How about hair samples and swabbing the inside of my mouth for saliva?"

Charles smacked his skull.

"Oh! Oh, yeah!"

"I also brought this."

Sophia grabbed her black bookbag, pulling out the plastic bag with her prison gear still covered in blood, staining the inside.

"Holy shit…" Charles said, stunned at the amount of blood in the bag.

"What's left of my prison gear. Hopefully, you can do something with this… also, I need to borrow some extra money… preferably cash… enough for a motel room and something to eat."

"Why don't you stay here?" Charles pleaded.

"Too dangerous," Sophia said, waving off the offer. "If the police or feds don't know I'm here yet, they will soon enough. I kind of beat up Craig Martin like almost an hour ago."

Charles, remembering Craig Martin, sat there with a dumbfounded, "Are you kidding me?" look as Sophia sat there acting meek. He decided to come back to that later.

"So you're just going to leave?" Charles asked with an irritated tone.

"I have to keep moving, Charlie," Sophia said, getting up and preparing herself.

"Why? Why did you shut me out?" Charles finally let out in frustration.

"Excuse me?" Sophia asked, stunned and taken aback.

"I knew you could never do something so horrible. Even when the verdict came down, even with all the bullshit evidence... I knew...

for six months after you cut me off, I came to see you every week, and you refused to see me... till I just gave up... why? After all, we've been through... why, did you do that to me?"

"I couldn't take it, Charlie," Sophia answered with a cracked voice.

Memories of him coming up to see her every week flooded her mind, and she had him turned away every week.

Sophia's eyes watered as she was guilty of something else: hurting her best friend.

"I couldn't take it anymore. Every time you or my parents came to visit, I saw how they looked at you... treated you... as if... you're friends with a murderer or you are the parents of a murderer. Then when you all left... I felt even lonelier than when you came. I wanted to kill myself... I really did because it was clear that I was never getting out no matter how many appeals I sent out; that's when I decided if I didn't win the first appeal... I wasn't going to appeal anymore... and I didn't want you or my parents to talk me out of it. I didn't have the strength for another forty... fifty years... I just wanted to go, and it was better the State took me… then I do myself in."

There was an awkward silence in the room as she wiped her eyes with her sleeve. Charles did not know whether to pat her on the shoulder, hug her, or use words to comfort her. Their friendship had lasted from college all the way into medical school. He was one of the groomsmen at her wedding; she tried to fix him up on countless dates with women she thought would make him happy, not knowing that the woman he wanted was the one he could not have.

From the arrest to trial to judgment, he was there with her until she entered Mountain View and cut off all contact.

Charles never stopped believing she was innocent, even when other friends and family thought she was guilty; he never stopped believing, even at the cost of his former position at Memorial Hermann.

He opted to walk up and put a kind hand on her shoulder, reaffirming their friendship.

"You're my best friend," Charles sighed, "and I just missed you... a lot... I thought I lost you. Anything you need, I will help you, and as far as money goes... one second. Don't run off or jump out the window."

He walked away and entered his bedroom, throwing the lights on; it sounded like he was searching for something in his closet. He returned with one of their old college duffel bags a second later, throwing it on his breakfast nook table. Sophia's eyes widened as he unzipped it to reveal several thousand dollars within it.

"Charlie... what the...?"

"It's your money... what was left... almost a hundred and fifty thousand give or take." He said with a nervous smile. "I kept it because... I didn't stop believing... you'd get out."

She could not stop the tears from flowing, shaking her head as she looked at her best friend, whose eyes also began to get glassy.

Before she could hug him, Charles turned away, wiping his eyes on his sleeve as it finally set in that his best friend was standing before him again.

"Okay… we got to stop this," he sniffled, "cuz… I'm half Asian, and I hate the crying stigma."

Sophia smiled, wiping the tears from her own eyes.

"Thank you."

She, too, was so sick of crying.

"But first things first," Charles said while wiping away the remaining mist, "Going to need you to strip."

"Excuse me?" Sophia asked, checking if she heard right.

"You said you wanted to know what's happening to you on a physical level," Charles said with a gesture while grabbing his medical bag, "so I have to give you a physical. Which means I need your current weight… height… etc. You know the routine… doctor. Come on, I've seen it all before."

"Okay."

Without hesitation, she unlaced and kicked off her sneakers. She started to strip out of her clothes from top to bottom. Hampton went into a mode of being stuck. He quickly noticed the changes in her. He was expecting a bodybuilder with layered muscle, but that was not the case. Aside from her cheese-grater abs, the rest of her body had a solid, lean muscle tone that did not take away from her womanly features; if anything, the transformation amplified them.

Sophia grew in height; Charles used to rest his arm on her head to mess with her. That was no longer possible. Charles's eyes could not help themselves as they slowly wandered from her sports bra down to her thong bottom.

In the middle of his gawking, Sophia gave Charles her medical diagnosis.

"My first theory is that whatever is happening to me has either slowed or stopped my ability to create myostatin, which rapidly increased my muscle growth and strength, Charlie? Charles?"

"Yeah... what?" Charles asked, partially in his trance of naughty thoughts.

"I was talking about the myostatin within me, slowing down, do you agree?"

"Yeah... yeah, it's a theory," Charles stammered, trying to catch up with the conversation.

"Well, I'm ready... where do you want me?" Sophia threw her hands up, inquiring, looking around.

The innocent question threw him off balance, making him look like a further blithering idiot.

"Uh... excuse me?" he slowly asked.

She was oblivious to why he was acting so sluggishly, so she tried to break it down for him, throwing in hand gestures.

"Where do you want me to "sit" for the examination?"

Charles finally snapped out of his erotic fantasy state.

"Oh! On the couch! Sit! Sit... on the couch... please."

Sophia gave him a weird look as she walked over to sit on the couch; she wanted to ask him if he was all right but decided not to for fear of getting another weird answer. Hampton shook himself back to reality, getting a quick glass of water from his Britta pitcher. He then grabbed his sphygmomanometer and stethoscope, taking a huge deep breath as he prepared to examine his half-naked, hot-looking best friend waiting on his couch.

CHAPTER 10

Mark and Dustin arrived at the Martin's house; the quiet residential community came to life in the middle of the night with officers, paramedics, agents, local reporters, and half the neighborhood. They both looked up to see the front balcony completely blown open and paramedics wheeling a half-conscious Craig Martin with handcuffs attached to him and the gurney he was on heading to one of the ambulances on the scene. They met up with the Sheriff's department's Chief, flashing their credentials before debriefing on the situation.

"What have we got here?" Mark asked.

To which the Sheriff answered.

"Nothing I've seen or heard of before."

"We're getting that a lot," Dustin returned.

"Domestic violence dispute interrupted by what was described as an Amazon wearing a black hood," the Sheriff reported. "Apparently, she tore the door off the back patio; we found it several yards away. The woman then ran upstairs, caught the husband pounding away on his wife, and grabbed him, putting him through one of the walls in their bedroom. She threw the sum bitch through the bathroom door and half of another wall.

Not before he apparently broke his hand and a chair trying to hit the woman; on top of the possible broken back and concussion, the paramedics said he might have. She then carried him to the patio, kicking out the glass doors."

The Sheriff turned, pointing to the balcony.

"Ripped the guardrail off with one hand tossing it, taking out the windshield to his car, and then threatened to drop him off the balcony while she held him by the neck. After leaving him shaking in his own body fluids, she leaped from the balcony down to the street where you see that crater by the wife's and neighbors' accounts. After that, she took off like a jackrabbit through that neighbor's yard, going god knows where. We actually have footage of that off someone's phone."

Dustin let off a sarcastic laugh, shaking his head in disbelief.

"I miss the joke somewhere?" the Sheriff inquired, confused and irritated.

"We believe the woman involved in this is our escape fugitive from Mountain View," Mark explained. "We're going to need a copy of that footage if that's okay."

"Well, off the record, I think she deserves a medal," Sheriff said bluntly. "I've got a file thicker than a Bible on that bastard and how badly he terrorized that poor woman inside. Chances are, if this woman didn't show up, I'd have to notify someone tonight that their child is dead. And would you believe it... she's finally pressing charges against him."

"Is she okay to speak with us?" Mark asked, respecting that this was partially the Sheriff's investigation.

"She's pretty banged up but coherent." The Sheriff motioned. "You can talk to her for a couple of minutes before they take her and her son down to county for an examination."

"Her son?" Mark inquired, not knowing a child was involved.

The Sheriff sneered in disgust, looking at the ambulance Craig Martin was in.

"Poor little feller was right there while that son of a bitch was beating his mother to a near bloody pulp."

"Question: you guys were called for the domestic dispute, right?" Mark raised, a little put-off. "What happened? Why'd it take so long to get here?"

"Believe it or not, we weren't called for any domestic dispute," the Sheriff said, quite disappointed. "We got the call of a home invasion when someone heard the crash on the balcony and saw this "superwoman" holding that jackass by the throat threatening to drop him."

Mark and Dustin's look of disgust mirrored the Sheriff's look. They thanked him before heading into the house.

"She goes from robbing a Goodwill store to stomping out a wife-beater." Dustin muttered, "This chick is all over the place."

"You want to check upstairs with the team," Mark asked, getting down to business, "or interview the wife?"

Dustin drew a breath in an attempt to contain his anger.

"You do the interview. If I see her, I might head outside and make sure someone doesn't make it to the hospital alive."

Dustin trotted upstairs to meet with the FBI and Houston forensic teams to survey the damage as Mark walked into the living room.

Instantly, he wished he had switched places with Dustin. Seeing a woman sitting on her couch covered in a blanket with a left eye the size of a golf ball and a possibly broken nose holding tightly onto her son with visible trauma in his eyes gave him the itch to kill someone. He had to bury that deep, put on his kid gloves and professional hat, and set personal feelings aside to obtain the needed answers.

"Mrs. Martin... my name is Special Agent Mark Armitage from the FBI," he introduced himself. "I'm very sorry about what happened to you. I was wondering if you were well enough to answer some questions for me."

Tammy slowly nodded as Mark pulled up a seat on a nearby ottoman to meet her eye level instead of towering over her, hoping to make her more comfortable than she already was.

He pulled an old-fashioned notepad and pen from his jacket to take notes.

"Can you tell me in your own words what happened?"

"My... husband came home tonight,"

Tammy recounted. "He works for this big insurance company and found out it was in serious financial trouble... possible bankruptcy like that other insurance company that was on the news."

"AIG?" Mark asked, engaging in the conversation.

She nodded as she continued her story.

"He started freaking out about how he could possibly lose his job... blamed me for just spending his money."

She held her son tighter as she began to tear up.

"He called me a dumb cow because I wasn't like his other friends' wives who held corporate jobs and could help pay for their day to day life. I... I said... but you wanted me to stay home, that I could have gotten a job... and then he got angry... called me a stupid bitch, and said if I thought changing bedpans could pay for this lifestyle... and then he threw his bottle of beer against the wall and hit me. I ran upstairs crying, and he chased me... I tried to shut the door to the bedroom, but he was stronger than me, and he barreled through the door, knocking me down… then he got on top of me, grabbing me by my throat, and he just hit me over, and over, and over again…"

Still fresh in her mind, the moment drew more tears from her.

"Our son came into the room crying," Tammy blubbered, "and he didn't even stop…"

Mark gave her a minute to compose herself as he pulled a handkerchief from his jacket and handed it to her.

Tammy continued her story while drying her healthy eye.

"And then she just came out of nowhere, she stopped him… she saved my life..."

"Super lady… made daddy… stop hurting… mommy…" Little Ethan meekly chimed in.

Mark cracked a smile and bent lower to meet eye level with him.

"Did she?" Mark asked with an enthusiastic tone.

"Yes," the little boy said with a nod.

Mark remembered he had to finish his investigation as he sat back up to continue gingerly questioning his mother.

"Mrs. Martin, did this woman say anything to you?"

Tammy thought about it for a minute.

"Other than for me to wake up from this hell I was in for my son... she knew my name. I remember her calling me by my name."

Mark gestured to the house next door.

"Do you remember a Sophia Matheson that used to live here?"

"Yes, right next door; she was very nice to me," Tammy said, mustering up a bright smile out of nowhere, "but this woman was much larger... Sophia was like my height... and... wasn't she executed; this week... for what she did to her husband?"

"Uh… yes, she was," Mark said with a textbook fake smile. "Listen, you need to go get checked out… here's my card… if you can think of anything or need anything, please give me a call."

Tammy nodded, taking the card.

"Thank you, Special Agent,"

Mark smiled as he gently rubbed the little boy's head.

"Take care of Mommy, Ethan."

The little boy waved goodbye as the paramedics escorted Tammy and him to the other waiting ambulance to take them to the hospital. Mark drew a sigh, more lost than ever; he then headed upstairs to see if Dustin had come up with anything. Sure enough, the upstairs looked worse from the inside than the balcony looked from street level.

"What do we have?" Mark dryly asked.

Dustin drew a sigh while turning to him.

"World War III in stereo. Blood

samples... possibly from both the wife and husband. I have to say I like her work... I know a couple of pedophiles and serial rapists I'd love for her to meet."

"Dennison came home alright," Mark confirmed.

"So, she just dropped by her old stomping grounds and happened onto this mess?" Dustin concluded.

"We need to get a team next door," Mark formulated, "see what she either found or was looking for."

"I'm waiting for when we find some actual clues as opposed to chasing our tails. This path of destruction makes no sense to me," an irritated Dustin said to his partner.

Out of nowhere, an older woman's voice from outside screeched.

"Excuse me! Excuse me!"

Mark and Dustin looked at each other, wondering, "What the hell now?" as they walked to the balcony to see one of the Sheriff's deputies attempting to calm down an irate elderly woman.

"Ma'am, I'm going to have to ask you to please calm down and step back," ordered the deputy.

"I just want to know when this will be over?!" she yelled. "This is upsetting my cats! I pay my taxes to live in a nice, respectable neighborhood!"

"Ma'am…"

Mark, finally having enough, decided to step in from his perch.

"Hey! You!" he barked at her. "Yeah, you!"

In her pink and white-flowered night robe, the silver-haired woman adjusted her glasses, looking up at Mark, who pointed to her, getting her and everyone else standing outside attention.

He approached the edge of the broken balcony as if to leap down on her.

"My name is Special Agent in Charge

195

Mark Armitage from the FBI. Did you call the Sheriff's department to stop the asshole that lives here from almost beating his wife to death in front of his kid?!"

"No… I did not…" the old woman stuttered.

"Then take your brittle ass back to your stupid fucking cats," Mark roared at her, "before I lock you up for obstructing a Federal Investigation! Then I'll shoot your cats! Don't talk! Go!"

The stunned old woman scurried back to her house close to tears.

"Anyone else got anything to say?!"

The old lion surveyed the street of onlookers daring someone to say something. Seeing that he was unchallenged, Mark marched back into the bedroom as everyone except Mercer, who had stopped to hear him tear into an old woman, scattered, returning to their work on the investigation.

Dustin walked up to him with a bit of

sarcastic advice.

"You really need to work on your people skills," Dustin exhaled.

"I hate people," Mark bluntly said.

"Even me?" Dustin asked with furrowed brows, pretending to be hurt.

"Especially you."

Mark walked off, heading downstairs before Mercer could respond to the ribbing.

"You're gonna remember you said that," Dustin muttered, "when you're crying at my funeral like a bitch… you…"

CHAPTER 11

With less than five hours of sleep after the incident at the Martins' house and then casing Sophia's old home looking for clues, only to come up with a couple of fresh fingerprints indicating that she was there, but nothing much else; Armitage and Mercer decided to take a break from hunting her. Obviously, she was in Houston and not going anywhere for some reason, so they focused on finding out what she was and if she had any possible weaknesses. They now stood within the Federal Bureau of Investigation Houston office's Forensics Department headed by Doctor Senji Kumamoto.

The doctor started his findings with the

basic theme of the investigation.

"I've never seen anything like this in my life."

"We've been getting a lot of that lately, doc," Mark sighed.

"To begin with," Doctor Kumamoto explained, "this blood should have killed the subject a hundred times over. It's literally saturated with adrenaline... twice the amount of possibly two full-grown bull elephants; this partially explains why her heart started again after the lethal injection and displayed the unbelievable, superhuman strength shown in the video footage. However, she should have dropped dead from a massive heart attack seconds afterward."

"Was it in the canisters?" Mark asked, hoping they were the key.

"Negative," Doctor Kumamoto confirmed, looking through his notes. "The canisters tested contained the usual sodium thiopental, pancuronium bromide, and potassium chloride used in textbook lethal injections. And she still would have died even if they were mixed; the adrenaline alone should not have saved her from the deadly combination of the pancuronium bromide and potassium chloride."

"So how did she produce that much adrenaline?" Dustin asked. "To survive a poisonous combo and two hails of bullets, one of which makes her both bulletproof and a thousand times stronger than before?"

"I think what I'm about to show you next will answer all of those questions," Dr. Kumamoto said.

He walked over to his computer, transferring the data to the widescreen on the wall with a couple of keystroke taps.

"What we're looking at are two DNA strands," Dr. Kumamoto pointed while explaining. "The one on the left is a normal human DNA strand double helix, atoms, etc. The one on the right is your subject's... it has a quadruple Helix... atoms and various other elements, many that I cannot find anywhere on the Periodic table. The nucleotides and chromosomes for the one on the left total in the millions while Dr. Dennison's numbers in the trillions, maybe even more. Each one with a possible application; also if we examine the blood itself as you see here comparing it to a regular blood sample."

The doctor punched some keystrokes, showing the blood under a microscope next to normal blood.

"The normal one has white blood cells and platelets," he continued, "while the quadruple helix one has neither white blood cells nor platelets. After examining your subject's blood closer, I found that the blood cells themselves possess the properties that make up white blood cells and platelets. It appears her normal red blood cells serve a multifunctional role of providing oxygen to the body, protecting it from disease, and repairing it when needed."

Mark and Dustin gave each other blank looks to determine precisely what the doctor said.

"So basically what you're saying, Doc, is she's not human?" Dustin concluded.

"I would have said that if I didn't see her blood before she went to prison," Dr. Kumamoto stated. "Dr. Dennison apparently was a regular blood donor. The hospital that employed her sent over a bag of her blood they kept in frozen storage. The one you're viewing on the left."

"So what you're saying, she was definitely normal before she went to prison," Mark asked.

Doctor Kumamoto nodded.

"From what I can determine, yes, that is correct."

Mark asked a follow-up question while pointing to Sophia's regular blood on the screen before motioning to the altered blood.

"So how could she be normal, and then become... this while locked up?"

"My only hypothesis is a form of virus," Doctor Kumamoto concluded with a shrug, "possibly a mutation; unfortunately, I will not know until I have run further tests. And no Special Agents, I don't know of any virus on Earth that can do anything like this."

Mark stood there, shaking his head, looking at the two samples on the screen in disbelief.

"Thanks, doc; let us know if you find anything else that would be useful."

Doctor Kumamoto nodded as he went back to his work. With a handful of files in his grip, Dustin and Mark left to head back upstairs to figure out their next step with the current information they had gathered.

"Well, at least we know the answer to what," Dustin sighed, "just not the how."

"We still need some more what, along with how who, and where," Mark grumbled.

"By the way, I didn't know you could lie so well."

Mark turned to Dustin, oblivious to what his partner was getting at.

"What are you talking about?"

"At the prison, when you told Dennison's parents that she was in contact with, and became a part of, a terrorist cell that mounted an attack against the prison and broke her out before her execution," Dustin smirked. "I'm surprised they bought that shit."

"What did you want me to tell them, Dustin," Mark asked, defending his position, "that their daughter was executed, and then came back to life a superhuman monster, was killed again and came back an even more powerful superhuman monster that busted out of prison and is now on the loose?"

Dustin shrugged.

"Maybe they could have told us something."

"Those people came to take their daughter home and bury her," Mark rebuked his theory. "They wouldn't have a clue as to what happened to her or how she got that way. Now, what do you got for me?"

Ignoring his friend bossing him around, Dustin thought to himself for a second.

"Got something on the C.O. that was

killed."

Mark stopped in the hallway to listen.

"Let's have it."

"Turns out our "fallen hero" wasn't squeaky clean at all," Dustin said while rummaging through his files. "He was awarded six citations while working at the Allan B. Polunsky Unit, one of them was for assisting in stopping a prison riot, but he also was charged twice for excessive use of force. Nothing came of those charges; he transferred to Gatesville, where he worked shifts between the regular women's prison and the Mountain View Unit. There he had over four complaints of sexual harassment, none of them proven, one complaint of sexual assault later dropped, and one complaint of rape which was an ongoing investigation."

"How was he still working there?" Mark asked.

Dustin rechecked his files.

"He was given desk duty until he was

formally charged, but guess who the victim was?"

"Sister Shareef," Mark answered while snapping his fingers.

"Close, but no, Rosanna "Bishop" Mendoza, the car thief sharing a cell with Sister Shareef," Dustin corrected. "She was also the person who filed the sexual assault complaint."

"She was also friends with Dennison," Mark added, filling in the blanks. "That's why she singled him out."

"Also, he was called "Big Buck" because he had a huge tattoo on his forearm of a stag mounting…" Dustin laughed.

"I get the picture, Dustin," Mark said, waving him off, not wishing to hear the details of a stupid tattoo.

Dustin got serious again.

"All of this is gravy if she was 'human'; we're no close to finding out what changed her or how to stop her if it came down to it."

"What about the assholes in black from the prison?" Mark asked.

Dustin screwed up his face looking through his files again.

"Stanley Slater, former SEAL Team Six Second Lieutenant with an I.Q. between 130-139, **he is** a special agent of the United States Government, but the division he's under is marked classified; he's got a "Do Not Approach" in his file."

"What the…" Mark said in disbelief at what he was hearing.

"The toad's boss, Arthur G. Rosen, is a Director," Dustin continued, "there is nothing on him… division is also highly classified under the United States Government, and he **also** has a "Do Not Approach" in his file."

"Holy shit," Mark said, totally stumped. "They really are the "Men in Black"… who the hell are these guys?"

Dustin sighed, shrugging his shoulders for the umpteenth time.

"I don't have the foggiest, but I'd love to know why I'm the only one doing the research regarding this case."

Mark answered while walking away.

"Keeps you from surfing for furry porn."

Dustin stood there in disbelief at his partner's comment.

"I… I only did that once!"

"Come on!" Mark barked.

Dustin cursed under his breath while power-walking to catch up with him.

As they neared the elevator to head to their temporary office, they ran into a young male agent who was apparently looking for them.

"Special Agent in Charge Armitage, sir," the male agent addressed him. "Executive Assistant Director King wants to speak with you and Special Agent in Charge Mercer ASAP."

"Why didn't he just call my cellphone?" Mark asked, searching for his phone in his jacket.

"Said he needs you to call him on the secure line," the young agent indicated.

Mark nodded as the agent walked off; he then turned to Dustin, who had his usual annoyed look, ready to spit sarcastic venom.

"I wonder what this will be about," Dustin said with a scowl.

Mark kept silent as he walked onto the elevator with Dustin, returning to the office they borrowed from an agent on maternity leave. An agitated Armitage stabbed away at the telecom in an attempt to set up the security line.

Dustin stood there, watching the train wreck, shaking his head.

"You forgot your secure line again, didn't you?" he sighed.

"No," Mark growled, jabbing the buttons with his finger as if trying to break it, "the stupid friggin thing isn't working."

"Move, man… move," Dustin ordered

while muscling him out of the way.

He dialed in to set up the line; he typed in his secure line code at the prompt before dialing the Executive Assistant Director's line.

"Don't feel bad; my kid taught me how to do mine," Dustin smirked.

"Shut up," Mark snapped back.

Executive Assistant Director King's voice came over the line within less than a minute.

"Armitage... Mercer?" his stern, coarse voice asked.

"What do you want, Doug?" Mark said bluntly, with no mood for B.S.

"Let's get to the point," King said dryly. "You came in contact with a Director, Arthur Rosen?"

Mark leaned further into the commlink to speak.

"Let me guess, you're gonna tell us about the "Do Not Approach" hanging out of his ass.

Who the hell is he, Doug?"

There was a slight pause as it was clear King did not appreciate Mark cutting him off. Mark, however, did not care what he felt.

"That information…" he began to say.

"Is classified, we know Doug!" the duo barked into the commlink, hoping it gave King an earache.

"Then get this through that one brain you two share," the Director snapped back. "This guy has the wrath of God Brimstone type protection… do not fuck with him."

"We're not handing over this case to some piece of…" Mark growled while slamming his fist on the table.

"No one is asking you to," the Director cut him off, reminding him who he was talking to. "Protection does not mean he can screw with the FBI either. This is now a dog race to the rabbit, if you know what I mean. If you get to her, she's ours… if you don't…well, from what I can gather from the ass-chewing I got from the top, he probably has the authorization to arrest and detain… probably even K.O.S… meaning she'll be his."

Mark and Dustin gave each other unsettled looks.

"Look, I don't like this cloak and dagger James Bond shit as much as you do," King muttered with an uneasy voice, "especially when it's our own people doing it to us. You got a job to do, whatever resources you need, bring Dennison in, and keep me updated."

As the Executive Assistant Director hung up, a frustrated Armitage hit the button to hang up on his end. A million and one questions were now swimming in his head, with no answer in sight.

"Why am I the only one asking the question of how the hell are we going to bring this chick in if we find her?" Dustin let out.

Correction, a million and two.

"Because you're the only one making sense in this goddamn world," Mark answered as he stared into space.

A somewhat disturbed look came across Dustin's face.

"That's not a good thing," he swallowed.

"No," Mark huffed, "it isn't..."

CHAPTER 12

Sophia was not having a good day. On Charles' insistence, she stayed the night; actually, he threatened to burn the one good pair of pants she had despite threatening him with bodily harm. He took the couch while Sophia took his bed, even though she was not tired; he reminded her that even Superman slept. It did not make sense to her, even when he tried to explain it. She just decided to humor him and go to sleep because she did not want to hear about Kryptonian mythology. After almost four years on a thin mattress and a harsh spring cot in a near-claustrophobic six-by-eight-foot cell, it felt nice to be in a warm, soft bed. Even though it smelled like Charles, she could "will" herself to sleep. Maybe because there were not many memories other than parties and the one day they had Thanksgiving at his apartment.

However, in the middle of the night, she woke up screaming and broke Charles' headboard while caving in a part of his wall as she scampered back into it, trying to brace herself. Her mental ability amplified her dreams. The horrible memory of the night Robert was murdered popped out of nowhere on her. It was the look of terror on his face as if he knew he was going to meet a gruesome end. The commotion startled Charles, dropping him to the floor; he was not dreaming. His superhuman best friend was sleeping in his bed.

The following day, she made breakfast, apologizing for destroying his bed. They agreed that she would go out for the day while Charles went to work, as usual, to not draw suspicion. He would test the blood and DNA samples he took from her; the saliva was easy, but her dreadlocks were as dense as steel, dulling one of his scissors and breaking another. Ultimately, she had to twist and snap a piece off to give him.

She walked the streets of Houston with no

fundamental objective at first other than to avoid familiar digs she used to go to, which was pretty easy because when she neared a friendly place, a memory would pop out of nowhere, making her turn right around. Houston was big, but she had forged a life there, and it would not let her forget it. Going to "friends" was out of the question. Other than Charles, everyone else thought she was dead to rights guilty, and she was sure they would not handle the miraculous change within her as quickly as Charles did. All of her family was back East in New York. Contacting them in any way, shape, or form would most likely alert the local and Federal authorities to her location. For now, aside from Charles, she was alone.

Instead of wandering around aimlessly until Charles got out of work, which heightened the chance of the FBI, police, or someone recognizing and spotting her, she decided to go to the one place no one would look for her and where she was sure she did not have a memory yet.

Houston National Cemetery, she could not attend the funeral, but she bought some flowers on the way. He never admitted it to her, but he liked sunflowers and lilacs. The caretaker was friendly enough to point her in the right direction. She took her time getting there as she neared it. Her heart fell deep into the pit of her stomach and never came back out.

"REST IN PEACE FIRST LIEUTENANT ROBERT OLIVER MATHESON... LOVING BROTHER WONDERFUL SON... YOU WILL BE GREATLY MISSED" April 1, 1973 – June 26, 2005.

Seven years of their life together were erased with the words on that tombstone.

Despite the justification, it hurt her to the point she could once again no longer hold back the tears. She knelt down and ran her hands against the tombstone; someone had been there maintaining it, probably Mrs. Matheson. She gently laid the flowers down and kissed the headstone. It did not help as she broke down crying. It was not fair; she should have been there. She should have seen his face before they laid him into the grave.

Anger and pain ravaged her heart; so many things were robbed, and she did not know why.

She raised her fist, wanting to hit the tombstone, but remembered she would probably smash it to bits.

Sophia let out a screaming sob, frustrated that she could not even do that. All she could do was clutch her belly, rest her head against the cold of the marble stone, and ride it out.

She sat there for hours, ignoring time itself. Eventually, the caretaker walked by and noticed her.

"You okay, Miss?" he asked out of concern.

Sophia came to her senses, wiping her eyes, and got up, dusting herself off.

"I'm fine, thank you."

She threw on a fake smile and prayed the old man did not notice her from some old news footage.

The caretaker, a friendly, slender older man with silver horn-rimmed hair, adjusted his glasses as he looked at the grave.

"I remember this young man," he said, wagging his finger. "Damn shame what happened to him. I heard his wife got what she deserved."

"Yeah, I heard too," Sophia huffed.

She looked off in a different direction. It would have been almost comical if it did not drive the dagger deeper.

"Can I ask how you know him?" the inquisitive old caretaker asked, no doubt making conversation because he had a relatively lonely and creepy job.

"He was my best friend," she sighed, "from college."

"Sorry for your loss," he said somberly.

"Thank you," Sophia smiled. "Take care of yourself."

She walked away, knowing that this was another place she would never return to.

~ ~

Back at Charles' apartment, she did not bother telling him where she went. It was just another memory she had to lock away. She was half a daze as Charles enthusiastically reviewed his findings that day. He ranted on for about half an hour until he realized she looked disinterested in what he was saying.

"Soph? Sophia? You okay?" Charles asked a little hurt she was ignoring him.

"Yeah, you said you never saw anything like this in your life, there was enough adrenaline in my blood to kill fifty men or the equivalent of twenty full-grown bulls, and I have a mutated DNA with a quadruple Helix," she recited effortlessly. "Please… continue."

His hurt expression turned to one of annoyance; having a superhuman memory also made her a smart-ass.

"As I was saying," he coughed, "the blood cells you gave me are very much alive and healthy."

Sophia gave him the "That's obvious" look based on the fact that they had covered the blood, not coagulating, after being exposed to the elements for days a half-hour ago.

"Yeah, I know we covered that… I also discovered that…"

Charles hesitated to get to his point.

"You also don't have any white blood cells or platelets."

Sophia Dennison furrowed her brows in confusion as she finally got into the conversation, switching to doctor mode herself.

"Then how am I fighting off…" she began to ask.

"Diseases and infections?"

Charles finished her question.

"I wanted to find out as well… so I introduced a common cold virus to the blood cells. Those cells wiped out the virus in a matter of seconds with extreme prejudice. For most of the day, I was like that kid that wanted to find out what else we could stuff down the toilet bowl before it clogged up… I introduced almost every strain of virus to your blood, including Ebola and HIV… and your cells destroyed them all."

"Great… I'm Wolverine," Sophia huffed.

"No,… you're better than him," Charles explained. "I decided to do it in reverse. I dropped one drop of your blood in a test tube of blood both infected with the HIV and the Ebola virus combined… your blood wiped out everything while replicating itself, both strains and the infected blood… it did it until it was the only thing left in the vial."

"So you're telling me I have the cure for every disease known to man in my blood, and I'm guessing that my red cells are not only fighting off diseases. They're also responsible for repairing my body at such a rapid rate now that I no longer need platelets… i.e., why there's no scar tissue when I heal," she said, switching to full doctor mode, leaving this morning in the past. "It still doesn't explain how my body recognizes a threat and then instantly changes to adapt to it."

"I've been thinking about the events of what happened during your execution and escape," Charles said hesitantly, "and I have a theory I'd like to try on you."

Charles pulled out a sizeable gun-like spray canister from a shopping bag labeled "Carter's County," to which Sophia knitted her brows again, not sure she wanted to be his guinea pig.

She slowly coiled back in her stool seat.

"What is that?"

"Bear mace," Charles said, swallowing hard. "Please... don't kill me."

"Why...?" she sneered.

Before she could ask what he was planning, Charles sprayed her in the face with a full blast of mace. Sophia screamed in agonizing pain, something she hadn't felt since leaving the prison. Immediately, she sprung to her feet, knocking over the stool she sat on, and hammered half of the breakfast nook right off. Hampton dived for cover to avoid one of her powerful swipes.

"What... the...!," she hollered.

"Just give it a second!" Charles begged.

"Give it a second?! You stupid son of a bitch! In a second, I'm gonna break your neck once I can…!"

Instantly, Sophia's eyes began to fill up with white foam. The foam then turned into a liquid form, running not just from her eyes but also from her nose. She drew back and hacked up a massive spit of thick yellow stuff at Charles' feet, making him coil back in disgust. As she wiped her face with the sleeve of her jacket, she realized how quickly the pain had left her and that she could see clearly again. Without hesitation, Hampton hit her with another blast of the bear mace. Aside from the irritation of getting wet, this time, it had no effect on her as it did before.

"You're gonna keep going till I make you eat that, right?" Sophia growled, baring her teeth.

Charles quickly stopped tossing the can far away before handing her a kitchen towel. She snatched it from him, wiping her face.

"Sorry, really sorry," he feverishly

apologized, "but this proves my theory… you're not a Marvel… you're a DC."

"What?" Sophia asked again, not familiar with his comic book jargon.

"Fanboy reference… actually, you're kind of both since you have…!"

"Charlie…" Sophia said, putting a hand up, stopping him. "I don't care."

"Right," Charles coughed, getting back to business. "Basically, your body not only makes you immune to all forms of diseases and gives you extremely hyper-regenerative healing. It improves and builds defenses, ensuring that you can't be physically hurt the same way again… during the execution, they put you to sleep, stopped you from breathing, then they stopped your heart, but brain activity usually continues for a couple of minutes to hours."

"Fighting to stay alive," she added.

"This means the source of this defense mechanism making changes to your body is most likely your brain. It probably has developed some higher independent function commanding your body to build defenses when attacked; it's the most logical theory. My guess is the Sodium thiopental knocked you out because it wasn't an initial detrimental threat to your system. You would have probably woken up after the pancuronium bromide, but then you got hit with the potassium chloride," Charles hypothesized.

"This "higher independent function" knew it was under attack and determined that a massive adrenaline rush would jump start your heart and lungs, restoring oxygen and nutrient to the brain while it dealt with the toxins within you. I'm also guessing your cells can analyze foreign threats to your system and send data to your mind, which dictates how best to handle the danger.

Again, this is all theory; when you got shot up, just as if it would be a virus, the cells probably analyzed the slugs still within you. This higher independent function probably determined that the best way to prevent an injury like this again after your cells repaired you were to increase your skin's density to repel bullets in the future. I wouldn't be shocked if it took some of the properties of those slugs and just added it to your genetic code to do it; naturally, it would have to do it to the rest of your body, like your bones, muscles, and other organs for you to properly function, which is why you increased in weight…"

Sophia shot him another dirty look. Charles remembered how she almost fainted when she found out she weighed four-hundred-eighty-seven pounds due to the density increase.

Superhuman or not, a woman's weight was still dangerous territory. Charles made a mental note never to bring up her weight again while trying to show her the brighter side of her predicament.

"Which is why… you have great superhuman strength, among other things," Charles swallowed hard.

"And it kind of makes sense, physically due to exercise and nutrition we're far more superior than our ancestors' thousands of years ago… our bodies possess chemicals and properties that are capable of taking us to a superhuman state… we see it every day in athletes, gifted people, and hormonal imbalances like gigantism. Your body can just do it without the negative side effects that can kill you. It also does it on a maximum level. Pain is definitely one of your triggers... I didn't know to what magnitude, so I went with bear mace just to be sure," Charles explained with a big smile.

Sophia glared at him, still not finding the humor in being blasted with bear mace. Charles stepped back a bit, making another mental note to stop putting his foot in his mouth around her.

She decided to change the subject before she hurt him.

"So if I hadn't been executed or shot..." she hypothesized.

"You would be well... you... without your additional abilities," Charles gestured, "but with a very... very long lifespan... you'd probably outlive everyone on this planet... at your current stage, I'd say you definitely will... I don't even think you'll even age at this point."

Sophia walked over and sat on Charles's sofa with a blank look and an unimaginable weight in her eyes. It was a misconception that everyone would be thrilled about living forever. She feared death like anyone else; however, the possibility of living forever was unnatural. Charles somberly walked over, sitting on the arm of his lounge chair to be there for his friend.

Sophia finally spoke without looking up.

"Charlie... the only thing I can think of that can do this is a virus..., but I can't possibly see how I was infected."

Charles had a face as if he wanted to say something; he knew how she was infected, but he decided not to go there as she was not in a great place.

He got up, sitting on the arm of the sofa, getting closer to her.

"It's not like you'd know, this isn't the type of virus that makes you sick... you can't get sick... you're like a female David Dunn."

"That's another fanboy reference?" Sophia asked with a smirk.

Charles hesitated, choosing his words

229

carefully.

"Uh… yeah… the point is, I think you're skating over the possible origin of this entire situation… all of this leads back to one night and one obvious person that this is all about."

Sophia bowed her head, looking at her feet, knowing what Charles was leading to, the night when everything changed for her. In her gut, she knew that whatever was happening to her had to do with the sci-fi assassins who murdered her husband. Everything leading up until now had to do with something Robert knew, saw, or had.

"I was trying to avoid contacting people for help," Sophia sighed, "but I'm not getting anywhere at this point. Clearly, these people I'm looking for are from some military branch, mercenary division, or terrorist cell… I need someone from that world. I think I know who to talk to. The problem is I'm pretty damn sure he's not going to want to talk to me."

CHAPTER 13

Mark and Dustin sat in the video room eating dinner while watching footage of Sophia Dennison from almost four years ago. The footage was of her entering the bank where she and her late husband kept their joint checking account. They also looked through the footage of her withdrawing money from the ATM the day after her husband's murder, driving through the toll booth heading to Oklahoma, and checking into the hotel at the airport.

On the table next to Mark's Big Mac were grizzly photos of the late Lieutenant Robert Matheson, reports taken from the crime scene, and a disc with video footage of Sophia's

interrogation after her arrest in Oklahoma.
Dustin munched on his big salad with a sour look
on his face. It was unclear if it was because he
had to eat rabbit food while his partner gorged
away on fast food or that they were watching
footage from a much-closed case.

"Tell me why again we're looking at
evidence from an open and shut case from four
years ago?" Dustin asked, finally indicating the
reason for his sour puss.

"Know thy enemy," Mark recited.

"You start with that Sun Tzu shit; I'm
gonna hit you with my big salad," Dustin
warned.

Mark turned to Dustin with a glare that
read he wanted to backhand him. He pointed out
why he was going through old files and footage.

"It baffles me how you became an FBI
agent; under almost sixteen hours of on-going
interrogation, she couldn't give account for
withdrawing the money from the ATM or
checking into the hotel."

"She couldn't give account for murdering her husband either," Dustin dryly volleyed back.

"But she did admit that she and her husband did make love that night," Mark said while munching on a fry.

"Big whoop," Dustin snorted, mixing his big salad into the balsamic vinegar dressing. "DNA and fluid proved that, like the DNA and fingerprints on the wedding knife."

"Yes, and the video footage and the eyewitnesses," Mark noted before driving his thought home. "But through her entire interrogation, her story never changed... she kept saying she didn't remember. All that damning evidence and her story never changed."

"Reports from the psychologist who examined her stated she could have gone into a psychotic episode," Dustin reminded him. "A blood rage where one doesn't remember anything."

"But the forensics report said she took her time killing her husband," Mark said. "It looked like she picked spots on his body to stab a total of forty-one times… that he basically died an agonizing death while bleeding out."

"Your point?" Dustin dryly asked.

Mark wagged a fry in the air, pulling his thoughts together.

"First of all, she's a neurosurgeon; if this was all about money, she could have thought of a million other ways to kill him without being suspected. Why murder him in such a sadistic, barbaric way knowing she would be hunted down and caught? You don't have to be a master criminal to know this was pure amateur bullshit. This is something you do if you want to get caught… or someone is setting you up."

"No other DNA, foreign fibers, or fingerprints were found at the scene or on the murder weapon," Dustin recited the case files in a zombie-like tone. "No sign of forced entry and no footprints from another party to suspect foul play from someone else. They even checked for foreign footprints and vehicle tracks outside the premise just to be sure, which is a lot considering they had the only possible suspect in custody."

Mark went back to the footage of when she walked into the bank.

"Then explain to me this, the defense's key argument at the time Dennison supposedly opened her private checking account. Dennison keyed out of the hospital at 12:05 PM for lunch and went over to the Subway for her usual six-inch Teriyaki chicken on a honey roll with Doritos Ranch Potato Chips and a bottle of water.

The security cameras were not working for some reason that day, but two of the food prep people and the cashier came forward to testify that she was there, not to mention she had a receipt for the transaction with the time stamped on it, which she kept in her car. She had her lunch on the hospital's front lawn and then punched back in with her security key card at 12:45 PM. The timestamp here on the video shows that she walked into the bank at 12:15 PM and didn't leave till 12:38 PM."

"Again... your point?" Dustin groaned, no longer in the mood to play Law and Order.

"She didn't take her car with her. Cameras

showed it still in its parking spot. Her bank is on the other side of town, a good forty-five minutes in traffic. How did she get there and back in that short amount of time?" Mark asked.

"Uh… taxi?" Dustin returned.

"Not one cab driver in the whole of Houston could confirm that they drove her to the bank and back on that day," Mark said.

Not waiting for Dustin to attempt to refute his building theory on the case, Mark pulled out a report from the Subway restaurant, slapping it down in front of him. He pointed to a highlighted section.

"This report says that the security cameras were checked on January 15, 2005, for maintenance. They were up to code, three weeks before this incident. Two of them were only a year old. What are the odds that all six cameras fail to record the day this woman is obviously in two places simultaneously during her lunch break? On top of that, how much did they say she transferred between accounts the night she murdered her husband?"

Dustin sighed, grabbing a file to confirm.

"2.9 million."

"Dustin... Federal law states anything transferred over ten thousand dollars is a red flag," Mark reminded him, "no one is allowed to transfer that amount of money online, even between their own accounts. You have to go into a bank to make that type of transfer. And she did this with a regular Dell laptop? She's got a Master's degree from Texas Southwestern for Neuroscience, not a hacking degree from the Masters of Deception. So how did she become Jonathan James in one night? And why wasn't this office tapped?"

"It was," Dustin shrugged, "but it was clear that this was a case of domestic foul play, not drugs or terrorism. As you said, she somehow managed to transfer the money between accounts in the same bank; it wasn't wired overseas. Based on that, it was a State case, not Federal."

Mark glared back at his friend.

"Dustin... this woman somehow broke

through her bank's firewall and transferred over two million dollars online with a laptop. No one thought to bring this woman in and find out how she did it?! How big of a red flag needs to go up to know that there is something seriously friggin wrong with this whole case, and it's not from a couple of days ago?!"

Mark sat back, summating his final point.

"At the prison, when she resurrected the first time, she repeated over and over again that she remembered. Call me crazy, but I think she remembered what happened that night. I think she remembered who really murdered her husband."

Dustin finally nodded in agreement.

"Interesting theory, which we'll never know unless we can find her and bring her in to ask."

Dustin reached over to grab some of Mark's fries, only to get a hard smack.

"I told you about reaching for my food; get your own," Mark snarled.

"You know Bethany's got me on this damn diet because of my cholesterol," Dustin pleaded. "I just wanted a couple."

"Not my problem," Mark said, denying his friend while stuffing a handful of fries in his mouth.

The telecom went off in the office, stopping the conversation of stealing food as Mark tapped the answer button, switching it to speaker mode as he munched away on his fries.

"Speak," he muffled between chews.

"Sir," said the agent on the other end, "we've located Sophia Dennison."

Those four magical words almost caused Armitage to choke on his fries as he tried to speak with a full mouth.

"See," Dustin wagged a finger at him, "God don't like ugly."

"Where?" Mark coughed, ignoring his partner's stupid comment.

"She's at Dr. Charles Hampton's home;

239

agents ID'd her from the video footage at the Martins' house," returned the agent. "Apparently, she's made contact with him."

"Is she still there?" Dustin demanded to know.

"Yes, sir," the agent acknowledged, "but the agents in the field just indicated that she's leaving to see someone else."

"Who?" Dustin asked.

"She didn't say," the agent answered.

"Tell them to continue surveillance on her," Mark instructed, "and to not engage her under any circumstances, is that clear?"

"Clear, sir, will maintain surveillance," confirmed the agent before cutting off.

Mark and Dustin looked at each other with some form of relief.

"Well, at least we now know where she is," Dustin sighed.

"Yeah," Mark huffed, "Now we just have

to figure out how we're going to bring her in."

"Yeah... you think about that," Dustin snorted.

CHAPTER 14

11:15 PM, the constant ringing of his doorbell forced former Marine Second Lieutenant Kenneth Scott out of his den to see who was stupid enough to come to his door this late when his children were in bed.

Finally, after serving three tours in Iraq, the Lieutenant attempted to assimilate himself into society. Although he was one of the lucky ones to return physically unscathed, the horrors of war-ravaged him in other ways; tonight was one of the few nights he could sit quietly and feel at peace. Whoever disrupted it would find him in a foul mood when he opened the front door.

"Ken… who is it?" asked his wife, Elizabeth.

Irritation draped over her face as she stood at the foot of the upstairs to their two-floor house.

"I'm about to find out," Ken shot back. "Go back to bed."

She ignored his order. It was hard living with him since his return. She understood the duties and burdens of being a soldier's wife; enduring the unknown possibility of being a widow with children or the wife of a cripple was not easy after almost three tours. Sadly, although spared the first two, the Kenneth that returned was not the man she married nearly six years ago. The body had returned intact, but the soul never made it back, and it was slowly marching their marriage to the grave.

"Who is it?" Scott barked, standing at the door, not bothering to open it.

The person on the other side did not bother

to answer as they continued to lay into the
buzzer. He reached into the silver chrome
umbrella stand, pulling out the jet-black
Louisville Slugger ball bat from the row of
umbrellas.

"I said, who the fuck is it?" Ken asked
again, a bit more forceful.

"Ken…" Elizabeth emitted a nervous
feeling that something was not right.

"Liz, I said go back to the bedroom…
now," Ken snapped at her again.

He was not in the mood to deal with her
and the asshole disturbing their household.

She refused to move as the person on the
other side refused to answer and stop ringing the
bell. Having reached his limit, Lieutenant Scott
flew the door open to come face-to-face with the
intruder on his doorstep. A very tall figure in a
jet-black hooded Gothic-like midriff jacket
covering their face with a white tank top shirt,
blue jean-like leggings, and black and white
Converse sneakers stood at his door. A great
uneasiness came over him as he gripped the bat

in his hand.

"You want to tell me why you're on my damn doorstep ringing my bell?" Ken barked again, demanding an answer from the hooded person.

"Long time no see, Ken," rang out a familiar voice.

Though Ken's face read irritation, a cold chill ran down his spine as he clutched his bat tighter.

The height and build threw him off, not to mention he could barely see her face under the oversized hood, but there was no mistaking the voice.

"Sophia?" he asked with a quiver of rage.

She lifted her head so he could see her face in the porch light. Ken could feel his body trembling uncontrollably. He fought the temptation to take her head off with the bat and beat her to death on his porch.

"Stopped by to see how the family was doing... and to talk," she said, ending the awkward silence.

"You're supposed to be…" he began to say.

"Dead? Yeah, I have been dodging that bullet a lot lately… but I didn't come here for small talk… I came here for answers… I want to know who murdered my husband."

Kenneth looked at her in disbelief that she dared to come to his house any night, asking such a question.

"You did, you crazy bitch," he snarled, "and I hope you burn in hell for it."

"Ken! Who is it?!" a frustrated Elizabeth raised her voice, demanding to know who was at their door.

"Go back to bed, Liz… now!" Ken shot back, officially losing his patience.

"Still see you haven't changed much," Sophia sighed. "You're still a prick."

Ken narrowed his eyes at her as he pointed his bat at her chest, nearly touching her.

"The only reason I'm not beating the shit out of you till the cops get here," his lips quivered, "is because my kids are upstairs. When I slam this door in your face, I will be calling them… so you best not be here before they get here, or I change my mind."

True to his word, Kenneth backed up and slammed the door in her face before locking it.

He turned to look up with irritation at his nervous and equally exasperated wife at the top of the steps, looking down at him before heading back to his den. He was not expecting his door to smash open, causing him to leap out of his skin as Elizabeth let out a terrified scream. Ken turned around with widened eyes, shaken with disbelief, as Sophia casually strolled through the now-disheveled doorway into his home.

"What the fuck?"

"I thought I told you last time you and I got into it, and you spoke to me that way, I'm not your wife."

"Are you out of your damn mind, bitch?!" Kenneth approached, pointing the bat at her

247

again.

She calmly snatched it out of his grip with her left hand using "slide of hand" speed.

"Don't point your damn bat at me," she sighed.

Not impressed by her unbelievable speed and newfound jail muscle strength, Ken went to grab for her, only for Sophia to grab him by the wrist during mid-reach.

She bent it back while applying pressure equivalent to a mechanized vice grip, forcing the highly-trained Marine to his knees.

"You're... breaking... my... fucking wrist," Scott hollered in pain.

"Sorry... I still don't know my strength yet," Sophia returned with a girlish smile.

Kenneth watched in disbelief as Sophia crushed his Louisville Slugger into two with just her bare left hand; he was so fixated on the spectacle of power he forgot his wife watching, terrified at the top of the steps.

"I'm calling the police!" she screamed.

"Go ahead, Liz!" Sophia sarcastically advised, not looking up at her. "While you're at it, make sure they bring the SWAT and the National Guard too!"

Sophia dropped what was left of the bat on the floor, looking Ken dead in the eyes to let him know that it was really her and that she meant business.

"But I'm not leaving till you tell me who killed my husband," Sophia growled, "and where I can find them. So you decide now if you're going to tell me... or if you want a firefight right here on your doorstep. Either one is fine with me."

"Okay... okay... let's talk," Ken shuddered, finally giving in. "Liz... no... no cops."

"Ken!" Elizabeth yelled in disbelief.

"Mommy!"

A frightened child cried; one of the Scotts' two children awakened from the commotion going on in the house.

"Liz! The kids... please... go see to the kids," Ken begged. "And no cops... **do not call the cops**... Sophia and I are just going to talk."

Upon hearing his agreement to talk to her, Sophia released Ken, allowing him to nurse his wrist as he rose to his feet.

Ken gave her a quick glance.

"You're taller than I last remembered."

He then motioned to his entranceway.

"You wanna get what's left of my damn door?"

She watched him enter his den as she returned to the entranceway, closing the broken door. Its weight ensured it did not swing back open, but the entire door frame needed replacing. She went to Ken's den, feeling Elizabeth's glare down at her from the steps.

"Nice to see you again, Liz," she addressed her, not looking up.

She was unsure Liz would call the police despite Ken telling her not to; at that point, she did not care. Sophia did hope for the sake of her children and their house. She would not do anything stupid.

Memories of bridal and baby showers appeared as she walked through the house. She also saw the countless football parties Robert dragged her to, and she disliked football. Though the mental bombardment was not as bad, she realized being unfocused and in a familiar place caused memories to jump at her like gangbusters. Nearing the den, she did the counting game to push it down.

She saw Ken placing his injured hand into an ice bucket while holding a Beretta M9 cocked and ready to fire with his left. She was worried about the wrong person doing something stupid. The scene did help get her focus back.

Sophia shook her head, both disgusted and disappointed.

"Figured you'd do something stupid like this."

"Who the hell are you?" Ken demanded while taking the safety off the gun.

"Thought we settled this at the door," she glared at him, almost wishing he would pull the trigger.

"Bullshit!" Ken bit back. "The last time I saw Sophia Dennison, she wasn't no goddamn Amazon bitch kicking in doors, catching punches, and crushing bats with her bare hand... so for the last time..."

Scott took aim.

"Who... the... fuck... are... you?!"

Sophia could have just rushed him and taken the gun away or walked right up to him while he emptied his clip on her, but that would have the police there in minutes, and she needed answers, not more violence.

Slowly, she walked closer to him, looking Ken dead in the eyes as she prepared to run down their history.

"September 21, 1994; we were at Christian's Tailgate; Rob spotted me on campus two days before that and finally built up the courage to talk to me. You weren't with Liz at the time; you were busy hitting on a waitress with strawberry blonde hair and a huge rack. You and Rob had joined the Marines R.O.T.C. program together. You met Liz your second semester of college at the Kappa Gamma/Sigma Alpha Epsilon party; you both broke up at the end of that semester because she caught you cheating with Becky Olson in your dorm room, but then you both got back together at the start of senior year."

Ken pretended to be unimpressed by her run-down but lowered his gun as she continued to go through their history. Sophia wagged a finger at him as she continued.

"And even though you and I couldn't stand each other because I thought you were just a self-centered womanizing son of a bitch who never took life seriously, you gave one of the most beautiful speeches at our wedding, you also proposed to Liz that same night. Then you almost cheated on her again with the stripper at your bachelor's party two days before your wedding because you wanted to have Grave

Digger instead of a limo.

Rob threatened to end your friendship if you did… and walked out of the bachelor party early. You showed up in a drunken stupor at our doorstep in tears begging for forgiveness. You swore on Buster… your prize black Labrador Retriever's life… you didn't do it. Two years later, he suffered from Osteosarcoma. You stood by his side for almost two hours after they put him down."

As she spoke the truth and secrets only the real Sophia would know, he slowly released the hammer to the gun while putting on the safety.

"On April 15, 2003, when you and Rob were to be deployed for the first time, I said to you, remember that you have a wife and a newborn son. And that's not just your best friend; he's my husband, the love of my life, and the father of my future children, so make me a promise on your worthless friggin life…"

"To make it home… safe… the both of us," Ken finished her sentence.

"I can't explain to you what happened to

me," Sophia said sternly. "What I do know is I did not murder Robert. What I need to know from you right now is what military, mercenary, or terrorist force sports a symbol of a Grim Reaper sitting on a large skull while holding a scythe in one hand and a smaller skull in its other hand."

Her symbol description visibly shook Ken, letting Sophia know she had come to the right person. What caused her some concern was when he almost dropped his gun, trying to lean against his liquor cabinet for support. Ken wasn't easily shaken by anything, and this rattled him to the core.

"Say that again?" Ken asked, swallowing hard.

"The night my husband, your best friend, was brutally murdered; there were three individuals in our bedroom decked out in black like a bunch of sci-fi ninjas," she began to go into detail. "I managed to see the symbol embossed in black on the left shoulder of one of them. Barely able to make it out with what little moonlight was in the room… it was of a Grim Reaper wielding a scythe and sitting on a large skull while holding a smaller skull in its other palm…and judging by the look on your face, you know who owns that emblem."

Ken took in a reasonable amount of air before laying his gun atop the cabinet.

He removed some ice from the bucket, dropping it into a Scotch glass. He then grabbed a bottle of Black Bush Irish Whiskey and poured.

"Want some?" Ken offered her.

"This isn't a social call, Ken," she said impatiently.

Ken ignored her, taking a sip of the Black Bush, licked his lips, enjoying the taste as he took another deep breath.

"What I'm about to tell you," he swallowed.

"Is confidential bull…" she rolled her eyes.

"No… no confidential bullshit," he cut her off, "because there is no record of this… anywhere… it's more of an urban military myth... boogeyman type shit."

"What are you talking about?" she sneered, not in the mood for riddles.

"The symbol you described," Ken paused, thinking of the best way to explain to her, "belongs to the D.E.A.D."

Sophia stood with a perplexed look on her face.

"The...'Dead'? What some Special Ops Team with the flair for friggin George Romero movies?"

"They're not Special Ops," Ken said, fighting to make her understand, "they're not even black Ops... they're not even fucking soldiers... they're highly trained killers that do not exist."

"Make some goddamn sense, Ken!" Sophia yelled, losing her patience. "I don't have time for the wordplay!"

Ken locked eyes with her again. Part irritation and fear were written all over his face as he clutched the half-drunken glass. He partially whispered his retort, thinking someone might hear him.

"Jesus, you gain muscle and lose your brain locked up?! There's no other way to explain this! These guys are said to be the fucking hell hounds of the United States government... a rumored Death Squad."

"Death Squad?" Sophia repeated in disbelief.

Ken swallowed hard before continuing.

"They're said to kill mercilessly on command; there is no record of their origin, no "official" record of their exploits if you want to call them that. Who they are, who commands them, or what branch they fall under. They're deadlier than any military unit in the known world... no one even knows what the fucking D.E.A.D. stands for! I don't even think Bush knows they exist."

"So, how do you know their names?" Sophia steely pressed.

"You only saw their left side, right?" Ken

motioned. "On their right side, each of them apparently has another patch with one letter that spells out the word "dead" between the four of them."

"Several years ago in Rwanda, some months after the Genocide, some poor bastard from the Impuzamugambi and his entire regime of over three hundred was attacked and wiped out in one night. Their camp burnt to the ground. With his dying breath, he described the same emblem you saw and was able to see the patches on their right arm. He said God had judged them for the evil they had done by sending something far eviler than the Devil himself. Guess that makes sense considering the military police found him crucified upside down and skinned to his ribcage so the vultures could feed on his insides."

Sophia, being a visual person, began to sway and shudder from his disturbing tale. Ken swallowed hard as he finished his account.

"He had the words "Cry out for God to end your life" carved into his forehead; they did that after they asked him if he believed in God."

Sophia shook her head, fighting to expunge the sick image from her mind.

"How do you know all of this?"

Ken's eyes went almost blank as he prepared to go to a darker place.

"Like I said... unverified reports... rumors... drinking stories... if you're in some branch of the military or a conspiracy theorist, you've heard the stories, but what solidified it for me was something on my third tour... our squad was on patrol in Ramadi. Got a tip that there were some insurgents in this small residential town... we roll on in, and from the beginning, something just wasn't right; it was 11 AM in the morning.

There wasn't a person on the street... no kids playing or running around, and dogs were whimpering and whining... we thought we were being set up for an ambush. We waited for fifteen minutes before we went knocking on the first door... got a sick feeling when no one answered, so we kicked it in... the minute you walked in, you could smell the stench of death and blood in the air... went into the bedrooms, and there they were... family of five... their throats slit from ear to ear."

Kenneth trembled as he took a big sip from his glass; Sophia could see that he had relived that moment right before her.

"We went to about five houses, each one the same thing. Some were killed on the toilet... in their living room... kitchen... shower... When we got deeper into the town, we found a few outside their homes done in the same way... and these bastards got creative... some were slit from chin to groin... some had their head cut clean off and placed in their laps. Men... women... children."

Ken gave a nervous chuckle as his eyes got glassy, making him take another deep sip. His bottom lip began to tremble.

"There were so many we had to call in for back up to check the whole town. Relatives and friends started to come in from buses from neighboring towns... and then the screaming and crying started. Some thought that we were responsible. When we got to the fifteenth house... we found a mother and her two daughters… heard crying in a closet… it was a little boy, no older than Sam. He was in the closet playing to get away from his sisters nagging him when he fell asleep… when the kid woke up… he heard scary voices in a language he didn't understand and saw black figures. Watched as they cut up, his mother and sisters… didn't see their faces, but as one passed by, he saw a picture on their left shoulder of a skeleton in a cloak with a big blade… sitting on a skull… holding a skull."

Kenneth appeared as if he was about to have a panic attack as his eyes scanned everywhere within his den except Sophia's face.

"Medical team came and picked the kid up after that. Haven't seen him since… said they took him to his relatives in a neighboring town or something. Four- hundred-thirty-two fucking bodies… ten out of that number were identified as insurgents we were looking for… an entire town wiped out in one night, and there were no signs of a struggle and not one shot was fired…as if the entire town was sleeping… and they just walked in and butchered them all."

Ken closed his eyes, shaking his head to

rattle the horrible visions from his skull.

Sophia knew how he felt at that point.

He quickly threw back what was left in the glass, trying to get down to the last drop; he wiped his eyes and buried his chin in his chest so she could not see the emptiness that was now within them.

"Never in my life had I seen any shit like that," Ken whispered, shaking his head, "and I've seen some shit…"

"I'm sorry," she said consolingly.

No one in her mind should ever witness something so horrible.

"Yeah…" was all Ken could say.

Sophia instantly recognized the thousand-yard stare. Like Robert, he never really came home; worse, he was carrying a massive cross on his shoulders. She forgot about their differences for a minute, standing there as a friend and a listening ear.

"I was sent home early because I just

couldn't let go of what I saw that day," Ken explained his last tour of duty. "Asking too many questions… trying to piece shit together. Did you know there are currently at least forty-four military conflicts worldwide?"

"I did not know that," she said, joining the conversation.

"You think everyone is watching who's killing who? You think everything is televised?" Ken began asking rhetorical questions he did not expect her to have answers for. "Rebel forces with just a handful of guns and explosives eventually topple a military regime. Think they did it all by themselves or did they get a "little help"? Did you ever wonder, except for the first tower bombing and 9/11, why foreign attacks on U.S. soil are almost nil? You think it's just because of our "powerful military presence" in the world because we have nukes?"

"You're saying it's because of these people?" Sophia asked.

"If you knew your enemy had the keys to the gates of hell itself and could send something so evil with the capability of finding you no matter where you hid. Something that could not be stopped and could kill you slowly in the most intimate ways that you fear most… would you fuck with him?" Ken asked her with a dazed look.

"So how do I find the gates of hell?"

As much as she did not mind playing his shrink, Sophia remembered why she came to speak with Ken and that she did not have time to hang out and root through his demons.

"Before I was sent home, I started doing some research," Ken continued. "Myth states the D.E.A.D. was around since the Vietnam War, maybe even before… and it's always been a team of four."

"Team of four?" Sophia asked, remembering that only three were in the room with her and Robert.

"Four horsemen of Apocalypse," Ken clarified. "Biblical type shit."

"That would make them in their fifties; this team seemed young," Sophia said, comparing notes. "And there was a woman on their team."

"That's the other part of the myth," Ken explained. "It's always a four-man or person team... when one is killed or "retires," they replace those members immediately with someone else... but it is always four."

"I only saw three," she cited again.

"Don't know what to tell you, maybe one was doing lookout somewhere," Ken said, shrugging his shoulders, "but all stories talk about four... but like I said, that's all word of mouth shit. Campfire stories told on patrol."

"You said there were conspiracy theories about them?" Sophia asked, thinking that he checked those leads.

"Yeah," Ken said as the fearful look returned to his face, "I tried that route when I got back home. There was nothing out there... not a website... not even a blog, and I found out why. I sent an email blast to a bunch of conspiracy theorists thinking someone heard something. Some flat out didn't respond; what was scary were the ones that did. Very aggressive emails telling me to never write or ask about the D.E.A.D. again, and then they blocked me."

"Why?" she asked.

"This went on for about three days. One day I found a note on my truck windshield telling me if I wanted the answer I was looking for to go to the 59 Diner, sit in a booth, and have their big breakfast. I went there, ate, and waited for an hour. I was about to leave when this skinny kid with a bald head, black sweatshirt, and jeans jumped into my booth. He told me to shut up and listen. That he was not going to give me his name. He told me to stop asking about the D.E.A.D. and to stop researching them. He said a couple of years ago, a guy put up a website about them and started making theories, drawing from real stuff and bullshit."

Ken started to have the jitters again as he continued his story.

"A lot of people, especially in their "field," subscribed to his site, including him. Then, one night, he said the entire website was gone. Not one trace of it was on the web. He started searching for it, talking to other subscribers he'd friended about what happened. Twenty minutes later, he got an email from the owner of the site. When he opened it, the email said, 'Do not talk about us ever again,'…five seconds after he read it, the email disappeared from his inbox. He then said he tried to send an email to other people he knew who visited the site, asking if the same incident happened to them. Before he could hit the send button, the email deleted itself, and a new email popped up with no sender address saying 'Read.' When he opened it, it only had two words… 'Last warning.' Then that one disappeared from his inbox."

"Didn't he call the police?" she asked.

"I asked him the same thing," Ken said, gripping the liquor table behind him to stop from shaking. "He said he dialed 911 and thought he got an operator… started to tell the person what happened. Whoever it was on the line said to him, 'What part of last warning do you not get?' then the line went dead. He said after that, he never spoke to anyone about what happened.

Two months later, he read the same guy

who owned the site died of carbon monoxide
poisoning in his house. It was ruled an accident,
but he knew better. He told me, for the safety of
my family and myself, to forget about the
D.E.A.D. Then he got up and ran off. I never saw
him again, but I didn't stop. And if you want to
know why I'm shaking like I'm fixin' ta piss
myself. Two weeks after I spoke to this kid, I
saw him on a missing person's report on the
news."

Ken paused a minute to try and suppress
his uncontrollable shaking.

"His name was Michael Evans, I called
the hotline number that night to speak with
someone... the person on the phone told me...
the kid's dead... you and your family will be too
if you don't stop. Then the line went dead."

Ken looked as if he was about to collapse
as his legs shivered. He appeared to want another
drink but was too afraid to move.

"I took his advice after that," he
swallowed.

Sophia went blank, realizing how Ken's

story applied to her.

"They set up his murder... like they set me up."

Ken turned to look at her with a dazed expression.

"What?"

"They killed Robert and then set me up as his murderer because of whatever he knew... or was looking for," Sophia said with the same expressionless tone.

She was not there as she pulled the pieces together to see the more prominent, horrible picture.

Kenneth's eyes widened as he emerged from his trance, realizing what she was saying.

"Holy shit..." he shuddered.

As she looked up at him, tears began to pour from Sophia's eyes.

"Did you tell him?" she asked with quaking lips.

"What?" Ken asked, bewildered at Sophia's question.

She slowly walked up to him.

"Did you tell Robert," Sophia asked with a bass-filled voice, "about the D.E.A.D.?"

Before Kenneth could react, Sophia, within arms reach of him, snatched him by his jeans pants and lifted him into the air like a rag doll.

The former hardened Marine freaked out at how freakishly strong a woman who used to stand at stomach level to tell him off was.

"What the fuck, man?!" Ken howled.

"Did you tell him about the D.E.A.D.?!"

Ken gripped her wrist to stabilize himself in the air as he locked eyes with her.

"Of course, I did; who else was I going to tell?! I was losing my shit over it! He told me to let it go, get my focus, and just think about the job and coming home!"

"Oh my god…"

Sophia trembled as she held him high; she gasped as if her legs were about to go out from underneath her.

"All this time… you knew… you… selfish son of a bitch… you knew about this… you got my husband killed… **you** got my husband **killed**!"

Ken violently shook his head in denial, realizing what she was saying.

"Nu-uh. Rob told me to forget about them! Rob told me to forget about them! Why would he go looking for them?! Sophia! I swear to God! He didn't tell me! I didn't know!"

"You promised me!" she wailed. "You promised!"

She screamed as he slammed him up against a wall.

Ken broke down, not fighting her, as the revelation that he could have possibly gotten his best friend murdered over something he confided in him was too much even for him to stand.

272

"Sophee... I didn't know," he blubbered, "...I swear to god... I did not know..."

She wanted to smash him through the wall until he stopped moving but slowly lowered Ken back to the floor, where he bawled over. She turned away, grasping her chest as if she had a heart attack. The pain in her stomach returned as she covered her face, shaking like a leaf while she wept.

Her focus was officially gone as she saw her husband standing before her, smiling with a cigar in one hand and a glass of Cognac in the other. Ken and he were christening the den after the housewarming.

She remembered jokingly reminding him about cigars causing low sperm count, while Ken reminded her of the imaginary sign on the door that read, "No women and no whining." Therefore, she had to leave for violating the rules.

"Go away," Sophia whispered, whimpering. "Please, go away."

It was not fair; she was a decent person;

she did not want these powers or this crazy existence. She wanted Robert back…to have his children; she wanted to grow old and die with him. Now he was gone, and she was alone with haunting memories she could barely control.

What was killing her most was if what Charles said about her being truly immortal were true, she would never see him again.

She walked away to get some distance between herself and Ken, in fear that she might punch his head off. She took in some air, wiped her face, and counted in her head again to make the vision disappear. It was not easy, but the mental apparition disappeared. In its place, a horrified Elizabeth stood at the door of their den.

"What did you do?" Elizabeth shuttered close to her own tears.

Sophia thought she was addressing her when, in actuality, she was looking at her husband.

"My God, Ken," Elizabeth asked with trembling lips. "What did you do?"

"Liz, please go back upstairs," Ken begged.

He turned away so as not to look her in the eyes.

"I'm not going anywhere," Elizabeth firmly threw back at him, "I am your wife… you should have told me. Days and nights, I waited thinking today, or tonight I'd hear that knock at the door. That I'd have to tell your babies, you weren't coming home. I earned the right for you to tell me. You should have told me!"

Her words made Ken stoop into a ball and cry harder.

With focus back and patience out the window, Sophia grabbed him by the front of his sweatshirt, forcing him to his feet. She braced him against the wall, looking him in his bloodshot, tear-stained eyes.

"Stop your damn crying," she barked at him. "You don't have the right to cry. You two selfish assholes and your secrets, not even thinking about the people you claim you love. You two are responsible! You destroyed your wife's trust, and I was executed over this bullshit! Now I have to fix your messes… so I need you to soldier up right now and tell me what else you do know so I can find your best friend, my husband's murderers. Now think! After you spoke to Rob about Ramadi, did you contact him again?"

"No." Ken shook his head. "I swear to god no."

"Are you sure?" she pressed him. "Think. Did he contact you? Voicemail, instant messenger, email, Facebook, or Twitter?"

Ken made sure to look her dead in the eyes.

"Sophia, that was the last time I spoke to Rob before he was murdered. I swear…"

"Don't you dare swear on the life of your children," Elizabeth cut him off, pointing at him with a warning, "don't you dare do it."

She released him, walking away, running her hands through her dreads in frustration. If that was their last conversation, the trail was now officially four years cold.

Sophia bit her bottom lip, realizing she forgot to ask him what could start a new spark.

"Ken, before you spoke to Rob that final time… did he ever talk to you about a… super soldier project?"

Sophia had lied to Charles. She had an excellent idea of how she was infected. She did not want him falling deeper down the rabbit hole to hell with her, which was where she was going.

"No, he did not," Ken said, wiping his eyes as a visible chill ran down his spine, "is… is that what?"

"You ever know me to crush ball bats with my bare hand before this?" she asked sarcastically. "Three months after Rob came home, he was going to a V.A. hospital for physical therapy for his injuries… the Michael E. DeBakey VA Medical Center. Within six months, he went from walking with a severe limp, barely able to raise his arm, and popping painkillers for the mind-numbing back pain to doing a 3K run and bench-pressing almost two hundred and fifty pounds. I was so happy that he was getting better; I didn't think anything of it... I thought it was the combination of physical therapy and his desire to get better."

"Rob was always pretty tough..." Ken nodded, acknowledging.

"What if it was something else that was making him better?" she questioned. "Something that's now inside of me?"

"I think I talked to him once about his physical therapy before our last talk. He said it was coming along, but he didn't go into detail," Ken confessed.

"Maybe they were testing this... drug or virus on him while he was there, and he found out something about it that was dangerous," she began to formulate. "I've been having some tests run on it with the help of Charles Hampton, and so far, other than the abilities I acquired, there have been no real negative effects. He said the night before he was killed, Robert would "burn" for what he did. Do you know what that might mean?"

"I don't know, Soph," Ken said with a shrug. "Rob got blood on his hands while over there just like me... up till then, both you and I know he'd never killed anyone before. If I have a nickel for every time I talked about burning in hell while drunk... well, you know."

Ken turned to look sheepish and ashamed, while his wife just looked at him, unsure what to think of him, not because he served his country, but because of his lies and keeping the truth from her.

Realizing she was officially out of viable options, she came to one conclusion as she massaged her forehead.

"Then there's only one other option," she sighed.

"What?" Ken asked. "You're going to break into the V.A. hospital?"

"No," Sophia said sternly. "I don't have to when I can go to the one person who can fill in all of the blanks."

Ken already knew whom she was talking

about by her tone.

"General Matheson?" he stammered, "you don't think?"

"I think he'd be crazy enough to put Robert in such a program," Sophia deduced, "and I think Robert would be stupid enough to enter such a program for his father. He recommended Rob to that hospital... he's the key to all of this."

"You don't think he knew about..." Ken nervously swallowed.

"I don't want to think about what he knew or didn't know. I'm at the point where I want some answers... my gut tells me he can give them to me."

"Whoa wait... you're really going to go ask him?!"

Ken held his hands up, motioning for her to think about what she planned to do.

"You do know if he doesn't know anything about this, this is the man who believes you brutally murdered his son, and this is the

280

general we're talking about."

"And?" she asked with a "What's he gonna do about it?" look, making the battle-tested Marine all the more nervous.

"You do know what this means," Scott quivered, glancing at his wife and then at Sophia before looking down at his feet in shame and fear. "If everything's as fucking insane as it is... is true."

"What?" Sophia asked, a bit scared to hear his answer.

Ken hesitated before saying the words.

"Our own government is authorizing executions on its own people... killing United States citizens."

CHAPTER 15

On September 5, 2008, she left early before Charles got up, not telling him where she was going. She left a note saying she would be back soon. It was the third lie. She told him the second one after letting him know what she learned when visiting Ken and Elizabeth. He asked her what she was going to do, and she motioned to go to the V.A. hospital to follow leads on Robert's treatment if there was any. She hated lying to him but did not want him to know what she had planned because she knew he would try to talk her out of it or go with her. This was something she had to do alone.

Sophia's stomach was in a knot as she walked through the luxurious neighborhood of West Lane, heading to house address number seven. She was shocked that patrol cars had not pulled up already to ask her what in George Bush's name she was doing in the neighborhood.

She always dreaded going there; it was intimidating; he was intimidating. General Bernard Matheson was as hard as a rusty nail and as daunting as a nuke. Sophia used to think he was a Sith Lord because his mere presence made people uncomfortable, but that was what one expected from the man with a billion-yard stare who earned his stars and stripes on multiple battlefields.

He probably was not home; chances are he was down at Fort Bliss in El Paseo or the Marine Barracks in Washington, DC.

She huffed as she walked up to the house; sitting in the driveway among other cars was his restored 1965 Pontiac G.T.O.; if he was in El Paseo, he would have driven it, and if he was in D.C., it would have been in the garage covered up; the man's routine was predictable after all these years.

Sophia's attention was quickly averted from the G.T.O. to something else all too familiar. It made her blood boil when she saw it. An extremely rare, fully restored 1969 ZL1 Camaro was initially painted metallic sea blue, her favorite color; someone had bastardized it with a generic black and white color scene and the license plate "SO FLY."

"You son of a bitch," she sneered in disgust.

Also, among the vehicles was a black BMW X5 S.U.V.; she found it odd all the cars were there, especially on a Friday; everyone on shore leave usually came over for a traditional family dinner on Sunday. It looked like everyone was there except Marcus, the eldest, and his family. He was no doubt still over in Iraq. Last she remembered, he was a Sergeant First Class, which meant Alexis and Peter were in the house with their family, and she could not stand Peter.

She walked up the driveway, taking her time to run her hand across the body of the ZL1. Images of the days and nights Robert toiled away working on that car and the day he showed her the new paint color, which she picked out, filled her head. She was officially enraged, which was probably not the logical way to go considering she was walking into her former in-laws' house, the convicted murderer of their son and brother, now accusing their husband and father of having knowledge of the real killers. However, tact was out the window after bearing witness to the constant violation of things that emotionally meant something to her.

She stood at the doorway of the Brick Veneer Stucco mini-mansion. Fear crept back, sitting on her shoulder. After her episode at Ken's house last night, she was unsure what state she would be in walking into what used to be her "third home." Aside from the car she purposely channeled, memories did not bombard her like before if she went to someplace familiar.

It did help that while Charles slept during the night, she practiced until dawn how to better control and suppress it. It appeared to manifest itself in extreme cases of distress. Using the meditative state of Yoga, Sophia taught herself to move through memories as if watching television.

Sophia even learned she could fast forward, reverse, and freeze a memory with a simple thought to look at it in detail. The focus of her lesson was to shut it off and keep it shut unless needed. She could not afford to have a repeat at Ken's house.

She remembered the last time she saw any of these people sitting opposite her behind the prosecution, rejoicing when she received the death sentence. All except Mrs. Matheson cried when she heard the verdict, not of joy; she was losing another child that day.

There would be no wondering how they would react to seeing a ghost before them. It was happening now. Sophia pressed the button, waiting for the bell-like music to play through. The fact that memory did not leap out at her was a good sign. It meant she had it locked down.

She pressed it again. The older woman's voice rang out as Sophia went for number three.

"I'm coming! Hold on! I'm coming!"

A sweaty chill washed over Sophia; she
had time to blitz out of there and find another
time and place to confront the General. Coming
too far was what rooted her where she stood.
Slowly, she bit her lower lip as the glass front
double Oakwood doors opened. Mrs. Matheson
was the same as she remembered her, a little bit
older, but the same. Her black and silver hair was
cut in a bob style. She still wore the silver
spectacles with the chain her mother gave her.
She was dressed like a typical grandmother in
her pink Polo shirt and baggy grandmother jeans;
Sophia got emotional when she saw her smiling
again.

"Yes... how may I help you?" Mrs.
Matheson asked, adjusting her spectacles.

"Hi... Ma."

Mrs. Matheson's smile changed to fear
and bewilderment; she was not so old that she
could not recognize a voice, especially one that
still called her "ma" like that.

Her voice quivered as she said the name.

"Sophia?"

She remembered that her hood was still on, pulling it from her face. Her new height and appearance threw Mrs. Matheson off, but there was no mistaking her former daughter-in-law standing in front of her at her door. Feeling a bit faint, she lost her footing.

Sophia was fast enough to catch her so she did not hurt herself.

"I got you, Ma," she nervously breathed. "I got you."

Sophia walked her over to the foyer area, setting her down in the sitting chair. She checked her pulse to make sure she did not have a heart attack.

"You feeling any tightness in your chest?" she gently asked. "Any pain in your arms or legs, or shortness of breath?"

Mrs. Matheson shook her head.

"No,…no."

She was so shocked to see Sophia kneeling before her that she responded without realizing what she was saying. It was a surreal moment for both of them.

Until a highly nasty voice ruined it all.

"Get the hell away from my mother!"

Sophia did not even have to turn to see who it was; his voice was like battery acid to her brain, and just thinking about the ZL1 further infuriated her.

"Hello Pete," she said as her nose twitched while she rose to her feet.

Peter Matheson was the fighter pilot of the family; in her mind, he was also the designated asshole, forever vying for his father's affirmation and respect, sometimes at the expense of others.

General Matheson had great respect for all military branches, considering his bloodline ran through all of them. Still, he was a Marine, and there would always be a special place in his heart for the Corps and anyone in his family who took up the mantle of the Corps. Robert was the only one to do so.

Marcus and Alexis joined the Army, while Peter joined the Air Force. Despite his other despicable traits, which entailed womanizing, unhealthy competitiveness, and being an all-around jerk for no good reason, he had the aptitude for flying with near-unrivaled precision.

Personally, Sophia believed the Master Sergeant was just too puss to survive actual combat on the ground, which is why he opted to become a Nintendo pilot. She had taken great pleasure in reminding him of that over the years whenever he had crossed the line of getting on her last nerve.

As Sophia turned to face him, she saw the gang was all there: Alexis, her husband Jeff, who happened to be a Navy Seal. Peter and his girlfriend Trisha (No military affiliation unless gold-digger became one in the last four years she was locked up), who was now the shock of all shocks Mrs. Peter Matheson by the massive wedding ring spied on her finger. Oh, yeah, she remembered. She could not stand Trisha either.

"I see you're still swinging for Daddy's nutsack by your teeth," Sophia smiled, firing off the first insult. "Tell me… how long was my husband in the ground before you violated his blood, sweat and, tears with your grubby little paws?"

"That's **my** brother's car," he snapped back at her. "He would have wanted me to have it!"

Her eyes narrowed as the urge to pounce on him built within her.

"No, he did not."

"Why are you here, Sophia?"

Alexis, the youngest and only daughter, jumped in between the childish argument demanding an answer.

"How could you come here after what you did?"

Sophia softened when Alexis stepped in; she loved her like her little sister; she was one of her bridesmaids. Alexis never believed Sophia was capable of killing Robert; she knew how much she loved him. Her conviction did not sway until the trial when she saw the bank's video footage, the A.T.M., and at the hotel.

Sophia remembered Alexis springing to

her feet, screaming for her death as she sobbed tears of utter betrayal; never more did Sophia want to die on the spot than on that day.

"I came here to see the General," Sophia softened up a bit when she spoke to her, "and I'm not leaving here till I speak to him... I believe he knows what happened to Robert..."

"We all know what happened to Robert," Trisha said, butting in, snapping her neck. "He married a greedy murdering bitch like you."

"Whu ya, call me?! Bitch?! Say it again... I dare yu," Sophia shifted into the Caribbean slang of her mother. "Say it again and see whu happens to yu! Ya, jancrow dog, you. Say it again!"

"I ain't afraid of you!" Trisha fired back.

"Yah, little, what's it not! Ya should be!" Sophia returned, warning her. "Yah really should be!"

"Sophia... look... I don't know how you managed to escape," Jeff jumped in, trying to be the voice of reason, "but you need to turn yourself in."

"Thanks for the advice, Jeff, but for your information, I didn't just escape from prison," she said, deciding to educate him. "I was executed, shot several times, and I fought my way out taking on at least fifty of Gatesville's finest... so, no... I'm not going 'back to prison.' Now I'm tired of this 'Soul Food' shit! Where is Bernard?! And don't tell me he's not here. I saw the G.T.O. outside. Where are you, Bernard?! Bring your sorry ashy-crusted ass out here! We need to talk! Bernard!"

Noted to all in and out of the household, especially Sophia, General Matheson despised two things: disorder, especially in his house, and the other was someone other than Mrs. Matheson calling him by his first name.

"How dare you come into this house," the man said, finally standing before her.

Well, a reasonable distance from her, he still had a stone-chiseled demeanor that commanded respect. Physically, he could still run a 3K relatively quickly, but his age was showing. He seemed smaller in his blue Polo shirt, tan khaki pants, and black suede slippers.

Or it could just be that Sophia saw him differently from her new height advantage, which she found weird that no one commented on remembering what she initially looked like.

"I dare because I believe you know who really killed Robert," Sophia said, getting to the point, "and I believe you know where I can find them."

"Bernard," Mrs. Matheson asked, completely confused, "What… what is she talking about?"

"I have no idea what she's…" General Matheson started to say dismissively.

Sophia cut him off before he had a chance to deflect.

"I want to know about the D.E.A.D… Bernard."

The room went dead silent, as the only ones still confused were Mrs. Bernard and Trisha; her demand even took Peter aback.

Alexis turned to her father, looking for an answer.

"Daddy...what is she talking about?"

Sophia decided not to wait for him to come up with a lie.

"The night Robert was murdered," she began, "I woke up to see his murderers. Three people covered from head to toe in some black hi-tech outfits you see in a comic book. Two men and a woman, who was holding the knife from our wedding cake sitting on top of Robert, ready to stab him... on their left shoulder was a black embossed symbol of a Grim Reaper... sitting on a large skull holding a Scythe in one hand and skull in the other.

I just came from Kenneth Scott's house last night, and he confirmed not only their name but that he witnessed their handy work... on his last tour, he and his squad came across an entire town in Ramadi that was massacred by these individuals... the only survivor, a little boy described to him the very same symbol I saw."

The silence became more awkward as the

295

General stared her down with a scowl on his face, making everyone uncomfortable because he was not refuting what she just said.

"Daddy... is what she saying... true?" Alexis asked again, stunned at what she just heard. "Daddy, say something!"

"Do you expect me to respond to an old wives tale?" he scolded his only daughter. "A conspiracy theory? This is the United States of America... there is no such thing as a Death Squad secretly sanctioned by this country! This is the woman who murdered your brother in cold blood for our family money, who got her information from a man who was dishonorably discharged during his last tour!"

Something Ken forgot to mention, no doubt because he was too ashamed to talk about it, and probably why there was an unspoken tension between him and Elizabeth; it's the ultimate kiss of death for a serviceman, especially a Marine, and Sophia knew how much Kenneth loved the Corps.

"That's right," General Matheson pressed. "Dishonorably discharged for threatening a superior officer with his firearm and conduct unbefitting a Marine officer! The man's an alcoholic undeserving of the title Marine!"

"You expect me to answer wild accusations supposedly backed by a man such as him? Ask her why she didn't come forward with this information during her trial!"

"Because it was blocked from my memory with whatever they injected me with that night. Funny that memory came back, but I still don't remember going to the bank, the A.T.M., driving through the toll to Oklahoma, and I don't remember checking into a hotel," Sophia returned fire, going on the defensive. "Then again, I also didn't know that you put Robert into some goddamn super-soldier program!"

It was a Hail Mary; everyone would think she was nuts until she was forced to show them what she was capable of. The General remained stone-faced, not flinching an inch from her accusation. The man was a solid poker player; she was now counting on a confused family filled with questions to force his hand.

"Super soldier program?" Peter emitted an

idiotic laugh. "You mean like Captain America and shit… you joking, right?"

General Matheson mocked her, grinning in disgust.

"Prison has obviously left you delusional and more twisted."

"You want to see delusional and twisted?!" Sophia hissed.

She advanced to rush him, cracking the tile floor with a step. Peter and Jeff moved to get in front of her, not realizing what she did, but Alexis saw it. In that instant, no one existed other than her and the General. All she saw was how quickly he stepped back when she moved forward.

The man who fought in countless occupations, the epitome of what it meant to be a hardcore Marine, backed up to a woman's advance.

"Sophia! You need to calm down!" Jeff ordered her.

Peter started flexing on her, ready to fight.

"You trying to run up on my father in his house?! Are you out of your cotton-picking mind?!"

"Crackin, they good floor with your roach stompers!" Trisha slipped in.

"Sophia, please stop!" Mrs. Matheson pleaded.

Sophia, however, did not hear any of them; she had tunnel vision on the General.

"Why'd you backup, Bernard?" she asked with a quivering voice. "Big bad Marine with almost every branch of the military under one roof, why'd you back up?"

This time, the General did not answer; Alexis looked at her father and saw something she had never seen in her twenty-eight years of knowing him... pure, unadulterated fear.

"You know," Sophia bared her teeth, "you son of a bitch... you know what I've become!"

Sophia saw red as she advanced full speed ahead for the General. Jeff was the first to try to take her down. To his shock and dismay, the six-foot-five, two-hundred-sixty-pound Navy Seal quickly discovered that no training could prepare him for the six-foot, several-hundred-pound female powerhouse. She overpowered him, grabbed him by the front of his khaki pants, and hoisted him high with her right arm.

"Holy!" Jeff screamed.

"Oh my god!" Mrs. Matheson cried, freaking out.

Trisha quickly coiled behind an antique chair in fright.

"Oh shit, she dun turned supa thug!"

Alexis was beside herself in disbelief at what she was witnessing. She turned to her father to see that even though he still displayed fear, he was not shocked at what he saw, only angered and defenseless.

However, Peter was not impressed with the display of power as he prepared to throw hands with her.

"Bitch, you think you got some jail muscle. I'm afraid of you?!" he snarled.

Sophia cared about Jeff and did not want to hurt him despite it all.

"Go ahead, Captain Nintendo," she smirked while taunting, "take ya best shot…"

She really wanted to hurt Peter.

"No! Don't take the shot, man! Do not take the shot!" Jeff yelled, begging him.

An enraged Peter narrowed his eyes.

"What did you just call me?"

It was like a tick to Peter being called that.

"Peter! No! Stand down! That is an order!" the General yelled at his son.

"Peter!"

Alexis also joined in, trying to bring him to his senses.

"Bitch ass Nintendo pilot flying pussy," Sophia sneered.

Peter exploded, putting all his weight behind the punch; unlike Craig Martin, she was

301

not shocked when he hit her. She just stood there, took the six-foot-four man's blow to the jaw, then watched him drop backward on his rear, clutching several broken knuckles.

"Oh! Oh god! My hand! Oh god!" he hollered, rocking back and forth.

Sophia ignored him as she lowered Jeff back down to the floor. As Sophia advanced toward the General, the big man backed up against the nearest wall, no longer wanting any part of her.

General Matheson stood there trying to keep himself from shaking, visibly trying to remain rigid. She was within six feet of him when Alexis jumped in her way with her hands up.

"Sophia, please stop," Alexis cried, begging her.

"Get out of my way, Alexis," Sophia growled. "Don't make me hurt you."

Alexis threw her arms around Sophia, holding her tightly. She bitterly wept.

"You're not going to hurt me, sis, I know you'd never hurt me… like I know you didn't hurt Robert…"

Sophia grabbed her, wanting to throw her off. She tried to get to the General to strangle the truth out of him, but Alexis held her tighter.

Tears poured from Sophia's eyes as she finally broke down, letting out an agonizing wail.

After almost four years of hell, screaming innocence, and going to her death with no one believing her, the truth finally revealed was too much for even her. She dropped to her knees, sobbing as Alexis followed her down to the floor, still holding her and crying.

It broke Mrs. Matheson's heart again.

She turned to her husband, demanding an answer.

"Bernard… what did you do?" she bawled. "You son of a bitch… What did you do?!"

"Sophia Dennison!"

Mark Armitage's voice came via a

bullhorn outside.

"This is the F.B.I. and the entire Houston Police Force! We have the house surrounded. You are ordered to come out with your hands up and surrender!"

It saved the General from having to answer to his family.

Sophia looked around, confused about what was happening, as multiple lights flashed outside around the house.

"We knew you were coming," Alexis confessed to her. "The F.B.I. was here early this morning... they told us to keep you in the house till they surrounded it so you couldn't escape."

Sophia was still in a daze, suffering from emotional overload.

"How's that possible?" she asked, "Wait... why are you all here? It's not Sunday..."

Tears flowed from Alexis's eyes as she started to cry again.

"Marcus was killed in Iraq during an ambush. We've been here since yesterday."

"But ma… came to the door… just fine," Sophia uttered.

"She has early-onset Alzheimer's. She doesn't remember Marcus. She barely remembers me…only some people," Alexis explained.

Sophia instinctively turned to the large picture of the Matheson family in their traditional military garbs. Marcus was the oldest of the four, followed by Robert, Peter, and Alexis. He was one of the best people she had ever met; he loved and treated her like a little sister from the first day Robert introduced her to him. She fell out because of the news, triggering her "condition."

Memory after memory began to appear everywhere: the day Robert introduced her to the family for the first time, the holidays she spent there, the day Robert and she told them of their engagement. The day her parents flew down to meet his parents for the first time. Barbecues and the laughter of children running, so overwhelming was the attack it left her on her knees in a near-catatonic state.

Alexis, noticing something was wrong, gently shook her.

"Sophia," she pressed with concern, "Sophia... talk to me."

"Alexis... get away from her," General Matheson ordered his daughter.

"Dad... shut up!" Alexis spat back at him, "Sophia talk to me; what's wrong?"

"Nancy, the kids..." she managed to get out.

She could barely hear Alexis through the mixed noises in her head, crashing her senses.

"They're not here," Alexis responded, choked up with tears, "Removed for their safety and Nancy's pregnant again... the house is surrounded... you have to give yourself up."

Alexis' words of surrender brought her to her senses. Surrendering was not an option; it would not end with her walking out in handcuffs again until she found them. She remembered what she taught herself last night. As she concentrated, the memories disappeared until she could hear the original present sounds in the room. She could once again feel Alexis's touch on her hands.

Sophia shook her head.

"No... I'm not going. I'm not going back till I find them."

Alexis, accepting the impossible, gently cupped her face.

"Then, you have to run, run..."

Sophia knew what she meant; the last thing the house needed was a firefight on the front lawn. She had to protect the people she loved and cared about... even Peter and Trisha. Sophia rose to her feet in control again. As Alexis stood with her, she realized the dramatic changes in her.

Sophia silently leaned down to place her forehead against hers for a final goodbye. She stopped her walk toward the main entrance to lock eyes with the General one last time. It was to let him know this would not be their final meeting.

"Conversation to be continued." Her lips quivered as she pointed in his direction. "I will see you again... real soon."

Sophia headed to the door as Alexis took over, looking at her father with betrayal and disgust. She remembered to shoot Trisha a dirty look, making her cower further behind the oversized old chair for some "protection"; she quickly walked over to Mrs. Matheson, kneeling in front of her and holding her hand.

"Ma... I got to go," Sophia smiled.

"I'm so sorry," she wept. "Baby, I'm so sorry for what we've done to you..."

"Ma... you didn't do anything to me." Sophia caressed her cheek, reassuring her. "I love you... I got to go, but... I love you..."

She quickly kissed her hand before heading for the front door. She slowed down as she saw through the glass doors the multitude of cars and law enforcement littering the lawn. Butterflies filled her stomach as she took a deep breath, grasping the doorknob before flying it open and stepping out.

"She's coming out! She's coming out!" an officer screamed.

Sophia walked onto the lawn, surveying the sea of personnel, vehicles, and guns aimed at her. Residents of the neighborhood tensely watched from their yards and windows. The way she saw it, if she tore through the least path of destruction, she would be gone before any of them jumped in their vehicles and gave chase.

Armitage stood there with bullhorn ready and made sure no one foolishly opened fire, creating an unneeded combat situation.

"Dennison hands up! Get down on the lawn! There's nowhere to run!" Mark ordered.

He prayed that she would comply.

"She's gonna bolt," Dustin muttered.

"She's not gonna bolt," Mark shot back.

Slowly, Sophia raised her hands as commanded, surveying the land. She spotted two squad cars with the least amount of bodies covering them.

Seeing that she was complying, Mark gave a mental prayer of thanks to a God he had not spoken to since he was an altar boy.

Mark followed up with his third order.

"Down on the floor, Dennison! Down on the floor!"

He found out that day God was up there, hacking a loogy on him. A fake smile grew on her face as Sophia went halfway down, allowing the agents to move closer. Her face switched to a sneer as she exploded, kicking up dirt and grass on the lawn, knocking two agents out of the way. They would be thankful later that they had body armor on as they hit the ground hard.

"She's bolting! She's bolting!" Mark yelled, scrambling.

"I told you!" Dustin shouted, running with him.

Gunfire erupted, but none of them would touch Sophia as she put it into overdrive, charging like a bull toward the barricade of squad cars.

Mark bellowed on the bullhorn, seeing the direction she was charging.

"Get out the way! Get out the damn way!"

BOOM! was the sound that sent everyone in the area of impact ducking for cover as Dennison smashed through two unmanned squad cars, sending them both into an almost three-hundred-and-sixty-degree spin. Once again, she went into a full-out sprint, jetting out of the residential area for the main street.

Those who were able and brave scrambled, getting into their vehicles to begin pursuit along with Mercer and Armitage already behind the wheel of their issued car leading the chase.

Dustin shook his head in disbelief, holding on for dear life as Mark drove.

"This shit cannot be happening, this shit

cannot be happening, man!"

"You took a drink today?" Mark asked.

"No!"

"Neither did I... this shit is happening."

Mark gritted his teeth, pushing the gas pedal to the floor, trying to catch up with the woman outrunning them on foot.

~ ~

Back at the Matheson's house, General Matheson exited his home with two luggage pieces, heading for his car. Mrs. Matheson chased after him, demanding answers, while Alexis chased after her mother, followed by Jeff, bringing up the rear.

"Mom! Mom!" Alexis frantically called to her.

Mrs. Matheson blocked out her daughter, now obsessed with chasing down her husband, who she still remembered.

"Where are you going, Bernard? Where

are you going?!" she screamed at him.

As he reached for the car door, she managed to jump in front of him, grabbing him by the front of his shirt and trying to shake him.

"What did you do, you son of a bitch?!" she yelled in his face. "Tell me what you did!"

"I did what I had to do for my country!" he fired back, refusing judgment even by his wife.

"Who murdered my baby?" she frantically howled. "Who murdered my baby?! You bastard! Who?!"

She slapped him hard out of frustration, angered him enough to grab her. Alexis jumped in, beating his hand off her, getting between them to protect her mother.

"Don't you dare touch my mother..." she snarled at her father, giving him a direct order, "get out of here and never come back."

The General sneered before opening his car door and throwing his bags in. Hopping into the driver's seat, he quickly backed out of the driveway before speeding off.

"God help you if you had anything to do with this, Bernard!" Mrs. Matheson screamed her lungs out. "God, help you!"

She broke down, crying in her daughter's arms, who held her close as Jeff put a comforting hand on his wife's shoulder.

~ ~

Back at the chase, fast as they floored their vehicles, the fleet of pursuing police and F.B.I. could not catch up with Sophia, easily clocking a hundred miles an hour or more. She could have probably gone faster by right, but there was the great fear at her current speed that she would accidentally slam into an unsuspecting car, hurting someone.

As she spied, the helicopters that flew overhead, no doubt broadcasting the unbelievable spectacle of her version of the O.J. chase on foot. The last thing she needed was to be filmed accidentally killing innocent people while trying to escape Five-O. She needed some distance between herself and the authority and decided to head to the nearest highway to get it.

"Looks like she's headed for Interstate 10," Dustin pointed out as he hung onto the strap inside the car as Mark drove like a maniac.

"We got to stop her before she gets on there," Mark muttered, pushing the 2008 Impala to its max.

His mind went through a thousand scenarios to end the chase. Every one of them had an end result that spelled disaster.

"With what, the bazooka in my ass cheeks?!" Dustin sarcastically barked.

"Why don't you stop acting like a bitch and think of something, man!" Mark howled. "I can't drive and do everything!"

"You want me to do something? Fine!" Mercer yelled back, removing his seat belt.

He turned to throw his rear into the windshield, going for something in the backseat. He came back around brandishing a Heckler and Koch MP5 locked and loaded.

Mark glanced at the combination and saw a bad idea.

"What the hell are you going to do with that?!"

"Something!"

Dustin leaned half his body out the window, taking aim the best he could from a moving vehicle doing close to eighty, and pulled the trigger, trying to unload rounds from the Heckler into Sophia's back. Several pierced through her mid-riff leather Goth jacket and shirt, but none penetrated her skin as they bounced off like previous rounds.

Sophia turned quickly to shoot Dustin a dirty look for ventilating the only articles of clothing she had in her possession and then picked up speed, darting onto Interstate 10.

Mark quickly drifted the car, leaving skid marks to exit onto the highway while grabbing onto Dustin, who almost fell out.

"Get your ass in here!" Mark barked.

Dustin fell back into his seat, checking his rounds with a disgusted scowl.

"Any other bright ideas you want me to

come up with?"

"There's got to be a way to stop her…" Mark muttered.

A Dodge Charger patrol car blasted right by them on a mission, cutting off Mark's vocal train of thought.

Mark's face twisted in disbelief.

"What the…"

Dustin raised an eyebrow.

"Looks like someone's got an idea."

Mark seeing an idiot attempting a dumbass move, got on the C.B.

"If he's thinking of doing, what I think he's doing…Someone tell that idiot in the Charger ahead of us to stand down!"

"Go suck an asshole, F.B.I. man!" came over their C.B. from the State Trooper in front of them. "While you two are holding each other's dicks, I'll show you how to shut this freak showdown!"

"How's he know we're holding each other's dicks?" an insulted Dustin turned to his partner, asking.

Mark growled, ignoring his partner's joke and stepping on the gas.

"We got to stop that dumb fuck before we're a wreck on a wreck on this interstate!"

In front of them, Sophia was moving way beyond a hundred miles per hour based on Armitage's speedometer, indicating he was pushing his car to ninety. She had gotten better at maneuvering around objects at incredible speeds without realizing it.

It made it easy for her to move around vehicles, considering they were going with the flow of traffic; also, cars literally began to part like the Red Sea at the sight of a woman on foot moving faster than most vehicles on the highway with a fleet of police cars attempting to chase her down.

Sophia thought that smashing through their barricade with considerable ease and out running the F.B.I. and Houston's Finest on the busiest highway on foot would give them a hint to back off. However, they were unbelievably relentless despite witnessing the impossible taking place in front of their eyes.

Maybe they figured she would eventually run out of gas and hit the wall, but there was no wall for her, and her tank would never run low from what it seemed.

Their tanks would run low before hers, giving the ten-year veteran State Trooper in the souped-up dual turbocharged Hemi-powered Charger motivation to put the pedal to the metal to end this quickly.

"Time for some jungle bunny roadkill," the State Trooper said with a grin.

The trooper's car inched behind her, hoping the reinforced grill guard would clip and trip her up so he could run her over. No one would dispute he was not doing his duty.

As his vehicle moved in for the kill, Sophia, sensing something approaching from behind, simply moved out of the way while maintaining her speed. Royally pissed that his initial plan did not work, the trooper decided to take a more direct approach swerving his car into her like he would do with a regular vehicle during a car chase... he would soon wish it was another standard vehicle.

The Dodge Charger met unstoppable force as Sophia stopped the car from slamming into her with one arm, grabbing it by its hood while breaking the passenger side window with her thumb. She took the terrified trooper for a ride at her current speed, pulling the car along with her.

"Jesus Christ!" the trooper screamed.

Pulling out his issued sidearm, he fired repeated shots that bounced off her.

Fed up with people putting bullet holes through her clothes, Sophia lost it, reaching down and grabbing the bottom of the car.

"Awwww shit!" she yelled to herself.

She had meant to flip the car over on its driver's side, stopping it to a screeching halt.

Once again, not in complete control of her own strength, Sophia sent the vehicle flying over the guardrail into opposite oncoming traffic a good forty feet up, high enough to know that there was a slim to nil chance the officer inside would survive when it landed.

There was also the great possibility the vehicle might land on another car or cause a massive wreck, injuring and killing many people.

She could not allow that to happen as she slid to a halt, leaving a trail of smoke while kicking up concrete; in just two steps, she launched herself toward the falling nearly three thousand-pound vehicle, catching it in mid-air.

Her landing was too awkward due to the vehicle's sheer size, but she got her feet underneath her as she came down on one knee. Oncoming traffic stopped abruptly, causing a few minor rear-fender benders at the jaw-dropping scene.

On the other side of the guardrail, every patrol car on her heels screeched to a halt. Civilians, special agents, and local police exited their vehicles, watching with their hearts in their throats as Sophia rose to her feet and gently lowered the Dodge Charger onto its four wheels. The State Trooper inside righted himself and quickly wiped his eyes while sniffling as he looked around, making sure no one saw his state.

As Sophia slowly walked around the vehicle, the authorities on the other side finally came to their senses, drawing their firearms on her. Before Sophia was thirty to forty, screaming men and women ordered her to get on her hands and knees as she slowly placed the hood to her Goth jacket on her head.

Some people turned their children away, fearing what would happen next, while others continued watching; others went further, pulling out their cellphones to record the scene for a YouTube or Facebook exclusive.

Mark stood there with his gun lowered for the first time, unsure what to do; something told him to see if he could talk to her, reason with her to come in, except the gap between the two sides made it impossible for him to cross.

Before he could put thought into action, someone in the sea of pointed guns lost it, causing everyone except Mark and Dustin to open fire.

Screaming and yelling came from the civilians off to the side, watching as bullets from all types of firearms pelted and ripped through Sophia's clothes, only to fall like coins to the ground as they slammed against her hardened skin.

Seeing that ricochets were getting closer and closer to the native Texans watching on the side, Mark decided enough was enough, grabbing the bullhorn inside his car.

"Cease-fire! Cease-fire! Goddammit!" he screamed. "We have civilians in the damn vicinity! Cease-fire!"

The shooting ended abruptly with the target still standing, her clothes a lot worse for wear, but she was no doubt still standing and unscathed. Sophia took her time backing up to the guardrail behind her, as every person looking back could feel her narrowed gaze. She was deliberately allowing people to take one final good look at her.

"No woman should have that much power…" a male civilian driver from within the crowd uttered.

She then effortlessly hopped over the guardrail, dropping two hundred feet below. Civilians all left their vehicles, clamoring to the barrier, looking down to see her land safely at the bottom, creating a sizable crater on impact. She casually sped off in a direction where no vehicle, both land or air, could follow her. Armitage walked as close as possible to the guardrail, unable to cross due to the enormous gap between his side and the other highway.

"What was that? What the hell was that?!" Mark yelled, finally losing it on Interstate 10.

"We'll find her again…" Dustin said, attempting to calm down Mark.

"And do exactly what, Dustin?!" Mark roared while throwing his hands up hysterically, pointing at every agent and officer who fired a shot. "If you haven't noticed, every damn shot from those dumbasses over there is all over the goddamn interstate! Why didn't she kill him?!"

Dustin looked around, confused.

"Kill who?"

Mark continued his pointing rant.

"She threw his car into the freaking stratosphere! Could have let it crash and burn into oncoming traffic for the perfect diversion, but she stopped and does a superman save on his worthless ass! She could have torn us apart back at her ex-father-in-law's house... yet she chooses to run... where in that is a woman who butchered her husband over some money?!"

Dustin shrugged, giving his partner the only suitable explanation he could think of.

"Maybe she found Jesus."

Armitage looked at Mercer as if he was about to shoot him; he then marched back to his patrol car.

"Where are you going now?" a frustrated Dustin asked.

"Going to find out why she came back to Houston once and for all," Mark yelled. "Bring

Lieutenant Kenneth Scott in… and get me Doctor Charles Hampton… now!"

~ ~
~

St. Luke's Episcopal Hospital, nurses, doctors, orderlies, and patients inside the break room huddled near every flat-screen television to view the interstate incident.

As reporters talked to commuters who gave their account of the phenomenon during Friday rush hour traffic, Charles Hampton was the only one who stood way back with a visibly worried look on his face. Only he knew it was his best friend on that interstate, outrunning the police and throwing patrol cars like Tonka toys. As he wondered her whereabouts after the death-defying jump played for the umpteenth time, he jumped out of his skin at the sound of his "Pocket Full of Sunshine" ringtone.

"Hello? Hello?" Charles whispered.

"Charlie… it's me," Sophia spoke, holding a payphone.

Hampton looked around as if all eyes were on him and then scurried off to find a safe place to speak.

"Oh my god… are you alright?" he stammered.

"I'm fine… clothes look like shit," she joked, "but I'm right as rain… found the last working payphone in the world…"

"I'm glad you're in a joyous mood while I have a heart attack watching you do your version of "Hulk Smash" on national T.V.!" He raised his voice a bit, scolding her.

"I'm not running anymore, Charlie."

"What?" Charles asked, now confused.

"I am tired of running like I'm guilty when I know damn well that I'm not, and I don't have to. I'm not running anymore. I'm not going to find Rob's murderers while hiding in the shadows and ducking the police and F.B.I. every two seconds. I have to call them out and really go hunting for them."

"How will you do that?" Charles asked.

327

Sophia looked around before answering.

"I don't know yet, but I'm going to figure something out."

"Let me come and meet you. I could bring some clothes and money, and we can figure this out," Charles proposed.

"No... Charlie... I don't need you to come, and I'm good at money... I took some out of the bag... the rest is yours," she thanked him.

"I don't want the damn money," Charles fired back at her, frustrated.

"Then just hold it for me," she calmly returned, not looking to argue with him, "but I need you to do me a favor."

"You name it," he said.

"The samples you took from me," she requested, "I need you to destroy them."

Charles paused as if hit with a body blow; apparently, he did not expect "I need you to do me a favor" to mean that.

"Soph…" he swallowed.

"Charlie, whoever killed Rob over this will kill you if they find out you have it. They can work behind the shadows without prosecution; they are that treacherous. I couldn't live with myself if that happened. Not to mention it is dangerous. I know you see it as the ultimate cure, but it's just too dangerous at the end of the day. I am dangerous… can you imagine more people like me in this world, people like the ones who killed Robert? I think he found out how dangerous this was and tried to tell people… and they killed him for it. I have to finish what he started. I have to stop them for him."

"You have five minutes for this call. Please put in fifty cents to continue," interrupted the automated operator.

"Charlie, time is almost up, and I have to go. Promise me you will destroy it."

"I… I promise I will," Charles sighed, giving his word, "but what are you going to do?"

"I don't know yet, and it's better you not know," she huffed. "I got to go, thanks for

329

everything. I love you."

"Sophia!" Charles yelled, forgetting where he was.

The phone went dead before he could respond. His heart leaped out of his chest from the last three words. He knew Sophia probably meant it in the context of them being best friends, but he wanted to tell her he felt more, that Charles always felt more for her, and how much of a coward he was for not acting on his heart and telling her.

For making excuses for something always coming up, things never being the right time, who she was dating, or that she was in court facing a death sentence.

The regret he carried after she married Robert, he thought she was lost to him forever. Right there in the mother of all insanity, he had an opportunity to tell her how much he loved her and, no matter what happened, to ensure she returned to him. His one chance was cut off by a pay phone. He looked up, thinking that if God existed, He was a cruel, practical joker.

"I love you, too," he said, letting all the air out of his chest.

~ ~

On the other side of the ended conversation, Sophia composed herself, adjusting her bullet-riddled clothes. Some bullets caught in her clothing, and dreadlocks fell, hitting the floor like coins. She walked back out into the front of the diner with all eyes fixed on her. When she jumped from the interstate, she just took off and kept running; Sophia was not sure how far she ran, but she was sure it would be a while before anyone would find her.

She lied to Charles for the fourth and probably final time. Sophia already had a plan. She did not want him involved anymore or talking her out of doing it because it was indeed an insane idea, and she was already scared and unsure it would work. The first thing to do as she walked up to the now nervous waitress behind the counter was to find out where the hell she was.

Sophia gestured while putting on the most innocent smile possible.

"Excuse me, how much for some coffee and a bagel with cream cheese?"

"Two dollars fifty cents," the waitress nervously answered.

"Okay," she nodded calmly.

She slowly pulled out the money from her jacket pocket and placed it on the counter; in the process, some more bullets caught in her clothing fell onto the floor. It also did not help much that the twenty-dollar bill had a bullet hole.

"And I'll take that to go… skim milk with four sugars," she said, smiling while pretending everything was normal. "You can also keep the change… uh… could you tell me exactly where I am?"

"Waco…" the waitress answered, looking her up and down.

Sophia nervously smiled, nodding; yep, she'd run pretty far.

She then dared another question.

"Do you know what direction Washington,

DC is?"

"Do you need a bus station or airport?" the waitress asked.

"No…" Sophia smiled, "just need the direction."

~ ~

On almost the other side of the country, within the secret and fortified Mount McLoughlin, Director Rosen stood in his situation room alongside Dr. Archifeld Zimmerman, watching an unedited replay of the confrontation on Interstate 10.

On the theater-like screen, various different takes and angles of the footage played from distant and zoomed-in frames as analysts and lab technicians with technology never seen in some of the most advanced scientific facilities in the world attempted to study and assess Sophia's extraordinary abilities in hopes of finding a chink in her armor.

"She is amazing," Dr. Zimmerman beamed. "She is holding a current speed of a hundred and ten miles per hour… I believe she can go even faster! The density of her entire anatomy must be greater than that of steel or tungsten! Pupils indicated that heart rate is at forty beats per minute while blood pressure is operating at 120 over 80, no over-exertion whatsoever!"

"Fascinating Doctor Zimmerman, now how do we capture her?" Director Rosen calmly inquired.

The doctor shrugged while scratching his head.

"Physically, I don't even think it is possible. Even with the BAMs."

"Then we have no choice but to go with plan B," Director Rosen said, contemplating.

Almost as if on cue, Director Rosen's phone went off, playing his ringtone Hot N Cold by Katy Perry. He slowly rolled his eyes as he pulled his Wi-Fi headset from his pocket, placed it on his right ear, and turned it on.

"Bonjour," he answered.

The Director massaged his nose as he listened to the distorted and incoherent ranting on the other side of his headset.

"Well, sir," the Director explained to the person on the other end, "considering this is the first time we've encountered such a situation, you should respect the fact that it takes time to devise an effective plan to deal with said situation."

The Director massaged his nose again as he listened to more distorted and incoherent ranting, waiting for it to end.

"Somehow, she's managed to go off radar, preventing us from tracking her. That shouldn't be for too long." Director Rosen reassured, "and when she does show up again, we will be prepared for her. Yes, sir… yes, sir… good day, sir."

Director Rosen quickly pulled the headset off his ear, rolling his eyes while looking to the heavens.

A bewildered technician turned to him in confusion.

"Sir... we are tracking her; she's in Waco."

"I know that," Rosen returned. "I just wanted to get him off the phone."

Ms. Barrett walked in with apparent news.

"Sir, we have located the package. Agent Slater and assigned team have been dispatched to acquire it."

"Excellent, Ms. Barrett," the Director praised her. "How goes the unit's training?"

"Steadily... #4 was not taking it seriously," she answered. "I was forced to give him a bit of motivation. I estimate that they should complete their training two hours before the forty-eight hour time period you gave them."

"Thank you, Ms. Barrett; please continue to monitor their training along with real-time updates on Ms. Dennison's whereabouts. Dr. Zimmerman, let us discuss the procedure once we've captured her."

CHAPTER 16

Doctor Charles Hampton sat quietly, looking around at the sterilized interrogation room that was no different from one of the many examination rooms he had worked in, aside from the sizeable dull silver table, three chairs, and a two-way observation mirror. He wondered if Sophia felt like this when they took her in. Charles imagined it was probably a million times worse.

No more than thirty minutes after he finished speaking to her, federal agents walked into his place of work for the second time and allowed him to be escorted out with or without handcuffs. Charles chose the latter as he sat in the room unrestrained… for now. Nervousness began to set in as he tried to tap a tune on the table with his nails while his right leg twitched uncontrollably.

He was about to get up and walk around when the door flew open. Armitage barged in with a face that could split stone, which made Charles' heart beat faster.

The last time someone interviewed him about Sophia was almost three days ago in the safety of his own office. The female agent who came with a couple of files presence and mannerisms was a billion times nicer than the old bruiser before him.

Mark looked at him as if he had stolen something from him, grabbing one of the chairs on the opposite side of the table. He purposely dragged it around, making an ear-splitting screeching sound before placing it right next to Charles. Mark took a seat using the back of the chair as an armrest while staring right through Hampton. Charles tried not to make eye contact with Mark, believing he was peering into his soul. Sweat trickled down Charles' forehead as he stared at the table.

"Dr. Hampton," Mark said as calmly as possible, "what did my agent tell you after she interviewed you in your office?"

Charles slowly turned his head to look directly at a man with the demeanor of a puma, and he was the kill. He swallowed lightly, not making any sudden moves and thinking before he spoke.

"Um… excuse me?" he slowly asked.

He was not trying to play dumb; his mind went blank from fear.

Armitage exploded out of his chair, startling Hampton, who almost fell out of his. He marched over to the interrogation room door, flying it open.

"Agent Morella Sanchez! In here! Now!" Mark barked.

Morella Sanchez, an agent of five years, walked in with her brunette hair pulled back, adjusting the black square glasses on her face. She looked just as nervous as Hampton, although she tried not to show it.

"Sir?"

"What did you tell Dr. Hampton on September 3rd, 2008, after you interviewed him at 15:00 hours, which is 3 PM in his office?"

"That if he was to come in contact with Sophia Dennison, he was to alert us immediately," she relayed.

"Because?"

"Aiding and abetting an escaped convict is a Federal crime," she cited. "punishable up to two years or more in prison…"

"Thank you, now get out," Mark ordered.

"Yes, sir."

Sanchez quickly scurried out of the room.

Mark slammed the door shut, walking back over to Hampton. He set up his chair and sat to stare him down like a cobra again.

"Almost half a day after that conversation, I have Intel that Ms. Dennison made contact with you," Mark said calmly, "and you did not contact this office, which means you broke the law."

Hampton made another hard swallow, moistening his severely dry throat. Seeing that the slightest thing could set him off, he decided to see if he could reason with Mark the way one would a bear.

"Look…Agent Armitage," Charles said, slowly choosing his words carefully, "if you're trying to intimidate me, it's working, but if you want me to tell you where she is or what she has planned. I do not have a clue. She contacted me after what happened on Interstate 10. She told me she wasn't running anymore and that she would find the people who really murdered her husband. She told me she didn't want me involved anymore; Sophia didn't tell me anything; she just said goodbye and hung up the phone. I swear that's the truth."

"Who does she believe murdered her husband?" Mark cynically asked.

"Not believe… knows… her husband was murdered by three people, two men, and a woman," Charles explained. "She believes the woman did the stabbing because she saw her sitting on top of him holding the cake knife from their wedding. They're called the D.E.A.D. She described them as wearing some ninja-like black sci-fi armor and a symbol on the left shoulder of a Grim Reaper holding a scythe in one hand and a skull in the other sitting on a large skull."

Hampton's description caught Mark off guard and sent a sickening chill down his spine.

Charles caught it.

"You know what I'm talking about," he swallowed, "don't you?"

"She used that name and described that symbol to you?" Mark pressed Hampton.

"To the tee, another thing," Charles clarified, "along with her physical abilities, which you've probably witnessed firsthand, she can remember everything that she's ever read, saw, or heard in her entire life; her mind is like a supercomputer allowing her to access any memory she has at will. I don't know if you looked at her files, but the reason why she kept saying she had no memory of opening an account, withdrawing money from an A.T.M., or driving to Oklahoma is that she never did those things. Call me crazy, but I believe someone else looking like her did those things to frame her."

Armitage knew that Hampton was not feeding him a line of bull. He had put enough of the fear of the Federal Government in him so he would not lie to him. As he looked into his eyes, it was also clear Charles did not care about jail time; he wanted to clear his friend's name.

"You sit here… think about what you did," Mark scolded him, "and I'll be back to decide whether to charge you or not."

Mark got out of his seat quickly exiting the interrogation room so Charles could not see him sweat. Mark speed-walked to meet up with Mercer to deliver shaking news when Dustin came from around the corner from his own interrogation, looking just as pale as Armitage.

"You won't believe what the good Lieutenant just told me," Dustin started.

"Tales about the boogeymen?" an unnerved Mark guessed.

"What the hell is going on Mark, what did we just walk into?" Dustin whispered at his wit's end, "a U.S. government-issued Death Squad… what the?"

"What did Lieutenant Scott tell you?" Mark asked, comparing notes.

"Oh, about a massacre in a town in Ramadi, Iraq," Dustin threw out, visibly disturbed, "where an entire freaking town was wiped out. He believes his best friend, the late Lieutenant Matheson, was killed by the very same individuals who did the massacre for either doing his own investigation on them or over a super-soldier program, which would be so easy to call bullshit on except for the fact that his widow single handily made us look like bitches on Interstate 10."

"Back up," Mark asked, now confused, "what super-soldier program and what massacre in Ramadi?"

Dustin tried his best to break it down verbatim.

"Almost four years ago, three days before he had his last conversation with Matheson. Scott and his squad entered a town in Ramadi looking for insurgents. He and his squad found an entire town wiped out in the middle of the night; the assassins apparently slaughtered everyone with just bladed weapons. A little boy survived the massacre and described a symbol on one of the assassin's left arm of a...."

Mark finished his sentence.

345

"A Grim Reaper with a scythe in one hand and a skull in another sitting on a large skull… Dennison described the same thing to Hampton."

Dustin nodded.

"Lieutenant Scott said she told him they were in their bedroom the night her husband was killed, a woman and two men."

"Has he been in contact with her today?" Mark asked, praying he was.

Dustin shook his head.

"He said no, and I believe him."

"Why didn't he come forward with this?" Mark asked beside himself.

Dustin looked at Mark, wondering how he could ask such a stupid question.

"The guy was court marshaled and dishonorably discharged for trying to uncover the truth. He was then "warned" of severe repercussions if he leaked a now "highly classified mission" to anyone; that's what happened. Seriously?! American soldiers "happen" to stumble upon a town brutally massacred, how do you think that's going to go over?! No doubt, there are a million and one gag orders burying this incident deeper than I did the neighbor's cat!"

Mark nodded in agreement.

"What about this super-soldier program?"

"Speculation, Matheson was murdered while Scott was overseas," Dustin sighed. "At least a month and a half after the incident in Ramadi. He never spoke to him about a super-soldier program. Dennison told Scott that her husband was receiving treatment at a V.A. hospital and that she noticed he was getting significantly better from his injuries. The reason she went to her ex-father-in-law's house was that she believed General Matheson was responsible for enrolling him into this alleged project since he was also the one who recommended him to the hospital."

"Which VA hospital?" Mark asked, preparing to send agents there to investigate.

"Records show he was going to Michael E.

DeBakey VA Medical Center," Dustin said.

"We need to get his records and whoever he saw while he was there. I'd also like to get a personal interview with General Matheson," Mark quickly decided.

"You know this is walking right into military territory," Dustin cautioned.

"I don't give a rat's ass if we're stepping into the Pope's territory," a fed-up Mark responded. "It's time we get some real goddamn answers... it's time we get the truth."

CHAPTER 17

September 6, 2008, 5:00 PM Eastern
Standard Time,

"Low profile... low profile..."

Sophia said to herself repeatedly as she
walked with her head down in the streets of DC.
She had been undetected for most of the day
since arriving yesterday early morning.

After the battle in Texas and making it to
the nation's capital, she decided it best to stay
under the radar until she figured out her next
step. As she told Charles, she had taken some of
the money he had kept for her, lining the back of
her former Goth jacket with bailout money if she
could not return to his apartment. It was also why
she gave Mercer a dirty look when he shot her in
the back during the chase. Luckily, the semi-
automatic bullets from his Heckler & Koch did
not riddle all of her spending cash.

Sophia found a seedy motel to take a
much-needed hot shower and stay off the streets
until morning, where she could shop for some

much-needed clothes. Not that she did not stop to change her shot-up outfit before getting to Washington; her black and white Converse, which served her faithfully since she acquired them in Cypress, finally gave out halfway between Arkansas and Tennessee.

Sophia stopped at a Sports Authority in Memphis to purchase two decent running shoes, a running outfit, and a new book bag.

When businesses opened in DC, she went on a part shopping, part recon mission.

While casing the neighborhood and targeting the building of her harebrained scheme, she purchased some new black jeans, a pair of cute mid-heel boots in her size, a new black hooded sweatshirt, and a blue slim racing jacket. In her hand was a bag full of other items she purchased and something to eat from Taco Bell.

Now, she was heading back to the motel; Sophia felt it was best to stay off the streets, especially in the Nation's Capital. Her confrontation with the General got her no vital information about the D.E.A.D or any leads on finding them. And although she escaped, the incident on Interstate 10 plastered Sophia's name and face all over the news. Her public appearance as an escaped convicted death row fugitive did not serve her cause and made many people afraid of her. She needed to figure out a new tactic to achieve her goal.

Sophia thought about seeing her parents one last time, but that was now out of the question. She figured their house would be crawling with agents and probably the military; the last thing she needed was to bring a firefight like Houston to where they lived. They would have to go on without seeing her for a bit longer.

As Sophia roamed Good Hope Road, she did not notice that she walked past some "brothers" gawking and making catcalls, beckoning her to come over and talk to them. She just kept walking, heading back to her motel room where she could get her thoughts in order.

"Well, fuck you, ya nasty bitch!"

The disgusting insult came from one of the men in the group named Deuce.

Deuce stood about six-foot-six with two-hundred-seventy pounds of pure muscle in a black ribbed tank top that appeared as if it was struggling to stay on him while his jeans pants fought to stay up under his rear, revealing his blue and white striped boxers. All Sophia heard was the buzz of a bug she could crush. Sticking to her keep a low profile mission was the only reason she was merciful.

"Nobody wants yo funky…" he began to boast.

Before Deuce could finish his following lewd sentence, Sophia turned on her heels, dropping her bags, and was airborne a good twenty feet up. When she landed, it was with a double ax handle smash to the hood of his custom Escalade with the trimmings.

She figured it was his, considering he stood beside it while pumping Black Rob's "Whoa" from its custom system inside.

Sophia remembered she hated bugs, especially the annoying ones who did not know when to stop buzzing.

The impact was equivalent to a fifty-ton

construction beam dropped from one hundred feet up, caving in the front of the SUV, obliterating the engine, blowing out his two front tires along with his front window, and crushing his two front custom twenty-six-inch rims. The back end of the SUV shot up as if it was doing a handstand before crashing violently back down to Earth.

Deuce stood in the same spot he was in, not moving an inch, covered in fresh new sweat as his associates, who were laughing and giggling at his remark earlier, lay sprawled out on the floor, beyond terrified at what they just witnessed.

The neighborhood became alive as people stuck their heads out of their windows or ran out from wherever they were to see what had happened. Sophia pulled herself off the top of his obliterated SUV with her hood covering the upper half of her face.

She turned and walked up to a traumatized Deuce, getting face to face with him.

"Who's the bitch now… bitch?" Sophia calmly asked.

She did not even wait for him to answer with an apology or plea for his life. She turned, walking away, picked up her bags, and sped off.

The second she left, the masses came flocking around to witness the destruction Sophia unleashed on Deuce's vehicle as his friends flocked around him frantically, asking if he was all right. Deuce stood silent with a blank, distressed expression, looking in the direction Sophia departed. Six buildings away, Sophia turned into a back alley and fast-walked out of it into the street with her hood still up and head down, trying to keep a low profile once again.

She cursed herself for losing her temper. The overgrown punk son of a bitch was not even really worth it. She could have walked away and ignored him, but the minute he opened his mouth, it was like claws in the back of her brain, and she just had to take him down several pegs.

However, her male castration via "vehicular manslaughter" had drawn attention to her current location sooner than she wanted. She knew she had to go up against the law again, and Sophia was serious about not running, but she still needed to pick her battles, for the time being, staying under the radar.

The entire country, probably the world, would soon know about her and everything happening under their noses. For now, constant movement and staying incognito until the right time had to be her religion. For breaking one of the commandments, she had to leave the state and find another place to crash and burrow in until the mayhem she caused cooled down.

~ ~

Director Rosen sat at his desk on the other side of the country, holding a broken piece of a banana while a black and white spider monkey greedily reached out to grab it.

"Remember Cornelius," Rosen baby talked the monkey, "do not grab… do not…"

Despite his command, the little spider monkey snatched the piece of the banana from his grip, quickly chomping down on it as he looked up at the Director, who just smiled, wagging his finger at it.

"Naughty little spider monkey," he

playfully reprimanded him, "naughty... naughty..."

In the middle of his playful scolding, his telecom emitted a high-pitched ringtone, startling the monkey a bit.

The Director rolled his eyes with annoyance as he answered it.

"What is it, Ms. Barrett?"

"Sir, the target has been spotted during an incident she caused in the nation's capital."

"In less than twenty-one hours," Director Rosen said to himself, "most impressive..."

"Sir," Ms. Barrett began to interject, "the team has also completed the operator training."

"And the other matter?" Director Rosen asked, talking in code.

"Agent Slater is en route with a team to collect the package as we speak," Ms. Barrett confirmed.

"The minute he's confirmed pick-up,

ready the team, and the necessary equipment for a trip down to Washington DC," Director Rosen instructed.

"Sir," Ms. Barrett asked, a bit concerned, "you're going to attempt an extraction in the nation's...?"

"Thank you for carrying out your orders, Ms. Barrett."

The tone in Rosen's voice hinted for her to do her duty and not to question him.

"Yes, sir," she said, taking the hint.

The Director turned off the telecom as he broke off another banana piece, holding it up for an anxiously waiting Cornelius.

"Daddy's going to capture a god," Director Rosen smirked, "isn't that wonderful Cornelius? Yes, it is... don't grab... don't."

~ ~

Six hours and forty-four minutes later, Mark and Dustin stood on Good Hope Road, inspecting what was left of the SUV belonging to

Deuce. Around them, agents and reporters subjected themselves to the hood interview accounts of the woman who laid waste to Mr. Deuce's vehicle with a single superhuman blow.

Taken from the account of the typical street interviewee verbatim.

"Yo, son, I saw it with my own eyes, son. Shortie took two steps and leaped into da mafuckin stratosphere an shit, den came down on homie's whip on some incredible juggernaut destruction type shit like blouw! An I was like, "Ooooooooo shit!" Blew out da nigga's windows and everythang... den she just rolled off his shit, called him a bitch and took off like Flo Jo on speed dataway! Left him cryin and shakin next to his busted up whip and shit... wit snot runnin out of his nose an shit... I ain't neva seen no shit like dat son!"

Deuce's interview went a bit differently.

"I was standing next to my vehicle talking to some old acquaintances when this woman came out of nowhere and accosted me, and then obliterated my vehicle! Honestly, I don't even think she was a woman!"

Deuce nervously answered the agent, interviewing him with the demeanor of a polished and refined man.

"Acquaintances?"

Tru Dat, one of Deuce's friends, shot back at him.

"Who da fuck you callin' "acquaintances"?"

The agent he talked to actually learned that the hardcore thug known as Deuce's real name was Nathanial Walters, a Harvard graduate working on his master's degree and an attorney for a very reputable law firm living in the prestigious Georgetown area of DC. The agent derived that Mr. Walters was just a wannabe thug who occasionally hung out with his going-nowhere friends from the old neighborhood to boost his ego.

It also did not help that Mr. Walters gave his acquaintance Tru Dat the "talk to the hand" sign, officially losing all street cred.

"Please!" Deuce yelled back, "I am

talking to a federal agent here! Please!"

"Dat's why supashortie wrecked yo shit… bitch," Tru Dat answered back.

Nathanial Walters ignored him, wanting to know what the federal agent he was talking to was going to do about his car.

"I am a taxpaying citizen, a corporate attorney for Pendergrass and Munich, and I need to know what you intend to do about this? What am I supposed to tell my insurance company?"

"Tell em da truth," Tru Dat laughed, "Supahead Randy Savaged yo shit!"

"You can walk home!" Walters yelled while frustratingly pointing at him.

"You walking home too, bitch," Tru Dat shot back.

"We're trying to do everything we can, sir," the agent said, trying to calm the situation. "Just need to ask you a few more questions."

"Well… at least now we know where she is," Dustin huffed.

Mark glanced over to Dustin as if he wanted to take out his service piece and shoot him when Executive Assistant Director Douglas King walked up to them, none too happy. A former military man hailing from the Army Special Forces, he wore the traditional military crew cut, which matched his granite exterior. Like Mark and Dustin, he worked his way through the ranks but knew when it was time to get out of the field and let the young blood take over while he sought a leadership position for better pay and a corner office.

Half of him respected his two senior officers because they were war dogs just like him. The other half wanted to take them behind the tool shed because of their dual lack of respect for authority and old-dog mentality.

His patience was nonexistent, seeing as how the situation that was supposed to be contained in Texas had traveled from the Midwest to the nation's capital.

"Enough is enough," King muttered, "I'm heading this case… Sophia Dennison has now been moved up to the very top of the most wanted list… we're locking down DC… kill on

361

site… that's the order."

"And how do you expect to do that Doug," Mark asked, not even looking at his boss. "When bullets have no effect on her? You gonna start issuing out tanks to us?"

"That's Executive Assistant Director," King reminded him, "and in case you haven't noticed, your goddamn fugitive is now in the nation's goddamn capital!"

"And this is our fault?" Mark snapped, "because we've dealt with superhumans before, so we should know how to take her down, right? Because we forgot to carry the green rock that went with our goddamn service pieces!"

King squared off with Mark, standing toe to toe with him.

"No one is blaming you, Mark. However, if all this is getting to be too much for you, you can go home, Special Agent."

Mark gave him that "you can't drag me away" look as Dustin placed a hand on his shoulder, gesturing to calm down if he wanted to stay on the case.

"Now, allow me to reiterate this again," King issued his final order, "Sophia Dennison is officially a terrorist of the United States of America at the top of the list, which means you are authorized to use any means necessary to find her and to stop her! The order is to kill on sight… that means if you need a fucking tank to take her down… get one. Is that clear?"

"What about our report?" Mark bit back, grinding his teeth.

"The one implicating a decorated four-star general is in association with a fictional death squad under this government corroborated by a dishonorably discharged soldier, a friend of the terrorist fugitive, and the terrorist fugitive herself… how should I answer that?"

King glared with sarcasm.

"Let me simplify it for you… there is no death squad and stay the hell away from General Matheson… is that also clear?"

King marched away, not waiting for a

response. Mark bowed his head, fighting to control his rage. Dustin moved in front of him to block him from possibly tackling King from behind and beating him in the middle of the street, although the older man looked like he would give Mark a hell of a fight.

"We'll strengthen the security around the capital," Dustin began shooting off ideas. "Get birds in the air, drones, cameras, and all the manpower we can muster... we'll find her."

Mark let out a frustrated laugh.

"And do what, Dustin? Besides, piss her off and cause billions of dollars in mass destruction trying to stop her, not to mention getting a lot of people hurt or worse?"

Dustin looked around, baffled.

"Why the hell did she come here in the first place? Why not New York or LA like they do in the movies? It's as if she's looking for a fight."

Mark took a deep breath and released it, finally calming down as he answered his partner.

364

"That's exactly what she's looking for; she believes a government-sanctioned death squad murdered her husband and turned her world upside down; what better stage for a confrontation than right here? She's here to call out those responsible."

"So, what do we do?" Dustin asked his partner, hoping he had a plan.

Mark's face revealed he had none. He sighed while shrugging his shoulders in defeat.

"We wait for the shit to hit the fan... and pray we don't get buried by it."

CHAPTER 18

8:50 AM Monday Morning, September 8th, her little antic had placed D.C.'s entire capital on high alert two nights ago. All around her were heavily armed officers and soldiers on almost every corner. Squad cars and personnel vehicles drove up and down the city while helicopters scanned the air; she could have sworn she even saw a drone or two.

The heat was so bad that Sophia jumped two states away to avoid detection. It did not matter; the objective was always to wait for Monday to initiate her plan.

~ ~

She remembered the day before promising
to wage no war on a Sunday; instead, Sophia
found another motel to set up camp. She changed
her clothes, putting on a pretty, long, yellow
flowing summer dress with white sling-back
wedges and a small purse she picked up. She
would later leave everything in a bus stop locker
with the rest of her belongings that she did not
need to carry for the mission.

After Sunday, it would no longer matter if
Sophia returned for them. She found the nearest
Pentecostal church to visit, taking part in the
sermon, killing half the day. The homily was
God's miracle, and the incident at Interstate 10
somehow became a part of the pastor's speech.

Sophia thought it would have been
amusing if she could have stood up and informed
the congregation that the person he was talking
about was standing in their midst, but she opted
to make goo-goo eyes at a little girl with pigtails
staring back at her from the pew in front.

A mother beside her asked if she could
kindly hold her eight-month-old while she got

his bottle from her bag. She nervously obliged, clutching the child, who stared back at her with inquisitive eyes.

The child appeared more fascinated with her dreads as he reached out to grab one handling it. The innocent act made her eyes gloss over. His mother noticed the sadness her eyes could not hide.

She leaned in, whispering in Sophia's ear.

"Your time will come… God has a plan for you. You just have to believe."

Sophia wanted to tell her with a smile that God screwed up her plans four years ago, using the F-word as the verb. She opted to smirk and thank her. If He did exist, Sophia had a grudge against her Creator. She was there because it was less likely for F.B.I. agents or local authorities to storm one of His houses during a service looking for her. It was the least He could do for her. She became the designated babysitter for the rest of the service, left a substantial offering, and vanished before anyone could ask her if she accepted Jesus Christ into her life.

Sophia stopped by a small mom-and-pop diner and had a stack of pancakes and eggs with sausage on the side and a glass of orange juice to wash it down for brunch. She finished her meal with a slice of homemade apple pie and a strawberry milkshake. Sophia then just sat there looking out the window and around the diner at the people, while from time to time thinking of happier days. She made sure to leave a very nice tip before departing.

Returning to the motel, Sophia changed her clothes and spent the rest of the day into the night studying her own self. A local junkyard was the perfect training ground. After the guard dog realized there was no way his teeth would pierce her impenetrable hide and decided to behave itself, she got to work. She needed to know how fast she was, how strong, how durable, and if her new mental capabilities could be used for anything other than accessing memories. If she was going into combat, Sophia was going to be prepared.

~ ~

Back in D.C., everything was business as usual. People scrambled to work, unconcerned with the heavy security, making it a bit easier for her to get around; she got into a D.C. taxicab and drove to her destination.

It also helped Sophia wore a lovely navy blue two-piece business skirt suit with an ivory blouse underneath, black pumps, and a book bag. Glasses pulled the outfit together; she figured it would work for her if it did in the comic books. She exited the cab and looked at her target, the CNN news station.

"No more hiding," Sophia said to herself one final time.

She also knew there was no going back; everyone would see her once she did this, which meant everyone would be coming after her.

Sophia walked across the street with a crowd rushing to work to avoid detection from officers with full-body armor, assault rifles, and police dogs stationed at the corner. A scene people have grown accustomed to since 9/11. She headed up the steps and entered the lobby to the directory to find the news station's exact location. One of the guards, a stocky baldheaded Caucasian man with a salt and pepper goatee, watched her from the minute she entered the lobby and had an awful feeling in his stomach despite her business attire. The ninth floor was her destination in the eleven-story building. As she sailed across the lobby heading to the turnstile, the guard discreetly moved in her direction so as not to cause any alarm.

"Excuse me, Miss, may I help you?" he asked politely.

"No."

"May I ask who you are here to see?"

"No."

"Miss, I'm going to have to ask you to…" he firmly began to order her.

Before he could finish his request for Sophia to either comply with some information or leave, she gripped the turnstile in front of her and, in one single motion, ripped it from its foundation, holding it in the air with her bare hand.

She then crushed it, causing everyone, save for a few and the guards behind the reception desk, to run out screaming.

"You think they're paying you enough to stop me?" she asked.

The guard looked at the crushed turnstile in her hand with pieces of tile dropping off it to the floor before giving her the obvious answer.

"No."

Sophia released the turnstile, dropping it with a hefty thud to the floor before heading through the open area she created. A younger, slimmer guard wearing a faded hairstyle fretfully approached the older guard as he watched Sophia walk toward the elevator banks.

"What should we do?" the younger guard asked.

"Call everyone."

"The police?"

"No," the older guard ordered. "Everyone."

~ ~

At the F.B.I. Washington Field Office - 601 4th Street NW, Dustin lay sleeping on the couch in their dual office while Mark sat at his desk with a cup of black coffee in his grip. It had been almost forty-eight hours before any of them got any rest.

Mark rifled through the investigation files that had grown bigger and bigger since the case began. The mystery included files stating Lieutenant Robert Matheson was treated at the Michael E. DeBakey VA Medical Center. Still, no doctor, nurse, physical therapist, or even janitor could physically confirm he was ever treated there.

No one had heard of the doctor or physical therapist on his files, nor could anyone explain how the apparent ghost files got into the system. Clearly, someone wanted people to believe he was getting treatment at that facility to mask where he received actual treatment.

On top of that, General Matheson was impossible to locate, would not give an interview, and could not be touched per King's orders, which meant he had something to hide.

Mark appeared to be at his wit's end, buried with more questions, finding no answers to help him burrow out of the grave that was suffocating him.

As he contemplated burning everything on his desk, including Dustin, who was snoring up a storm on the couch, the door to his office flew open.

A frantic female agent barged in to deliver the news they had waited for all night into the morning.

"Sirs!" she yelled.

Dustin sprang upon instinct, still half-asleep, as Mark got out of his chair, grabbing his body armor, getting it ready to put on after he strapped on his shoulder holster.

Mark pulled out his service piece from his desk while asking her questions.

"Where?"

"CNN News Building... 820 1st Street!"

she confirmed.

"Get everything not bolted, down there now," Mark ordered.

"Sir, Executive Assistant Director King has already given that order."

Mark nodded as she ran off to prepare herself.

Dustin, wiping the cold out of his eye, got to his feet and grabbed his vest, strapping it on.

"At least she didn't go to Fox…" he mumbled.

"Kill the jokes and get your shit on…" Mark grumbled, not in the mood for early morning banter.

"Well, what the hell is the plan?" Dustin muttered. "Besides blowing the whole building to shit with her in it?"

Mark answered while shoving his pistol in his holster.

"I'll think of one once we get there."

~ ~

Back at the CNN building, Sophia knew they would probably cut the power the second she entered the elevator and opted to take the building emergency evacuation stairs.

Impatiently, she tore the steel door to the stairs from its hinges, tossing it aside. As officers from the outside entered the lobby from the commotion she caused, she removed her heels and thought of a particular martial arts movie where the hero took great leaps covering large distances.

Of course, the hero performed the stunt by Wire-Fu. Sophia could duplicate the same technique minus the wire and harness, clearing each staircase quickly as she headed to the ninth floor.

The training last night allowed her to hone her abilities better. Sophia learned that her nervous system and muscles could duplicate any action or movement she had ever seen with just a thought, as long as it was within reason of her physical capabilities.

Aside from denting parts of the stairwell with her bare feet when she landed, Sophia quickly turned each corner, completing the process repeatedly, moving from floor to floor as she quickly closed in on her destination. Back in the lobby, the officers on the scene received instructions via radio to stand down, evacuate, and secure the area. She had to go from the fifth-floor to the sixth-floor stairs to continue her ascension to the ninth floor.

Sophia decided to walk the last two flights. Without hesitation, she flew through the emergency doors. Since CNN owned the entire floor, finding what she was looking for was not hard.

The receptionist was the first to see her and got an equally lousy feeling in her gut, like the guard downstairs. It got worse as Sophia headed in her direction.

"Excuse me… can I help you?" the receptionist asked with a bit of an attitude.

"Bad feeling" did not acknowledge her as Sophia passed her, heading through the doors into the station's office area.

The receptionist took it as extremely rude, getting to her feet.

"Excuse me!"

Sophia walked through the sea of office cubicles, looking for the newsroom itself as the receptionist followed behind her, sounding like an ankle-biter.

"Excuse me! Excuse me! Whoever you are, you can't be back here!"

"Oh, yes, I can," Sophia sang back in defiance.

People got up from their desks or poked their heads out of their offices to see the commotion.

As she searched for the newsroom, one of the staff members, probably a reporter, got out of his seat and tried to step in her way.

"Excuse me," he sternly asked, "where do you think…?"

Sophia calmly swiped him out of the way, gentle enough to not injure him but powerful enough to send him flying five cubicles down, hitting the carpet floor hard, forcing everyone to get to their feet. The display of power stopped the receptionist in her tracks. She now understood that Ms. Dennison was not the one you wanted to trifle with or follow.

As she made another cubicle turn in her search, a much taller and stockier staff member sporting glasses stepped in her way.

"Hey, you can't..." he forcibly began to state while holding his hands up.

He apparently did not get the memo about not getting in her way; Sophia decided to educate him by grabbing the nearly six-foot-four man by the front of his pants and hoisting him into the air like a rag doll.

A chorus of screams rang out in the office from shock as the now terrified man held onto her arm for dear life.

"J-Jesus Christ!!" he screamed.

Sophia calmly looked up at him.

"I'm going to ask you once, the

newsroom… where is it?"

He quickly pointed in the direction she needed to go; Sophia then steadily walked him over to a nearby seat, setting him down. He looked up at her with timid little childlike eyes.

"Don't move," she ordered him with a pointed finger.

"N-no ma'am," he promised, rapidly shaking his head.

Sophia quickly glanced around to see if anyone else would challenge her. Finding none, she made her way to the entrance of the newsroom itself.

The receptionist quickly rushed toward the staff member, who was still sitting in his seat with his head down.

"Joshua, are you okay?" she frantically asked.

"She told me not to move…" Joshua whimpered, visibly shaken. "I'm not moving."

Inside the newsroom, all eyes were fixed

on her as Sophia walked toward the set. The news anchor Carol Costello, in the middle of her news report, looked like a deer in headlights as the woman she was reporting on stood before her. Luck was on both women's sides that day.

Mrs. Costello, originally based out of Atlanta, did her show in Washington to cover the financial crisis, the election, and the mayhem Sophia was causing since Friday. This meant Sophia could do what she came to do, and Mrs. Costello would be a part of the exclusive of possibly the century.

The production manager was still oblivious to what was happening and screamed to go to commercial.

"Who the hell is that on my set?!" she roared.

One of the production assistants took the initiative to walk onto the set, which made Sophia roll her eyes.

"Hey, who the hell are you?! What are you doing…?!"

Once again, Sophia grabbed him by the front of his pants and effortlessly hoisted the young man high.

"Oh! Oh, god!" he screamed.

It set off a chain reaction within the studio, including the production manager, until Sophia turned around, allowing her to see her face.

"Holy shit... that's... that's Sophia Dennison," she stammered.

"The escape death row inmate?" asked one of her staff members.

"No, your mother..." she shot back at him for asking a stupid question.

Sophia calmly looked around, taking off her glasses while still holding the young man in the air.

"Excuse me, anyone looking for an exclusive?"

"Get her whatever she wants... Now!" the production manager ordered, "and contact all other stations to switch over to us right now! I want this broadcasted throughout the entire country in two minutes!"

~ ~

Back outside, Dustin and Mark rolled up to an invasion in front of the CNN building.

"Wow… they actually got us tanks," an impressed yet disturbed Dustin said.

Two M1 Abram Tanks sat flanking one another with turrets aimed at the front entrance of the building. Positioned around the tanks were A.V.Rs and two Mobile Command Vehicles. A sea of F.B.I., army military personnel, and SWAT in their respective combat gear scattered around, taking their individual position. The duo exited their vehicle to the sound of a helicopter soaring across the D.C. sky.

Mark spied King in all the commotions, coordinating with the Chief of Police and the Sergeant Major to position snipers and M60 machine guns for a crossfire attack. He quickly marched over with Dustin, bringing up the rear to quell the madness before it got further out of hand.

"What are you doing, Doug?" Mark barked over the mayhem. "You gonna bring the entire building down on top of her?"

"That was my plan!"

Dustin pointed to himself sarcastically, wanting credit.

"We're doing whatever is necessary to put an end to this today," King announced. "Whatever happens, Sophia Dennison does not walk off the steps of that building!"

"She was doing a buck ten in Texas on foot out running a fleet of squad cars on Interstate 10. There's no friggin way those turrets are going to hit her," Mark informed King, "and if they get lucky, and you do wound her, not only is she going to heal, but she's going to be impervious to shellfire. She gets stronger every time you try to hurt her."

"We intend to use concentrated firepower on her," Sergeant Major Abram instructed, "aiming strictly for the head and torso area until she goes down."

"With all due respect, Sergeant Major, you haven't been watching YouTube," Mark updated him. "We tried the firing squad method. It didn't put a dent in her! All you're going to do is have a ton of ricochets and get a lot of people hurt!"

"So, what should we do, Special Agent?" King asked, putting Mark on the spot.

"For almost six days straight, all everyone has ever done is shot at this woman," Mark advised. "Why don't we attempt to do the dumbest thing in the world and try to talk to her?"

"Talk to her?" King said, not appreciating Armitage's sarcasm.

"I volunteer to do it."

Mark raised his hand.

"What do we have to lose?"

An F.B.I. agent stuck his head out of one of the command stations, trying to get everyone's attention as he yelled for King.

"Sir! You might want to get in here! CNN is about to put her on the air!"

Without a word, King, Armitage, and everyone else in the huddle made a beeline to the command station to see what was happening upstairs.

~ ~

Inside the newsroom set, Sophia stood ready as CNN, now scrapping its previously scheduled show, prepared to introduce her live from their studio, allowing her to tell the world what was on her mind after being on the run for almost six days.

Sophia swallowed hard and carefully clutched the microphone so as not to crush it by accident as a pool of sweat washed over her. She found it ironic that she barely broke a sweat after all the running and fighting, but standing there, she could feel it dripping down her back from nervousness. Sophia was still human. Hopefully, those watching would see that as she prepared to address the entire country and beyond in less than a minute. With her heels back on, Sophia nervously smoothed out her suit to look

386

presentable on air.

The production manager gave the cue to begin the broadcast again.

"Ready in five, four... three... two... one."

"Good Morning, again," Carol Costello began, "we are interrupting this regularly scheduled news program for this exclusive statement from Sophia Dennison, the escape death row inmate fugitive from the Mountain View Unit in Gatesville, Texas, who has been on the run for almost six days evading local police, the F.B.I., and quite possibly the military. Somehow she has managed to make it to our newsroom, and would like to make the following statement here live, so without further interruption... Sophia Dennison."

The camera panned from Costello to Sophia, who looked like a deer in headlights. The knowledge that millions of people were probably watching her put a painful knot in her stomach.

~ ~

At the Gatesville Women's Prison, inmates almost rioted as they cheered her on, rejoicing in the mess hall. Bishop was the loudest, jumping up on one of the tables, screaming at the top of her lungs as she performed the Crip walk.

Sister Shareef just sat there with a broad smile as tears flowed.

She looked up and pointed a wagging finger.

"You are awesome."

~ ~

In a small town in Missouri, recovering from both her wounds and broken life, a mother watched in disbelief on her parents' living room couch holding her son. He pointed at the television at the woman who had saved his mother's life a couple of nights ago, the same woman who once lived next door to her.

"It's super lady, Mommy!" Ethan gleefully pointed.

Tears fell from Tammy's eyes with a smile on her face.

"I see... I see..."

~ ~

In Houston, a nearly broken family, minus their Patriarch, huddled together to hear the truth about what really happened to the brother they all loved and missed from the only other person they now knew within their hearts loved him to the end.

~ ~

While in Mount Vernon, New York, a mother fell to her knees with tears in her eyes and a father sobbing equally for joy, beholding a child they long thought was lost to them standing alive and well.

"Thank you, Jesus!" Mrs. Dennison cried uncontrollably. "Thank you, Jesus! Thank you, Jesus! Thank you, Jesus!"

~ ~

Back in the studio, the set behind the

rolling cameras was crowded with every staff member from CNN watching Sophia like hawks, which did not make it that much easier for her as they prepared to hang off her every word. She closed her eyes, imagined what she wanted to say for all those years, and then opened her eyes again.

"My name is Sophia Dennison," she began, "formerly Sophia Matheson... four years ago I was convicted of the murder of my husband, Lieutenant Robert Matheson, and sentenced to death by lethal injection... and despite what you heard in the news... I did not escape... I was executed for that crime almost six days ago..."

Throughout the news station were whispers and nervous looks while masses huddled wherever a television or streaming device was transfixed on what she was saying.

"Don't ask me to explain the unexplainable," she continued, "I don't know why I am still alive... standing here before you... what I do know... is that I didn't kill my husband."

Sophia took a slight pause as confidence began to build back within her.

"My husband was murdered by a black Ops death squad known as the D.E.A.D., which was created by our very own United States Government. There are four individuals on this team… only four… they have committed acts of murder and violence around the world on behalf of our government in secrecy for years… they brutally murdered my husband for reasons that I do not yet know, then framed me for his murder. I don't expect anyone to believe the words that I say, and at this point, I don't really care…"

A stone coldness grew on Sophia's face as she made her final statement, which was clearly a declaration of war.

"I came here to let everyone who has been looking for me know that I'm not hiding nor running anymore… and I will not be going back to prison. I came here to let those four individuals who took my husband from me and turned my life upside down know that I may not know your names or your faces, but I do remember your voices and the emblem you wear on your uniform. A Grim Reaper sitting on top of a large skull holding a scythe in one hand and a skull in the other. I want you to know that when I walk out of this building, I will be coming to hunt you down and to kill all four of you and anyone else responsible… that's pretty much it… thank you, and have a nice day."

With a wave and a nervous smile, she walked over to the broadcast desk, put the microphone down, picked up her bookbag, and proceeded to leave the set as a very bewildered Carol Costello looked at the cameras, unsure how to follow up with Sophia's mind-blowing statement. People moved as Sophia proceeded to walk out of the studio and office to take the steps back down to the lobby. She decided to take her time, knowing what awaited her outside, going to the bathroom first to change.

~ ~

Mark looked an unnerved King in the eyes inside the command station to get the okay to try to end this peacefully.

"You've got ten minutes," King massaged his left eyelid in frustration, "you only… and if she walks through those doors without her hands behind her head ready to surrender… you better not be there."

Mark bolted out the door with Dustin following him.

"What the hell are you going to say to her?!"

"I don't know…" Mark shrugged while running. "Please come in and talk to us and not wreck half of D.C. I'll think of something… just have my back on the ground and make sure no one does something stupid to get me killed."

Agents and soldiers received the radio command, allowing Mark through the perimeter. He ran up the building steps, hoping to meet Dennison to talk her down before she came out to the full-on assault.

~ ~

As expected, when Sophia finally reached the ground floor level, it was now a ghost town, save for one lone man standing in the lobby by the security desk wearing a bulletproof vest with F.B.I. printed in white on the front. His gun was holstered, which meant he was probably there to negotiate; the flashing lights outside indicated that the party had arrived in full force.

Sophia changed, leaving her clothes and book bag in the bathroom upstairs, putting back on the blue slim leather racing jacket she wore on Saturday, along with some black leather biker pants and black military field boots. She prepared for possible combat and needed a material that could take a little more beating than her old attire.

"I thought this lobby would have been filled with a SWAT team," she casually said to Mark.

"We're looking to not have a repeat of Gatesville," Mark returned the casual banter, "and every other place you've been."

"I didn't catch your name," Sophia asked, curious about the lone F.B.I. agent sent to talk with her.

He officially and formally introduced himself.

"Mark Armitage... Special Agent in Charge."

As she got closer, she looked outside and raised an eyebrow.

"Is that a tank I see outside?"

"Actually, there are two... M1 Abrams," he corrected her.

To which she answered with a nod.

"Impressive."

As she finally reached the security desk, Mark could not help but step back. She was only an inch short, probably shorter without the combat boots she wore compared to him. He factored her outfit masking the superior physical specimen she had proven to be these past few days, but he was still expecting someone more immense, more powerful, and intimidating; not that her actions did not make her daunting; her appearance confirmed that he was never chasing a monster or killer. He saw the face of a young woman slightly hardened by circumstances; he saw someone's daughter.

"You were the one on the bullhorn," Sophia wagged her finger at him, "who was screaming for me to surrender at my in-laws' house and for your people to cease fire on the Interstate."

"You're the one who made me and almost every law enforcement branch in Houston look like bitches on YouTube," Mark smirked.

Sophia blushed while looking down at the floor.

"Sorry about that."

Armitage cracked a smile; in his mind, he thought this was good; the proverbial ice was broken, and he had a better chance of talking her down.

Sophia got to the point.

"You here to asked for my surrender, Special Agent Armitage?"

"I'm here to ask you to please come in and talk to us," Mark requested.

"See... no... sorry," Sophia replied,

shaking her head, refusing. "The last time I was brought in to "talk" was almost four years ago. For practically sixteen hours of that "talk," the Houston legal system tried to force me to confess that I murdered my husband. And when I refused, I was tried, convicted, and sent to rot in a box living like less than an animal in semi-solitary confinement for almost four years before they put a needle in my arm. Do you know what semi-solitary confinement is, Special Agent? It's less than two hours a week of human contact except for a C.O. barking orders at you... oh... I forgot about the county physician who comes in every six months asking if a death row inmate has suicidal tendencies... so, no... I don't feel like coming in to talk."

Strike one, Armitage thought to himself. He needed to shift this conversation back to an upbeat, something positive, anything for her not to walk out those doors.

"Let's talk about something you are guilty of, your next-door neighbor who you roughed up and almost dropped out of a window."

"Yeah, did you see his wife's face?" Sophia reminded him. "He had stopped when my late husband promised to break every damn bone in his body the next time he put his hands on her… I was just keeping the promise."

"And what about the guard you killed when you escaped Mountain View?" Mark bluntly asked.

It was not his intention to push her buttons. This was his chance to find out who he was dealing with and fill in any missing blanks. It was also a delay tactic, giving him time to figure out how to defuse the situation if he could.

Sophia narrowed her eyes at the question of Buck Wilford. Mark braced a bit, thinking she would rip his head off for asking.

Sophia's lips quivered with rage.

"That 'guard'… raped one of the only two friends I had in that hell hole… he had it coming."

"And then some," Mark finished her sentence. "Sister Shareef told me the same thing."

Sophia leaned against the security desk, countering with a sneer.

"Well, here's something she probably didn't tell you. That son of a bitch confessed to me what he did the night before I was to be executed."

A savage curveball out of nowhere were the words fired out of her mouth. Mark was not sure he was on strike two or three, but he was sure the conversation was officially downhill. At this point, his best bet was switching baseball to boxing. Let her talk while he did the rope a dope.

"A year and a half ago, he sexually assaulted her in the laundry room," Sophia explained. "He knew how to maneuver the cameras the night before to create a blind spot between the large dryers where no one can see. Buck also controlled the work schedule to put her where and when he wanted her.

Rosanna was doing a two-year for a first-offense grand theft auto charge, and as tough as she talked, she wasn't built for prison, and he knew that. Wilford promised if she didn't drop the charges, he'd sic the Sisters of the Arian

Nation on her, and they'd make her life a living hell even if he were arrested."

"He told her he'd make sure she'd never get out of prison. That he'd find a way to keep her there or make sure she was carried out in a body bag, and even though Sister Shareef promised to protect her, she couldn't guarantee twenty-four-hour protection, especially when Buck had friends who could have the work schedule changed on his behalf. So she dropped the charge, said it was a misunderstanding, and forgot about it."

She took a minute to get her anger under control as she continued to tell Mark more about the infamous Buck Wilford.

"He waited a month before she was supposed to get out to teach her a 'lesson,' and because he missed the way she 'smelled down there.' He knew so close to her getting out she wasn't going to say anything… he said telling me was a 'gift' I could take to my grave."

"How did he get desk duty?" Mark asked, engaging in the conversation.

"Sister Shareef told her niece, who's a District Attorney in Austin, and she put pressure on the DA in Gatesville to file an inquiry," she answered. "Buck told me it wouldn't stick. He also promised Sister Shareef would be joining me soon for being an uppity bitch sticking her nose in his business, and I dare you to ask me why I, a death row inmate, didn't come forward with this information. I managed to slip her a letter about it in the Bible I gave her before my final walk; it's useless to her now."

"So to save your friend, you took matters into your own hands," Mark concluded.

"Wasn't planned," Sophia shrugged. "I didn't go looking for him, especially with all hell breaking loose that day... but when I saw his nasty greasy ass between me and three or four concrete walls to freedom. With nothing to lose, I decided what the hell."

He was unsure if she was taunting, sizing, or attempting to get some form of rise out of him. He did know that time was winding down, and King was a man of his word.

Mark decided a bit of a reality check was

in order.

"Ms. Dennison..." he chose his words with a slow gesture, "I'm here to make sure no one gets hurt."

"No, you're not, Special Agent, you're trying to handle me," Sophia said sarcastically. "I double majored in psychology, and I think you know by now... I can't get 'hurt' so easily."

She was verbally beating him into a corner.

"You came in here trying to see if you could restore order and reason, to try to put this little problem in a box like so long ago. I'm sorry to disappoint you... that's not going to happen today."

"I'm not here trying to put you in some box, Ms. Dennison," Mark defended himself. "Look... clearly, a lot of mistakes were made..."

"That's what you're going to tell me, Special Agent? Mistakes were made? The system wasn't perfect?" Sophia snorted. "When I was like ten, my mom had a crystal swan broach with gold accents that she accused me of taking. When I told her I didn't take it, she said I was lying and must have lost it. I got an ass-whooping and sent to my room without dinner.

For almost an hour, I cried until my baby sister walked up to my mom wearing the broach in her hair, asking her why I got a beating. When my mom came in my room, no matter how much she hugged me and told me she was sorry, I could not stop crying, nor be consoled."

A sneer formed on Sophia's visage.

"**That** was a **mistake**... but you want to negotiate, Special Agent? Here are my terms."

Sophia stretched out her hands in a passive position while making her request.

"Give me back my husband, and I will surrender."

To which Mark responded.

"Excuse me?"

"I believe I'm still speaking English," she returned, "and before you say my request is impossible, remember impossible is standing right before you. I think it's an uncomplicated request... I don't want my four years back... I don't want my job back, or money, or my possessions... I'll even forgive the State of Texas for killing me. If you can give me back... my husband, Robert Matheson... I will surrender..., and you can do whatever you want with me... that is all I want... can you do that?"

In all of Mark's entire life, he'd never felt more uncomfortable than at that moment. He did not see crazy in her eyes, or he hoped. Therefore, if she did not have a case of insanity, she knew very well that her request was impossible. What was the correct response to such a demand? He thought.

"Ms. Dennison..."

Mark began swallowing as hard as Hampton did when he interrogated him. She waved him off before he could start with a reasonable explanation that would not get him killed.

"Stop, that was an unfair and unreasonable request," Sophia half apologetically recognized with a hint of sarcasm. "Here's another proposal. You go outside to your superiors and tell them I will surrender if and only if they find and turn over the members of the D.E.A.D. to me."

Once again, Mark felt uncomfortable; the request went from resurrecting the dead to making the tooth fairy appear. Not that he did not believe they existed with all the evidence he had and Sophia's worldwide statement, but there was no way of materializing individuals that were initially campfire stories soldiers told five minutes ago.

"Ms. Dennison…" Mark started again with a weary swallow.

"You gonna tell me the United States Government doesn't negotiate with terrorists, Special Agent?" Sophia smirked.

Mark briefly brandished a face that said he was a bit insulted; she would think he would say something that stupid.

"If you are… remember… United Nations General Assembly in 1994 defined terrorism as a group of persons or particular persons committing criminal acts intended or calculated to provoke a state of terror in public. For political, philosophical, ideological, racial, ethnic, religious or any other nature that they may deem justifiable," she cited.

Now, she insulted him by reciting something she probably read off Wikipedia, remembering what Hampton told him about her super memory.

"Now you can charge me with manslaughter or second-degree murder. Breaking and entering, evading and eluding or trespassing." Sophia said while motioning to her surroundings. "I'll even cop to breaking out of prison, although technically, I think I served my time when I allowed the state of Texas to execute me. I have not committed a terrorist act, nor am I a terrorist. All I want after all the hell I have been through is justice, which is not too much to ask for; as I said upstairs, I am not going anywhere until I find those responsible for murdering my husband and framing me. So there are only two options, Special Agent… you can march back out there and tell your superiors to move heaven and hell to get me the people I want…"

Sophia leaned forward a bit with a scowl to get her point across.

"Or I walk out there and find them myself, and all of you can 'try' to stop me."

Mark put his head down in defeat. Sophia knocked him out several rounds ago, and they were nearing the ten minutes given to him. He also knew that no one outside would agree to her terms, and she would not bow.

"You know... that's not going to happen," he said quietly.

"Then there's nothing more to discuss... is there, Special Agent. By the way..." Sophia's eyes became glassy with tears of pent-up rage, "how you feel right now... powerless... that's how I felt... doesn't feel good, does it?"

"I'm sorry," Mark somberly returned, looking at his shoes as his shoulders felt heavy.

"You didn't murder my husband or turn my world upside down," Sophia returned, "so why are you apologizing?"

Mark chose his following words carefully.

"Ms. Dennison, there's no way we could have known…"

"That's the problem, Mark… Can I call you, Mark? 'We' didn't know," Sophia said as she wiped her eyes. "We the 'people' too busy watching American friggin' Idol, or House Wives of whatever state I could give a shit about to ask the question, 'What the hell' is my government doing while I sleep at night. We let people who we elect claim they have our best interest at heart bend us over a table doing whatever they like while we're texting our B.F.F.

We don't do a damn thing till it hits the fan, and even when we're drowning in it, we still do nothing. Sanctioned Death Squads coming into our homes in the dead of the night, killing our loved ones, and framing us for it is just the extreme side of it, but my eyes have been opened, and now it's time to open everyone else's for good.

So again, thank you but no, Special Agent, as a former card-carrying member of the Republican Party, which **killed** my parents. I waited for the system to come to its senses and see my innocence to the very end when they strapped me on that table… I'm going to have to decline to come in and talk to the likes of you… no offense."

Armitage looked into her eyes and saw no longer a shred of reasoning. How could there be after what she described being put through? He thought about criminals he muscled with the power of the Federal law backing him, how small and feeble they felt when he put the hammer down on them, even though they deserved it. His power was now tiny and weak against an innocent woman scorned, with the power of a god coursing through her veins.

Diplomacy was officially dead.

"You're not good at negotiations, are you?" Sophia plainly asked.

Mark huffed, flicking imaginary dust from the marble security counter.

"No, I guess I'm not."

Sophia turned, looking again out the glass doors.

"Two tanks out there, huh?"

Her spirited enthusiasm forced a smirk on his face.

"Yeah..." Mark nodded.

"Probably should have brought three. They got snipers? And those mini-gun things like in Predator?"

"Something like that," he grunted.

"Gonna mess up my outfit," Sophia frowned, looking at her gear, "you know I just bought this on Saturday?"

"Listen, there are kids out there," Mark went in with one final plea, "husbands and wives caught up in this mess doing their duty... is there any chance you could... not..."

Mark was at a loss for words; this was no regular negotiation. She was not holding hostages, nor did she have a bomb or a biological weapon.

She was the weapon, an exceptionally strong one, and here he was, standing there, pleading with her not to walk through those doors and possibly hurt good people outside for the sins of a failed system. Sophia looked into his carved out, worn eyes that probably hadn't seen a good night's sleep in years, including the days he was chasing her, and saw goodness in a hardened face.

Sophia smiled, deciding to do him a solid.

"So, if you were to talk me down? What was supposed to happen next?"

"You coming out with your hands behind your head, ready to kneel and be restrained," Mark motioned, grateful she was willing to work with him.

"That again?!" Sophia derided, remembering his first attempt at the General's house. "Well, that's not going to happen, but I think I can do something to make sure not a single shot gets fired…, and no one gets hurt… radio your people… tell them I will come out with my hands up behind my head."

As she moved to head to the entrance, Mark cautiously put his hand out to stop her, asking one last question.

"I got to know," Mark swallowed, "everything you said upstairs about the..."

"All true, but I think you knew that," Sophia confirmed as she looked into his eyes.

"One last question," he threw out. "Why did you decide to talk with me for so long?"

She gave him a simple, pleasant smile and answered.

"Something told me you'd probably be the last nice person I'd ever get to talk to."

She turned, heading to the door as Armitage stood there dumbfounded and guilt-ridden. He had lived in a world that hardened him to the fact that evidence ruled and the justice system, though faulty, was fair.

There was nothing fair about what the system did to the young woman who smiled at him and walked out to meet several hundred guns pointed at her. He had no right to ask her to surrender and subject herself to that system that had blatantly failed her on many levels.

He was not religious; he only visited church after his altar boy days for Christmas and Easter when his ex-wife dragged him there, but Mark had to wonder as he watched her walk off. Had things gotten so bad that the Man upstairs, who remained silent for so long, allowing His children to figure out their own mess, decided that this one time enough was enough, and it was His time to intervene? Did He spare her life... so she could shatter an already broken system?

Realizing he was getting philosophical while she was almost near the door, Mark grabbed his radio from his belt to let the outside world know.

"She's coming out with her hands up."

King yelled over the other end.

"What? You're not walking her out?!"

"Negative," Mark answered before turning off his C.B., "and we're gonna see why..."

Sophia pushed the glass doors open, walking out into a three-ring circus. Every cop, F.B.I., C.I.A., SWAT, and military personnel in the capital and some neighboring states. All with guns trained on her.

Behind them, broadcasting both state and worldwide, was every news station. Finally, behind them was another sea of fellow citizens of the District of Columbia watching curiously to see her get taken into custody or gunned down in front of their very eyes. She also remembered the two tanks moving their turrets into position to blow her away if she made any sudden moves.

King stepped forward, roaring his command over the bullhorn.

"Sophia Dennison! Get down on the ground now! Do not make us shoot you!"

She rolled her eyes at his orders. Finally, taking her time to take it all in, Sophia slowly put her hands up, placing them behind her head.

Seeing she was complying, King followed up on his first order.

"On the ground now! Now!"

Slowly, she got to one knee while King signaled for a team to move in and bring her down, but before they got within ten feet of her, Sophia would make them believe… that a woman could leap buildings in a single bound.

The air left the lungs of everyone watching over every device that had television capability as Sophia exploded with a leap that took her into the skies of Washington, D.C. It looked as if she was flying as she cleared at least ten skyscrapers before descending back into the city. Sophia created a sizable pothole in the middle of Pennsylvania Avenue on impact, which caused a taxi driver to come to a screeching halt as she pushed off again back to the skies.

Back at the news station, Mark strolled through the doors to see the dumbfounded look of everyone, including King.

Dustin was the only one looking at him as he walked out, asking.

"What the hell happened?"

To which Mark replied with a shrug.

"She didn't want to come in."

Sophia took off once again with a scream

of exhilaration into the air of Washington DC from the streets of New York Avenue, where bystanders stood beside themselves, watching the unbelievable spectacle before them.

As she soared through the sky of the nation's capital, she got lost in the euphoria of being unbound. Sophia was not really into comic books growing up; her imagination was built on playing doctor with her Barbie and Cabbage Patch dolls. However, she had seen her fair share of superhero movies and became in awe of the fantastic abilities they displayed in celluloid films. She was basking in the dream of a million comic book enthusiasts worldwide to be more than human....

On her subsequent descent into the streets, she had planned to go higher, soar further, to see if she could actually achieve flight until something shot her violently out of the sky like a sparrow hit by a 12 gauge.

Sophia took the hit on her left side from the unbelievably powerful projectile. It sent her into an unrecoverable tailspin, clipping the rooftops of two buildings before landing on downtown Washington's streets. She took out two parked vehicles and created a sizable crater on impact between a local pizzeria and a gym, shattering the glass in both storefronts.

"Target is down," #1 confirmed, "move-in quickly to subdue and extract… and remember to put your jammers up… we don't want this shit on YouTube…"

The high-pitched ringing in her ears finally subsided as the smell of smoke and something burnt filled her nose, choking her. Everything was blurry, and everything hurt. She had not felt this pain since her escape from Mountain View. Not even the bear mace was this bad.

For about a second, Sophia thought she had cracked several ribs, but the fact that she could slowly breathe easier meant they either held during the impact or did their regenerative healing thing. The ringing in her ear was replaced by multiple voices, the sun beaming down on her minutes ago covered by "shadows."

Finally, coming to her senses, Sophia realized a crowd had formed around her of D.C.'s concerned citizens. Some were concerned, while others had their phones up in her face, taking pictures and videos.

She could make out someone asking if she was okay, that an ambulance was on its way and not to move. Other questions were if she was an alien, a mutant, or a stunt double for a movie. In a minute, she wanted to tell them to get the hell out of her face when the screaming began to ensue. The crowd scattered like roaches when the lights came on.

Sophia's vision finally returned to see them descend from the skies above and hover several feet off the city streets, kicking up dirt and trash while vibrating the store windows around them.

They were massive, at least thirteen- to sixteen feet tall, with two digitigrade hind legs. That, along with their four-finger appendages gripping the rifle-like cannons aimed at Sophia, made their appearance look alien. The glowing white eyes did not make them appear any less inhuman.

However, the black urban military colors on their hulking metallic hides were a dead giveaway that this was not any close encounter, and there were four.

All the motivation Sophia needed to rise to her feet.

"Wow… she looks pissed… wonder why?" #2 asked casually.

"Could be she remembered us from a party way back," #3 gleefully said, brandishing a sadistic smile within her cockpit, "and we weren't nice to her…"

"Thought I said to cut the shit…" #1 ordered.

He switched to external audio to address their target.

"Sophia Dennison… you have five seconds to surrender and comply before…"

An enraged Sophia leaped into the air, ignoring #1's order, looking for blood, only for #4 to shoot her out of her midair assault.

This time, it was a shot to the gut, sending her through the 10th floor of the building she just crashed into. #2 and #3 joined in concentrating firepower into the tunnel #4 made with Sophia. Screams of terror emitted inside the building as poor souls ducked for cover. The crowd on the street scrambled, trampling over each other to get to safety. Those foolish enough to stay and try to record the events were frustrated that their cameras and cellphones were not working on recording what they believed to be an invasion from another planet.

"Cease-fire! Cease goddamn fire!" #1 yelled at his trigger-happy team. "You want to dead level the entire building?!"

~ ~

Mark's car screeched to a halt several blocks away, on the outside of the military blockade now set up at New York Avenue. They jumped out, running up to an equally clueless King as smoke rose from afar.

"What the hell is going on, Doug?"

Gunfire, which Mark had never heard in his entire life, echoed from the same direction as the smoke.

"Apparently, there's a massive firefight going on between your girl and something huge!" King reported gritting his teeth. "Four of them!"

A cold sweat washed over Mark at the sound of "four."

"So what the hell are we doing?!" he pressed.

"We are waiting for backup to show up!" King answered.

"This shit will be over by the time "backup" shows up!" Mark snapped back.

"Weren't you the one saying we weren't equipped to deal with something like this?!" King willingly fired Mark's own words back at him. "I'm not risking one agent's life on this madness; not even yours... we're waiting for military back up! You try and cross that barricade, and I will shoot you myself."

King revealed his sidearm to Mark, daring him to test him.

"Can't we at least get some eyes in the air

to tell us what the hell is happening?" a frustrated Mark asked.

"We have eyes in the air… but they can't relay a signal back… something is interfering with communication on a large radius," informed an Agent coordinating communication between the nearby teams. "Radios, cellphones, cameras, everything is acting screwy, even radar! That's why the military isn't coming in yet. They can't tell what they're attacking!"

Mark cursed in frustration as he looked at the black smoke rising from the chaotic direction to the heavens. He was powerless to do anything and bothered by the fact he was genuinely scared for a woman he had just met a couple of minutes ago.

~ ~

Back at McPherson Square was a battleground. Black smoke and flames billowed out from the side of the obliterated building while people inside, either injured or terrified, spilled out from the entrance of the skyscraper, running for cover, searching for help, or both.

"Intel coming in from command, government, military, and local police both evacuating and blocking off this area within an eight-mile radius," #2 reported. "We've got a window of fewer than twenty minutes to wrap this shit up before we see some heavy guns coming."

"Fine, then let's secure the target or what's left…"

#1's orders were cut short again.

The sound of a sonic boom shattered almost all the windows within a five-block radius. Actually, what cut #1's words short was a vicious hit from what could only be described as a flying tackle propelling him through the building behind him by a tiny and powerful unidentified object. Not even his teammates saw when he took the hit, leaving their presence. They were left with a near-deafening pop of the sonic boom, shards of glass raining down on them from above, and the now muffled hollers (or screams) of #1.

The other side of the building that Sophia drilled #1 through exploded with the sight of a massive machine coming out back first with a small-enraged woman gripping its chest plate with both hands.

The force of her initial charge ended as they sailed across the street, crashing into another office building before falling to the streets below, taking out whatever was unlucky to be under them on the way down.

#1 sat rattled within his mech's cockpit, trying to get himself together.

Already up, Sophia sprang on top of his machine, raining down trip-hammer blows as she screamed.

"Son of a bitch! I'll kill ya! I'll kill all of ya!"

She concentrated her punches on what appeared to be the head of the mech, caving the side of its skull. The blow shorted out the visual camera on the left side of the machine. #1, in a fit of desperation, managed to swat her off, landing her on a parked car. He struggled to right his mech and find his weapon.

"Got to get up! Got to get up! I could use some fu (static) help!" #1 yells his distress call.

While he was attempting to stand his machine, Sophia had already shrugged off his backhand, rolling off the car she landed on. She decided to take that very same car and swing it like a bat, taking out #1's legs from behind and landing him on his back again. She then leaped into the air, violently clobbering #1's mech with the 3,565 lb. vehicle as he desperately tried to cover up.

"Goddammit! Somebody get this crazy bitch off of me!" #1 hollered.

Sophia growled as she took what was left of the Nissan Maxima, slamming it again into #1's downed mech before coming under heavy fire from his teammates, finally arriving on the scene.

"Light this bitch up!" #4 howled.

This time, Sophia stood defiantly against the barrage of firepower on her, as she used her right forearm as a shield for her eyes against oncoming shellfire. Vehicles hit nearby exploded, sending shrapnel flying all over the place. The trio in the air decided to spread out, making it hard for her to pick a target as they concentrated their firepower on her from different angles. Her clothes became the worst for wear from the vicious volleys that now ricocheted off her impervious form.

"We're not making a fucking dent in her!" #2 gritted his teeth.

"Switch to plasma heat rounds!" #3 screamed. "Remember the ten-second capacity recharging delay between shots!"

Following their operators' mental commands, the BAMs quickly switched out the magazines to their rifles. The guns locked and loaded automatically, emitting a high humming sound and bright orange light.

#3 was the first to fire a volley of sheering energy, which Sophia took head-on with her forearm. She felt the blast down to her spinal column and the smell of burning leather and flesh.

"Ow…" she managed to get out while

426

staggering backward.

Two more volleys from #2 and #4, hitting her side and shoulder, sent her flying into a parked car behind her. She screamed and gasped at the excruciating pain of her flesh being charred down to the muscle.

"We got her! We fucking got her!" #3 squealed.

"Getting her doesn't mean stopping her! Look!" #4's voice emitted over her audio system.

True to #4's words, Sophia rose again due to her initial wounds healing in the order she was shot. Confidence filled her once again as she knew she would be impervious to their energy volleys once fully healed. She started advancing toward #4 when #2 fired another round, which Sophia deflected with her forearm.

To her horror, she felt the same excruciating pain again of her arm scorched for the second time. Sophia instinctively dived out of the way as #3 and #4 fired rounds, one hitting her in the meat of her thigh. As Sophia clutched her burnt leg, she saw #1's rifle locked on her from the corner of her eye.

In her head, she screamed, *"Move, dammit, move!"* forcing her body to do what her mind commanded. She dived through the storefront window of a Chinese restaurant as #1 lit up the sidewalk.

~ ~

Far off the battlefield in his black Sikorsky private helicopter, which doubled as a command center, Director Rosen observed the action smilingly.

"So... you do have a weakness."

~ ~

Back at the now war-torn McPherson Square, #2 dropped out of the sky, impacting the street and opening fire on the Chinese restaurant, forcing Sophia to scramble to her feet and dive over the counter; she covered up now gripped with fear.

What was happening? Why was her defensive invulnerability not kicking in? Her regenerative capability was clearly working, but the pain was far too much for her.

This was not a comic book, nor was Sophia a hero or a soldier. She was a wife, a neurosurgeon, a girl from a regular family out of little Mount Vernon who just wanted a simple life.

This was crazy, colossal machines shooting at her, trying to kill her. She wanted to go home; she just wanted to go home.

Just then, Sophia remembered she no longer had a home because of the individuals outside. Images of how defenseless and terrified Robert was just before they murdered him filled her head.

The final image of his face looking at her with tears in his eyes, the four years of agonizing hell she went through before they stuck the needle into her arm. The image of her dying for a crime she did not commit stoked the fire back in her.

"Get over yourself," Sophia thought, *"you wanted this! You called them out on live T.V.!*

You wanted to fight! You wanted this! You wanted this!"

Her defensive invulnerability may not work, but her other abilities did, as Sophia willed herself to her feet and charged to the back of the store. She needed to distance herself from them, so she smashed through the back door, taking her to the alley.

Out of the way of gunfire for a few seconds, Sophia took the time to reaffirm herself.

"You're not human anymore… you're more… so start acting like it."

The sound of thrusters and heavy metallic footsteps meant the hounds would be on her soon. She needed more distance, but not before snatching up a three-hundred-pound old cast iron manhole cover. Sophia then quickly smashed through the steel door of the building in front of her. Sure enough, #2 hovered overhead while #1 stood in front of one of the alley's entrances, hunting her.

"She's in the next building! Move into position!" #1 barked, scrambling.

Sophia ran from the back, where she crashed through a beauty parlor where the patrons and employees huddled together, hiding. They screamed as she walked into the middle of the floor.

"Sorry! Sorry!"

Sophia tried to calm them; she quickly noticed a woman with a bright orange and red hairstyle and gestured.

"Love the colors!"

She quickly crouched down and shot through the ceiling, going four floors into a dance studio where little ballerinas, their teacher, and parents huddled together, screaming and crying.

Sophia rolled her eyes, looking up, not amused at another cosmic joke.

"Really? Really?" she sneered.

Before Sophia could give her Creator the finger for constantly jamming her up, #2 hovered with his rifle aimed at her, ready to blow where she stood to pieces, and she could not allow that to happen.

With a thought, Sophia remembered Allen Dempsey from college, who had a talent for throwing a Frisbee with such insane accuracy that he could hit a football in midflight as she hurled the manhole cover with the velocity of a patriot missile.

An unsuspecting #2 took a manhole cover smack to the face of his BAM, spinning it in midair. This gave Sophia the advantage she needed to charge and crash through the front window, jumping on #2's machine's back, getting a good grip, and ripping off the back thrusters, keeping it propelled in the air. She remembered seeing the move done in some superhero cartoon as a kid, thought it was a good idea, and executed it flawlessly.

"Oh shit!" #2 screamed as he dropped into the street below like a stone.

#1 took aim to blast Dennison out of the sky, but not before she threw the thruster still in her hand at him as he opened fire.

The plasma charge from his rifle blew the

thruster up in his face, blinding him. Sophia remembered that she thought it was a good idea from a movie she saw as a teenager and executed it flawlessly.

Sophia landed before a burning #1, attempting to swat the flames out, and charged at him. As #3 and #4 rushed into position, Sophia coiled up and leaped, exploding off the concrete and slamming into the BAM taking it into the air, drilling it into the side of a building-rattling #1.

Because of her close proximity to #1, #3 and #4 were forced to watch as Sophia somehow managed to perform a one-arm shoulder judo throw in midair on the BAM, weighing several tons, dropping it back first on top of a parked S.U.V. before landing herself.

"Screw the order," #3 growled; "kill the bitch...now!"

#3 and #4 took aim-opening fire as Sophia continued her offense. She remembered the Flash live-action T.V. series on C.B.S. She was forced to watch with her younger brother because they only had one television in the living room.

Surprisingly, she thought it was somewhat cool, although she acted bored when she watched it.

Sophia mirrored Barry Allen's superhuman speed on the first try, though not as fast as the special effects used to give John Wesley Shipp the fictional superhero's ability.

Using her newly learned Barry Allen moves, Sophia combined her speed with football and basketball player memories, using fancy footwork to evade barrages coming at her. It was like going for a touchdown or layup as she quickly ducked, spun, and dipped through the hail of firepower, destroying the block she was on in an attempt to kill her. The duo's targeting system could no longer lock on her due to the speed at which she was moving. Sophia decided to make a mad dash for #3.

"She's coming this way," #3 shuddered. "I can't get a lock on her!"

#4 gave chase, trying to line up a shot before Sophia reached his teammate as #3 backed up as far as she could; her mech's back thrusters scorched the building behind her.

#3 fired repeated volleys, which Sophia dodged, juked, and jived until she was out of range. #3 cursed as she hit the thrusters, taking her upward, but Sophia once again used her powerful legs to become airborne, getting face to chest with #3's machine.

"Shit…" a frustrated and outmatched #3 said.

While this happened, #4 lined up a kill shot to the back of Sophia's neck, ignoring the bring back alive order and knowing he could possibly blow away his teammate.

"Mine… bitch…" he said, licking his lips.

He did not calculate Sophia dropkicking #3 into the building behind her. She sent her halfway through it while using the momentum to launch herself backward into a spin at #4, delivering a crushing flying shoulder charge, knocking him into an insane tailspin.

He screamed while bouncing around in the cockpit.

"Holy shit! Holy shit! Holy shit!

Holy shit! Holy shit! Holy shit!

Holy shit! Holy shiiiiiiiiit!"

The force of the hit sent him flying about fifteen blocks before hitting the streets, where his machine bounced violently off the concrete, destroying everything in its path, going another five blocks before coming to a rest. Black smoke began to seep out of his mech's damaged areas as #4 slumped in his cockpit seat, rattled and dazed.

Sophia, brandishing a confident smirk, descended back down to the streets. She was doing it; she was winning. She was beating the giant mech killer robots.

Before Mountain View, Sophia would have been like everyone else, running, screaming, cowering for safety. Here she was in the middle of it all. No longer running, she was fighting and winning.

For a split second, Sophia felt unstoppable until she remembered there were four of them as a recovered #2's mech leaped into the air with its cannon for a rifle aimed right at her. Then,

Sophia remembered that she could not fly, which meant she was a sitting duck in midair.

"Oh shit…" she said, breathing heavily.

Point blank range, despite trying to cover up, Sophia took the hand cannon's blast, the length and size of a Harley Davidson. She felt the sheering heat again as it scorched her skin and clothing. The force of the impact propelled her through an office building, sending people screaming and diving for cover as she exited out the other side, hitting like a meteorite, destroying everything in her path unintentionally while bouncing off the concrete, creating human-size craters before coming to a stop in a heap.

Smoke wafting from her caused her to choke again as she slowly rolled to fight back up to her feet despite being in agonizing pain. Her skin felt like it had first-degree burns, while her lungs filled with smoke and acid. Her vision was blurry; she looked like a train ran over her, dragging her nonstop for about five miles straight.

Sophia was so out of it that she could not react to the BAM crashing down on top of her.

Smoke and debris flew everywhere, some shattering windows and taking out parked cars as people ran, ducking and looking for cover from the war zone.

As the smoke cleared, those brave enough to peek out and look could see Sophia trapped underneath the foot of the massive BAM belonging to #3.

"Where's that puffed up chest now, bitch?" she said, going external with her taunt.

Sophia groaned and growled as she managed to get her hands underneath her and perform a push-up, getting space between her and the ground. #3 growled as she tried to crush Dennison under her machine's foot, but Sophia refused to budge as she managed to get her feet underneath her. She then used her piston-like legs to explode with enough force to hurl #3 off her, landing her several yards away on her back.

#2 cut her offensive attack short as he sprung from nowhere, driving a crushing bi-pedal foot into Sophia's chest, drilling her further into the crater. It was amazing how the ground did not give way altogether, dropping them into the sewers of D.C.

A determined Dennison covered in dirt and blood from wounds that had already healed growled again as she gripped the bipedal toes of the humanoid machine standing on her, pushing her further into the crater. Sophia struggled even with #2's cannon trained on her again at point-blank range.

"You move super-bitch," #2 warned, "and you die... doubt you can survive me unloading several rounds in your face at this range."

"What... part of me... killing all of you... did you not get?!" a defiant Sophia yelled.

She ripped the bipedal foot of #2's mech in half, spilling an unknown red fluid all over her.

It forced #2 to scream, feeling the neural feedback. It felt as if she actually did rip his foot in two. #2 still managed to pull the trigger, but not before Sophia lurched forward and stuck her entire arm up the barrel of the mech's gun, causing it to blow up right in front of them.

The force of the explosion, along with shrapnel, sent a badly damaged #2's machine crashing to the concrete, while Sophia also dashed to the street by the impact, letting off a blood-curdling scream, clutching her charred right arm. Tears of rage ran from her equally badly burnt face as she watched her arm, with half the skin burnt, reform before her very eyes while #2 desperately tried to stand his now smoking machine on its badly damaged foot.

#1 and #4, both no longer with aerial capability, came running down West Virginia Avenue, joining #3. Sophia, once again fully healed, rose to her feet. With no more words wasted, they opened fire on her, but instead of outright dodging, she made slight movements, and short speed bursts zipping out of the way, dodging the barrage of cannon fire. As they tore up the street, she weaved through shot after shot, getting closer to them; it was a clear message Sophia sent to them. She would kill them… and nothing on Earth could stop her, not even them.

"We need to fall back… now!" an unnerved #1 muttered.

Just as #1 gave the order to retreat, Sophia,

like a lioness on the hunt, launched herself plowing into #2, barely able to stand, taking his machine completely off its compromised feet.

#2, in desperation, tried to throw a right from his back to knock her off him, but Sophia, proving to be much faster and far more powerful, caught the mechanical fist eight times the size of her own hand and crushed it in her grip. The neural feedback made him scream again as if she turned his actual hand to powder. Sophia then grabbed the machine's arm by the forearm, getting another good grip, and ripped the entire arm off, sending the weird fluid that looked like blood flying everywhere. Within the machine's cockpit, #2 hollered again in pain as if she had ripped his arm off while sparks and mini-explosions erupted around him.

"Fall back now," Director Rosen ordered, coming over #1's audio system, "lead her to the rendezvous point."

"Sir... #2," #1 stuttered.

"Is dead as of right now."

Director Rosen coldly gestured to the

technicians within the helicopter.

Lights and a female mechanized voice went off in #2's cockpit.

"Self-destruct sequence has been initiated... self-destruct in five seconds..."

"No! No! No!" #2 screamed.

Outside, Sophia, with her bare hands, tore open the machine's chest plate and got a glimpse of the black-clad human she had seen four years ago in her bedroom. One second before, the BAM blew underneath her with the torn-off arm, delivering a force that would leave no recognizable trace of the machine or the pilot. The strength of the blast sent her flying while taking out half the block around her. The other three mechs staggered backward, barely shielded from the explosion that had now claimed #2.

"I have now bought you some time," Director Rosen instructed #1. "Fall back to the rendezvous point before she comes to... I will take care of the rest."

"Sir..." #1 confirmed; he then motioned to

#4 and #3, "you heard the order… let's move out."

#4 and a livid #3 turned tail and ran following #1 as a now smoldering Sophia knocked six blocks away by the blast rose to her feet off a now smashed-in BMW X5 courtesy of her. Aside from the hit to the leg she took earlier, her leather pants weathered the battle. Her now torched jacket, however, did not survive.

She looked around and noticed Nathanial Walters, a.k.a Deuce, in his business suit, quivering and trembling in a store entrance, looking at what was left of the parked X5 she stood on.

"My car…" he stammered.

A replacement for the vehicle she wrecked, Mr. Walters, realizing her eyes were on him, went faint, collapsing to the concrete floor.

Sophia hopped off the wrecked luxury vehicle with a shake of her head, quickly noticing a mannequin wearing a red midriff leather jacket in a storefront where the glass was shattered.

Sophia leaped into the display area, pulling out whatever charred bills she had in her pockets and tossing them at the foot of the mannequin. She then unzipped the now-one-armed jacket she had on, which fell apart due to the scorching heat from the explosion, tossing it away. Next, she tore off what was left of the still smoking blue skintight short-sleeved Under Armour shirt, quickly revealing her red sports bra covered chest.

Sophia quickly took the jacket off the mannequin, throwing it on. It was a snug fit, but it would have to do as she zipped it up.

Clothed again, she hopped out of the storefront and exploded into the sky with a leap, now hunting the remaining three D.E.A.D. members.

Despite the head start they had on her, Sophia could see them booking for their lives down Maine Avenue. She planned her next leap for the Reflecting Pool, and from there, she launched herself further to cut them off before they got to the Jefferson Memorial.

#1 had the lead as #3, and a badly

damaged #4 trailed behind him. People scattered, screaming for safety as the trio turned quickly on 14th street, clearly heading for the Memorial.

"Keep moving! We are almost there! We're almost there!" #1 yelled, gunning his BAM.

Almost would not be good enough as the sound of what could only be described as a Tomahawk missile grew louder before a massive impact cratered a portion of 14th Street, sending chunks of the road their way.

The trio backed their machines up in defense mode as Dennison casually hopped out of the crater she created, dusting herself off.

"Hey... where yawl goin?" she asked. "Don't you all wanna see how much my life has changed?"

Sophia advanced, cracking her knuckles while the trio of the most advanced machines unknown to man reversed in fear of the walking female juggernaut now playing the grim reaper.

As she prepared to charge for another

round, a blast of dust and the whirling sound of a black Sikorsky helicopter appearing in the sky overhead interrupted her. Slowly, it descended between an irritated Sophia seeking vengeance and the remaining disheveled D.E.A.D. looking for sanctuary.

Knowing in her heart that inside the descending craft was the head of this sick and twisted operation, she allowed the copter to land safely so she could come face-to-face with the person who orchestrated the ruination of her life.

The winds died down as the helicopter finally came to a rest. Sophia stood unimpressed as the door slid open and storm-trooper-like soldiers in black full body armor hopped out by the dozen, circling her at a wide radius.

Finally, the Director stepped out with a calm smile and a manila folder in his hand. Special Agent Slater brought up the rear, holding what appeared to be some form of restraints behind him. Sophia's left eye began twitching at the sheer gall the Director displayed.

"Sophia Dennison, you're gonna have to come with me," Director Rosen said plainly.

"Is that so, and who the hell might you be?" she snorted.

"You know 'who the hell' I am," he returned. "I'm the man responsible for who you are, and you need to come with me."

"To coin the phrase," Sophia fired back, "you and what friggin army?"

Director Rosen, with no fear, walked right up to her.

"I don't need a 'friggin'" army; all I need is this."

Director Rosen handed her the manila folder, which she snatched from him, flipping it open. Her eyes widened, and she staggered back, trembling, unprepared for what she saw inside of it.

Inside the folder, Sophia looked at the picture of a little girl with hazel eyes and her complexion with thick, curly black hair, wearing a light green jumpsuit with a pink flower imprinted on the front and a pink shirt underneath, sitting in a small chair in what appeared to be a sterile room.

There was a blank, expressionless look on her face, which was close to fretting. She had seen it in pictures her parents had of her when she was young, but those piercing hazel eyes forced tears from Sophia's eyes, making her heart heavy. They were Robert's eyes.

"Now... before you do anything stupid..." Director Rosen warned.

It was too late; Sophia snatched him by the front of his suit at breakneck speed, thrusting him into the air. The shock troopers and D.E.A.D. in their machines immediately trained their high-tech rifles on her, but Rosen threw up his left arm for them to stand down as he calmly looked down at her from her grip.

"Where is she?!" she screamed.

A crackle and whimper came from her voice; despite her power and strength, the Director now knew he was in control.

"In a facility in Oregon... on the other side of this country," he informed her. "What you don't see in that room is a man waiting to decapitate her if you don't comply with my orders."

It was as if his words had sapped her strength as she reluctantly lowered him back to his feet.

The Director smoothed out his ruffled six-thousand-dollar custom-tailored jacket.

"We figured out that was the only permanent way to dispatch someone like her. If we put a bullet in her skull, she'd just become like you. It's still a theory, but she would be our first test subject. Anyway, we've wasted enough time roughhousing in our nation's capital."

Agent Slater walked up with the restraints.

"I doubt these will keep you fully restrained, but they should be strong enough to hold you and allow us to do whatever we have to do to your daughter should you step out of line," said the Director.

He then leaned in, whispering to her.

"So I advise you to be a good little girl

from now on."

As the Director took the folder from her, Agent Slater placed the high-tech restraints on Sophia, who was no longer willing to fight. They looked like large cannon shells covering her forearms and hands while the shells connected with a malleable thick metal bar. He opened the panel on one of the cannon-like shells, flipping on a switch and turning up a digital dial to its highest level. Sophia's face winced as she began to feel intense pressure on her arms.

"Feel that?" Director Rosen said with smiling fascination. "That's an electromagnetic field delivering a gravitational force of several hundred tons. A normal person's arms would be crushed to dust, but apparently, that's nothing for a big girl like you... shall we?"

Sophia stared the Director down with eyes stained with tears and thoughts of murder. She straightened herself up as best she could as she walked with her head held high to the helicopter. The Director smirked as he realized what Sophia was playing at. She was the Alpha female, and regardless of the restraints, no threats could take away or diminish that fact. As long as she continued to carry herself as a threat, the playing field was still level. So she thought.

As the Director watched as she entered the helicopter, he turned to Special Agent Slater.

"Tell those three idiots to get those mechs back to the hanger," Director Rosen coldly snapped, "then get the other one."

"Dead or alive?" Agent Slater asked.

"Dead if they find the samples and any data he has... alive if they don't," Director Rosen ordered. "We must locate those missing samples at all cost... it was already a pain lifting the samples and data from the F.B.I. Houston office... tell them if they have to, kill anyone that's with him if need be."

"Yes, sir. What about all the commotion here?" Agent Slater asked, looking around.

"Come now, Agent Slater," Director Rosen smirked, "we're the United States Government. We convinced the entire nation to go to war looking for W.M.Ds... in time, people will think this was some promotion for a blockbuster movie."

"And if they don't?" Agent Slater asked.

Rosen shrugged.

"We'll still be fine."

~ ~

About two miles from the extraction point, Mark stood chomping at the bit, ready to go. The second he saw the ominous black Sikorsky helicopter flying overhead, he knew who it was; the pieces to the puzzle came into place, revealing a very dark and terrifying tale that basically said the Constitution and Bill of Rights combined were no longer worth the ink and paper they were written on.

Mark could not allow that to happen, not on his watch, not after all he sacrificed. An unsettled Dustin watched as his partner looked like a linebacker with a roid case waiting for his coach to send him in.

King, however, had him; Mercer and the rest of his agents stand down while he tried to speak with his boss, Director Stan Miller.

"What are we doing? What are we doing?! They are going to take her away! They're going to take her away, goddammit!" Mark frantically yelled.

King ignored him, listening to the man in command on the other end of his phone.

"Yes, sir… yes, sir. I understand, sir… it will be done…yes, sir."

King closed his phone with a grim look that made Mark want to vomit because he knew what he would say.

"Orders are to stand down. The fugitive has been captured. Sophia Dennison is no longer our problem."

"No! No! No! This is bullshit!" Mark roared, going into an unsuspecting rage. "Who are they, Doug?! Who the hell are they?!"

"I said this is over!" King yelled fiercely.

"She's a United States citizen with rights!" Mark yelled back.

King delivered his final warning to end the conversation.

"I don't know what she is! But she is no longer our problem, are we clear on that Special Agent?"

"Fuck you!" Mark howled, refusing to end it getting in his face. "It's not over!"

"Someone get this son of a bitch out of my face, and calm him down!" King yelled.

"Move me, Doug!" Mark spat back. "You goddamn coward! You…"

Before he could finish his third insult laced with a slew of vulgarity, three agents grabbed him, pulling him out of King's face.

It forced Dustin to step in, pulling the agents off his partner. He grabbed Mark, who lunged at King.

A bigger and stronger Dustin hauled him away.

"Mark, stop! You gotta stop, man!"

"Get him out of here before I take his badge, Dustin!"

Mark screamed at the top of his lungs, fighting to escape his friend's grip.

"You fucking coward! Our badges are worthless if we let them take her! They're fucking worthless!"

Mark struggled until he heard the whirl of the helicopter once again, making his heart sink.

The fight was taken out of him as he looked up to see the Director's helicopter fly off, taking Sophia god knows where, never to be seen again. At that moment, Mark reached his breaking point.

"Get off me, Dustin. Get off me… I said, get off of me!"

Mark exploded, breaking away from his friend.

His head was buried deep within his chest; his heavy heart had sunk so deep into his gut it felt like it would never come out again. He turned to walk away.

"Where you going, man?" Dustin asked, throwing his hands up.

"I'm going home…" Mark quietly replied.

Dustin followed behind him, trying to understand his outburst.

"Mark, talk to me, man, don't just…"

"I wanna go home, Dustin!" Mark shot back, shouting. "I haven't been home in almost seven days… and I want to go home… I just want to go home."

Mark walked off, heading to his vehicle, ripping off his vest as he flew open the door. He chucked it into the back seat, hopped in, and sped off as Dustin tried to catch up with him, not even thinking about how his partner and friend would get home.

He drove in a daze, his mind filtering everything that went on for the past several days. In the blink of an eye, the world had gone insane, and the person he chased for the past six days was the sanest. It made him drive faster; never in his life did he want to go home so badly.

CHAPTER 19

Mark pulled up to the small Victorian-style home. He quickly got out of his vehicle, locking it up. Mark even ignored the piled-up mail filling his mailbox. He just wanted to get inside his house as he fumbled with his keys, finally unlocking the door so he could be still and away from the world.

He thought it would take it away; being inside his house would take away that lousy feeling working its way down to his bones, but it did not. The quietness only amplified what he felt to nauseating levels. He marched over to his bar for a drink. He poured a glass of Bourbon almost to the rim and went to take a sip. A taste he used to savor with a good cigar at the end of the day was like battery acid to him with a side of ass. It officially made him rage as he threw the drink across the room.

"Goddammit!" Mark screamed at the top of his lungs.

The feeling was now in his bones as he thought about what Dennison said before she walked away from him, that he was the last nice person she believed she would ever speak to. Mark looked around his house, painfully realizing how empty and lonely it was.

On the mantle of his fireplace was a picture frame with a photocopy of his divorce papers. A poor taste of a joke as it sat next to other pictures that outlined his life, photos of his ex-wife, Michelle, long since gone, along with their twins, Annie and Penny. Mark walked over to the mantle, now holding the picture clutching his heart. He fought back the tears as he remembered why the words hit him so hard. He was not a nice person.

~ ~

Eight years prior, there was life in his house, the regular life expected of a family of four. Back then, Mark did care about moving up the ranks. He had just been made Special Agent in Charge and desired to be either an executive assistant director or director one day, which meant taking on high-profile cases and working some late hours.

Sometimes, it also meant missing occasions and family events. Other times, it meant forgetting not to bring your work home. It did not bother Michelle initially; she was a former elementary school teacher who decided to be a stay-at-home mom when the twins were born. It was the usual understanding that he was working hard to provide for them all. She could take a missed or forgotten anniversary or birthday here or there.

Like everything in life, things change, especially when children age. Penny was more like him, a little rough around the edges for a very loud and active girl into sports like baseball and martial arts. She wanted a pellet gun when she was ten just so she had a weapon just like him. Annie was more like her mother: quiet, soft, and very book-smart.

So it was only natural when one who was so much like her father became disappointed when he started to miss her games and track meets regularly, while one was disappointed she got little of his attention. As any mother would react, it was okay if he did it to her; she chose to love and stay married despite his faults, honoring

the "for the better or worse" deal. It was a
different story when he did it to her flesh and
blood. Michelle knew Mark was a good man
who loved her and the children in his own way.
She fought with him so much to save him from
making possibly the biggest mistake of his life.

Sometimes, he sat and took it, giving a
mutter of an apology and, in his eyes, a
justifiable explanation. Sometimes, he bit back,
howling and preaching the importance of his
work to keep monsters off the streets. It took
time and some sacrifice, and no one complained
when his success spelled promotions, which
meant better living for all.

Michelle would always ensure to interject
somewhere in the argument, usually in the end.

"You're going to regret not being here."

He would always end it walking out of the
bedroom to his daughters' room, mustering up
some apology while giving them a lighter
version of his explanation.

They would say it was okay, and they
understood. The next day, Mark would do

something to make it up to them, taking them shopping, to the zoo, or to a movie; once, he screwed up so bad he had to fork out for Disney World.

Eventually, children grow up, and the "It's okay, Daddy" turns into "Whatever, Dad." Gifts and trips begin to lose their luster, and the time does come when they do not have time for you. Mark got a taste of what he dished out over the years and did not like it. He tried to spin around the Earth in his best efforts, turning back time. It only worked in the movies. He had to weather the storm he knew that he brought on himself. It was not easy, but eventually, it did ease, and sunlight poked holes through the dark clouds over him. Once again, the hand of trust extended to him, and he reached for it one morning during breakfast.

"Oh, Penny, remember I have that job interview for that teacher's position at the Dunbar High School this afternoon, so you're going to have to take the bus to your karate class," Michelle reminded her daughter.

"Ma... it's Tae Kwon Do..." Penny corrected, rolling her eyes.

"You know what I mean…" she said while making another pancake.

"I can skip out of my science club and go with you," Annie offered. "Then, mom doesn't have to double back to pick us both up."

"Or… you can go to your club… I can pick Penny up," Mark said out of nowhere, "wait for her, then pick you up, and all three of us can get some ice cream for dessert tonight; come home and help your mom make dinner."

The female trio of the house looked at Mark like he was the elephant in the room, not just because of what he offered, but because he rarely spoke during morning breakfast anymore other than to say "Good Morning," "I love you," "Study Hard," and "Goodbye" sometimes with a kiss depending on his mood.

"What?" Mark said with a shrug. "I'm a Special Agent in Charge; Dustin can carry my workload for half the day; the man owes me his firstborn for all the favors I do for him. It's not a problem."

"Mark, you don't have to…" Michelle

softly pressed.

It was a light gesture for him to opt out; she actually wanted him to.

"Yeah, Dad, it's..." Penny chimed in.

"Dude, I haven't been to one of your classes in like ages," Mark persisted, "be nice to see if you're now tougher than your old man."

Another awkward moment dropped on the table as Penny cocked an eyebrow.

"Did you just call me, "dude?"

"Yeah, he did," Annie smiled in disbelief.

"Ain't that the term now?" Mark asked, acting cool. "Or is it dudette or shortie?"

"How about none of those terms," Penny waved, begging her father to stop.

Laughter and banter were back at the table, lost since the girls entered their preteens. Mark saw Michelle with a smile and a small breath of relief. She saw her family coming back, and it made her happy.

2:30 PM, Penny was where she was supposed to be, but Mark was not.

There was a break early that morning in the Eduardo Mendoza case, the head of an up-and-coming Brazilian Cartel known for trafficking weapons, drugs, white slavery, prostitution, and the extortion of minors. A business meeting carried out by one of Mendoza's high lieutenants with a foreign diplomat from Somalia for a deal on black market firearms and drugs to finance their ongoing civil war had gone down that day, and they were there with a team to finally make the collar and bring the lieutenant in. Mark decided to sit in on the interrogation, forgetting that his daughter awaited him.

At 2:45 PM, Matthew Anderson, a senior in Penny's high school and a student at her same dojo, saw her and offered her a ride. She took it, seeing her chance to catch a ride with her long-time crush as an excellent opportunity to muster some courage and see if he possibly liked her. Before she drove off with him, she would borrow his cell phone to call her father.

Not recognizing the number, Mark would

not pick up, sending it to voicemail, continuing his interrogation, forcing her to leave a message.

"Daddy, I know you must be busy," Penny whispered, "it's okay… this guy from my class, Matthew, offered to drive me, so I'm going with him. When you finish what you're doing, you can pick me up, we can still come back and get Annie, and we'll just keep this a secret between us. Love you, Daddy."

Penny drove off with Anderson in his Ford Mustang GT. After getting six blocks, Matthew, having the green light and driving within the speed limit, would have his car broadsided on the passenger side by Austin Campbell going sixty miles per hour in a twenty-five-speed limit, a thirty-eight-year-old stockbroker with a habit for afternoon cocktails with a side of cocaine and three DWIs already under his belt.

Matthew's car would flip over eight times before coming to a stop, despite wearing seatbelts and an airbag; Penny died instantly, while Matthew Anderson passed away on his way to the hospital; Austin Campbell survived with only six stitches to his skull; his blood alcohol level was 0.21.

Mark got Penny's message at 3:05 PM after he had finished his interrogation and acquired Mendoza's lieutenant's cooperation in obtaining key shipment locations for his contraband. It was an exchange for not spending the rest of his life in Federal maximum prison. An agent told Mark the news at 3:07 PM.

He went home to a sobbing, distraught wife who hugged him tightly as he walked through the door a destroyed man. Annie would not go near him. A week later, they buried Penny; her Sensei gave them the brown belt she had worked so hard for at her funeral.

Michelle never blamed him for what happened and never asked him why he never showed up when he promised to pick up their daughter. She got a job working at the high school. Annie stopped talking to him altogether. Life went on like this for six months as Mark did the only thing he could do: throw himself deeper into his work to hide. The later he came home, the less he had to see their faces and know he failed them.

One night, he walked into a dark house, noticing things were missing, but there was no forced entry. Annie's room was bare. Mark entered his bedroom with everything still there except Michelle's belongings; on the bed were divorce papers and a note that read, "My daughter is dead, and now my husband is dead. Annie and I cannot live in a tomb."

He never went looking for them. He sent an agent to do him a favor and ensure they were safe. Michelle had rented a two-bedroom apartment for them on the other side of town.

He sat on the papers for at least a month before signing them. He waited at the high school one day as she walked out.

She was stunned to see him walk up, fearful he would make a scene.

Mark handed her the papers, saying three words.

"Are you okay?"

"Yes... I am," Michelle nodded.

He looked around, not making eye contact with her.

"Is Annie okay?"

Michelle nodded again, trying to make eye contact with him.

"Yes…"

Mark looked down at the ground, shook his head, and mumbled, "Take care of yourself."

He walked off, leaving her standing there. It was not clear if he thought she would run after him screaming, crying, and slapping him for acting the way he was, for closing up, shutting down, killing Penny, but she did not, and that was the last he saw of her or Annie.

~ ~

As Mark looked at his copy of the divorce papers in the picture frame, a wave of rage came over him.

"Stupid! Stupid fucking old man! Stupid!"

Grabbing the frame, he smashed it against the mantle, sending glass flying everywhere before throwing it across the room. He should have been there. He should have fought for what really mattered. He should have clawed, kicked, and hollered, begged if he had to.

As he stood there, Mark came to a decision that would probably change his world forever. He reached into his pocket, pulled out his phone, and dialed a number he never called before. It rang a couple of times before going to voicemail.

"This is the Hudson residence," a soft female voice said, "we're not in right now, but please leave a number and a brief message. We will get back to you."

Mark drew a deep breath before finding the words he wanted to say.

"Michelle… Annie… hi," he said nervously, fumbling with his words, "you guys must be out or something. I hope you're both safe. Listen… I'm… I'm sorry; I wasn't there, and I know it's too late. I know… I always thought… one more case… one more mission… that I was working for a better tomorrow, a better country. Some shit you hear in a stupid commercial, and I believed it… so much that I forgot what was most important."

The tears began to roll, an emotion the old Army vet had not felt since losing his parents and Penny.

"I fu... I messed up... really badly," Mark finally got out. "I messed it all up. Everything I fought and sacrificed for... it was all for a lie, all for a damn lie. I just wanted you both to know that I have to go away... to do something right for a change. If I get back... when I get back... if it's okay, I'd like to tell you this in person... and if for some reason I don't. Annie... the second greatest day in my life was when God gave me you and Penny... and the only reason why it's the second... is because you giving me the privilege to share my pathetic life with you, Michelle, and giving me two awesome kids was the greatest day of my life. I regret every day I didn't cherish either one of you. I'm a stupid slow old man, but I get it now... I get it now... I love you both."

Mark hung up his cell and wiped his eyes with his sleeve. He had wanted to say more, but he knew the answering machine would cut off the rest of his message. He hardened his heart dialing another number; the person picked up after two rings.

"Nick… how you doing?" Mark asked.

"Mark, what's going on, man?" his old friend said with concern. "Saw it all over the news; you guys had some crazy shit going on in the Capital today, you okay?"

"I'm good," Mark confirmed. "How's the family?"

"They're good; boy's growing like a weed," Nick chuckled. "I'm about to break my daughter's iPhone one of these days. Susan asked me yesterday if I spoke to you."

Mark smiled.

"Tell her I miss her meatloaf."

"You're the only one who'll eat that shit," Nick joked. "But you didn't call for small talk… did you?"

"I'm asking if you and your boys in the FAA can check and confirm the whereabouts of a black Sikorsky private helicopter," Mark said, finally getting down to business. "It would have landed after 2:30 PM at either a commercial or military airport here in Washington or another airport on the East Coast... preferably private or military. I also need to know if any aircraft took off from that same airport and its destination... specifically private and cargo planes."

"You okay, man?" Nick came back with the same concerned voice at the start of the conversation. "You never "ask" me for anything... you usually demand."

"I'm fine, Nick. I'm also asking for one more favor. I'm going to need a pilot and plane once I get this information... like tonight. Ex-military, willing to fly with no questions asked."

There was a pause on the phone before Nick responded.

"I'll see what I can do. You sure you're okay, man?"

"I'm fine, Nick, just fine... as soon as you can."

Mark hung up his phone and went upstairs to pack.

473

His phone went off due to an incoming call; the ID said Doctor Senji Kumamoto. An eerie feeling told him to pick up. Mark answered as the hairs stood up on the back of his neck.

"Dr. Kumamoto?"

"Special Agent Armitage… glad I got you… I have been trying to contact you all day. I finally got your number from someone in your office," Doctor Kumamoto said with great concern, "someone has stolen all of the samples and data from the lab this morning concerning Ms. Dennison."

"What? How?" Mark asked in disbelief while having a good idea who did it.

"We're still trying to figure that out," Doctor Kumamoto said, "but I called to tell you after compiling Ms. Dennison's entire medical history. I found something very interesting."

"What is it?" Mark asked.

CHAPTER 20

Mark walked the tarmac of College Park Airport, heading blindly into the unknown without hesitation.

Sure enough, Nick came through; he confirmed that a black Sikorsky private helicopter did land at Leesburg Executive Airport at Godfrey Field in Loudon County, Virginia. A private corporate plane took off thirty minutes later; its destination was the Oregon City Airpark, typical that it would be all the way across the damn country. An almost six-hour flight made the trail considerably cold. Not that it was stopping him from going; Nick also came through with a pilot and a plane. Ex-military, as usual, would not ask any questions and would get him to his destination. An advantage Mark needed, considering he was carrying a mixture of his old military, FBI gear, and all the guns and ammo in his possession.

He drew a heavy sigh, walking to the plane with his bags as the last person he wanted to see stood in front of him with a not-too-happy look.

Dustin walked up to him with the intent to slug him.

"What the hell are you doing?" he spat at Mark.

"How'd you find out?" Mark asked, dodging his question.

"You're frantic ex-wife and daughter called and told me you left some insane message on their answering machine," Dustin seethed. "I put it together that you weren't somewhere putting a bullet in your skull. I then called Nick threatening to come to his house and beat his ass in front of his wife and kids if he did not tell me where you were. Now, what the fuck are you doing?"

"You know damn well what I'm doing," Mark fired back at him.

Dustin moved closer, getting in his face.

"Exactly what you were ordered not to do."

476

"This is not your concern…" Mark began to tell him.

Dustin shoved him backward, sticking a finger in his face.

"You selfish son of a bitch, it is my concern!" Dustin raged. "Let's start with Michelle and Annie, who still give a shit about you, and then there's me who's supposed to be your partner, then let's add the fact that you're jeopardizing your entire career as well as your life if you fuck with this guy! If he kills you, he cannot be touched! So you tell me why I shouldn't knock you on your ass and drag you out of here in restraints till you come to your senses?"

With no time to get into fisticuffs with Dustin, Mark pulled a folded piece of paper from his pocket and handed it to him.

Dustin snatched it out of his hand, opening it up to see a picture of a little four-year-old girl with hazel eyes and thick, curly black hair wearing a Catholic schoolgirl outfit. The photo was on a printout of an Amber Alert for Kimberly Stone.

"She had a daughter... that's why she surrendered," Mark informed his partner while pointing at the picture.

Dustin looked at the picture and then at Mark for the first time without the information in his grasp.

"What are you talking about?"

"Sophia Dennison was pregnant while on trial," Mark explained. "Doctor Kumamoto was running into a dead end with the blood, so he pulled all of her medical files and found out she was pregnant while in Harris County Jail during her trial. Dr. Hampton wasn't just visiting her as a concerned friend; she got the request to appoint him as her designated obstetrician."

"Say what?" Dustin erupted, stunned and frustrated over the never-ending madness.

"The baby was reported coming out stillborn. He signed the death certificate and, by Dennison's wish, had the body cremated. Something seemed funny, so I dug around in the birth and adoption databases, narrowing the field down to a month... he wasn't even subtle about it… Hampton signed a birth certificate for this little girl the following day at a closed adoption to a couple in Boston, Massachusetts."

Dustin stood there in disbelief at yet another puzzle in this crazy affair.

"Why would they fake her baby's death?"

Mark shook his head before going on.

"I don't know. What I do know is almost thirty-six hours ago, Mr. and Mrs. Brian and Jamie Stone were both found dead in their home in Boston. No forced entry, DNA, or fibers found at the crime scene… both dead from carbon monoxide poisoning and the child… this child is currently missing."

Dustin began formulating a plan that involved going to King with this new information for the first time.

"We need to…"

"I'm more than six hours behind; I don't have time for the red tape."

"Then I'm coming with you…" Dustin

479

demanded.

"No, you are not!"

A furious Mark with very little patience got in his face.

"You are not going to make Bethany a widow or leave Kyle, Marcus, and Angie fatherless. You're going to start answering your goddamn phone when your family calls you! No matter how stupid or petty it is! You're going to stay here and watch my back, especially if I don't come back. Tell Doug what I found, and make sure I don't disappear in some propaganda cover-up bullshit."

Dustin stared down at the man who was the godfather to his kids, and as much as he wanted to argue with him, he knew the truth. He had to stay.

Dustin shook his head.

"I know this is all messed up, man... but why? Why does it have to be you?"

Mark looked up at the dark, starry sky as if the answer was there.

"Because I didn't sacrifice everything for a country where good people are butchered in their sleep," Mark grunted, "while their loved ones take the fall for it… and no one points a gun in my face and gets away with it."

Mark passed Dustin, no longer looking to stop him. He paused, placing a hand on Dustin's shoulder.

"The rest of the files are printed out on my desk at home. I was going to leave you a message about them. You know where the key is. Give me a six-hour head start, and then get them to Doug… open his damn eyes… make him listen."

"Tell me you're coming back," Dustin said with a heavy heart. "Tell me you're coming back, and I'll do it…"

Mark patted his shoulder before walking off to the plane.

"I'm coming back."

It was a half-lie, he said, leaving his friend standing there; if Mark had it his way, he would do everything in his power to come back, but even armed to the teeth, his fate was not up to him. He was still left with all the fear and uncertainty in the world in him.

Uncertain if he would find the Director, Dennison, or even the little girl, he feared that he might not return from wherever he was headed, fearful because this was not him on tour in some unknown foreign country. This madness was going on in his backyard.

As he walked up the steps boarding the plane, he heard Dustin yell at the top of his lungs.

"Yay tho I walk through the valley of the dead… I shall fear no evil!"

Mark finished the prayer they always recited when heading out into the shit.

"Because I will be the baddest son of a bitch in that valley… Amen."

CHAPTER 21

September 9, 2008, after almost seven
hours between the flight and traveling via a 1990
Honda Civic he acquired from a used car lot for
six hundred dollars in Wilsonville, Mark pulled
into the town of Klamath Falls. The trail was not
cold… it was arctic. After landing in the Airpark
Aviation Condominium in Aurora, he confirmed
with air traffic control and ground crew that a
Bombardier Challenger 300 did land, followed
by a Boeing C-17 Globemaster III. Five minutes
later, two M1070 truck tractors with M1000
heavy equipment transporter semi-trailers pulled
onto the tarmac, where three massive containers

were unloaded from the Globemaster onto the trailers. Finally, a female occupant in some weird type of restraints exited the Challenger 300 with armed guards; all of the occupants of the private jet immediately boarded another waiting black Sikorsky helicopter heading south, followed by the military transports, no doubt taking the I-5S.

After almost five hours of driving, hoping he could play catch up and come up with basically nothing, Mark needed to get his bearings, find a lead, a breadcrumb. Being up for almost twenty-four hours, minus the three-hour nap on the plane, he pulled into the Black Bear Diner in Klamath Falls, Oregon, for some black stuff. He hoped to ask the locals without alarming them if anything significant and weird rolled into their town that day.

Mark quickly looked at his phone, contemplating turning it back on to check his messages, but thought it best not to take the chance. It would take a second for it to be on; Doug would know his location and have agents down on him faster than he could sneeze, so he was forced to purchase a car in cash instead of renting one. The only way he would complete his mission was to stay off the radar.

As Mark entered the diner, the locals raised their heads or turned their necks to acknowledge he was at the door before returning to their business. Armitage found himself sitting at the counter where he knew the regulars usually sat. The waitress behind the counter walked up to him with coffee and a friendly, bright smile, obviously happy to welcome a new face into their establishment.

"How are you doing today?"

She pointed to her nametag.

"My name is Carolann; I will be your waitress today."

He smirked with a nod.

"Mark, please to meet you, Carolann."

"Would you like some coffee, Mark?" she chirpily asked.

"Yes, please, black… two sugars."

She quickly poured him a cup and finished

placing two sugar packs to distribute into his coffee as he saw fit. She then put a menu in front of him and pulled out her pad to take his order.

Mark narrowed his eyes quickly, looking over the menu.

"I'll have a vegetable omelet, please, and a side of orange juice."

"Coming right up," Carolann said, taking his order.

Ten minutes later, Carolann was back with her perky smile, his omelet, and orange juice.

"Here you go, sweetie," she beamed.

"Thank you."

Mark looked around for the ketchup to throw on the omelet before digging in.

"So what brings you to Klamath Falls?" Carolann asked, making small talk.

Mark used it to see if he could get some Intel from a local.

"Vacation," he said in between bites, "decided to do some camping and hiking... get some nature and clean air in me."

"Where you from?" Carolann asked with a bright, near-obnoxious smile.

He needed a trick answer for an honest question, seeing how the vehicle he pulled up in could no way be a rental car. Only an oddball buys a vehicle in the same state he is going on a camping trip or hiding something.

"Sacramento," Mark said dismissively.

"Wow," Carolann emitted with some shock, "that's a heck of a drive!"

"People I've spoken to told me it's worth it," he shrugged, "especially for the experience."

"You headed to Gilchrist State?" she asked, leaning flirtatiously forward and showing Mark much cleavage.

"Considering it," he said while remaining polite, "or Sun Pass."

"Well, if you're going to Gilchrist or

Mount McLoughlin by Upper Klamath Lake, be careful," Carolann warned. "The black bear population has been growing in those areas... they stay away from folks for the most part, but they love wrecking campsites looking for food."

"Good to know," Mark said, lying through his teeth about doing any camping.

Just as she walked off to attend to other patrons, Mark put his nose to the floor and saw if he could sniff out a breadcrumb.

"So, are there any military bases around here?" Mark asked innocently while taking a bite out of his omelet.

The question caused her smile to fall slightly as if she was trying to hide obvious concern for what he just said; Mark saw a possible breadcrumb. His suspicion became bigger when some of the locals within earshot gave him a dirty look from the corner of their eyes.

"Why do you ask?" Carolann inquired with a partial smile and a nervous tone in her voice.

"No reason, really," Mark shrugged. "While driving up here, two huge military trucks came up behind me on the US-97 bearing down hard; rattled me so much I have to pull over. As I said, I planned to do some hiking and didn't want to make the mistake of walking into some restricted area... would really suck if I got shot or something."

He finished cracking a genuine smile to put her at ease.

Carolann's bright smile came back full blast.

"There's a National Guard Army base in Ashland, that's probably where they were headed, but there are no bases in this area."

"Good to hear," Mark returned.

He kept the fake smile while cursing inside as he lost the breadcrumb again.

Carolann moved in closer to have a more private conversation with him, again showing much cleavage.

"I'm really sorry," she whispered, "I

thought you were one of those conspiracy theory people."

"Excuse me?" Mark responded with genuine confusion.

"Every now and then, someone asks about "secret government bases," Carolann explained. "Fans of our local conspiracy theorist…"

"Local nut job is what he is…" the patron to Mark's left interjected.

"Be nice, Bernie," Carolann scolded him before returning to Mark. "He's talking about Eric Dunbar… he runs this conspiracy theory website out of his home called "Break the Iron Curtain." He believes that somewhere in Mount McLoughlin is a top-secret US government facility where they do experiments unbeknown to the public, like cloning or creating high-tech weapons… he goes up there from time to time looking for it…"

"And ends up back in town the next day drunk as a friggin skunk either on his lawn or in front of my shop talking about how high tech soldiers grabbed him and 'drugged' him." Bernie added in disgust and contempt, "One time he and this tree-hugging broad from New York who was a so-called believer was arrested for being drunk, high, and butt ass nekkid in Veterans Memorial Park downtown... disgraceful."

Mark leaned back, pretending to be startled.

"Wow, drunk... high... and naked... I guess I'm going to Mount McLoughlin then."

The joke made Carolann and Bernie chuckle; however, Mark smiled because he finally got his breadcrumb. Eric Dunbar was not a hack; he saw behind the iron curtain and knew something was shitty at Mount McLoughlin, and it was not the bear droppings. He had to find him and find out what he knew.

Mark finished his omelet, juice, and coffee, said his thanks and goodbyes, leaving a decent tip, and left, heading to his car to figure out how he was going to find Eric Dunbar with no help from the Bureau or the ability to walk into a local police station and ask for help.

Mark figured he could walk into a library

or cyber café if there was one in town, but how much more downtime would that take off his search for Dennison and her daughter?

With minimal resources at Mark's disposal and time against him, dread came over him that he would never find them in time to do anything.

"Who are you?" a voice said behind him.

Mark slowly turned around to see a slender man in his mid to late twenties, with fiery red hair underneath a black skullcap and a matching full, unkempt beard. The hollows of his eyes meant he had not had a decent night's sleep in a long time; he also had a few bruises that were healing. He seemed quite agitated in his black long johns and blue coveralls three sizes bigger than he was.

"You said you were from Sacramento," the young man said, pointing out, "but your temporary plates are from Wilsonville... so who are you?"

"Eric... Dunbar?" Mark guessed, "you were in the diner? No one..."

"People talk about me whether I'm there or not," he said flatly. "They don't acknowledge that I exist because of the things I allegedly did… you didn't come here to go camping or hiking… are you one of them?"

"One of them?" Mark asked.

Mark had a good idea who he was talking about; he just wanted to hear him say it.

"One of the agents from the base hidden in Mount McLoughlin," Eric said, getting agitated, "the ones who've been fucking up my life and making me look like the town loon."

"No… my name is Special Agent Mark Armitage from the FBI," Mark confessed, also putting it out there, "and I need to find that base… there's a woman and a young child who was abducted by those people, and I need to find them and stop whatever they plan to do with them."

"How come you're here by yourself, Special Agent?" Eric asked with a head tilt, unsure if he believed him.

"Just like you, no one believes me or has the balls to do something about it," Mark earnestly said. "What happened in DC yesterday was because of those people. They're violating people's rights for their own agenda, they murdered the little girl's adoptive parents and just took her, and they have her biological mother. The woman you probably also saw on the news. I have to help them. Will you help me find them?"

Dunbar looked over Armitage's shoulder, noticing Carolann and some patrons looking out the window being their nosy selves.

"When you leave this parking lot," Eric said with a low tone, "make a left and drive down four blocks, make a right and then wait for me. When I walk away, turn around and shrug your shoulders like you were just confronted by a nutcase."

Without another word, Dunbar walked off, Mark doing precisely what he said, and turned around, seeing a concerned Carolann, Bernie, and a couple of other patrons looking out the window. He shrugged his shoulders with a smile, waved, hopped into his car, and drove out of the

494

parking lot following the directions given to him by Dunbar.

As Mark reached the destination and pulled up to the park, Eric Dunbar came out of nowhere, hopping into his car. He turned on his radio and pushed the volume way up. Apparently, the Civic Mark bought was a "Fast and Furious" type car because the custom speakers were nearly deafening. Vexed, he went to turn the music down until Dunbar slapped his hand away, holding up one finger and telling him to wait.

He pulled out a small pen and pad from his coveralls. He wrote feverishly without looking at what he was writing.

He then held it up for just Mark to read.

"I'm bugged, somewhere on my body that I can't see!"

An average person would have thought he was nuts. Mark would have thought Eric was nuts had he not witnessed the things he saw the past few days.

Dunbar went on writing something else without looking at it.

"They may probably be onto us now; Mount McLoughlin is one hour from here. Drive and follow my hand signals to where we need to go."

Mark nodded as he shifted the clutch into first and pulled off with one eye on the road and the other on Dunbar's hand gestures, which would guide him to his destination. The breadcrumb was leading him to a trail that was thawing out. Would he make it in enough time to make a difference was another question?

CHAPTER 22

Mark accomplished the hour drive in less than forty-five minutes behind the old tuner car with Dunbar guiding him. Luck was on his side as he could evade speed traps while taking sign language directions from his passenger, who believed someone implanted him with some surveillance bug relaying data back to somewhere.

After finding a remote spot, Mark, already out of the Civic, suited up, putting on his old military fatigues before throwing on his F.B.I. tactical armor. He then loaded up with two Glock

23s, an M4 Carbine, and a Heckler & Koch MP5; he then strapped on several needed ammo belts. Mark thought about turning on his phone and texting Dustin to alert him to his position, but if Dustin could find him, they could locate him. He needed to stay under the radar just a bit longer.

"I can talk now," Eric said with enthusiasm. "What do I get to carry?"

"You get to carry your ass back to town after you point me in the right direction," Mark instructed.

Eric's face contorted.

"Hell no, screw you; I'm coming!"

"Listen, kid, these are very dangerous people," Mark said, getting serious with him. "They see you coming with me; they're not going to knock you out and play some stupid prank on you… they're going to kill you, and I don't need your blood on my hands. And if you are bugged as you say you are, they probably know we're here right now and will know our position the second we enter the forest."

An unfazed Eric leveled with him as he fidgeted.

"You know how this all started? My dad used to take me up to a cave in Mount McLoughlin to explore when we went camping up here... before he died of colon cancer. One day I went up there just to go to the cave to remember him and the great times we had together; a so-called park ranger came out of nowhere and advised me not to go up to the cave because the bear population was heavy there. I told him I'd take my chances.

Next thing you know, after a couple of yards, I blacked out. That's when it all started. First, it was just dropping me off at my campsite... I thought I was going crazy and thought it was aliens, but they kept upping the ante. Finding ways to embarrass and humiliate me in front of my friends and family, I knew I wasn't crazy, that there was someone up there who didn't want me to see or know what they were doing."

"Why did you keep going back?" Mark asked.

Eric looked down at the ground, kicking some dirt around.

"My dad never gave up. Even when the cancer was killing him, he kept coming with me on these trips... so how could I?"

He raised his head, looking Mark in the eye.

"Also, I knew there was something just wrong about whatever these people are doing, and you confirmed it, so you're taking me... or you can walk around these woods finding this place yourself."

Mark glared at him. He did not have time to argue, so he reached into his bag, grabbed extra body armor, and handed it to him. He then pulled out a Remington Model 870 shotgun with a case of shells.

"Put this on," he ordered while handing him the vest and shotgun, "standard issued, ever shot one?"

"Dude," Eric grinned. "This is Oregon."

"Take the keys to the car, the sign of a

firefight you get the hell out of there, get to this vehicle," Mark instructed. "Drive, and don't stop driving till you hit the town. When you get there, you call the second number on this phone."

Mark reached into his pocket, handing him the keys and phone.

"The password is Penny," he continued, "all lowercase, you tell my partner Special Agent in Charge Dustin Mercer everything that happened, you got it?"

Eric nodded, tightening the straps on the body armor.

"I got it... I got it."

"Lead the way... but stay close!" Mark warned him one last time.

With a shotgun in grip, Dunbar led the way as Mark quickly put the rest of the gear he could not carry in the car, locking it up before following him. He prayed the kid really did not have a bug on him.

Part of him knew he would regret taking the kid, but time was against him, leaving him a minimal choice; he had to find that base and try to save them.

~ ~

A half-hour later, they were deep in the forest, heading toward the mountain. Mark had to grab the kid several times to reel him back as he checked out their perimeter, ensuring there were no unsuspecting snipers or traps. He figured that was how they were taking the kid down. The last thing he needed was to go out like a light and find himself in an embarrassing predicament with the kid or worse.

"We're almost near the area where they take me out," Eric whispered to him, "sometimes they stop me cold… sometimes they let me get a little further before putting my lights out. Last time they just came out of nowhere and started kicking my ass."

"Say what?" a startled Mark whispered back.

"Yeah," Eric confirmed, "they had on some crazy heavy body armor like storm troopers from head to toe."

502

"Thank you for now mentioning that," Mark whispered harshly, "and stay close; the last thing I need is to carry your ass while we're getting shot at."

At that point, so deep in, they moved from tree to tree, hoping to be less of a target. Mark was uneasy. His old military experience told him there were eyes everywhere, but he could see nothing. At least the Predator displayed some silhouette before gutting someone. If they were out there, these people were ghosts in every sense of the word and patiently waiting for the right time to attack.

"Dude," Eric whispered again, "I've never been this far in... we're almost to the cave... maybe they left or something."

"Yeah... may..."

Mark was about to answer when he saw the silhouette. A green laser pointed at Dunbar's neck, naked to the untrained eye.

The old dog still had the sight; he also knew that if Dunbar had a laser on him, he had one. He booted Dunbar in the ass sending him flying face forward before diving himself. He was not fast enough as a bullet or dart hit him from behind, luckily in the back of the vest.

"Dude! What the…!?" Eric howled.

Mark ignored Eric's temper tantrum over kicking him, quickly grabbing and dragging him around the thickest oak tree he could find before putting a portion of his body out with his M4 Carbine to shoot at who or whatever was taking a shot at them.

The objective was to rattle them into making a sound so they did not have time to set up another shot and take them out. His shooting was apparently pretty close to the sniper's proximity because he heard something unnatural echoing back; he continued to fire near the sound.

Off away, a pack of five Shock Troopers in heavy camouflage body armor stood by as bullets fired from Mark's M4 whizzed by them, hitting the trees. Two shots luckily struck two of them in their chest plates of nearly impenetrable armor, which was probably what Mark heard.

"Intruders have made our position," the Lead Shock Trooper instructed his unit, "switch to live rounds… move in… move in."

Heavy gunfire erupted back at them, ripping into the trees. Mark fired back but knew he could not hold their position long.

He quickly grabbed Dunbar by his vest, looking him in the face.

"Remember what I told you?!" Mark yelled.

A terrified Dunbar shook his head in obedience.

"Then go! I'll cover you! Go! Go! Go!" Mark screamed.

Eric fought past his fear and ran back in the direction he came, moving from tree to tree to avoid the barrage of bullets flying. Mark returned fire and began to move, too. He hoped to draw all the attention to him and away from Eric. He also hoped someone else would hear the commotion and call for help.

Mark moved while returning fire, a bit

winded, sliding behind another big oak ripped to
shreds by automatic gunfire. The old man was
used to chasing people down, not running and
ducking for cover. He quickly changed the clip
to his M4, locking and loading as he sucked up
as much air into his lungs to get a second wind.

"Come on, you sons of bitches," Mark
gasped, "let me see your faces… so I can blow it
off…"

He went to aim and shoot when a
hummingbird whizzed right up to him, the last
thing he expected in the middle of a gunfight,
until he realized in disbelief that it was
mechanical. Its eyes blinked red as it let out a
high-pitched noise that got louder before he
could react.

"Oh shit!" he yelled.

Instinct told him to run for it, which he
did. Still, he did not get enough distance between
himself and the flying robotic assassin as it
detonated with enough concussive force to throw
him several feet, slamming into one of the great
oaks of the forest.

Mark's head rang, and everything went blurry. The veteran in him quickly grabbed body parts, checking to see if anything was missing. The limbs were still attached. Everything was still there. His vision returned enough to know they were already on him from different angles.

Armor and weapons he had never seen before, one of them had what appeared to be a hi-tech version of a mini-gun. They definitely looked like stormtroopers but more terrifying and ruthless. Mark slowly raised his hands, fearing the worst.

"Target has been captured... prepare to terminate," the Lead Shock Trooper ordered.

"My name is Special Agent Mark Armitage of the F.B.I.!" Mark yelled at the top of his lungs, "you are under arrest for charges of murder and kidnapping of a minor! Agents now know where I am, and they will be coming for you and for me! Believe it... you sons of bitches!"

It was a last-ditch effort for a condemned man, but it was enough to have the Lead Shock Trooper turn and talk to whoever was giving him commands from behind the scenes. With one swift motion, the trooper pulled out his sidearm and fired a shot into Armitage's neck without hesitation, only it did not feel like a bullet. The world started to go black. He imagined this was probably what Dunbar's world was like.

Mark heard the trooper utter one final sentence before going into the darkness.

"Secure the perimeter; bring the transport so we can take him back to base."

~ ~

The light slowly came back into Mark's world, along with the taste of cottonmouth. He braced himself for probably being butt naked with something stuck in him in the intersection of the town of Klamath Falls for all to see, but that was not the case. They removed his body armor along with all of his gear and weapons. He was in chained shackle restraints. Under arrest was his second thought, prepped for agents coming to take him back to D.C. to face disciplinary action for going rogue.

His room was more of a sizeable sterile

conference room with a large silver table stretching from one end to another. One of those commlinks he hated using sat in the middle, with highly uncomfortable chairs one would see in the Jetsons and a huge flat-screen monitor.

Two guards wearing lighter black armor versions of the ones that captured him stood at attention on opposite corners of the conference room, confirming his suspicions that he had made it alive inside of the base in somewhat one piece.

Mark adjusted himself in his seat, bending forward to shake the cobwebs off; his movements did not make the guards jump at all, which meant they were highly trained to expect the unexpected, not the obvious. In his current state, he would not fight his way out of that conference room. Even if he got lucky, they would gun him down the second he exited the room.

Mark's best hope was to sit tight, gather as much information as possible, and pray that Dunbar made it out to contact Dustin, who would be there with some agents on the ground looking for him.

"Any chance a guy can get some water around here?" Mark asked.

Still no reaction, but he really did need water; the cottonmouth was getting to him, and he did not have anything other than the breakfast that morning. The door in front of him slid open, and his prayers went up in smoke.

Eric Dunbar was a little bit worse for wear, and in chained shackle restraints as he entered with another guard bringing up the rear.

"Sorry, man… I ran as fast as I could," a disheartened Eric said. "Everything just went black again…"

"It's okay, kid," Mark smiled. "It's okay."

The guard gave Eric a sharp tap on his shoulder with the butt of his rifle to keep moving forward, escorting him to one of the chairs where he sat. The guard then positioned himself by one of the vacant corners of the conference room.

A minute went by before Mark turned to Eric, asking a question.

"They give you water when you woke

up?"

"Uh… no," Eric answered, giving him a weird look.

Mark shook his head.

"Me neither, what a stingy joint."

A minute later, the door slid open one more time. The devil himself walked through with his entourage of Agent Slater and Ms. Barrett, bringing up the rear holding her tablet, still walking in her trademark pink flip-flops.

Mark stood up, ready for anything; Dunbar did the same, trying to mimic him in looking tough. Rosen, however, ignored Mark altogether and made a beeline straight for Eric.

Director Rosen walked up, grinning with his arms open.

"Eric! Eric!" he beamed. "You made it, Eric! You **finally** made it!"

Mark and Dunbar looked at each other with utter confusion as an approaching Director Rosen gave him a warm hug, rubbing his back. It was like some twisted scene from Willy Wonka and the Chocolate Factory... the Gene Wilder version.

Director Rosen let out a sigh of relief as if they were old college friends.

"Great to see you, Eric... finally great to see you in person."

"Yeah... okay," Eric answered with an unnerved smile, "who the hell are you?"

"Come on, Eric! Veterans Memorial Park." Rosen gestured with a hurt smile, trying to jog his memory. "The police chief's patrol car... candy store... City Hall."

Mark turned to a now livid Eric.

"City Hall?"

Dunbar bared his teeth.

"Son of a bitch had me drunk on a bench in my boxers wrapped around a goddamn blowup doll."

Mark shrugged.

"That's not too bad."

"It was a male doll," Eric seethed.

"Candy store is my favorite," Director Rosen beamed, wagging his finger while walking away. "Francine, the store owner, didn't know whether to laugh or be mortified with you sleeping in the jellybean pit in just a diaper and bib."

Rosen chuckled and sighed as he shook his head, clasping his hands with fatherly pride.

"Eric, you're like my Wile E Coyote, time and time again venturing up here looking for us, no matter what embarrassing, humiliating, or hysterically funny situation we left you in after we bag and tag you. Well... here you are, you've made it... you're not crazy, or some drunken reprobate. This is a covert government facility with the sole purpose of creating advanced weaponry, ensuring that the United States of America remains a Superpower in the world for like forever."

After finally giving Eric his golden ticket, Rosen sadly lowered his head. He inhaled deeply before releasing it.

"Unfortunately, as wonderful as it is to see you, Eric, you now know far too much."

"So, what," Eric nervously smirked, "this is where you blow my brains out?"

Rosen mockingly waved at him for making a ridiculous assertion.

"Come now, Eric... I told you... I like you, but we are going to do something to your brain... Ms. Barrett."

As the guards moved into position around Armitage, Ms. Barrett looked at her tablet, typing something in. Instantly, Dunbar's face went blank as he dropped to the floor a drooling catatonic mess. Mark lost it, attempting to rush the Director. The hindrance of his restraints allowed the guards to quickly overpower him.

"You son of a bitch," Mark roared, "what did you do to him?!"

"Nanites, Special Agent," Director Rosen sighed, "nanites."

"How do you think we were able to stay five steps ahead of him? After his third attempt to breach our perimeter, we decided it was best to keep close tabs on him. You were right; we did know you were coming. We were considering notifying the local authorities to deal with you, especially with the 'firepower' you came with but seeing how resourceful you've proven to be, we couldn't risk bringing more problems to our doorstep, so we decided to deal with you in house."

The Director walked over, kneeling beside Eric, rubbing his head.

"These are in their early stages, the programming for something so small to do complex things is complicated, but these were given the specific functions that allow us to both hear and see everything around him, as well as track him. In this case, they performed a high-precision lobotomy leaving him in his current yet somewhat functional vegetable state. One day they'll be able to permanently correct erectile dysfunction in men."

"You fucking monster!" Mark shrilled, fighting to get free.

Director Rosen got up and moved closer to Armitage with an irritated, bewildered look.

"I'm a monster?" he snapped at him. "You blaming me for this, Special Agent?"

Rosen pointed at him, baring his teeth.

"This is your entire fault. You brought a civilian to a highly classified government facility jeopardizing national security when given strict orders not to pursue this case any further. You did this to Eric. I could have you shot for treason."

"You tell me, where's the national security in murdering a family and kidnapping a little girl, you sick piece of shit?!" Mark spat back.

"An unfortunate necessary evil that had to be done to ensure the creation of the ultimate defense for this country, Special Agent."

Director Rosen somberly turned to Ms. Barrett.

"Please take Mr. Dunbar out of here… make sure he's found in a hiking accident. Make sure there's an anonymous payment to cover his medical expenses... make it look like a bunch of his conspiracy theorist followers pulled together on his behalf... looks good... pay off any debts he may have too... it's the least we can do for him."

"Yes, sir."

She motioned to two of the guards who shouldered their rifles. They walked over, grabbed Dunbar off the floor, and dragged him out as Ms. Barrett followed them.

"Also, bring in Ms. Dennison," Rosen added to his request, "might as well have her present since I hate repeating myself."

He turned to Mark.

"You want the James Bond treatment," Rosen said with narrowed eyes, "you got it."

A minute later, after Ms. Barrett walked out with Dunbar, the doors flew open again, with Sophia walking in. Her arms and hands still donned the huge shell-like restraints. She wore her battle-worn clothes from yesterday, flanked by four heavily armed Shock Troopers. The remaining members of the D.E.A.D. brought up the rear partially out of their gear. She appeared to be relatively calm and relaxed despite her current predicament.

"You alright?" a concerned Mark asked.

"Doing good... pretty... pretty... pretty good," Sophia nodded with her best Larry David impersonation. "You come here to rescue me?"

"Yeah," he nodded.

"Good job," she said with a sarcastic smile.

"If you two are done with the plot filling banter," Rosen interrupted.

"Allow me to quickly explain why you "Are here, and you..."

Rosen pointed to Sophia before pointing to Mark.

"... should not be here. Project EVOlution or the Olympus Project, as it was known back then, was started simultaneously with the

Manhattan Project in 1942."

"You mean 1939," Sophia snidely corrected.

Rosen turned to sneer back at her.

"Yes… give or take a year. You see, our government at that time realized that the Nazis were right… for us to remain a superpower in this world, we as a nation had to evolve not just on a technological level but on a physical level as well. So while one division was creating weapons of mass destruction in the light for all to see, this division was kept in the shadows working on creating advanced weaponry and biological technology to would make us forever independent of nuclear arms."

Rosen began to walk around.

"You see, after Hiroshima and Nagasaki, we came to the obvious realization that nuclear warfare is ineffective. Sure, you can drop a bomb and devastate an entire country… kill millions, but at the end of the day, you end up destroying billions upon billions of dollars in land and natural resources. At the end of the day, war is about making a profit… and it does not pay if you blow your profit to shit. Germ warfare and dirty bombs hold similar problems… that on top of the possibility of accidentally infecting your own troops and country is just too damn high… you don't need to see '28 Days Later' to reach such a conclusion."

"Love that movie by the way," Rosen stopped to add, "conventional warfare, though not as destructive, still costs and is one of the reasons why this country is now in astronomical debt due to our current leader putting two wars on a credit card. While our enemies, who don't even spend a quarter of what we currently spend on defense, still achieve very high and effective body counts. That's because as "hardcore" as we claim to be, our enemy is more hardcore with no fear of death and no remorse for who they kill as long as it's in the name of their god and achieving their objective. The only logical solution is to take death off the table in regards to us. That is why we have been feverishly working on upgrading the age-old tool that has won wars for centuries and is cheap… man."

"Another damn super soldier project,"

Mark muttered in disgust.

"Not 'another damn super-soldier' project," Director Rosen mocked Mark's voice. "A superhuman project... and to build the perfect superhuman, it's been concluded that it needs to be done on a genetic level. Drugs produce temporary changes with long-term, extremely harmful side effects... sometimes fatal. Cloning, although unethical to the bleeding masses, is one option but takes too damn long. Only in the embryo stage can we achieve successful gene alteration; we need effective soldiers like yesterday."

"But by creating a virus that when injected into the body would destroy, replicate, and mimic the functions of whatever cell it encounters... becoming a superior cell in every shape and form of the way... we could create a superhuman from the inside out in a matter of days," Director Rosen proudly said.

"Sounds like the perfect version of the AIDS virus," Sophia snorted.

"How's the saying go? Can't make an omelet without breaking a few eggs?" Rosen coldly said to her. "Unfortunately, the homosexual community got a bad rap due to an infected agent with an uncontrollable heroin habit, which we thought was suppressed in a time when idiots who did that shit shared needles. Back in the early stages of the project, there was a process each D.E.A.D. agent had to go through before they were injected with the virus, so it did not reject and kill them by attacking their immune system. Those that did not go through the process... well, you get the idea."

"We did our best to try and contain it, but in the end, we were forced to cover our tracks and cleanse the rest of the agents in our stable," Rosen sighed, shaking his head, "set our D.E.A.D. project back two years... but that's what happens when you recruit a junkie serial killer."

Sophia and Mark had mirrored looks of grimace, realizing what Director Rosen was talking about as they looked into the eyes of the remaining D.E.A.D.

"That's right, people... members of the D.E.A.D. are beta testers for a more superior and elite America," Rosen finally introduced them. "The Disavowed Extermination Assault Division was created after the Vietnam War. Once again, our government realized that there were monsters in this world so terrifying and so ruthless they could not be dealt with by regular soldiers, nor were regular soldiers capable of executing certain unnerving tasks needed to deal with such monsters."

Rosen motioned with pride.

"So we went looking for the most homicidal sociopaths in this country, made them dead on paper… virtual ghosts. Genetically altered, trained, and equipped them with the most highly advanced weaponry no one has ever seen before. We then sent them out with one command… to kill and slaughter any and anyone we saw as a threat to the national security of this country."

Mark motioned to the remaining members of the D.E.A.D. in total disgust.

"So you spit on real soldiers by turning these sick…"

#4, having enough of Mark's mouth, walked over and took the air out of his lungs with a gut shot, doubling him over. The enhanced punch was powerful enough to lift him off his feet, dropping him to his knees.

#4 went to pull him up for another one, but the Director waved him off.

"You put... this country's trust into the hands of these murderous scumbags," Mark coughed, getting it out.

Rosen walked over, patting #1 on the shoulder.

"These "murderous scumbags" are still Americans serving their country, and I trust them far more than I trust you. Especially since each of them is implanted with the same nanites that were injected into Mr. Dunbar."

"You're out of your goddamn mind..." Mark sneered.

"You're out of your goddamn mind," the Director mocked him again. "Aren't we playing the hypocrite... you were a soldier once, Special

Agent. You know firsthand the ravages of war. If
there were a way to save one soldier from dying
on the battlefield... if you could stop coffins with
flags from coming home, would you not take it?
I'm saving the economy and making sure all of
the young men and women we send into battle
come home alive and in one piece. You tell me,
wherein that am I out of my goddamn mind?"

"Because I fail to see the 'good' in **them**."

Mark motioned to the D.E.A.D.

"Turning a bunch of psychopaths into
unstoppable monsters who murder and butcher
innocent..."

"Dear God, stop... please stop with the
holier than thou speech."

Rosen shook his head, rubbing the bridge
of his nose.

"Who do you think was flying those
planes on 9/11? You think they were soldiers?
Studies show that the average 'terrorist' has seen
their first dead body or body parts up close and
personal by the age of five. Their playtime is

poking rotting corpses with sticks. That same terrorist has either killed or seen a person killed by the age of thirteen. While almost ninety-five percent of the U.S. soldiers have neither seen nor killed anyone in actual combat… why do you think many of them are in a 'f'ed' up state when they get back? As of 2008, we've had the largest suicide rate for servicemen since 1980, one hundred and twenty-eight confirmed suicides by serving Army personnel and forty-one by serving Marines."

"We figured out a long time ago that the perfect killer is not one that is trained or condition. It's one that is naturally born with the joy of killing," Director Rosen said, driving the point home. "I personally find it far more productive than having them out there cutting up little girls in the Midwest, wasting taxpayers' money on a trial, appeals, and accommodations for either a life or death sentence."

#4 raised his hand.

"I'm more partial to cutting up whores," he interjected.

Everyone turned, giving him a dull glare.

"Just saying," #4 shrugged.

Mark slowly got back to his feet.

"So this is what it's all about? Huh? Taking a dump on the Constitution? Murdering anyone who stands in the way of your quest to create a Master Race? Is there a color requirement or a dollar amount to get an 'S' on your chest?"

It was a tactic to buy some time to think of something to get them out of their obviously impossible situation.

"You think I'm Oliver North?"

Director Rosen laughed.

"You think we spent the last almost seventy years busting our asses to become gods to sell it off for some printed paper, metal, stones... oil?!"

Rosen's smirk transformed into a sneer, signaling that he was insulted.

"I should shoot you myself on mere principle... especially for implying that I'm a racist, my banker is black goddammit."

"I told you we're here working to save "American lives," if Russia wants to make their own Ivan Drago," Rosen chuckled, "let them figure it out for themselves along with the rest of the world. This one the good ole U.S. of A is strictly keeping for ourselves … which is why you should be rejoicing… a dawn of a new day Special Agent… soldiers like you use to be will soon be just like her."

Rosen walked over, motioning to Sophia.

"The only thing we'll need a military budget for is some cool, highly durable uniforms. Who needs to spend billions of dollars on tanks or fighter planes when you can drop five of her into a hot zone? You need to stop thinking of this as some stupid comic book hero-villain situation. Our enemies have promised that they would not stop if it takes five hundred years until they destroy this country. We're just making it where we're still standing five hundred years from now to laugh in their faces when they finally realize they've failed miserably and need to bow down."

"What we are doing right here, right now,

is for the good of this country," Director Rosen emphasized. "The only way to do that is to reclaim our spot as a true superpower of this world… by speeding up evolution and becoming the image of what we were modeled from… God Himself."

"So, my husband was butchered for what?" Sophia finally asked, joining in the conversation. "Exposing your quest to turn men into gods?"

Director Rosen sighed as he turned with an emotionless look to address the living goddess in the room.

"Your husband was 'executed' for betraying his country and his unit when he planned on leaking classified information about this division to the press."

"You're lying," Sophia smirked in disbelief. "What would…"

A wave of emotion ran through her as Sophia's legs buckled underneath her, dropping her on her rear.

Sophia slowly shook her head, wanting to believe it was all a lie, but the pieces to the puzzle, when formed, revealed the only clear picture; the Director's words placed a stamp on what she knew was the horrible truth… why Robert knew he was going to burn.

The Director walked within a safe distance of her, stooping down to look into her dazed, teary eyes.

"Finally figured it out, huh… the reason why there were only three in the room that night," Rosen sighed heavily, "was because #4 was sleeping right next to you… actually, his call sign was #2, but you already knew that, didn't you… deep down. I can tell you it wasn't my idea to make him a part of this outfit… that blame belongs to his daddy for breaking protocol to get him in here."

"The… General?" Sophia seethed with rage in between the tears that fell.

"Yes, the General. The job application requires that you are a one-hundred percent grade "A" murdering psychopath," Director Rosen explained, "but daddy took it pretty hard that his little Marine couldn't be all he could be anymore. So we were forced to make an exception… even had to wave off the nanite implant, which fucked up moral a bit… but he is the head of this division."

"I'm still just one pay grade below the general," Director Rosen sighed with a shrug. "Your husband did have promise. The virus repaired his injuries and enhanced him quickly… you wouldn't have known because he wore prosthetics to make him appear still injured. So while you thought he was going to rehabilitation, hanging out with friends, or screwing someone else. He was halfway around the world slaughtering whole regimes with the rest of us via our orbital jump program, which would take too long to explain… the initial plan was for him to eventually divorce you… but after the job in Ramadi…"

"Oh… god no," Sophia sobbed while bent over.

"Yeah… anyway… like I said… not a job for 'regular' people." Rosen huffed while shaking his head. "And as I predicted, his conscience kicked in. We found out he contacted this reporter about the Ramadi attack and exposing this operation. Over sixty years worth of good work, this whole division possibly being compromised by your dry snitching husband could not be ignored... not even by his own father."

The Director's reveal even made Mark sway in disbelief.

"No fucking way."

Rosen turned to Mark, acting somewhat surprised.

"Yeah, even I didn't think the old man had the sack to give the order. If it's any consolation, I wanted to get him done in the field. A random mugging gone bad... it was the old man's idea for you to take the hit... personally, I think the whole thing's bullshit... holding you responsible for his son's military downfall."

Rosen rose once again to his feet.

"But I'm not one for getting into family drama."

"So... my husband infected me that

night?" Sophia finally asked. "That is what made me like this?"

"Close, but no, doctor, we can't take full credit for what you are," Rosen said, waving her off. "You see, the current virus we created is only capable of enhanced attributes... strength, speed, endurance, healing within a couple of days. We were far from our final goal, which is you. Making sure we didn't duplicate the mistakes of the past, the new strain we created does not infect humans during sexual intercourse or through blood transfusion like the strain of old... we, however, did not foresee procreation and conception."

Mark jumped in, attempting to wrap his brain around what Rosen said.

"Wait, you're saying..."

"You're not the first superhuman, Ms. Dennison," Rosen revealed, "your daughter is."

He pointed at her, still sitting on the ground.

"The missing ingredient which we've tried

to avoid, but obviously couldn't get around was fresh new cells. The virus just didn't like consuming and replicating aged cells. We found that the younger the subject, the better the replication process, and as you can imagine, there's only so far we can "ethically" go when it comes to testing subjects. The night you and your husband did the deed was the night the virus within your husband found what it really wanted… fresh new cells to consume and replicate from."

"I don't understand," a confused Mark asked, "so how did she…"

"Our good Dr. Zimmerman's hypothesis is that some form of symbiosis occurred between her and her daughter during the nine months of pregnancy. It probably detected stress levels within you, which could have led to a miscarriage. I guess there is nothing more stressful than being on trial for the murder of your husband with a possible death sentence. Therefore, as a defense mechanism, it replicated all of your cells to ensure that you were able to carry her to term."

"It was also how we were able to figure

out your daughter was still alive," Rosen informed her. "There's no way you could be who you currently are, and she not survive."

Sophia did not answer him as she sat there looking at the ground.

"Very clever still how you were able to fool all of us, even the General."

Rosen wagged his finger at her in admiration.

"It wasn't because we didn't have the technology or the information within our grasp to find out. It was because the General didn't believe you were sneaky or smart enough to pull off something like faking your own daughter's death. Guess the joke was on him."

She still did not answer him as the Director continued.

"Currently, your genetic makeup is superior to hers because of all the trials and tribulations you went through, but from the blood sample we took from her, it shows she has the potential to reach your capabilities and far beyond you if 'pushed.'"

A smile formed on the Director's face.

"The cool part for us is that through the whole ordeal you endured, the cells within you can and will replicate all aged cells. But to answer your question, your daughter saved your life... not your husband."

Sophia remained silent, trying to wipe her face with the sleeve of her jacket, her dreads now covering any visible expression on her face. Now tired of the dramatics, Rosen clapped his hands together to "liven up" the atmosphere.

"Okay, now that we have done the whole James Bond tell-all master plan crap... time to get down to business."

Rosen snapped his fingers, pointing at Mark.

"You... we're going to put into a little cell for now. Until I decide whether it's best to lobotomize you or just kill you for being so damn nosey and unruly."

Rosen then pointed to Sophia.

"And you are going into a shiny egg-like container where we have a nice little sharp pointy device capable of piercing that thick hide of yours so we can take enough samples to make more of you."

"You're not going to do anything to him," Sophia said plainly, "and I'm not going anywhere."

Rosen decided to remind her of his trump card.

"Excuse me? You seem to forget we have your little girl."

"Yeah, you do… for all I know, she could be dead the minute I step into that 'egg.'"

Sophia shrugged.

"She could be dead right now, so what's to stop me from breaking these restraints and killing every last one of you in this room… except for him."

Sophia motioned to Mark, who nodded with appreciation.

"Thanks."

Rosen pointed to her.

"If you're expecting me to bring her in here as proof, you are out of your goddamn mind."

"No… I know you're too smart for that, but I also know everyone in here is terrified of what I am capable of." Sophia smiled. "Especially if I think I have nothing to lose… so here's the new deal."

Sophia gestured to Mark again.

"He lives. I see him walk out of here with my little girl… and you can do whatever you want with me… as you said… my genetic makeup is currently superior to hers… it's what you need to make more of me… so you really don't need her."

Director Rosen narrowed his eyes, pointing at her again.

"You promise to play nice?"

"Like a good little 'girl,'" Sophia said

coyly.

"Fine," Rosen sighed. "You got a deal."

Sophia glanced over to Mark, their eyes locking briefly; they knew as soon as they got her in that chamber she was dead, and they were definitely going to kill him.

#4 brazenly walked up to her, pulling her to her feet.

"Come on, sweetness, time to…"

It was over in one motion; the once standing #4 fell like a slab and lay dead at Dennison's feet with half his skull caved in and his neck snapped. Because Sophia's hands were still shackled with the heavy, high-powered restraints, she clearly killed #4 via a head-butt.

"Holy… fuck," #1 uttered.

Sophia shrugged her shoulders with a disturbingly innocent look on her face.

"Oops."

A beyond enraged #3 pulled out her

sidearm, walking up to Dennison to empty a set of rounds in her face.

"Holster your weapon, #3," Rosen ordered her.

"But, sir," she screamed, "this fucking bitch…!"

"Killed #4 in front of us… yeah, I saw that," Director Rosen said dryly. "Nobody told his dumb ass to get that close to her when she clearly said **on live T.V.** she wanted to kill the four of you… now holster your weapon before you send a ricochet around this place hitting me."

#3, with teeth bared, trembled as an evil, sinisterly grinning Sophia looked her dead in the eyes. She did not need to utter a word, as #3 knew all too well what she was thinking… two down.

Director Rosen stepped over the body of #4, moving #3 out of the way to face Sophia. He shook a finger at her.

"Do that again, and I'll have Mr. Slater

over there, cut your daughter's little head off
with a dull hacksaw… and have it play over this
facility's P.A. system for you to hear while you
tear this place apart searching for her. You
wouldn't want any more blood on your hands
like your friend Dr. Hampton or Lieutenant Scott
and his entire family."

Sophia's eyes widened in shock as she
gave off a nervous laugh; tears formed in
disbelief at what her ears were hearing.

"You're lying," Sophia fretfully snorted.
"You… you didn't…"

"Yes… I very much did," Rosen said with
a sarcastic sadness. "Dr. Hampton knew way too
much about your physiology, while Lieutenant
Scott knew way too much about the D.E.A.D.
than he already knew thanks to you."

"But Elizabeth… the children," she
shuddered.

"We knew his wife knew everything,
especially since she saw you ripping their door
off its hinges with your bare hands," Director
Rosen continued with his sardonic, gloomy act.

"The children were... unfortunate collateral damage... but we had to make their deaths look like an accident... and aren't there enough orphans in this country?"

Sophia lowered her head, weeping as her body shook; her restraints cracked and creaked with its feeble attempt to keep her secure. She wanted to slaughter everyone in the room save for Mark—saving the Director for second to last. Her daughter's safety kept her feeble and obedient.

"I'm going to kill you," Sophia whispered loud enough for him to hear her.

"Yeah... no... I don't think so," Rosen said dismissively.

"You forgot people know I'm here in Oregon; they're looking for me. There's evidence of what you did," Mark reminded him.

"No, they're not," Director Rosen laughed. "You went rogue Special Agent, you disobeyed direct orders, and now you're being hunted by local and state authorities."

Rosen strolled over to him, delivering his version of what could possibly happen to him.

"Whether you turn up captured or dead is entirely up to us. As far as evidence goes… you have none. I told you there were higher powers behind this, and you should just let it go. You think you'd learn your lesson after your daughter, Penny."

Mark's eyes widened as the Director's words knocked him on his ass.

"Read your psyche files after your mandatory sessions to see if you were still deemed fit to remain a field agent."

The Director shook his head in disgust.

"You just couldn't let that interrogation go to pick up your own daughter."

An irate Mark lunged at Rosen, screaming at the top of his lungs. The soldiers flanking him again overpowered him. Mark frothed at the mouth, clawing the air to get to Rosen.

"You son of a bitch, I'll kill you! I swear to god I'll kill you for saying her name!"

"Wow… everyone wants to kill me today," Director Rosen sarcastically shuddered, acting hurt. "Giving me a complex… get him out of here and get her prepped. We're already behind schedule with this nonsense."

CHAPTER 23

Mark was led down a hallway by a triple-armed guard detail passing a series of cells. His initial rage over the Director conjuring demons within him had subsided; he had to focus and figure a way out of there. If what the Director told him was correct about no backup coming because he was being labeled a rogue agent, there was a chance Mark was not leaving the mountain alive. He would be lucky if he ended up like poor Eric Dunbar, although his fate appeared to be worse than a death sentence.

One of the guards opened the cell while one trained his rifle on him as the third removed his restraints and shoved him into the cell. There was no chance of fighting his way out; he had to wait for another opportunity. The first guard aimed his rifle at him as the cell door closed. Mark listened to the fading of their heavy boots as they walked away.

He examined the cell, looking for a way out that clearly had none, when he heard a groan from the unit across. A fellow inmate meant a possible fellow ally.

"Hey! Hey! Anyone there?" Mark yelled. "You with me, buddy?"

He heard shuffling from behind the cell door as the person he attempted to communicate with struggled to get up. Two hands finally gripped the bars in front of the small cell door window as Mark's eyes widened while staring into a dead man's face.

"Doctor Hampton?" Mark said in disbelief, "they said they killed you!"

Poorly worked over but very much alive was Charles Hampton, from what Mark could judge from the limited view he had.

"Those bastards damn near tried," Charles groaned. "I was at home watching the news about what happened in D.C... next thing I knew, I passed out, and I woke up to a right cross from a big nasty looking son of a bitch with a horrible disposition."

Mark figured it must have been Slater; he fit the bill for cruel and unusual punishment.

"Why'd they take you?" Mark asked.

"They're looking for the samples and data I have on Sophia. She told me to destroy them, and I was, but something kept telling me it was too valuable to destroy."

Charles sighed, a bit disappointed he did not do what she asked.

"So I sent them off for storage, which, trust me, is not easy to do in an age where everything is tracked, and you're almost watched 24/7. It's probably why I'm still alive because I think they would have killed me if they found it."

"Like they killed Lieutenant Scott and his family," Mark said disgustingly.

"Are you serious?" Charles asked in disbelief.

"From what I can tell, yeah, and it looks like we're stuck here till we can find some sliver of a chance out of here," Mark said, running his hand across the door to his cell. "So how about passing the time by telling me why you helped Dennison fake her daughter's death?"

Charles drew a sigh, which only made him cough due to his battered ribs. Since his fate was clearly up in the air, it was time for Agent Armitage to hear his confession.

"Four months into her pregnancy, she started to have nightmares, reoccurring dreams of her daughter as an infant crying hysterically looking for her while walking around aimlessly in a warzone littered with corpses wearing nothing but just a bloody American flag. She said every time she had the dream, it was the same, except the flag got bloodier and bloodier, the bodies started to look like friends and family and were stacking higher, and her cries became louder to the point of shrills. In her culture, recurring dreams were omens... she was sure that the dream meant she had to keep her daughter away from the General at all costs."

"Her father-in-law," Mark confirmed.

"General Matheson's entire family legacy is military, dating back to the Civil War, I think," Charles said with a nod. "All four branches and all serving in every known conflict. He's the only one ever to achieve the rank of four-star General. She knew if he had his way, he'd influence her daughter to join the military, and she didn't want him to do to her what he did to Robert."

"She married a soldier but hated the military?" Mark asked.

"Exact opposite… she respected the military a lot, and she loved Robert, but she knew that he wasn't meant to be a soldier," Charles explained. "Physically, he had all the makeup of one, but it wasn't in his heart, she said. Robert was just doing it to please his old man; he loved and respected him to no end."

Charles shrugged.

"He figured he'd do his four years, have it under his belt, get his dad off his back. Get his trust fund and start the custom car restoration company he wanted. Who knew 9/11 was around the corner. Let it be said he wasn't the same man coming back."

Charles coughed as he clutched his still-aching ribs.

"During his first tour. Sophia said every
time she spoke to him, it felt like his soul was
dying bit by bit. I saw it too in a video message
he sent, but she hung in there with him praying
for the day his tour of duty would be over, then
the General 'somehow' got him to enlist again…
'Mathesons are in till it's over… till every man
comes home,' and all that bullshit."

Mark listened with disgust because it was
apparent the General and he had similar traits,
while Charles went on with his story.

"Sophia wanted children… but she didn't
want to have them with Robert over there, so she
waited. You can imagine what happened when
she found out he reenlisted and was going back
over… they argued every day. General Matheson
paid her a visit to 'educate' her on being a
'proper' military wife. She had a couple of
uneducated words for him that day… anyway…
Robert went back over, and then he got injured."

Mark knew what happened after that from
his conversation with the Director.

"Sophia said she'd rather die with her baby and burn in hell than let the General have her, and if I didn't help her, she'd find a way to kill herself and the baby because she wasn't having an abortion."

Charles swallowed with a rattled look in his eyes.

"I knew she'd do it, and I knew she knew how to do it. So we got an attorney to help appoint me as her doctor. I was also given power of attorney to facilitate a closed adoption for her when the baby was born and found a very nice family. We told no one what we were doing... when she went into labor, we told no one. I delivered the baby and signed a birth certificate giving the child the adopted parents' name and then a death certificate telling everyone else the baby was a stillborn due to complications and that Sophia wanted the body cremated by her wishes. It was a million to one chance, but everyone bought it. We probably wouldn't have pulled it off without her money."

Mark furrowed his brows at Charles' revelation.

"Her money?"

"The joint accounts concerning her and Robert were all frozen," Charles recalled, "but Sophia had almost over a million-and-a-half dollars in a personal savings account before Robert was murdered. Before he went to Iraq, he paid off the house and both the cars. Sophia didn't want for money… they were living comfortably off his trust fund and military pay.

She took her paychecks from Memorial Hermann and just saved a bulk of them. She also had investments and stock options. Robert advised her to keep it in a separate bank due to all the identity theft going on. Her name was also in the house with Robert. That is why her killing Robert for money was all bullshit. Anyway, she liquidated it all and put me in charge of using it to pay for or pay off whoever needed to be paid. She spared no expense to keep her daughter hidden from General Matheson."

"Well, I got news for you, Doc," Mark revealed, drawing a heavy breath. "These sons of bitches murdered that nice little family you found, and they have the little girl."

"What?!" He coughed profusely. "Why?!"

"The little girl is actually the first superhuman," Mark informed Hampton. "Dennison inherited her powers from her child while she was still in her womb somehow... her husband Robert was recruited by his father, General Matheson, to become a part of this superhuman death squad known as the D.E.A.D., which are apparently beta testers for a much larger superhuman project. They killed him for trying to expose the truth and framed Dennison for his murder."

A stunned Charles braced himself against the door, fighting to stand up while absorbing the news that gut-checked him.

"Oh god, I know what her dream was about...the little girl, the bodies... she killed all those people shedding blood for this country."

"What?!" Mark asked.

Charles began to babble while forming calculations in his head.

"If what you're saying is true... Wait! It all

makes sense! That's why Robert didn't want to sleep with Sophia when he got back!"

Mark attempted to keep up with Charles' ranting.

"Say what? Make sense, man!"

"For months after getting back from Iraq and the hospital after his injury, he refused to touch her; Sophia thought it was due to the P.T.S.D. Then she thought he was cheating on her. He was probably afraid whatever was within him would be passed onto the child!"

"How do you know they weren't having sex?" a mystified Mark asked.

"She's my best friend," Charles returned. "She tells me everything. Anyway, that little girl has the potential to be a thousand times more powerful than Sophia if nurtured and developed... possibly god-like."

"I don't think they're looking to develop her abilities," Mark muttered while examining the cell door again, "they seem more interested in stealing them... like they plan to do to her mother."

"That's even worse! Wait, Sophia's here?!" Charles said, officially flipping out.

"Yeah, she's here," Mark confirmed. "They plan on harvesting her cells for the virus so they can make more of her."

Charles pounded against his cell door in frustration.

"We've got to get out of here. Doesn't someone know you're here?!"

Mark sighed, sadly remembering Eric Dunbar.

"Someone knows what state I'm in, but they won't find the exact location, not in time. The person who could have given them my location was lobotomized right in front of me… for now, we just have to sit, wait, and pray for a miracle… if they still do exist."

~ ~

Sophia had already settled into her confines in a different section of the base. They

were a lot bigger and cleaner than her cell at
Mountain View. The jail cell was constructed of
some pure metal alloy: titanium, tungsten, or
both. The door to her confines was massive and
vault-like. The only two sitting areas were the
metal toilet on the other side of the room and the
folding steel cot attached to the wall; there were
no windows.

As instructed, Sophia removed all her
clothes and showered under supervision, which
was uncomfortable. She slipped on an extremely
skintight red, white, and black sci-fi bodysuit
complete with attached booties that they put in
her cell. There were three black metallic ports on
each of the arms and legs and four on the suit's
spine. She figured they were the insertion points
for the injection needles taking the samples from
her, which would be one hell of a trick,
considering there was not much out there that
could pierce her skin these days.

Sophia looked around the bare, sterile
white room with the typical fluorescent medical
lights. The only other color beside her and her
little-to-the-imagination bodysuit were the four
black orbs planted in each corner of the room,

watching her every move.

Slowly, Sophia strolled over to the heavy sliding door she came through. She placed her hand on it, pushing forward a bit, making a handprint in the metal. The force of her push made the metal door emit a hard creaking sound. It caused the four orbs to turn red with four beams locked on her. She removed her hand from the door as the rays remained on her, tracking her for another fifteen seconds before shutting off and returning to normal.

Even if she was fast enough to smash through the door, as explained by the guard who led her into her cell, there were motion sensors and cameras throughout the entire facility, most importantly, the hallways.

Sophia also did not know where they were holding her daughter, which meant she was a prisoner again for the time being.

She pulled down the folding metal cot attached to the wall, rolling onto it. Surprisingly, it held her weight; she closed her eyes and concentrated on Charles, Ken, Liz, and their children, Sammy and Ashley.

Sophia tried to focus on their good times: Charles and her graduating medical school together, Ken's speech at her and Robert's wedding, Liz's pregnancy with Sammy, who she held in her arms, followed by Ashley.

Various other memories flooded her head, causing tears to pour; she curled up into a ball and wept bitterly. They were all dead now because of her and the mess she brought to their doorsteps.

It was memories of Charles that broke her heart. He never gave up on her; he never stopped believing in her, and Charles was always there whenever she needed him, even when she pushed him away and did not feel the same way about him that she knew he felt for her.

She was trying to protect and keep him away from all hell and madness, and she failed. She wailed as memories of the little time they spent together flooded her head, even the stupid bear mace incident.

"Charlie… I'm sorry… I'm so sorry… oh god… I'm sorry," Sophia sobbed.

Her best friend was gone because of the lies and deception of her husband, someone she thought she knew but did not. Memories of special moments and their deep love were mixed with the imagination of the nights he supposedly left to hang out with friends or needed time to himself but was off halfway across the world, murdering innocent people: men, women, and children.

Destroying their lives for no reason, just like the D.E.A.D. destroyed hers, all for his father's legacy.

Uncontrollable sobbing turned to blind rage as she rolled off the cot, screaming. Sophia ripped it from off the wall and flung it across the cell, smashing it into the opposite wall. She then turned and proceeded to hammer the metal wall. The force of her blows sent shockwaves throughout the facility; the orbs became red again, locking onto her, but she did not care.

"You son of a bitch!" Sophia screamed at the top of her lungs. "You stupid goddamn **lying** son of a bitch! I hate you! I hate you! I hate you!"

Blow after blow, Sophia rained down on the wall, leaving dents the size of craters. Her last punch pierced the metal wall, going straight through and hitting mountain rock. It was then she remembered her daughter. The night she gave birth to her, Charles was the one who delivered her.

Sophia remembered that she only cried a little when she came out, her little lungs, no doubt, quickly adjusting to the harsh air because of her genetics. She looked up at her as if she knew Sophia was her mother.

Sophia held her all night while the child looked at her until she fell asleep. The next day, Charles took her away to her new parents; she cried for almost the entire week. Sophia pulled her hand out of the wall, looking at her fist, and remembered what the Director said, that her daughter had saved her life.

Her husband was dead. Hating him now would solve nothing. No amount of vengeance would bring him, Charles, or anyone else back. Her daughter was alive, out there, and she needed her.

Sophia walked over to a bare, unscathed wall, sat down, and waited for her time.

~ ~

From the command deck of the facility run by various computer analysts and technicians, Director Rosen watched on the massive flat screen with satisfaction of the subsiding of Sophia's temper tantrum inside of her cell along with Dr. Zimmerman, Ms. Barrett, 3#, and #1, the two remaining members of the D.E.A.D.

"See... just a little moody." Director Rosen chirpily said, motioning to everything being okay. "Probably her time of the month. How goes preparation, doctor?"

"Based on the current D.N.A. sample we have of her, I am sure we will be able to extract viable blood samples of the superior, more compatible virus that can be used on future test subjects," Dr. Zimmerman confirmed.

"Excellent... when can we expect to begin the procedure?" Director Rosen asked.

Dr. Zimmerman estimated off the top of

his head.

"Another half-hour of calibrations, and we should be ready."

"Sir, General Matheson is on hold," Ms. Barrett announced. "He wishes to speak with you."

Director Rosen massaged his nose for the last person he wanted to speak to.

"Put him on the screen," he sighed.

General Matheson appeared on the screen with his usual stone-faced demeanor, wearing his service uniform.

"Report," he snapped.

"Procedure is scheduled as planned, sir," Director Rosen reported. "Subject is cooperating, and we should have samples within the next hour or so."

"After the debacle here, I have been forced to put out your fires, Rosen," General Matheson said distastefully. "Which directs light to a project not yet ready to be revealed, which also directs light… to… me, and I don't like the spotlight."

Rosen defended his position.

"Well, sir, with all due respect, this wouldn't have happened if…"

"Do not preach to me about past failures Rosen," General Matheson ordered, cutting him off. "I am a man who moves forward, and the fact is my bloodline was able to produce the results you failed to deliver all of these years; now… what of the child?"

"Safe," Director Rosen said flatly.

"Take care, Rosen… that is my granddaughter in your custody," Matheson warned. "Anything happens to her, and I would not want to be you. As for her mother, when you're done stripping the bitch… get rid of her… are we clear?"

Rosen again flatly acknowledged the General's orders.

"Crystal, sir… crystal."

The General signed off as Rosen massaged the bridge of his nose again, feeling another migraine coming on.

"I swear," Director Rosen groaned, "that man needs more fiber in his diet."

"Sir... after the procedure shall I begin scanning new candidates for the D.E.A.D. project," Ms. Barrett asked, "now that #2 and #4 are deceased?"

Director Rosen dismissively glanced at the other two remaining members.

"Negative. The D.E.A.D. project will be put on hold pending the trial tests of the new virus."

#3 glared at #1, then got up, walking off.

"I'm going to take a piss," she yelled out.

The Director scowled, shuddering, his face turning quickly to watch her leave before looking back at Ms. Barrett.

"Did she really need to televise that?"

CHAPTER 24

She sat on the floor, humming a little tune, something her mother used to hum to her as a child to help her sleep. She remembered being in a similar situation almost seven days ago, but that woman sitting paralyzed with fear was no longer there. Sophia waited with a lazy calmness for them to come for her.

As the door slid open, she did not even flinch nor look up at the sound of heavy boots filling the room as two heavily armed guards and two lab techs in light white versions of the guards' armor walked in. One of them, holding the restraints they had on her before, was visibly quaking with distress. One of the heavily armored shock troopers cautiously approached her, casting a shadow.

"Dennison… it's time," the first guard announced.

She rolled her eyes and then sprang to her feet, causing everyone in the room to coil back in either fear or precaution. She extended her arms without order, waiting for the jittery lab tech to approach her and fasten the gravity pressure restraints. The hum of the device meant it secured her again.

It did not stop her from moving so fast she was literally nose-to-nose with the lab tech.

"Boo," she whispered.

The lab tech let out a slight squeal as he fell to the floor while the guards in the room trained their rifles on her. It could have been that even though she was in restraints before, she killed an enhanced soldier with a head-butt to the skull.

"Why so jumpy boys?" Sophia asked with a smile. "Let's get this show on the road."

Sophia left the cell with her escorts, who rushed to keep up with her. The guards flanked her while the lab techs hung back a safe distance until they led her into an elevator, which took them several levels further down into the facility. The lab techs hugged the elevator walls until it opened up, and she was led out.

Sophia moved quickly, briskly, as she seemed to want to get there in a hurry. Her swift and constant stride forced her entourage to move double time with her. She marched with purpose as if drawn to the location. Unlike before, where she walked with fear and dread of the end, it appeared as if she looked forward to it, almost welcomed it. A smile practically formed on her face until she hit that final turn.

At least a yard from Sophia's destination stood #3, leaning against a wall, waiting for her. She appeared to have a dazed look, but when she turned to look at Sophia, there was pure hatred in her eyes, the type one would find in a demon. She had a walk as if she was drunk, but it appeared to be more with insanity.

"What the hell are you doing here?" the second guard asked.

#3 did not hear the guard's words as she

focused strictly on Sophia.

"How's it feel?"

"#3, answer me!" the second guard ordered again.

It was as if only she and Sophia were in that hallway alone. She looked like she had the shakes as she edged closer to Sophia, intending to pounce on her. Sophia smirked, wishing she would.

#3 asked her question in more detail.

"How's it feel to know that your Kill Bill vengeance riding off into the sunset bullshit with that little turd of yours was all for nothing? That in a couple of minutes, you're going to be nothing but period lumps in a Petri dish?"

"#3, cut the shit and stand down... now!" the first guard ordered.

Sophia knew what was going on; it appeared the sadistic bitch had a soft spot, and she struck it when she killed #4. It was the only apparent explanation for her erratic behavior.

"I wanna know how it feels to know that despite all your so-called strength and power, you failed to avenge that two-bit traitorous lying sack of shit for a man that I carved up like a turkey."

The second guard moved forward to get into #3's way.

"#3, I told you…!"

She violently kicked in his kneecap, breaking his leg in half, and then grabbed him, launching his skull first into a nearby wall, where he fell into a heap. A faint groan revealed that he was barely alive. The first guard quickly raised his rifle with laser sighting at #3's skull as the now terrified lab techs stood there unsure what to do. She was almost within striking distance- taunting Sophia.

"You're going to go through those doors right now, where these lab geeks are going to tear you apart bit by bit till there is barely anything left," #3 hissed. "I might just go do the same to that little girl of yours. Maybe I'll ask the Director if I can keep what's left your brat after they're done stripping her of what they need. I could be her mommy... dearest."

Sophia knew what she was after but would not give it to her; instead, she gave her the answer she was not expecting.

"You trying to get a rise out of me, little girl? You don't think I don't know what's going on here? You think you're some soldier? You believe they'll pin a Medal of Honor on you when all of this is done? You're an attack dog... less than a mongrel... another one of this country's dirty little secrets, a shit stain, due for a deep treatment. Nothing more than a number easily replaced and will soon be obsolete if they're successful in making more of me. No one will know who you are or be told the so-called 'deeds' you've done for your country."

Sophia leaned in closer, whispering, looking #3 in her soulless eyes.

"Yeah, I know I might die here today because your boss wants my very valuable DNA. But you... you're going to die because you'll now be worthless to him... just like your man, who I killed in front of **you**."

Sophia smirked.

"Tell me… do they have a nice little coffin for him all wrapped in a flag with a twenty-one gun salute? Or is he lying on a slab somewhere waiting to be chucked into a furnace-like the garbage he is?"

#3, visibly enraged, moved closer, baring her teeth. Her attempt to get under Sophia's skin backfired; Sophia was the one dousing salt into her open wounds. She wanted to drive her carbon-fibered dagger into her skull repeatedly if she knew it would not break on impact against her ultra-dense skin.

#3 leaned forward for one final verbal assault.

"When the police report said forty-one stab wounds, they were very accurate," her fuming voice quivered.

"And that little neurotoxin, the one that paralyzed his muscles but kept his nerve receptors all intact, it didn't just make him feel everything… it amplified it… like a cat's tongue. Poor little Marine tried to scream and cry out your name as you sat across the room from him while I did him… do you know he pissed himself? Your doctor friend had more balls than him… at least he only squealed like a pig when I slit his throat from ear to ear, but nothing gave me greater joy than dressing up and pretending to be you. The bank… the ATM… the drive to Oklahoma… the hotel… being in your skin… wearing your clothes… and imagining the look on your face when you saw yourself doing all those horrible things and not remember doing any of them. I almost creamed myself thinking about it."

Sophia leaned in closer, locking eyes with #3. Her voice became a growling whisper.

"The only reason you're still standing and breathing is because there's still…"

Before she could finish her sentence, #3 fired a glob of spit into Sophia's face. She grinned and braced herself, waiting for a reaction to see if she would lunge at her.

Sophia looked at her with a flat, blank, emotionless glare as she allowed the saliva to run down her face.

"Still, two more left," Sophia continued to say. "The other one... and the Director... before you die... and when you die... I promise you... you will suffer... and I will watch you die screaming."

Director Rosen's voice boomed over the PA system in the hallway.

"As much as I find this little verbal catfight entertaining, #3... get your narrow white ass out of the way before I turn that dumb blonde skull of yours into mush right in front of her... now."

A scowl of embarrassment was plastered over #3's face as additional guards and a med team showed up to care for the guard she had severely injured. She took her time lazily, moving out of the way and keeping her eyes locked with Sophia.

Once again, Sophia continued to her destination with eight guards and the original two lab techs. As the double doors slid open, it was, as she expected, another white-tiled sterilized room with those god-awful operating room lights.

She did not expect the massive black-chromed egg in the middle of the room. At least six technicians flocked around it for last-minute checks. They all stopped briefly to gaze at her, the superhuman they would soon harvest.

They came to their senses one by one, quickly returning to readying the egg-like chamber. Written on Sophia's face was "Let's get this over with," while her heart pounded against her chest plate. Being superhuman did not mean her fear was gone, that it would not eventually set in. Her continuation to advance was purely motivated by someone depending on her.

As they finally neared the pod, it cracked open in the middle, emitting a frosty smoke that bellowed out as the two halves slid open. Sophia saw a metallic cross table inside similar to the lethal injection table back at the Mountain View Unit, only this one had a metallic coiled harness and restraints for each of her limbs. For her head, there was a helmet comprised of a metallic crystalline material attached to a cylinder.

Just as she suspected, some ports aligned with the ports on her bodysuit. Sophia also noticed that the egg was attached to a cylinder base, leading down to an opening in the floor in the egg's shape itself. Her guess was once she was strapped in, the egg would close, lowering her down somewhere.

One of the technicians who escorted her to the room finally removed the restraints, allowing her to wipe #3's spittle from her face with her forearm and nurse her wrists, which had to endure kilotons of pressure.

An armored Shock Trooper tapped her back with the butt of his rifle.

"Get in," he ordered.

She ignored his order, still nursing her wrists, planted in place, refusing to move.

The Shock Trooper Guard tapped her much harder while raising his voice.

"I said get…"

Sophia responded with a vicious backhand to his helmet, not even looking at him as she sent him flying across the room into a wall before falling into a heap on the floor. Rifles again trained on her as technicians backed away to the nearest wall in fright. She continued to nurse circulation back into her wrists. It was one final act of defiance.

The Director's voice came over the PA system.

"Is there a problem?"

"You're damn right there's a problem," Sophia said, "I'm not moving an inch until I see my end of the bargain fulfilled."

"Very well," Director Rosen sighed.

One of the room monitors came to life, showing Mark Armitage holding Sophia's daughter's hand. Sophia's smile appeared then quickly disappeared as she saw the troubled expression on Armitage's face while the little girl looked around aimlessly without an apparent care in the world. The screen panned out to show them surrounded by Shock Troopers pointing their rifles at them; off to the side was Agent Slater in his own light Shock Trooper armor gear, brandishing a sizeable machete-like blade.

The remaining guards standing in the room with her swarmed in front of the only door blocking it. Sophia, now enraged, prepared to rush the entrance she came through, tearing whoever was in her way apart.

"That's not the deal!" Sophia howled.

"Go ahead... try it," Director Rosen dared her. "She will be dead by the time you get through those guards and tear those doors open."

"You backstabbing son of a bitch!" Sophia screamed, "That was not the deal!"

"Well, I am changing the deal!"

Rosen snapped back at her, going into a rant.

"You now see your daughter alive and, well, the deal now is you will step into that egg to ensure that her life continues. Frankly, I am tired of this drama."

"I am tired of the General... your dead husband, and I am tired of you standing in the way of progress. I have waited long enough and shall wait for no... more. So you have until I count to three, and then you can rip through those guards and tear open those doors because the next thing you will see is the guards on the monitor opening fire on your daughter and Agent Armitage. Followed by Agent Slater, lopping off your daughter's head with the blade in his hand, ensuring she can't regenerate and become like you.

Tear this place apart afterward; I really don't care because later, you will have to live with the guilt that your selfishness caused the gruesome death of your daughter. You alone will live with that guilt for the rest of your life, apparently for a long life span. So, now, the chamber… or mourning over a headless bullet-riddled corpse? One…"

Sophia quickly held her hand up.

"All right! All right…"

She wiped away tears of frustration and turned, giving in; there was nothing to think about. Her life was worthless in comparison to the life of her daughter, and she did not want Agent Armitage's blood on her hands either.

~ ~

She did not know that Armitage and a very much alive Charles Hampton remained locked in his cell. Mark Armitage removed his face to reveal one of the Director's many agents standing in for him behind the cameras. The Shock Troopers lowered their weapons upon Agent Slater's command.

"Feed has been looped… all clear," a technician reported.

Agent Slater walked over to the little girl, still brandishing the blade, looking down at her with a smile.

"See?" Slater smiled. "Now that wasn't so bad, was it? All make-believe."

The little girl did not answer him as she looked around with a fretful look on her face, unclear why she was in this place alone without her parents and with no knowledge that her maternal parent was about to lay down her life for her.

~ ~

Back at the lab, Sophia, with no assistance, stepped in and laid on the table. She could feel the cold of the steel through the thin skintight layer she had on, making the hairs on the back of her neck stand up. Cautiously, the technicians positioned her body, aligning the ports of her suit to the ones on the table.

They called on some of the guards to assist in moving her due to her immense weight. As her external ports fell into the table's interior ports, a technician flipped open a panel on the table, typing in a sequence code activating the table, which locked all of the ports together, fastening her to the table via the bodysuit. The guards who assisted the technicians joined the rest of their squad, watching their guns partially lowered as they applied the harness, restraints, and finally, the helmet itself.

Lights on the helmet, the harness, and restraints came on, serving a double function of keeping her restrained during the procedure while continually checking her vital signs.

~ ~

At his observation deck, Director Rosen

smiled as Doctor Zimmerman oversaw the final preps before the operation.

"You see, everything is fine," Director Rosen said, gesturing to Ms. Barrett. "All she needed was a little motivation."

"Would you have done it?" Ms. Barrett nervously asked. "Murder the General's granddaughter like that?"

"Yes, I would have," he said with no hesitation.

The fact that Rosen did not flinch or pause to think about the question unnerved Ms. Barrett; she tried her best to hide it.

"Does it trouble you, Ms. Barrett? Are you having thoughts?" Rosen asked.

Ms. Barrett answered with almost no hesitation.

"No, sir... not at all."

"Very good," Rosen chirped. "I do value your services, wouldn't want you to miss another Administrative Assistant's day. Dr. Zimmerman, whenever you are ready."

"Subject is secure, vital signs are online and monitored," Dr. Archifeld Zimmerman confirmed and ordered. "Activate fields and prepare to close and lower the containment unit."

~ ~

The lights on the helmet, harness, and restraints brightened as Sophia felt an immense pressure on her skull, wrists, ankles, and chest. It was similar to the field in the bonds she had on but a lot more powerful.

"No wonder the damn country is going broke," Sophia muttered. "They're making crazy shit like this."

It was a joke to take her mind off what would happen next. She knew what they were planning. They needed actual blood samples and fresh DNA to extract a pure form of the virus within her. To do that, they would have to pierce her near-impenetrable skin, and with no anesthesia on the planet capable of knocking her out, it meant she was going to feel every bit of it, which told it would hurt… a lot.

As the hatch closed and the pod lowered into the floor, with tears flowing from her eyes, Sophia said one final prayer with the time she had left.

"Lord... thank you for taking me this far... thank you for letting me see my little girl. Thank you for giving a sinner like me a little more time, even though she had vengeance in her heart. Now I ask of you one more favor... if my road ends today... please spare my little girl this same fate. Please..."

"Begin superheating syringes and moving them into position," Dr. Zimmerman directed.

Sophia did not know the pod she was in descended closer to the atomic fusion reactor, which powered the entire facility. The reactor's power channeled into the cylinder and into the pod itself, where it superheated spike-like syringes within the ports of the table. The power of the reactor would also deliver the force needed to drive the needles into her body. She could feel the heat building up from behind the table.

"Iridium syringes have been plasma superheated to 3.2 million degrees Fahrenheit, estimated 85 tons of psi force for penetration," the technician reported to Dr. Zimmerman.

"Initiate injection… now," Dr. Zimmerman ordered.

A button press cast Sophia into hell; white pain could not describe her sheer agony as the plasma-superheated syringe spikes pierced her arms, legs, and back, each straight down to the bone. It was so excruciating that she could barely scream or cry; tears poured down her eyes as she whimpered while her body shook violently from the spikes roasting her body from the inside.

"Doctor… extraction syringes have successfully pierced subject's skin," informed the lab technician. "Blood pressured has spiked to 200 over 190."

"Super-cool syringes," Dr. Zimmerman directed, "and then proceed with the sample extraction."

"Yes, sir," the lab tech acknowledged.

~ ~

With another couple of computer

keystrokes, Sophia went into spasm-like convulsions as the spikes within her body went from heat almost equivalent to the sun to sub-zero temperatures; she could see her breath with every exhale. She wished she could blackout, but her regenerative healing kept her awake through the ordeal as it fought to heal her.

She then felt fluid sucked from her body at a high-speed rate, each syringe attached to a thick tube that ran from the table in the pod, through the cylinder it was attached to, down to a secured lab filling five two-gallon canisters of her blood.

~ ~

"Samples successfully being extracted," the lab tech reported, "subject's blood pressure has lowered, but remains slightly elevated."

"Extraordinary," Dr. Zimmerman said to the Director. "She has already filled up each of the canisters half way… her regenerative capabilities are unparalleled."

An emergency message sensor appeared on a lab technician's screens in charge of periodically monitoring the pod.

"Sir! Something is dissolving the syringes within her body," the lab maintenance technician nervously informed.

An on-screen X-ray scan showed that the Iridium syringes, one of the hardest metals known to man, appeared slowly eroding within her body.

Dr. Zimmerman turned to the Director.

"Her body is going into defense mode, trying to protect itself. She will soon become stronger than the Iridium in her body."

The Director exhaled before taking control.

"I think we've got enough out of her, don't you think, doctor? End the extraction process and reheat the syringes to maximum capacity."

"Yes, sir," obeyed the lab tech.

Ms. Barrett turned away, officially uncomfortable with the scene as Sophia let out a blood-curdling scream to near insanity as the spikes were once again reheated to scorching temperatures, searing her once again from the inside of her body. Instinctively, she fought to break free. The restraints delivering kilotons of pressure to keep her restrained were now creaking and cracking as if they were about to snap any second despite her weakened state.

"Fire the cranial spike and flood the chamber," Rosen ordered.

"Firing spike, sir," one of the lab techs announced.

~ ~

In an instant, Sophia's eyes widened and dilated as a heated spike from the table's headrest fired through the helmet and pierced the back of her skull into her brain tissue. Her body went limp and consumed by the fusion reactor's raw energy below, now channeled into the pod for her destruction.

Only her bodysuit, designed to withstand the heat nearly equivalent to the sun, remained intact as the rest of her burned slowly down to the muscle and eventually to the bone. It was unclear if she felt anything after the spike pierced her skull.

~ ~

"Subject's heart in cardiac arrest... subject has now flat-lined," the lab technician reported. "Heart Failure at 13:56... Officially brain dead at 13:58... The subject is officially deceased at 13:59 PM."

"Shall we stop and extract more samples?" Dr. Zimmerman asked.

Director Rosen took a breath, finally glad the ordeal was over, before answering.

"No need. We have acquired all of the samples we require, and we have Dennison's daughter... incinerate all remaining material."

Dr. Zimmerman motioned to the lab technician to increase the atomic fusion incineration to quicken the destruction of Sophia's remains.

With a "somber" look, Director Rosen turned his back to the screen. He bowed his head.

"Thank you, Dr. Dennison. Your contribution to your country will not be forgotten."

HEARTBEAT...

Director Rosen's head slowly rose, thinking either his hearing was off or he heard feedback from the audio speakers. Still, it happened repeatedly, becoming more powerful with each second.

"What's going on?"

Rosen asked, visibly shaken and disturbed.

"What is going on?"

"Heartbeat and vitals have returned and are increasing, systems show subject is regenerating rapidly, atomic fusion is not destroying her cells anymore," the first lab tech nervously fired off.

"Sir! The reactor is losing power!" rattled off a second lab technician.

"Losing power?! How?! By how much?!" Director Rosen frantically demanded to know.

"By forty percent!" the second lab tech reported. "The subject is..."

"I know what the subject is doing!" Director Rosen yelled back at him. "Cut the power and tell me how she is doing it!"

"We're... we're trying, sir!" he frantically said. "Initiating emergency shutdown parameters!"

Director Rosen looked over to a now terrified, yet fascinated, Dr. Zimmerman, with his knuckles in his mouth. He muttered to himself as he ran a rainstorm of calculations on how life found a way again. The Director marched over to the doctor, grabbing him by his arm to shake him back to reality to find out what was going on.

"Doctor... what is going on? You confirmed that the cells could be killed by high plasma-based energy... fusion energy... because it did not have a solid form for her cells to analyze and defend against... what is happening?!"

"It needed time... and we gave it to it... it

needed time…" Dr. Zimmerman rambled.

Rosen feverishly shook him to his senses.

"What needed time?!"

"Her body… we… we got it all wrong…" Dr. Zimmerman hysterically chuckled.

The Director slammed him up against one of the supercomputers in the room.

"Make sense, man!"

The doctor timidly looked up, explaining to him,

"We… we thought that her brain had developed an independent higher function calculating and instructing the rest of the body to create defenses, so if we destroyed the brain, her body would die, but that's not the case… each of her cells has its own higher function. Like organic versions of our nanites but far more advanced, they work as a collaborative network, which means even if the vital organs fail, the functioning cells work together continuing repairs and building defenses."

"But why the massive energy drain?"

"It… it needed time to analyze the threat attacking it," Dr. Zimmerman continued. "Don't you see? The cells break down the material to analyze it so that it can build future defenses. Plasma rounds are pure energy, unlike a bullet slug lodged in her body. The second the plasma struck her body, it caused damage, burning and killing cells, and then dispersed, not giving her living cells time to analyze the attack and determine the best solution to defend against it. Energy, however, still has some mass to it! We've exposed her body to enough of it via the spikes and flooding the chamber giving it all the material it needed to analyze and come up with a final solution."

"What solution?!" Rosen frantically yelled.

"A… a new form of sustenance."

The Director swallowed hard at Doctor Zimmerman's answer.

"How is that possible?" Rosen shuddered.

"It's basic science," Dr. Zimmerman chuckled with uproarious fear. "Our bodies are made up of protons, neutrons, and electrons, the same properties that are within atomic energy... the average human body can generate between 10 and 100 millivolts of electricity. With hers beyond any fatal ramifications... it's the only logical choice."

Director Rosen went from being calm, relaxed, and collected to a man who appeared to be having a stroke with pants full of fecal matter. At that moment, the emergency lights came on via the backup electrical generators, as the power to the fusion generator shut down entirely. Still, it was evident and apparent that the damage was already done.

"We didn't kill her... we made her stronger," Dr. Zimmerman trembled.

Director Rosen shook the doctor one final time like an eight ball, praying he'd give him the answer he wanted to hear.

"What do we do?"

The doctor looked up, locking eyes with

the Director to give him their only solution.

"We... run," he whispered.

CHAPTER 25

Back inside, the pod was dead silent; the inside was still smoking from the raw power it was flooded with to kill its current resident. Sophia continued to lay lifeless, still locked in her badly damaged restraints despite readings dictating; otherwise, her body fully healed, including her pierced skull and brain. The Iridium syringes dissolved completely within her body, processed by her cells. She survived an event no ordinary human being could have endured.

Her face still appeared empty; the damage done irreparable despite her abilities. A faint blue light began to flicker in her eyes and then grow.

The pod she was in exploded, emitting raw blue energy that expanded. It took out whatever was underneath it, namely the partially powered reactor and everything above and around it, obliterating half the base while shaking the mountain it was in. It also forced the residents of Klamath and other towns to come out of their homes and places of business to view what appeared to be the destructive force of a miniature nuke ripping through the side of the mountain.

~ ~

Outside the Black Bear diner, patrons and staff walked out thunderstruck by the destructive force they just witnessed and the smoke billowing out of the once volcanic mountain.

"That's… Mount McLoughlin," Bernie nervously confirmed.

"They found Eric Dunbar up there an hour ago after his accident," Carolann said.

The two looked at each other, realizing the person of the town's ridicule was possibly screaming the truth about the mountaintop.

~ ~

Back at the base, the situation was total unadulterated chaos to the seventh level of hell. Still alive, personnel scrambled for their lives with the new objective... survival.

Back at the detention area, Mark staggeringly pulled himself off the floor. Apparently, part of the cellblock was right under the blast area.

"What the... Hampton! Hampton!" he hollered. "You dead?!"

"No! What the hell happened?!" Charles yelled from his cell.

"A... it could be Dennison... B... it could be Dennison... either way, all hell has broken loose," Mark formulated.

He examined his door; either by blessing or luck, it cracked open due to a malfunction or the force of the explosion.

He got a good grip, dug in, and growled, pulling on the door and opening it wide enough for him to slide through. He found Hampton's door cracked open as well, which meant it was definitely a malfunction throughout the entire facility. He went to work, pulling his door open, and Charles helped from the other side, finally getting him out.

"Thanks... so what's the plan?" Charles asked with a huff.

"Find Dennison's daughter... and get the hell out of here... in that order... you feel up to it?"

"Lead the way," Charles motioned.

~ ~

Upstairs at the control observation deck, the chaos continued. Due to the blast, debris dropped from the ceiling, killing two technicians instantly. The remaining technicians continued with their duties, rattling off damage reports.

"Over forty percent of the base destroyed from the initial blast, seventy percent of the facility systems are down," a male lab technician reported.

"Casualties reported on almost every level!" a female lab technician confirmed.

"Where is the subject?!" Rosen demanded.

"Don't know, sir. All surveillance systems are down... we're literally blind!" the first lab technician relayed.

"Sir," Ms. Barrett nervously beckoned, "General Matheson is on the line!"

The Director swallowed hard as he waved her over; she patched the call through her tablet, where a highly displeased General Matheson sat.

"It is all over the news!" Matheson roared. "What is going on over there?!"

Director Rosen tried to explain the situation.

"Sir... we've run into a slight situation..."

"Is she dead?!"

"Sir..." Director uttered.

For the first time, he was lost for words.

"Is... she... dead?!"

Director Rosen could not answer him because he did not know what was happening. For the first time in his life, he was not in control.

General Matheson gave Rosen a look as if he was a bug.

"You have disappointed me greatly, Director, and forced me to take matters into my own hands to clean up your mess. You have exactly twenty-five minutes to evacuate your location with all the materials and my granddaughter, and if I see you with one and not the other, you will wish you stayed where you were. Twenty... five... minutes."

The transmission ended with the Director swallowing hard, knowing what the General was referencing.

~ ~

In Washington, the general sat at his desk. He pulled a key from his shirt attached to a chain around his neck. Matheson snapped the chain off. He unlocked one of the draws with the key, revealing a digital safe. The General punched in a security code, opened the safe, and reached in, grabbing a black Land Rover military S8 3 cellphone with N.S.A. encryption technology. He slowly dialed a number and waited as it rang.

A male voice, on the other end, responded first.

"Sir."

"This is General Bernard Matheson initiating Deadman Protocol, Activation code Alpha Bravo Omega 61794385921783474969."

"Voice imprint recognized... activation code has been accepted...orders will be carried out, sir. Time of executed order?"

"Twenty-Four minutes," Matheson ordered.

"Yes, sir."

General Matheson shut off the phone, slowly placing it on the desk. He then turned to look out the window, clasping his hands together at the flag waving in the wind outside.

"For the good of the country," he

muttered.

~ ~

At the base, Rosen turned to Ms. Barrett with a look of fear.

He quickly turned to one of the technicians, still alive.

"Can you confirm if the helipad was destroyed, or is it still intact?!"

"Can't confirm, sir; surveillance is still down."

To which the Director ran over, grabbing him. He screamed in his face.

"Call the damn pilot and find out if he's still alive and if the helicopter and pad are still intact!"

"Sir... I've already done it... the pilot said the helipad was not badly damaged, and the helicopter is ready for departure," Ms. Barrett quickly confirmed.

The Director shoved the technician back in

his seat and pointed to her.

"Get Agent Slater," Rosen commanded, "tell him to meet us there with the child."

He quickly turned to Dr. Archifeld Zimmerman.

"Coordinate the move of the canisters to the helipad as well, four minutes! Now!"

He then gave his final order to the remaining technicians.

"Sound the evacuation alarm!" Director Rosen yelled.

~ ~

As the alarm blared, personnel and guards scrambled to evacuate. As a squad of guards ran together in formation, one straggled behind and became prey to Mark, who bum-rushed him, slamming him up against a wall. It was a struggle as a more formidable, younger soldier in body armor overpowered Armitage going for his rifle; Charles grew a pair and jumped on his back, trying to execute a rear-naked choke.

The guard used the back of his helmet-covered head to smack him in the nose, busting it open and then broke free, knocking him down with a spinning elbow. During the commotion, Mark managed to snag the knife from the soldier's boot and drive it underneath his chin as he turned around to deal with him.

The soldier gagged, choking on his blood as he fell into a heap. Mark crouched over to Charles, nursing a busted nose.

"You alright, man?" Mark asked.

Charles nodded while blowing bloody snot on the floor.

"Yeah... I don't get it. It worked on T.V."

Mark grinned while helping Hampton up.

"You didn't keep your chin tucked in."

Out of the corner of his eye, Charles saw two more soldiers coming around the corner.

"Look out!" he screamed.

Charles pushed Mark into a deep doorway

entrance before taking a hail of gunfire. Armitage quickly ducked down, grabbing the dead soldier's rifle and staying low. He returned fire, gunning down the two soldiers as the firepower from his rifle was the only thing capable of piercing their body armor for kill shots.

Mark quick checked the area to see if anyone else was coming, then grabbed a bloodied Hampton wheezing and coughing up blood, propping him up against a nearby wall.

"You gotta go, man... you gotta go..." Charles said, trying desperately to breathe.

"Not without the man who saved my ass."

Mark tried to help him up.

Charles stopped him.

"I'm done, man, and don't tell me I'm not... I'm a doctor..."

Charles cracked a nervous smile as Mark grabbed his hand, which shook as he appeared to be going into shock.

"Dr. Melissa Green… in Baltimore, she has… the samples and data… if you see Sophia… do not… tell her… I died here… would break her heart… promise me… promise me…"

Mark gave his word.

"I promise."

"Go… get her little girl… and get the hell out of here… in that order…" Charles coughed.

He took three more deep breaths before the light went out in him.

Mark closed his eyes and placed a hand on his shoulder, putting his head against Charles'.

"Another kid dead over this bullshit."

Mark picked up the rifle and detached the dead soldier's holster and sidearm, quickly snapping it on. He looked at the late Charles Hampton one final time before running off to finish his mission.

~ ~

At the helipad, which was still intact, Director Rosen power-walked with Ms. Barrett trotting behind, followed by four heavily armed Shock Troopers, two with mini-guns ready for anything. Agent Slater showed up with Sophia's daughter carrying her. Occasionally, the base violently shook with massive explosions going off. Director Rosen did not know if it was the aftermath of the first explosion or if something was coming. Either way, he was not waiting to find out.

As he and his entourage neared the black Sikorsky private helicopter to haul ass back to the airport, he was bewildered to see a petrified Dr. Zimmerman standing there as if he had seen the Devil himself.

"Dr. Zimmerman! Is the cargo loaded? Where are the pilot and extra security?!" Director Rosen yelled, wondering why he was standing there.

Out of nowhere, someone or something tossed the three bodies of the former guards, followed by the pilot from the entrance of the helicopter-like sacks of rice hitting the pavement. A cold chill went down the Director's spine as

#3 and #1 walked down the copter's steps, significantly different from when they last saw them.

They were taller, minus their body armor and usual weapons. Their skintight bodysuits revealed an outline of their new powerful physiques.

#3, due to her growth spurt, wore boots from one of the dead guards.

"A slight change of plans, Director," #3 said with a bright smile, "We're taking the blood... and the child."

"Ms. Barrett."

Rosen turned to her with no further stomach for insubordination.

Without hesitation, Ms. Barrett typed in the nanites' termination codes for #3 and #1, but nothing happened.

She typed it in repeatedly, but the screen displayed the same thing.

"NO NANITES DETECTED."

Ms. Barrett turned to Director Rosen with a horrified look as if she was about to wet herself.

The Director quickly turned to his Shock Troopers in desperation as Agent Slater backed away, putting down the child while drawing his Glock 23 from his side holster.

"Kill them!" Rosen yelled.

Dr. Zimmerman hauled tail on his little legs, cowering on the other side of the helicopter as the Shock Troopers with the mini-guns stepped forward and opened fire on #3 and #1 only to confirm what the Director already knew. The nanotech weaving in their bodysuit made them already somewhat bulletproof, but they still should have gone down to the blazing force of the mini-guns, especially with shots to the face. They stood there like metal pillars as the bullets created for piercing the densest of metals ricocheted off them. Signifying they were now officially impervious to conventional firepower.

Agent Slater did not even bother firing a shot as he moved farther back with the child to avoid ricochet. After bathing in their newfound power for half a minute, #3 and #1 moved in for the kill, forcing the other two troopers to open fire.

#3, facing off against the first mini-gun-toting trooper, grabbed the rotating barrel, crushing and stopping it cold. The bullets still fed through the barrel, causing the gun to explode in both the Shock Trooper's and her face. The Shock Trooper barely survived the explosion due to his armor, while #3 stood without a scratch.

As he tried to crawl away, she grabbed him by one of his legs, leaped into the air with him, and then came down, smashing the Shock Trooper into the concrete floor of the helipad like a child amid a temper tantrum breaking a doll she did not like. She then chucked him over the helipad platform to his death if he was not dead already.

#1 went straight to the point as he walked through the bullets bouncing off him. He snatched the mini-gun from the Shock Trooper's hands and tore it in two before him. The Shock Trooper then went for the automatic rifle on his back, but not before #1 grabbed him by the front of his armor and punched a hole through his chest.

He then pulled his arm out and took the Shock Trooper's body, launching it with one arm, taking out the one behind him, still trying to take him out with his automatic rifle.

#1 then leaped into the air and came down, delivering a crushing stomp to the back of the third Shock Trooper, breaking every bone in his upper torso for good measure and killing him instantly.

#3 used her newfound speed to finesse her next kill by blitzing the last Shock Trooper, who was now nervously firing away, unable to hit her. She sped behind him, performing a waist lock, and German suplexed him skull first into the concrete; #3 holding on rolled with him, taking the limp Shock Trooper up as his semi-lifeless body dropped his rifle.

#3 lifted him high in the air into a reverse military press.

"I always wanted to do this," she said with a savage grin.

She delivered a backbreaker, snapping the Shock Trooper in half like a twig before rolling him off her knee.

The helipad became as silent as a graveyard, with only the mountain wind blowing and the sound of a whimpering Ms. Barrett, in hysterical shock, still typing in the code to activate the Nanites, only for her tablet screen to come up with the same results. #1 walked up to her, taking the tablet out of her hand.

"I think you know by now… that's not going to work darling," #1 smiled. "Funny thing about this virus… it apparently kills anything it sees as a possible threat to the system… they were destroyed the minute we injected the blood into us."

Ms. Barrett broke down crying.

"Please… please."

"It's okay… it's okay… I just need the tablet."

#1 walked away, giving Ms. Barrett some sense of relief. He delivered a vicious backhand to her upper body, knocking her out of her flip-flops. The force of the blow sent her flying through the thick glass circular wall of the helipad at breakneck speed, where she fell several thousand feet, hitting the hood of a transport vehicle below, the final resting place of her lifeless body.

"But I don't need you," he sighed before motioning to #3. "I got the data."

The Director tried to slink away in the chaos only to run into #3.

She latched onto his throat, hoisting him high into the air.

"God, it's going to take a while for me to get used to this," #3 grinned.

Director Rosen gasped, trying to breathe.

"How... how?"

She pulled him closer, whispering in his ear.

"Arthur... Arthur... for all of your 'see all, know all, two steps ahead' bullshit, you still talk in your sleep. And your security is too lax when you're getting some. You don't think I know that you order the visual and audio features to my nanites shut down, so people don't see the ridiculous faces or sounds you make while you're sticking me? Sedatives also helped; guess where I put them?"

#3 slowly licked his ear.

"Hint: it wasn't the wine glasses you were licking it off of. With the nice fancy training I was given, I was able to rummage through your computer as you undetected and found what I needed.

Additional access code info on how the virus works; it was just a matter of timing. The original plan was to get you and Ms. Barrett in one of our regular play sessions tonight, knowing you'd be in a celebratory mood. I'd kill you both… and shut down the Nanites via her tablet, which the little bitch carries everywhere long enough for #1 to secretly breach the lab and get the samples."

#3 innocently shrugged her shoulders.

"The ruckus Dennison made screwed up our plan, which was disappointing because I really wanted the chance to roll around in your blood, but it made it easier for us to get to the samples when you had it transported here like I knew you would. With communication and surveillance down, you had no idea where or what we were doing. Luck was also on our side, as the late Ms. Barrett was too scared shitless about what was going on to check our whereabouts.

You apparently didn't care either, as it was clear you would leave without us... you didn't even notice #1 leaving the deck when all hell broke loose... so after we killed everyone bringing the samples here save for the Doctor, we injected ourselves with the blood... it bonded with us in minutes. Then, all we had to do was help each other shove our vanadium carbon fiber blades under each of our ribcages, and the virus just went to work... it hurt... a lot... but as you can see, it was totally worth it... apparently, because we're already enhanced, everything works faster... which is just dandy."

"You... have... no... idea... what...

you... have... done... dead... dead man."

Rosen uttered, barely able to breathe as she applied more pressure to his throat.

"You became a dead man when you made me stand powerless watching as that bitch killed #4." #3 growled with gritted teeth. "By the way... I may have been screwing you, but I was in love with him... lucky for me, I also love #1."

"We like keeping it in the family," #1 shrugged.

#3 bared her fangs at the Director, unmasking her rage and hatred.

"It's true, Arthur... we love killing... it's like crack or candy to us... but we love killing on our terms. You think you're any different from the pieces of shit you send us to kill? You sit in your high priced suit, never getting your hands bloodied while people like me go bathing in it willingly—changing the world as you reap the reward. It's not fair... and it's going to change."

"That's why we're taking the blood, the good doctor who has nowhere to run!" #3

616

screamed for Dr. Zimmerman to hear, "and the kid… we're going to create a world where only the truly fit and worthy survives."

#3 crushed and snapped the Director's neck with her bare right hand before dropping him to the floor.

"A world where we crush people like you… underneath our heels!"

She stomped on his skull, crushing it like a melon while caving in the floor underneath her.

Some blood splattered upon her as an insane grin appeared on her face. She then looked up at Agent Slater with the little girl. Slater took the hint that he was no match for the duo as he held his hands up with his gun dangling from his thumb and slowly backed away from the child.

"I don't want any part of this," Agent Slater swallowed. "You can take the little brat and…"

Before he could finish his sentence, the

ground exploded behind him. A hand grabbed him by the back of the neck and flung him like a ragdoll several feet at great speed, hitting the top entranceway of the helipad. He fell, hitting the concrete painfully and awkwardly.

The little girl quietly turned to see her mother standing tall with her dreadlocks covering her face, forcing #3 and #1 to back up, taking defensive stances. Her bodysuit's metal ports either melted off or were absorbed into her body, revealing not a mark on her where the Iridium spike syringes pierced her.

As Agent Slater weakly attempted to struggle to his feet, Mark finally showed up, pulling out his sidearm that he acquired and lit him up with two shots to the chest and one to the skull, thus ending Agent Slater.

"I told you... no one points a gun at me and gets away with it," Mark muttered, fulfilling his promise.

"You're late," Sophia said, not looking at him.

"Yeah, well... place is a rat's maze... had

to get past the rats," Mark explained.

"Take my daughter and go," Sophia ordered him.

Mark motioned to the remaining D.E.A.D.

"What about…"

"Don't worry about them. They belong to me now… go."

Mark nodded as he picked the little girl up. Without knowing him, she placed her arms around his neck, resting her head on his shoulder. He speed-walked off the helipad back where he came from. The little girl raised her head, watching Sophia, who continued to stare down #3 and #1. Armitage found the emergency stairs he originally came through, taking them back downstairs, hoping they lead all the way to the bottom and out.

"One down… one more to go," Sophia addressed #3.

"There's two of us bitch, much stronger than when you first came here," #3 warned her, "and if you choose to fight with us, we're only

619

going to get stronger… so why don't we just call this even… I took something from you… you took something from me… walk away, and let bygones be bygones… what do you say?"

"Things will never be even between us, and you'll never be stronger… then me," Sophia informed her.

"Cocky little slash aren't ya," #3 cackled, mocking her. "What are you, over nine thousand now?!"

"You know, in the movies… in the final scene… when the good guy and bad guy fight," Sophia stated, with her eyes closed. "Bad guy gets the upper hand during most of the fight… but the good guy in the last minute finds a way to win."

"This ain't a movie," #3 scowled, reminding her.

Sophia finally opened her eyes to reveal them no longer normal at all; it appeared as if her irises and pupils were utterly gone as her eyes had a deep blue glow from the raw energy surging behind them.

"You're so damn right about that," she glared.

Before they could even react, Sophia was face to face with #3; only a red, white, and black trail with a blue energy signature from her eyes revealed how she got from point "a" to point "b." She was now doing what John Wesley Shipp needed special effects to do.

Sophia grabbed # 3 by the front of her bodysuit in one motion, hoisting her into the air. With a spin, she flung #3 effortlessly into the helicopter, sending her and it through an unscathed portion of the circular glass of the helipad, revealing a still-cowering Dr. Zimmerman almost crushed. A stunned #1 reacted too slowly as Sophia zipped and stood before him with her hand inches from his face.

Blue energy burst from her pores, flowing into her hand, forming a blue ball of pure energy that grew in her palm to the size of a baseball and equal to her eyes' intensity. It was like falling into the deadly charm of a cobra.

"Now... you die."

These were the final words #1 would ever hear.

The sound of the blast was pure white noise, while the blast radius of the energy forming in her palm went from the size of a baseball to the height and width of a freight train. It engulfed everything in its path, including #1 and his screams. The blast tore through the facility, and then the mountain escaping to the outside, where it went God knows where before dissipating; not even ashes were left of #1, while two other explosions rocked the facility.

One was the helicopter falling to its destruction, taking out anything in its path in the process, which were several more levels of the facility not touched by Sophia.

The other was #3, hurled at a velocity equivalent to a railgun, sending her out the mountain's side like a missile projectile into the Oregon air.

She screamed her lungs out while throwing a couple of curse words in as she fell like a meteorite into the forest of the Sky Lakes Wilderness, hitting with the thunderous impact of a wrecking ball, destroying several ancient trees in the area. Her dense body created several human-size craters before finally stopping. As she tried to rise, she collapsed onto her knees, battered and bloodied, her regenerative healing not working fast enough to repair the damage done.

As she tried to fight to her feet, she heard the sound of a sonic boom exploding out of the mountain. She beheld the sight of an airborne Sophia flying out of the hole she created while blasting #1 into atoms. It was clearly not one of her regular super leaps as she hovered midair due to her energy dispersing at the bottom of her feet.

She soared down to where #3 landed, stopping again and hovering in midair; she slowly lowered herself to Earth, sending dirt and debris flying everywhere as a defiant and enraged #3 stood waiting for her.

When she was low enough, she dispersed the energy that gave her flight, landing gently on the ground to stand toe to toe with the last of the D.E.A.D.

#3, who had seen almost everything,

demanded to know in disbelief at what she saw.

"How…?"

"The energy from the reactor that was being used to kill me… somehow it siphoned into me like a charger to a car battery," Sophia confirmed. "Apparently, my body likes it. So much, it involuntarily blew me out of the pod, taking half the mountain to get to the reactor, which was below me. Cells just went to town, taking the rest of the energy. That's why there was no fallout… as for being the 'fastest woman alive' and the 'up up and away' I forgot to mention that I also cannot only remember but physically duplicate moves from anyone or anything I've ever seen in my life real or unreal, movies… television… video games… just with a thought."

#3 bared her teeth, trembling with rage and fear.

"If you think you can scare me…"

Sophia laughed, cutting her off without a care in the world.

"I don't really give a shit if you're afraid of me or not. I just know I'm going to beat you to death with my bare hands."

"Fuck…"

Before #3 could finish her vulgar sentence, a calm and cold Sophia, for the second time, was already in her face.

"No… fuck you," Sophia answered back.

And just as # 3 was not prepared to be flung through the facility like a pillow, she was not ready for the lightning-straight right punch to the chest that propelled her once again through the forest, shattering more trees as she came crashing back down at the foot of Mount McLoughlin by the now-abandoned security wall.

As she fought to her feet again, fighting to breathe after the cannon shot punch, she saw a red, white, and black blur approaching her with a speed that was uprooting trees. She barely covered up to defend herself as she was hit with a punch backed by a Mach 15 sonic boom, knocking her through the security wall back into the facility, obliterating everything in her path and almost sending her out the other side of the mountain.

The impact ignited various explosions and caused a section of the facility to come down. Debris and smoke rained down everywhere, some of it burying #3.

Sophia wanted to keep the battle at the mountain so no one else got hurt.

#3 managed to break free of the rubble that fell on her as she clutched her chest, spitting up blood. She was still regenerating, but her body could not keep up with Sophia's damage. The last mountain-destroying punch felt like she pulverized both her forearms to block the force aimed at her head. It was also clear that Sophia was pulling her punches; she could have easily obliterated her defense and punched her head off if she wanted to.

She wanted to drag this now one-sided fight out and make #3 suffer as promised.

#3 would not go quietly into the night. As Sophia walked through the smoke and rubble coming for her, #3 snatched up the most enormous slab of concrete debris that had to weigh nearly eight tons. She swung for the hills, hoping to knock her into the next town or stagger her. The slab just shattered on impact like glass hitting a tank.

"You wanna try again?" Sophia asked, taunting her.

#3 growled, taking what was left of the debris waffling Sophia's skull with it like something out of a wrestling show, but that piece just crumbled on impact against the immovable force.

She took what was left of the debris that was now half her body and launched it directly into Sophia's face with all of her might. It was like hitting her with soft, newly fallen snow. Now covered in dirt, rubble, dust, and debris, Sophia unscathed opened her glowing blue piercing eyes to look into the soul of #3.

#3, with quivering lips, gave the only answer stuck in her head.

"Fuck you…"

"You said that already," Sophia sighed. "Such a limited vocabulary you have."

#3 threw her hands up in ranting frustration.

"So, what now, huh? This the reckoning? Vengeance served cold and all that shit? You finally get your 'Kill Bill' moment. Well, then come on!"

"No," Sophia said, flat out to her.

"No?! What the fuck do you mean… 'no'?" #3 demanded, not loving being the one now toyed with.

"I want you to know this is no longer about vengeance. I'm not here to kill you for what you did to my husband… or for what you've done to me," Sophia calmly explained to her. "I'm going to kill you because you came after my daughter… that… is the only reason… why you die today."

#3 bowed her head and started to giggle as blood drooled from her mouth down the front of her bodysuit. Her giggle turned into a maniacal laugh as she wiped tears from her eyes with her forearm. No one would know if the tears were of fear or insanity. She became silent again; a growl emitted from her as she rushed Sophia with all her might, kicking up dust behind her.

A vicious boot to the gut by a much faster female titan upended her. Sophia did not stop there as she grabbed the front of her hair and knocked the taste out of her mouth with a thunderous right, sending a couple of teeth flying. As #3 spun around, Sophia slammed her with a second bone-crushing right while executing a "flash step," moving to the opposite side and hitting her with another freight train punch.

After Sophia's two brutal hits, #3 was nearly out on her feet. However, she was not finished as she caught #3 from falling, shoved her backward, and unleashed an attack on her with moves straight out of a fighting video game.

The former neurosurgeon, who had not taken even a Tao Bo class, took the highly-trained death squad assassin to school. She remembered and pulled from the countless kung fu movies she watched and the weekend video game marathons she had with her husband while in college. That and her unbelievable speed and strength made her an unstoppable combatant.

At that point, Sophia was toying with her as she leaped into the air, faking her with a 360-degree roundhouse kick; it was a setup for a 360-degree legsweep, sending her into a tailspin, but before #3 could hit the ground, Sophia clobbered her with an explosive spinning backhand fist, swiping her out of midair. The force of the hit sent her crashing through several walls, again shaking the facility.

~ ~

Elsewhere in the facility, Mark staggered, cradling Sophia's daughter as he tried to make his way out, nearing the bottom of the base.

"Sweet baby Jesus... I'm too old for this shit," Mark groaned to himself.

Out of nowhere, Mark was close to having a heart attack as the screeching spider monkey belonging to the late Director Rosen jumped on top of him, almost making him fall down the stairs. He was about to grab the animal and fling it away when Sophia's daughter took the monkey in her arms, cradling it as it clung to her.

Mark shot Cornelius a dirty look as he continued descending the stairs.

"You better be the last surprise in this goddamn place."

~ ~

Back at the fight, as #3 staggered to her feet, Dennison, the flying scud missile, slammed right into her, taking her for a ride. She took pleasure in putting her through additional wall after wall until they came exploding into the quad of the complex behind the now destroyed security wall.

Sophia was not done with her yet as she angled her trajectory, dragging #3's body across the hard concrete, creating a shallow trench. Satisfied that she probably took half of #3's skin off her back, she quickly took her up into the air. She then executed a spinning nosedive, aiming for a rather sizeable, armored personnel vehicle below them.

#3 fought to break free from Sophia's iron grip with her own strength, but it was all for naught as the strongest of the two with the ability to achieve flight drilled them into the vehicle.

The brutal impact ignited the diesel within the vehicle, causing an explosion and sending flaming shrapnel everywhere. Some of it hit a nearby fuel supply, causing a devastating chain reaction of detonations, which took out almost every vehicle in the vicinity and another part of the facility.

Smoke and fire roared and bellowed everywhere. A large piece of smoking debris flung from the initial crash site's wreckage was #3, bouncing off the pavement before rolling to a painful rest.

"Oh... oh god," #3 groaned in agonizing pain.

Out of the flames and wreckage strolled Sophia, casually swatting flames off her now slightly torn and burnt skintight plug suit. It was still highly durable despite the punishment it endured.

"Oh… you calling for God now… you think He's listening?" Sophia inquisitively asked.

"Wait… wait!"

#3 pleaded as she stumbled backward, holding her hand up beggingly with genuine fear in her eyes.

"You don't understand! It was…"

"Your job? Was that what you were going to say?!" Sophia screamed. "You gonna tell me you were just following orders?! Or maybe you wanna tell me about how ya daddy beat the shit out of your momma and molested you? How you had such a hard life? Go ahead! I dare you to tell me that it won't bring my husband or my life back! That it won't erase the four years of hell I had to endure because of you!! And then… you not only threatened my kid… murdered my best friend… you spit on me!"

Her eyes glowed brighter and more intense with rage.

#3 just stood there looking at her.

She imagined this was how her victims looked when they begged for her mercy and found none. How many cried, sobbed, and whimpered through their words as they attempted to bargain for their lives. Lives she thought were worthless, puny... quickly extinguished and forgotten. Murder was an erotic pleasure for her. She happily bathed in the blood of the innocent and the guilty with no regrets. Here she now stood, attempting to reason with one whom she had inflicted the most significant offense.

One who she just told in intricate detail less than an hour ago how she took great pleasure in obliterating her life; it did not matter if #3 confessed that she did not kill her best friend, the now late Charles Hampton; the other evidence was too overwhelming.

#3 was already tried and convicted. This was now her long walk. No appeal in the world would change her fate.

"What?!"

Sophia roared loudly enough to emit a low-level sonic boom with her vocals. It shattered every glass in her vicinity, causing a mini avalanche on the mountain base.

#3 stared at the unstoppable force, void of all reasoning, and hated her for making her beg for her life.

#3 sighed while rolling her eyes.

"Well... since you're not willing to listen to reason."

She stomped the ground in defiance, cratering the floor as she raised her hands, getting into a stance ready to bang. If she was going to get the beating of her life, she would get it fighting back.

Sophia also got into her stance; she looked like a seasoned combatant as she etched closer to #3, ready to strike. Out of nowhere, she channeled some of the pure raw energy now stored in the cells of her body into her fists, causing them to glow as she clutched them; the intensity of the heat faintly burnt the sleeves of her plug suit.

#3 could feel the heat from her fists and

shook her head in disbelief, thinking she was in some crazy anime movie.

"Just don't hit me in the nos…" #3 requested.

BLAM!

Before she could finish her sentence, Sophia faked her out, blasting her in the face. Not with her fists but with intense blue atomic eye beams, scorching her face and nearly blinding her.

#3 screamed in agonizing pain, unable to touch her smoldering face.

Sophia bared her teeth.

"That's… for Charlie."

#3 seethed, trembling as her face healed from the first-degree burns she received.

"Awwwwww…. u fuckin'… biter."

She roared, throwing a fury of combinations, which Sophia quickly blocked.

#3 appeared to be throwing faster, powerful strikes. She almost looked as if she was matching Sophia's speed. She seemed close to finding an opening until Sophia showed her the difference between them. She may not be the first, but she was still the most powerful as she effortlessly powered through #3's combinations, battering her with shockwave-shaking blows.

Her hands were like lightning twin pistons as she threw every punching combination she had ever seen within less than seconds, targeting #3's ribs, sternum, abdomen, and left and right jaw bone and nose.

#3 swung for the hills desperately, only for Sophia to catch her right haymaker. The punch's impact sent a massive shockwave through the facility, collapsing weakened structures. It still proved ineffective against Dennison's near-godlike strength.

Sophia snarled as she doubled her over with a body blow to the gut. She grabbed the front of #3's bodysuit, leaped into the air, and hurled her into the skies of Oregon. Sophia exploded into the air, going after her.

Several thousand miles up, she flew past a screaming #3 waiting to set her up and delivered another sonic boom-powered right cross, sending her spiraling back down to Earth. Sophia entered another nosedive with thrusters on full blast straight for #3. #3 crashed back into the facility, creating a colossal crater while emitting shockwaves again, causing tremendous structural damage.

There would be no rest for the wicked as a roaring Sophia pulled out of her dive but continued to fall, delivering a diving knee crashing down on top of #3, widening the crater and causing a second, more devastating shockwave. It created untold mass destruction and caused a minor earthquake that shook the mountain and most of Jackson County past Klamath.

Mark barely made it out the door into the hell outside, where he dodged flying chunks of debris the size of cars while cradling Sophia's daughter. Half the facility and mountain collapsed behind him, no longer capable of withstanding the brutality unleashed on it by Sophia's raw strength and power.

As he staggered over to the ballpark-sized crater, he witnessed Sophia standing over a beaten and broken #3, choking on her blood.

Sophia snapped her fingers to get her dazed attention.

"Hey… you bleeding on yourself. Wanna see something cool?"

Sophia raised her hand into the air. With a thought, she commanded her body to channel raw energy within her into a sphere in the palm of her hand once again, this time making it grow bigger.

#3 just looked up at her in disbelief; she knew she was doing it for the crack she made earlier. Of all the ways to go, this bitch was about to kill her with a one-handed Spirit Bomb.

Mark held her daughter at a safe distance, standing there watching imagination come to frightening reality. He turned the child's head away so she did not see what the mother she had never met before was about to do.

"Wait! Wait!"

A disheveled Dr. Zimmerman with cracked glasses screamed as he came running into the quad, somehow also surviving the base's destruction. He collapsed on his knees, completely out of breath.

"Help us! You have to help us! A nuke! He launched a nuke right at us!"

With another thought, Sophia dispersed the ball of unfathomable destructive force, which had grown to the size of a semi, so that she could hear what the Doctor had to say.

"What the hell are you talking about? Who launched a nuke?!" Mark demanded to know.

"The General, "Deadman Protocol" fail-safe," Dr. Zimmerman panted, "a contingency plan to stop dangerous subjects such as Ms. Dennison!"

"To launch a goddamn nuke at us?!" Mark yelled in disbelief.

"Mark… my daughter," Sophia warned.

"Sorry…" Mark said, patting the silent little girl's back.

640

"How long, doctor?" she calmly asked.

"We had twenty-five minutes to leave Oregon; two minutes ago, the missile was launched... I expect five minutes... once it reenters Earth's atmosphere!" Dr. Zimmerman confirmed.

Sophia turned to look up at the sky.

"Thank you, doctor... one more thing."

"Yes?" he asked, thinking she had a task for him.

The one more thing for the good Doctor was the last thing #1 saw: a huge flashing blue light before Sophia turned him to less than ash without looking in his direction.

"That's for the chamber," Sophia snarled.

#3 started to cackle, impressed, believing that she and Sophia were not so much different. Sophia stopped her laughter by bringing her foot down on 3's throat, smashing her windpipe while keeping her pinned.

"Well... I guess that doesn't leave us

much time."

Sophia removed her foot from #3's throat, grabbing her by her hair and ripping her to her feet.

"Wait, what are you doing?" Mark nervously asked, knowing time was running down.

"Figure if I can get to it and destroy it while it's in Earth's thermosphere, you won't have to worry about fallout," Sophia judged, acting as if she had done it before.

"So, why are you taking her with you?!" Mark asked, gesturing to #3.

"Because she's durable enough to stop a nuke," Sophia said, breathing deeply. "And this is a one-way trip for both of us."

"But you could just fly up there... blast it out of the sky or launch it back into space."

"And this would never end," Sophia debated back.

"But, no one can mess with you now!"

Mark argued. "You're the most powerful person…"

"And this would never end. As long as she and I are around, we're proof that man can become gods… and eventually monsters."

"Speak for your fuckin'…" #3 groaned.

Sophia quickly gut-checked her, taking the air out of her once again and her speaking ability.

"Nobody asked you jack," Sophia sneered.

"So committing suicide is your only answer," Mark asked, throwing up his free hand in despair.

"It's not suicide if you're saving the world," Sophia smiled, looking at him. "This is more of a sacrifice… only the three of us standing here alive know about my daughter… and soon there will only be one. One who I believe I can trust to make sure that no one ever knows about her… my daughter… died here on this base… can you make that happen for me, Mr. Armitage… can you grant the wish of a 'condemned' woman?"

"You have my word... I'll make it happen," Mark nodded.

"One more thing," Sophia asked. "At Charles Hampton's apartment,... in his closet is an old gym bag with our college emblem... the Goodwill..."

"The store manager said he forgives you... and I got you covered," Mark reassured her.

"The rest belongs to my daughter."

"You have my word," Mark promised. "What should I tell her when she asks about you?"

Sophia's tears glowed as they ran down her face.

"Tell her... the best thing I ever got out of this life... was watching her come into this world, and I said thank you... for saving me."

"She's right here, don't you want to..."

"If I do… I won't be able to leave… besides… I have a final image of how beautiful she's grown… that is enough for me… goodbye, Mark."

She turned to #3, squeezing her by the throat while looking her in the eyes.

"Remember when I said I'd watch you die screaming?"

With those words, Sophia leaped into the air with a gagging #3.

She channeled the energy from her feet's soles with enough distance between her and the ground, creating the thrust she needed to gain flight again. Before she took off, she turned back at the facility, hovering while extending her left hand. It appeared as if the world shook as Sophia channeled a ball of pure blue energy the size of a medicine ball.

"Holy…" Mark uttered.

His cue was to take the child and hop into the nearest unmanned vehicle, a still intact black, high-tech version of a Humvee. Luckily, it had the keys in the ignition as he drove like a bat out of hell, blowing through what was left of the destroyed security gate and flooring it. If the vehicle was built to do 230, he would get three times the speed out of it.

Sophia, deciding that Armitage and her daughter were at a safe enough distance, unleashed godlike fury on the facility, obliterating it. Except for some small gas explosions, only a massive cloud of thick black smoke wafted for miles as far as Los Angeles, along with the intense blue light. She scorched the facility from the face of the Earth while bringing down Mount McLoughlin in the process. Satisfied she destroyed the complex and everything contained within completely, Sophia rocketed away with #3.

~ ~

Mark looked to the sky while driving to see if he could get one more glimpse of her.

"That's my mommy," said the silent little girl out of nowhere, looking up at the sky with the spider monkey in her lap.

Mark slowly turned to look at the little girl, who he thought mute with fear.

She pointed up at the sky.

"That's my mommy... flying up in the sky..."

Her little words unnerved Mark as he gripped the steering wheel tighter, wiping his eyes that got blurry all of a sudden.

"Yeah, honey..." Mark grunted, "that's your mommy."

~ ~

High above God's blue sky, Sophia flew beyond the speed of sound as she searched for her target with a struggling #3 in the grip of her right hand, trying to break free. Even with the tremendous winds and thin air, Sophia could hear her screaming and begging.

"You don't have to do this!" #3 squealed. "You said it yourself! You're a god! We're gods now!! We can rule this planet! Make it how we want it!! You don't have to do this!!"

She ignored her engaging talks of godly rule as she stopped in midair, hovering. She searched the skies until the rocket finally came into view. The son of a bitch had actually done it, she thought to herself. Sophia cursed, hoping to take it out in the Earth's thermosphere, but it was now well within the mesosphere and nearing the stratosphere with astonishing speed.

"Goddammit!! You don't have to do this!!" #3 protested, still trying to break free from her grip.

Sophia clamped down on #3's throat, shutting her up while pulling her close to look her in the eyes.

"No, I don't have to..." Sophia whispered. "I want to."

With those final words, Sophia placed a vice grip hold on #3's throat with both hands as she launched herself toward the speeding missile with a screaming #3.

It would be over in a few seconds, but she took in the view of #3 with tears of rage in her eyes, struggling and roaring to get free. They were too high and moving too fast for Sophia to hear what #3 was saying anymore, but she imagined she cursed her and her ancestors to eternity.

Vengeance… Justice… whatever the name for it, Sophia had her fill as she closed her eyes. She said one final prayer in her mind, forgiving Robert for all he had done. Thanking him for the one good thing they brought into the world.

"I'm going home… I'm going home," Sophia softly sang, "I'm going home… I'm going home."

The world came to a standstill as the heavens became red and blue with flames for all to see.

CHAPTER 26

One year and seven months later... at the United States Disciplinary Barracks Leavenworth, Kansas, two correctional personnel walked alongside former four-star General Bernard Matheson, now in prison garb and shackles. Despite being charged with treason for willfully firing a nuclear warhead on his own country, which entailed the death penalty on top of the public humiliation and dishonor, he held his head high as best he could, still believing that his actions were in the best interest of his country.

In actuality, Matheson was a scapegoat; the incident in Oregon, the D.E.A.D. project, and any project EVOlution and Sophia records would be buried as best as possible, excluding the confrontation on Interstate 10 and the memorable battle in Washington, DC seen by many.

Despite Big Brother's reach, it was no match for freedom of speech, the vast power of the Internet, and the thousands of cell phones with video cameras. New conspiracy theories would arise, but the government remained silent on all matters except the General's deeds, hoping that bringing him to justice for his actions would appease the masses… it did not.

The two correctional officers lead the General to an interview room's doors, a stark stone room with just a long table and four chairs. Mark was sitting in one of the chairs on the opposite side of the table from him, reading one of the two file folders he had while waiting.

The General actually smirked as he took a seat sitting across from him. Mark did not even bother to look at him as he kept reading.

"Thanks, boys," Mark said. "If you don't mind waiting outside… this won't take long."

The officers nodded, departing, leaving the General and him alone in the room.

Mark sighed as he closed the folders, slapping them down on the table, now looking at the General with a semi-placid smile.

"Let me first say thank you very much for giving me an audience," Mark broke the ice, "dammit how rude of me... I should first introduce myself..."

"I know who you are, Special Agent Armitage," General Matheson nodded.

"Yeah, well, it will be former Agent in two weeks... retiring due to health reasons... you know radiation and me don't really mix," Mark explained, looking at him dead in the eyes.

"Sorry to hear that," Matheson replied with an unsympathetic tone.

"Yeah, well." Mark sighed. "I guess I have you to thank for that."

"What can I do for you, Special Agent?" the General asked, wishing to get to the point.

"Off the record... I was hoping you'd be kind enough to tie up some loose ends for me."

Mark reopened the file he was looking at, taking some of the pictures within, and tossed them out in front of the General to see; they were pictures of his lifeless son from the crime scene over four years ago. The General spread the photos out to get a better look at them.

"I just wanted to know what type of cold-blooded, heartless, piece of shit, son of a bitch orders the brutal execution of his son and then frames his wife for that murder. That on top of placing him in a super death squad," Mark flat out asked.

General Matheson did not answer him as he sifted through the pictures, looking at his dead son.

"I guess it comes from the same deep dark f'ed up place that would make you go and watch the execution of your ex-daughter-in-law."

Mark huffed as he threw out more photos revealing the General entering the Mountain View Unit and taking a seat on the witness side of the lethal injection room.

"Must have been quite a shock to see the woman you hated so much, who you blamed for the ruination of your son's military career, resurrect right before your eyes, refusing to die. At least I now know how the late Director Rosen and his goon squad knew to show up that day... because you called him."

Mark finished his detective-like summation, staring into the General's eyes, trying to find what little soul he had left.

"Do you have children, Special Agent?" General Matheson asked, leaning back in his chair.

"Yes... I do."

The General leaned forward, looking him back in his eyes.

"Then you must know... a parent's love for a child... and what a parent would do for that child. I have shouldered two burdens... one for family and one for the country. My family has served as soldiers for this great country since the

Civil War... my son... wanted to be a soldier. A proud Marine like I was... and that miserable bitch poisoned his mind instead of knowing her place... made him doubt himself and his duty to his country... my son was dead before he was injured in Iraq... and I, as his father, tried to breathe life back into him with the D.E.A.D. project."

"So that he could continue your **legacy**?" Mark scoffed.

"So he could continue the Matheson legacy," General Matheson forcefully corrected him. "A proud legacy of sentinels chosen to protect this country from all foreign enemies so that your children can sleep peacefully at night."

"A legacy that was apparently worth the life of your son," Mark returned, unimpressed with the General's little speech.

"The life of one... is not worth the life of millions... Special Agent," General Matheson returned; a sliver of emotion filled his eyes as he shifted in his seat. "Not even the life of my own son."

"I guess that's where we differ," Mark returned, "because I'd rather have the world burn than give up one of my own flesh and blood… and you're a lying sack of shit considering you were willing to kill millions all for one person… i.e., why you're in here."

"I don't have to answer to you, Special Agent… despite all of 'this.'"

The General looked around as if the facility could not hold him.

"I will still be remembered as a soldier who served and defended his country to the end."

Mark slinked back into his seat, shaking his head in disbelief; it was like looking at his former self in a mirror.

"You're right, 'General,' you don't have to answer to me."

Mark sighed, lurching forward to grab the pictures stuffing them back into the file.

"You'll be answering to the Devil if there is one when it's time for them to hang your sorry ass. I had a big, long final speech I wanted to leave you with but after looking into your eyes and hearing the garbage out of your mouth. I just realized how pointless it would be… you're just like me… another stupid old dog with the inability to stop shitting on people's lives."

Mark pulled three more pictures from the inside of his jacket, tossing them onto the table, a picture of the late Charles Hampton. A photo of the burning wreckage of Kenneth Scott's S.U.V. Expedition that blew up with him and his entire family, and finally, a badly lobotomized Eric Dunbar, forever a living, breathing vegetable sitting in a wheelchair.

"And there's only one road for stupid old dogs like us… the back of a tool shed… thank you for your **time**," Mark said as he rose to his feet while taking the pictures.

He knew they probably did not stir any guilt in his dark, twisted soul. He just wanted the monster to see his dirty work, the lives he destroyed, trying to secure his legacy.

"Can I ask you something off the record, Special Agent?" General Matheson threw out.

"Shoot," Mark said with a cough.

"My granddaughter… what happened to her?" General Matheson asked, carefully reading him for a reaction.

"Dead," Mark answered while giving him a cold, hard stare, "accidentally killed during the battle in Oregon."

General Matheson grinned as he searched his eyes.

"Is that so?"

Mark gave him a "Go screw yourself'" look.

As he picked up his files and prepared to leave, Mark went into a mid-turn, snapping his fingers as if he had forgotten something.

"Shiiiit! I knew I forgot something," Mark smiled, "again off the record… a final report just came out on the destruction of the base in Oregon. Now I'm just paraphrasing what the eggheads stated, "Though the force of the energy used for the destruction of the facility was extremely controlled… its destructive power was equivalent or possibly greater than the Fat Man, which detonated over Nagasaki."

Mark let out a light laugh, pretending to not notice that the General was not finding anything funny about what he was saying.

"Ain't that some shit? She was at an atomic level before she went toe to toe with that warhead."

Cold sweat appeared on the General's face as he realized what Armitage was getting at.

Mark leaned forward, placing his hands firmly on the desk to look the General in the eyes one final time.

"The more you hurt her…, the stronger she gets," Mark grunted, "the eggheads gave her a 30/70 survival rate. I'm more inclined to say if I were you, I'd pray for the needle to come… before she does."

On that note, Mark smiled, stood up, and turned, heading for the door.

"It's been almost two years!" General Matheson lashed out. "Almost two years and no body!"

"That's right... two years... and no... body," Mark mocked as he knocked on the door. "Guard... let me up out of this bitch."

"That's because there is no body! The bitch is ashes!!" General Matheson howled. "Burning in hell where she belongs! You hear me?!"

His words fell on deaf ears as the door closed, leaving him alone again. General Matheson looked down at the table, trying to find composure, but he could not stop the trembling nor get rid of the sick feeling that entered his stomach.

"Bitch is burning," General Matheson nervously muttered, "in hell... where she belongs."

~ ~

As Mark exited the facility and headed to his rental car, his cell phone went off. He quickly pulled it out of his jacket to take it.

"Hi, honey," he smiled. "Yeah, tell the

girls I'll be home soon... and bringing ice cream... I'll be on the next plane in an hour... yeah, back at 7 PM... love you."

Mark closed his cell phone, overtaken by another hard cough forcing him to clutch the rooftop of his rental car as he neared it. He pulled some cough medicine from his pocket, opened it, and took a swig to ease his throat. He hopped into his vehicle and drove off, exiting the prison facility.

Thunder overhead forced him to look up before he could turn onto the main road. The sound was not of a storm coming or a jet flying too low... one could easily see it was coming from a human figure streaking across the sky at unbelievable speed in a colorful outfit heading to an unknown destination. His senses diverted up the road to the sound of something moving at near supersonic speed. All he could make out from the blur that streaked past was that they were wearing silver and white and definitely running on two legs. A small sonic boom rocked his rental seconds after the person passed.

"Wait up bitch!!"

These were the words the speedster screamed while chasing the flight-propelled superhuman.

A dry smile came across Mark's face.

"Legacy." Mark chuckled.

He turned onto the main road, returning to the airport and home where he belonged. He turned on the radio, listening to CNN.

Ashleigh Banfield began her news report from 11 AM to noon.

"Moving from the near-crippling financial crisis here in the United States and around the globe, as the death toll from the Judgment Virus continues to rise worldwide, so does the growing superhuman population. Many continue to ask the question, are these signs of the times, the end of days? With us are a panel of well-known scientists and religious clergy to weigh in on this discussion."

~ ~

Several thousand miles off the West Coast the United States, at the bottom of the Mariana

Trench, a bright blue glow shined, cutting through the blackness, causing all sea life capable of surviving at that depth to flock around the source in curiosity.

Massive flounders and shrimp fluttered close to investigate the transparent blue sac that appeared to be a mixture of a jellyfish and an actual embryo sac, only to quickly swim away as they encountered the powerful shockwave of the heartbeat pounding within. In the center of the sac, a young woman with long dreadlocks slumbered curled up in a fetal position.

At a glance, the sac appeared to be bathing her with blue energy.

In truth, the uncontrollable energy emitted from her as she slept... the sac protecting her also protected the outside world.

"My name is Sophia Dennison, and I did not kill my husband..."

Eye opens...

In the beginning…

ABOUT THE AUTHOR

Kipjo K. Ewers was born on July 1, 1975. At an early age, he had an active imagination. By the time he started kindergarten, he would make up fictitious stories. One of his favorites was about a character named "Old Man Norris," who hated everyone except for him.

When he attended our Lady of Victory Elementary School in Mount Vernon, he continued writing and reading stories to his classmates. Sometimes, the children would laugh. His teacher, Mrs. Green, would remind them that some great stories they read came about that way.

After elementary school, he went to Salesian High School in New Rochelle, NY, and then to Iona College.

He would work for several major firms and companies in New York, but his passion was becoming a author/writer. Therefore, it is not surprising he decided to write his first book/novel.

Kipjo began working and creating a new superhuman universe, finding inspiration and solace in losing his first daughter due to an unfortunate miscarriage that devastated both his loving wife and him; he began writing a hero origin story now titled "The First."

After publishing "The First" in 2013, Kipjo wrote two more follow-up novels to the series, a spin-off novel titled The Eye of Ra and a romantic supernatural story titled "Fred & Mary."

Now known as the EVO Universe, Kipjo continues to write to expand the series and create new projects for the foreseeable future.

Thank you for reading and for your

support.

Made in the USA
Middletown, DE
06 October 2024